AF249040

SHA'DAA: PAWNS

CREATED BY
MICHAEL H. HANSON

EDITED BY
EDWARD F. MCKEOWN

INTRODUCTION BY S.M. STIRLING

Perseid Publishing
P.O. Box 584
Centerville MA 02632

Book design by Michael Hanson
Cover design by Helen Harrison
Cover image copyright © Helen Harrison 2012
Cover image: Paul Hakimata

ISBN-10: 978-0-9859351-6-0
ISBN-13: 0985935162

Published in the United States of America

THE SHA'DAA SERIES

Sha'Daa: Tales of the Apocalypse

Sha'Daa: Last Call

Sha'Daa: PAWNS

Upcoming Volumes:

Sha'Daa: Facets

Sha'Daa: Inked

TABLE OF CONTENTS

THE SHA'DAA SERIES i
TABLE OF CONTENTS iii
DEDICATION v
ACKNOWLEDGMENTS vii
INTRODUCTION ix
PROLOGUE: THE PAWN SHOP 1
CHAPTER ONE: FORCES OF EVIL 7
INTERLUDE ONE 45
CHAPTER TWO: ASYLUM.. 47
INTERLUDE TWO 63
CHAPTER THREE: HUNTER'S RUN 65
INTERLUDE THREE 79
CHAPTER FOUR: FALL FROM GRACE 81
INTERLUDE FOUR.. 99
CHAPTER FIVE: LIFEGUARD 103
INTERLUDE FIVE 119
CHAPTER SIX: DUST 121
INTERLUDE SIX 145
CHAPTER SEVEN: DOOR 790 149
INTERLUDE SEVEN... 165
CHAPTER EIGHT: BLOODSTONE 167
INTERLUDE EIGHT 185
CHAPTER NINE: SILVER AND IRON 187
INTERLUDE NINE 209
CHAPTER TEN: GLOOM 211
INTERLUDE TEN...237

CHAPTER ELEVEN: DOUBLE CROSS............................ 241
INTERLUDE ELEVEN 257
CHAPTER TWELVE: THE BOKOR................................ 261
INTERLUDE TWELVE 281
CHAPTER THIRTEEN: KEEPSAKE 285
INTERLUDE THIRTEEN 295
CHAPTER FOURTEEN: "THE SAGLEK INCIDENT" 297
    by Bruce Durham.. 297
INTERLUDE FOURTEEN 311
CHAPTER FIFTEEN: SOUL PROVIDER....................... 315
INTERLUDE FIFTEEN 327
CHAPTER SIXTEEN: TIME FOR A CHANGE 329
INTERLUDE SIXTEEN 345
CHAPTER SEVENTEEN: CROUCHING SEAL, SLEEPING
DRAGON 349
INTERLUDE SEVENTEEN.. 367
CHAPTER EIGHTEEN: NORTHLIGHT 369
EPILOGUE.. 387
AFTERWORD 389
AUTHORS I

DEDICATION

This book is dedicated to:

Those who love us, who have given us the space and time to write and dream.

ACKNOWLEDGMENTS

No man is an island, entire of itself. – John Donne

I'd like to take this opportunity to thank the small army of individuals who are responsible for this shared-world series making it into print:

ALL of the wonderful authors who have appeared in the three published Sha'Daa anthologies, to date.

Edward F. McKeown, Sha'Daa Editor/Co-Writer, whose fierce drive and professionalism have kept this project on track through some very tough times.

Author S.M. Stirling for writing the Preface that introduces this third Sha'Daa volume.

Sarah Hulcy, for her proofreading work on PAWNS.

Graphic Artist Helen Harrison for the excellent cover.

Finally, a humble bow to visionary publishers Janet and Chris Morris (Perseid Publishing) for showing faith in a rag-tag group of literary ronins naïve enough to think they could take on the establishment.

From the depths of my heart, I thank you all.

Michael H. Hanson

Sha'Daa Creator/Co-Author
Piscataway, NJ
Summer 2012

INTRODUCTION

By S.M. Stirling

Hell.

Literally, here!

The Hordes of Hell are about to ride out upon mankind, the Forces of Evil are trembling with eagerness at the doors of our dimension…

Oh, wait a minute. Actually they're not all eager. Some have become members of the Elks, or are involved with a fun crowd at the local High School (though granted, they're drinking the cheerleader's blood. Not enough to do any real harm!)

Others are tied up doing custodial work with incredibly annoying chipper young assistants. And there's a blood-diamond mine in Africa that's perfectly hellish enough without demons getting into the act.

Aliens and time-travelers are frantically trying to get out of Dodge, not least by buying help at a certain centuries-old Afro-Celtic swap and barter shop in Ireland. And the mysterious master of the deal… what's his part in all this?

Shared-world anthologies have a long and distinguished history in the science-fiction and fantasy world. This one has an intriguing premise; Armageddon is about to happen, as it periodically does. The walls between our world and the demonic realm are getting thinner and thinner.

When you think about it, Armageddon would be a big event; something on the order of one of the World Wars, only more so. The sprawling amplitude of having dozens of writers handle an event of this magnitude has the advantage of giving a view of it from many different points of view. As the blind men tried to find out what this 'elephant' was, nobody would have a complete or accurate view.

The danger with taking this approach is that it may fly out of control – lose coherence. The skillful use of framing devices in this series ties the separate stories together rather effectively.

So – enjoy the end of the world!

PROLOGUE: THE PAWN SHOP

by Michael H. Hanson

"A shopkeeper may initially refuse to quote a price for an item, suggesting that it is worthless. This obliges the customer to insist on paying, possibly several times, before a shopkeeper finally quotes a price and real negotiation can begin."

– Persian T'aarof

"Pawn, sell, trade, or sacrifice," Ashley asked, "what'll it be?"

"Sacrifice," the massive creature replied with a clipped Oxford accent, "and I want the big altar in the back, the ebonite one. None of your giant friggin' supper bowls in the basement, Ashley."

It was only 9:00 a.m. on a hot summer day, but already the Pawn Shop was doing a surprising amount of business. Eighty customers were huddled over transparent, armored display cases that stretched around the main floor like a hundred-foot-long horseshoe. All fifteen of Ashley's employees had been called in to help handle this sudden upswing in trade.

"They're Norse Hlautbolli, Gronk," Ashley said with a wink. "And show a little respect for the Odin-spawn, will you? They're some of my best customers."

"Pfagh!" Gronk laughed, adjusting his chartreuse tie and digging rebar-like fingers into the breast pocket of his dark grey and finely-tailored Gieves & Hawkes twin-breasted suit. He disrespectfully tossed three ancient Vitellius gold coins on the counter before carrying the exquisitely carved jade figurine into the back room. Built like an upright hippopotamus, Gronk strode away on polished leather shoes, each the size of an anvil. His bulk caused vibrations through the black granite shop floor with each step.

The pawnshop's proprietor pursed her lips. Gronk's little trinket had a resale value of at least twenty thousand pounds, if Ashley's emerald eyes had assessed it properly, and they always did. Five hundred years into the trade and there was rarely an artifact, tool, weapon, or piece of art that she couldn't slap a value on in less than a minute. The thought that Gronk was going to toss that ancient, beautiful work of sculpture into a force-fielded pyre that would burn at 800 degrees Celsius left a sour taste in Ashley's mouth. Gronk's future plans must have needed a great deal of karmic insurance to make him sacrifice so precious an object to his demon gods.

"Either you're losing your touch," came a deep voice from Ashley's left, "or you're growing soft on that big lunk. You know they say Gronk has a wife in at least eight different dimensions. Contemplating becoming number nine?"

Ashley, slim with an Olympic swimmer's physique, stood six foot two inches. Even so, this woman of obviously African ancestry had to look up to match eyes with the tall apparition on the other side of the shop's main counter.

"Benedict," Ashley smiled, "it's been, what, two hundred years, you old carpetbagger? I was beginning to wonder if you'd dumped me for another chop shop."

"Give or take a decade," he said, "and I go by Johnny these days."

"Since when?" Ashley asked.

"Eighteen forty-five, Anno Domini."

Topping six foot six, Johnny was gaunt with large hands. Caucasian, clean cut, with thick, but medium length jet-black hair, he was dressed in a mortician's suit, with black tie, long black trenchcoat, and a black fedora. The summer heat seemed to have no effect on him.

"Hey. Didn't your hair used to be brown?" Ashley asked.

"My hair has been every color in the rainbow, my dear," Johnny smiled, "just as I've been many ages, heights, and shades of pigmentation… but I've always been partial to black."

"And what's with the raincoat and hat?" Ashley asked.

"I love Bogie movies. Besides, cloaks are long out of style. And speaking of style, I've got some wares for you," Johnny said.

Johnny reached into his trench-coat and pulled out what appeared to be an overly-stuffed leather roll. He placed it on the counter and with a flick of his wrist, it unwound a full four feet. Displayed in two dozen pouches were a fantastic array of gold, platinum, and precious-jeweled devices that looked like a cross between surgical instruments and esoteric works of sculpture… assuming either occupation appealed to a billionaire dilettante.

"Oh no you didn't," Ashley gasped.

"Personal property of Atlantis' head engineer," Johnny said, "and to keep things simple, you get the whole lot for my short list."

Johnny tossed a small sheet of ancient parchment on top of the Quantum Crystallographer's maintenance kit. Scrawled in beautifully scripted Latin were ten items, artifacts of cunning design, distant origin, and questionable existence.

"You always did seem to know what I have in stock, Salesman," Ashley said.

"A bit early in the morning for formal titles, my dear," Johnny said. He displayed a shark-like grin, and the blaze of bright white teeth was marred only slightly by a single gold left lateral incisor.

"Can't say your mouth-bling is much of an improvement, either," she said.

Ashley bit her lower lip and ran her eyes suspiciously around her crowded shop. Vampires haggled with one employee over the value of a lovely gold and sapphire laden crucifix. One family of Alpha Centaureans desperately tried to purchase a laminated interstellar passport. Ancients were cashing in any antique in their possession for whatever gold and silver they could carry out. Demons of all varieties were lining up to hit the sacrifice altars. Ordinary humans were stocking up on esoteric weapons, and time travelers were dithering aloud about divesting themselves of any and all objects that could be labeled anachronistic. This growing crowd rubbed shoulders in unusually large numbers. Ashley had not seen this diverse a group of customers within her shop at any single time in, well, ever.

Ashley locked eyes with Johnny, struggling not to get lost in the twin pools of endless blackness that were his pupils.

"Not for nothing, but five centuries I've worked this counter, and you've never brought me a treasure like this," Ashley said, "and now, all these customers, all these trades and sales, not to mention the rush on sacrifices…. What the hell is going on?"

Johnny leaned forward and whispered a single word mere inches from her face.

"Sha'Daa."

A chill like an icy stiletto shot up Ashley's spine.

"Ohhhhhh shit."

* * *

CHAPTER ONE: FORCES OF EVIL

Edward F. McKeown

Rela held her victim against the gymnasium wall, her needle-sharp teeth in the young girl's neck. She concentrated as sweet blood flowed slowly into her mouth. Blood was the medium but it was life essence she drew out of Jennifer Sherwood. Rela prided herself on drawing the most energy with the least blood flow from those she fed on.

Satisfied, she drew back. With strength that belied her petite figure, she scooped up the cheerleader, who slumped against her, with one arm and the nearby gym bag with the other. She carried her over to the bleachers and sat the girl down.

"Sit up and be still," Rela commanded, brushing her own long, black hair from her eyes.

Jennifer swayed but followed the order. Quickly, Rela drew out a tube of Neosporin from her bag and dabbed it on the small punctures, covered them with band aids. Then she fished out a pint of Gatorade.

"Drink this and take these vitamins. You will double up on vitamins and fluids over the next day and eat as much spinach as you can stand," she glamoured. "If anyone asks you about the band aids you will change the subject. You will forget what happened tonight. We just chatted about boys and music."

"Yes, Rela."

"You showed me your cheers and expressed your sympathy about my being too sickly and weak to do them."

"You poor thing," Jennifer said dreamily, "Hemophilia and sun sensitivity…. I still like you, Rela."

"And I like you, Jennifer. Do you feel all right? Are you able to walk home?"

"Sure I am."

"Straight home and to bed," Rela ordered.

Jennifer nodded, rose and walked steadily out of the gym.

Rela smoothed her dark school uniform, then followed, shouldering her bag. "Note to self. Buy more Gatorade." She walked out into the quadrangle, looked up at the brilliant night sky. She drifted up into that sky a hundred feet over Jennifer as the cheerleader walked through the cool evening air. Rela watched her for any sign of weakness or unsteadiness but the cheerleader seemed fine. She also kept an eye out for anyone who might interfere with her last meal. East Baumfuche was a safe, small town but crime wasn't unknown. Woe to anyone who sought to molest Jennifer. Rela avoided killing humans for convenience, not morality. The vampire who had turned her had educated her on how to survive. The first trick was not to live for your fangs. Piles of bodies meant vampire hunters and hordes of other enemies. Rela had a practical forever if she didn't screw up.

But crime wasn't low in East Baumfuche only through the efforts of the police. Like most non-ACLU members, Rela had scant concern for the disappearance of muggers and rapists.

Jennifer turned into her yard, opening the white picket fence, and went up the stairs to the unlocked front door of her house. Rela nodded in satisfaction. Then, feeling sleepy and full, she headed home to her DVR, hoping to spend the rest of a quiet night under a blanket.

*

Stan Wozniak scratched his belly, which he had to admit was larger than was becoming for a werewolf. But it was hard since he was, quite literally, getting long in the tooth. Then there were all the temptations of running a bar like the Howler. Best beer and pizza in town. He'd chosen the wolf theme as a simple cover in case he or any of the Westies made a mistake in public. Truth was that these days, even the full moon didn't get that much of a rise out of the guys. Sure, they'd devour the occasional sheep and they'd cleaned out most of the stray cats from the neighborhood, but if it was raining the boys would as soon throw extra pepperoni on the pizza and stay in and watch "Sportscenter" on ESPN.

Evil really wasn't his bag anymore. He was a reservist. He did his monthly get together with the West Bumfuchian werewolves and two weeks each summer in Canada training with other monsters – full moon howl fests, cattle mutilations, the infrequent battle with a captive vampire. Nowadays most of the human hunting was being done in simulators, real state of the art stuff. It cut down on trouble with the RCMP. Stan impressed a lot of the younger werewolves with his stories of the old days and the scar he bore from the paladin who'd shot him with a silver bullet. Thank god it was a glancing blow that had passed right through, or he'd be dead.

He yawned and put down the glass he was cleaning. It was about time to tally the register. A flickering glow from the next room drew his attention. "Damn, did Charlie forget to close the fireplace damper again? Goddamn moron's going to burn the bar down."

Stan walked out from around the bar, heading for the main room with the huge fireplace, over which he'd mounted racks of antlers from moose he'd personally hunted. He froze in the doorway. In the fireplace, squatting on the flickering coals, sat a short ugly imp. It glared up at him.

"Hey buddy, make with the firewood. These coals are almost dead and I'm freezing my balls off."

Stan shook off the surprise and tossed the imp a few pieces of split oak, which it piled and blew on until the coals caught them. "Ah," it said, rolling in the flames. "I can feel my ass again."

"Not for nothing," Stan said, a sinking feeling in his gut that his Nexium wouldn't help, "but what do you want? I did my two weeks back in June."

"Ah, screw training, buddy," the imp said in satisfaction. "You're being called up for the Sha'Daa."

"What?"

"Active duty, Wolfie. We got the Apocalypse scheduled for the solstice." He looked disrespectfully at Stan's mid-section. "Better back away from the buffet, Wolfie. You got a lot of humans to slaughter. The Westies wolves have to take out West Baumfuche, you and a kid vampire are all we have to take out the East town. We're kinda stretched thin in the Heartland."

"Wipe out the town," Stan yelped. "I just joined the Rotary Club!"

"What the hell is wrong with you? It's the end of the world. Get with the program, Wolfie. You'll be getting your mobilization orders and attack plan shortly. Sharpen the fangs, Mac. It's showtime."

The imp gave him a sloppy salute. "Evil Forever." Then it vanished in a blast of gag-inducing smoke.

Rela lay back in her padded coffin and switched on Twilight. Human vampire stories always amused her. They got so much wrong. Vampires were nearly as varied as humans were. She, for example, could endure daylight, though it suppressed most of her other powers. It was so absurd to think a vampire needed to, or even could, drain all the blood from a human body. The suction needed would lift a bus.

Her eyes grew heavy and she figured on sleeping for a few hours when a thump brought her sharply awake. She sprang from the coffin and headed upstairs. A thump sounded again. She went to her door. Rela looked out of the side window. Visitors were rare for the solitary vampire.

Shock straightened her up. Thumping against her door was a huge messenger bat. She opened the door. The bat landed and morphed into a tiny female figure – shorter than Rela's mere five feet – black-skinned with yellow, glowing eyes.

"Vampire Rela," it lisped. "You have been called to battle for the Sha'Daa. You must report to your local coordinator for assignment."

"What?" she said. "The Apocalypse. Why? I mean why now?"

"Question not the orders of Hell," it hissed. "The times are set by the powers. You must destroy the life of this place."

"By myself?"

"All that can be spared are you and a local werewolf pack."

"No!" Rela stamped her foot. "I am not working with smelly wolves. They kill vampires."

"You are all Forces of Evil. Obey or suffer. Report to the werewolf who owns the gathering place called the Howling." The messenger morphed back into a bat. In seconds it vanished into the night sky.

The screen on Stan's phone lit up with the name, "Hotdog," alias Vince Master, leader of the West Baumfuchian Werewolf pack, which consisted of him, his brother-in-law and a cousin.

"Yo, Vince."

"Stan, dude, did you just get a visit from an imp from hell with a call up for the Sha'Daa?

"Yeah, I can't effing believe it. I just got the Howling running the way I want and now the big boys decide to end the world."

"Screw the world, buddy. It's going to end us."

"Vince, don't panic. We're werewolves, the baddest of the bad."

"Stan, don't be an ass. The game is rigged. We didn't take the humans 10,000 years ago when all they had were shamans and spears. Now they have tanks, planes, effing nuclear weapons."

"Vince, what are you saying?"

"There's a thumb on the scales. The game is rigged against Evil. We start winning and all of a sudden there's a volcano, a tsunami or a horde of magical elves on the side of the humans. Look at all the small battles we've lost since.

"Point is that each time there's a major battle between good and evil, us ordinary FOEs get it each time. If we win we have the Dukes of Hell lording it over us. Christ, that would be worse than the Republicans."

"Vince, I don't like political hate speech. We can disagree without being disagreeable."

"Stan," Vince yelled, "would you focus for Hell's sake? Me and the boys have talked it out. We're bugging out, heading for Canada."

"What, you think they ain't going to hold the Apocalypse in Canada?"

"They got a lot of big empty in Canada."

"Vince, the big boys don't like deserters."

"They don't like anybody. Come with us."

Stan rubbed his face. "But the bar, our lives, my friends –"

"You're supposed to eat those friends tomorrow."

Stan remained silent for a few seconds. "Nah, man. I don't know what I'm going to do, but running doesn't look like a solution."

"Don't be a fool, Stan. Get out while the getting is good. We don't win no matter who else does."

"Yeah."

"Look if you change your mind, get on your Harley and head up to Aberdeen, in Saskatchewan. Follow your nose when you get north of town."

"Okay. You and the boys look after yourselves."

"You too, brother wolf. You too." The phone clicked off.

To: Vampire Rela Aisah, Forces of Evil Heartland Division; Section Area

From: Commanding Demon FOE

All Forces of Evil are directed to commence offensive operations against Forces of Light from 12:01 AM on the night of the solstice. Under command of senior evil being Stan Wozniak (werewolf) you will slaughter, devour, or destroy as many of the FOL and their civilians as is practical regardless of personal danger or casualties.

Evil Forever

Commanding Demon F.O.E

Rela wandered about St. Lucia's School the next day in a daze. The Sha'Daa was to break out tonight. Her well-ordered world was coming to an end. She was so distracted as she crossed the quad that she didn't realize she'd walked right into Candace's overfilled pink sweater. The tall, buxom cheerleader had the biggest breasts in the school, possibly the school's history. She was also, unfortunately, a hugger and thought that Rela was her living Bratz doll. Before Rela could back away, Candace threw her arms around her, mashing her face back into the round softness and lifting her off the ground.

"Rela! Where have you been?" Candace said. "We've been looking for you for days. We're worried about you."

"Well put her down," Michelle snapped from behind Candace, before she suffocates." Michelle pushed her glasses back on her snub nose and rolled her eyes under her brown bangs.

"Remember the hemophilia," Barbara added. The slender, redhead seldom spoke over a whisper but she waved a finger at Candace.

"Oh, yeah." Candace let Rela come up for the air. She put her hand on the tiny girl's shoulder. "I forgot, Hemophilia must be awful. I didn't mean to be rough."

Rela hugged the big girl back. "No, that's all right. It's not that bad if I just stay out of the sun and get my transfusions."

"Poor thing," Barbara added, "living in that house all alone."

"Hey, it's not that bad," Candace said, striking a pose. "She's got us."

Despite what she was, or perhaps because of it, Rela was touched. The three girls had adopted her as a friendless orphan:

Candace the cheerleader, Michelle the brainiac and Barbara, who excelled at Home Ec and whose casseroles were the hit of the local church events.

"Hey, Rela, what's wrong?" Michelle, ever perceptive, asked.

"It's nothing," she said. "I was just thinking it was so nice to have friends and hoping nothing ever changes that."

"Nothing will," Candace declared, thumping Rela on the back. "BFF."

"If, you gigantic, big-boobed, bubble-brained blonde, you can remember to stop thumping her. She's delicate." Michelle pinched Candace.

Rela looked at her friends squabbling in their good-natured way, with Barbara the peacemaker trying to separate the mock combatants. In twenty-four hours I am supposed to slaughter all these people? she thought. How can I do that? Sure there are plenty of humans I'd kill without hesitation to live, to feed. But to slaughter thousands without feeding. That's unnatural. And these humans….

"Rela," Candace said, pulling her into the doorway. "Get out of the sun. You know it's not good for you."

Stan sat on the back porch of his bar, a Budweiser in hand. It was Sunday and mercifully the bar was closed and he could be alone with his thoughts. Or, well, he thought, I was alone. The hair on back of his neck rose as a familiar spicy scent bit at his nose. He looked up. Twenty feet above him and out of easy leaping range floated a pretty young girl in a St. Lucia school uniform. Her eyes glowed a deep red, her black hair floated about her. She demurely smoothed down her skirt as if to make sure he wasn't looking up it. Which he wasn't. She looked young enough to have made that creepy.

"You're my senior?" she said disdainfully. "Aren't you a bit hefty for a werewolf? You look like a biker."

"I am a biker. Come on down," he said, not bothering to conceal the weariness in his voice. "I'm in no mood to bandy words with a smart-ass vamp."

She remained floating out of reach. "Your people and mine have fought each other more bitterly than we ever fought humans."

"Now we're one big happy Force of Evil," he said, taking a long pull on his beer.

To his surprise, she laughed, a sound like Christmas bells on a bitter cold morning.

Down she came. The glowing eyes cooled to a red-brown. "We are so screwed. Aren't we? I mean it is so pathetic. The Sha'Daa is going to break out through no fault of ours, and we throw our fangs and claws against their science."

Stan shrugged. "Humans never see this sort of thing coming. We always do well in the early rounds."

"And never last in the late ones," she returned. "The Forces of Light are always lurking, wizards, shamans, priests of every denomination, Templars." She shuddered at the mention of the last. "The populace is ignorant, but the FOL prepare in secret just as we do."

"Are we ever meant to win," she continued. "And why? What is in this Apocalypse for us? What do we get? What sort of world do we inherit?"

"Don't worry too much about it. Here it's just you and me versus a whole town. I don't like our odds."

She raised an eyebrow. "I've smelled other werewolves in the area."

"They're gone."

"Where?"

He drank some more. "Away."

"Can we get some help?" she asked. "Where are the main attacks going in?"

He shrugged. "LA, New York, Vegas for starters. It may be a few days before anyone notices."

"You'd think we'd merit some help," she huffed.

He looked at her narrowly. "That what you want? Some outside monsters tearing up our town?"

She bit her lip for a second and studied him. "No. I mean it's not like I'm moral or that fond of the living, but I have it good here. I've invested so much glamour here that no one has noticed I've been in high school for 80 years. I get an annual supply of new virgins and…."

To Stan's surprise, Rela sniffled. "I have friends here. I've never killed any humans beyond the occasional mugger or would-be rapist. I've had more trouble with FOEs than with humans. Some of these girls are so nice to me. They make me cakes." She pulled out a tissue to dab at her eyes.

"I thought vampires cried tears of blood." Stand said.

"Why?" she returned tartly. "Do you cry tears of cheeseburgers?"

Stan snorted a laugh. Then laughed again, harder, slapping his leg.

She looked down at him, offended, then began laughing too. She sat next to him. "I sense in you a desire not to do this as well."

Stan studied her. "You and I are of this world. We may be part of what some call chaos or evil, but we're forms of natural things. These demons aren't of our space-time. Their bodies, their magics, even their wishes, aren't ours."

She smiled. "What a thoughtful werewolf you are."

"A guy can have back hair without being a Neanderthal."

"Well yuck, but continue."

"Do we really owe allegiance to these demons? I was born a werewolf, but no one ever asked me what side I wanted to be on. Why does it have to be FOE?"

"I didn't choose vampire," Rela said. "I was turned by a very old vampire who wanted a companion. I was sick and would have died, but I was not asked either. She who turned me was very unusual. She trained me until my bloodlust cooled and set me on a path of coexistence. I lost her to a troll in a Romanian cave, not to any human."

"You kill it?"

She looked away. "I was young, weak and frightened."

"Yeah, sorry," Stan put his beer down. "I don't want to do this."

"What choice do we have? Our own side will tear us to pieces."

"Hell," Stan said. "They can't even spare a familiar for East Baumfuche." He stood, decision made and depression dropping off him like snow off a wolf's back. "I'm not doing this. This is my town, my bar, my life."

She jumped up beside him. "And my school and my crypt!"

He put out his hand. "Put her there, partner."

Rela wrinkled her nose but took his hand. "Now we have to figure out how to do this and survive."

A blast of fetid air caught Rela and Stan by surprise as they sat at a table in the Howling, eating pizza. Before them stood a yellow-eyed, fanged, horned and tailed creature wearing an ornate vest, yellow pants and a fez. A satchel hung around his misshapen neck. It was the definition of ugly.

"Who are you?" Stan challenged as they scrambled to their feet. He stood ready to transform and leap upon the thing.

"I'm Fenis, adjutant to General Mahog, FOE, Central Sector Command," it snapped.

"I know you," Stan said. "You're the guy who was supposed to be running things around here. Every time there was a reserve meeting or some evildoing to be done, you were always off somewhere."

"Watch it with the insubordination, Hairbag. I always delegated things when I couldn't make it."

"Yeah, to my buddy, Hotdog, who said he hadn't seen you in forty years and he thought you were in the Bahamas."

"Well, now I'm back and the Sha'Daa is on. So stow the trash talk. I don't have much time to waste in this dung heap. Things have been going badly in this sector. I just found out your buddy and his werewolf pack has deserted. There's too much evil to do and too little time. Are you prepared to attack the town?"

"Not exactly," Rela said.

"What? The balloon goes up on the Sha'Daa at midnight," the demon growled, flexing his talons. He looked at them for the first time. "What are you wearing on your arms?"

Stan shifted his arm so the upside down red cross they'd hastily painted was displayed. "We're conscientious objectors. We can aid any injured evildoers, but not conduct offensive operations."

"But you're the only two evildoers here."

"And if he gets hurt, I'll be there for him," Rela said brightly, "even though he's a werewolf."

"And I'd be there for her, even though she's a vamp."

"Since neither of you is going to fight, the only injury you're likely to get is a hangnail," Fenis shouted.

"Sorry," Rela shrugged. "But you can report back to Mahog that we're not fighting."

"I can't do that," the demon howled, hopping from one clawed foot to the other. "He'll disembowel me for starters. Dammit, nothing is going right today!"

"Well," Stan said, patting the demon on the back, "that's why you get paid the big bucks. Good luck back at HQ."

The demon flung off Stan's arm. "Oh, no. You're not going to cast me into the pit so easily. Bad news for you cowards and shirkers. Mahog is heading for Omaha and he likes to show his touch with the line soldiers. He's passing through this town. What do you think he's going to make of your conscientious objector status? You'll be joining me in the disembowelment."

"Damn. This sucks," Stan mused. "A major demon coming here."

"Our only chance," Rela said, "is to fool the general into thinking that we're destroying the town."

"How the hell would we do that?"

"He's not going to be here long. What if we took him to the crappy portion of town, set some fires, put a couple of bodies around –"

"You keeping any?"

"No," she said. "I'm not a ghoul. But we wouldn't need many. I've got a thought on that. I think I know where we can get some help."

"What time is the general coming through?" she demanded.

Fenis stared down at her. "At about six a.m.. You don't have a lot of time for whatever gag you're going to pull. But all I can tell you is, if you can't persuade him that you're destroying this dump. I'll be the guy on the other end of your intestines, pulling." With a flash of the traditional foul gas, he was gone.

Stan looked at the diminutive vampire. "Please tell me you have a plan."

She grinned. "We're going to put on a show."

He groaned. "Anything but High School Musical."

Rela sped through the night sky, cell phone in hand, texting furiously. "Yes. Sneak out. Tell parents, school play, sleep over at my place. Life or death!!"

Candace, Michelle and Barbara were at the school by the time she arrived. Rela landed out of sight and raced up to the girls.

"Hey, Rela," Candace said, stretching in her brother's leather bomber jacket. "What gives?"

"Come around back where no one can see us." They followed Rela to the deserted spot that some of the girls used to smoke between classes.

"Girls," Rela said, dreading their reaction. "I need you to remain calm and focus on what I have to say."

Three pairs of eyes looked at her with concern.

"It's the time of the Sha'Daa, an apocalyptic battle between the Forces of Light and the Forces of Evil. It's happening tonight, right here in our town and all over the world."

The girls burst into nervous laughter.

Rela rose off the ground. Her power rippled through her, eyes glowed and fangs protruded. Her friends grabbed each other and screamed.

"Silence," Rela commanded, and her power cut their screams off in mid-breath.

"I am a vampire," she said, "but I have renounced the FOE."

"FOE?" Michelle squeaked.

Rela floated down. Her fangs retracted and her eyes cooled. "Forces of Evil. Listen, I know I've frightened you, unhinged your understanding of reality, but you must help me save our town from what is coming."

The girls released each other, looking back and forth. "You want to save the town?"

"Yes. I've lived here and attended this school for eighty years. I don't want my world to end."

"Eighty years in high school," Candace said. "Wow. I thought four was hell.'

"And no one's noticed?" Michelle asked, putting her hands on her hips.

"Vampires can glamour false memories. It takes a lot of effort, but every four years –"

"Wait a minute," Barbara said. "I've seen you in daylight."

Rela nodded. "I was taught to daywalk by a very ancient vampire. It suppresses most of my powers and I try to avoid strong light. Only those who do not slaughter innocent humans can do so. I've never killed an innocent. I feed only a little at a time –"

Candace stamped her foot. "Hey! Have you bitten me?"
Barbara and Michelle's hands flew to their own throats. They looked at Rela with accusing eyes.

Rela blushed and looked at the floor, scuffing a shoe. "Well, I have to eat to live too, you know. None of you were hurt."

"I'm… I'm sort of remembering now," Barbara said, rubbing her neck.

"It always did seem weird to me that so many of the girls had band aids on their necks," Michelle said.

"Neck, hah," Candace said crossing her arms. "That's not where you bit me. I got it on the inner thigh."

"You're so tall," Rela said. "It was easier…"

"Rela, that is sooooo gay."

"Candace, that was dinner, not sex."

"How old are you?" Barbara the peacemaker intervened.

"One hundred and sweet-sixteen," Rela said, exasperation creeping into her tone. "Anyway, back to that Apocalypse thing I mentioned. You know, end of the world – remember? We need your help."

"We?" Candace demanded.

"Stan Wozniak and I are all of FOE locally."

"Mr. Wozniak is a vampire?" Michelle said, goggle-eyed. "He rode to the last Rotary meeting with my dad."

"He's the assistant coach on the boy's softball team," Barbara added, dazed.

Rela waved her hand. "Mr. Wozniak isn't a vampire – as if – he's a werewolf."

More astonished faces.

"He is my so-called superior, locally – laughable though the thought of a vampire reporting to a werewolf is. We're supposed to destroy the town."

"Just the two of you?" Barbara asked.

"That's what I said!"

"Could you?" Candace demanded. "Bullets don't work on either of you."

Rela sighed. "We're both powerful and hard to kill. But this isn't an Elvira movie. We're both made out of matter. I won't die from a single gunshot wound, and neither will Stan. I'm not alive in the same sense you are and he heals almost immediately, but we can both be torn to pieces by guns, especially big Army ones, or hacked or burned. We're not invulnerable."

"How do we know this isn't a trick to get us somewhere isolated where you can have your way with our inner thighs?" Candace said.

"Ah, Candace," Michelle said. "We're already in an isolated spot, alone with her."

"Oh… right."

"Will you help me?"

Barbara's hands fluttered. "What can we do? You need the police, the army, the Vatican –"

"– are all going to be busy," Rela interrupted. "East Baumfuche stands or falls to FOE with us. Are you with me?"

Three sets of determined chins nodded.

An hour later, Candace pulled her father's big van up to the back of Miller's Department Store, passing the statue of George Remsen Baumfuche, the town's founder. The last of the staff were closing up the store. The setting sun cut harsh shadows in the alley.

"We need to let everyone get clear," Candace said. "You got your burglar tools ready, Michelle?"

Michelle pushed her glasses up her nose and waved her wire clipper. "Ready…"

A wave of faintness overtook Rela and she swayed.

"Are you ok?" Barbara asked.

Rela shook her head. "It's been too long since I had something to eat."

"Don't you mean someone?" Candace asked.

"That is the way it works."

Rela looked at Barbara.

"Why are you looking at me?"

"Would you, um… mind… if I took just a little…?"

"What?!"

"Candace needs to drive the truck and we need Michelle to take care of the burglar system."

"Oh, so I'm only good for a snack?"

"No we need you, but you could rest for a few hours, unlike the others."

"Is this really necessary?"

"Yes I'll need all my strength to face the challenges of tonight."

"Oh hell, if you must."

But Barbara's agreement was followed by fits and starts of giggling and pushing away and yelps of panic.

"Hey, Barb," Candace snickered, "if her lips hit your neck again, you're making out."

"Candace Mulroy," Barbara snapped, "you have a dirty mind."

But the distraction gave Rela the chance to get her fangs smoothly into the young girl.

"No, wait," Barbara cried, "I'm not ready. Wait, no."

Rela threw a little glamour on Barbara, both to ward off any pain and to keep the girl still. She focused as strongly as she ever had and drained what she dared drain. Quickly she withdrew her fangs and pulled out her band aids and Neosporin. "Pass the drinks and snacks back here."

She popped a Coke and handed it to Barbara. "Drink and eat as much as you can. How do you feel?"

"Woozy, a little sleepy," Barbara said. She looked at Rela with a mixture of fear and fascination. Feeding was a very intimate experience when remembered.

Candace and Michelle exchanged frightened looks, experiencing for the first time the idea that something might look at them as food.

"Okay," Rela said, refreshed and not wanting her friends to dwell on it. "Let's get going. Barbara, you stay in the van and rest."

"Don't have to tell me twice," she murmured as Rela hopped out of the van.

Candace and Michelle followed her up the street, toting their bags of tools and lights. They found a large electrical box on the back of the hundred-year-old building that was Millers. Rela broke the formidable lock on the gray box. "It's all yours," she said to Michelle.

"Come on, Brainiac," Candace urged. "Kill that alarm."

"Don't get your Double-D's in an uproar," Michelle said, studying the wiring.

"Just because you're flat as a –"

"Girls," Rela said.

Michelle started judiciously snipping. "That should do it," she said finally.

They ran over to the back of the shop. Again, Michelle went to work. "The things you learn in shop," she muttered as she tapped and prodded. The door swung open.

"Come on," Michelle said. They plunged into the building, as the girls pulled out their flashlights. Rela, who saw perfectly in pitch darkness, didn't bother. They found what they were looking for in the storerooms at the back. Mannequins lying in stacks, some assembled, some not. Most were nude.

"Guess we need to steal some clothes, too."

"I don't feel right stealing from the Millers," Candace said.

"We are trying to stave off the Apocalypse, at least locally," Rela replied, waving her hands. "Michelle, get some clothes. Candace, help me get these mannequins into the van."

Rela and Candace grabbed up ersatz humans and went to the back. Candace woke the sleeping Barbara and moved the van up to the back door. Then they ran back in. Rela loaded mannequin after mannequin, then wondered where her two friends were.

She found Barb and Candace carefully going through racks, selecting outfits.

"What are you doing?" she exclaimed.

"You said get clothes," Candace returned.

"I didn't say go shopping. We don't care what they're wearing."

"Rela, no one will believe it if the clothes don't look right."

"These are demons from a hell dimension. They don't know what the Gap says is fashionable this year!!"

"Okay, okay." They began scooping up jeans and tops.

Stan moved to the back of the town morgue and slipped in through the back door. To his surprise, it wasn't even locked. Small towns, he thought. He made his way to the back. East Baumfuche didn't have that many deaths in a week, but two drunks had been killed in a car crash on the highway. Nobody had claimed the bodies. It was rumored that the two unknown men might have been on the run from the law.

Stan found the bodies in the back and quickly put them on a gurney and pushed them to his huge black Hummer. "Sorry, guys. No disrespect intended but if you save a whole town-full of people, it may go better for you in the great hereafter."

Stan loaded the bodies and drove off to the bad side of town. Next he needed as much gasoline, flares and other flammables as he could get his hands on.

After setting up some contrived scenarios for the locals, Stan pulled up to the rundown strip mall beside the train tracks that held the "Twin Peeks" adult store. Rela floated down from a nearby tree and hopped in the Hummer. He checked his watch. "Show time. Those old barns in the back country should be burning now. That will keep the volunteer fire guys out of harm's way. I set a charge on the cell phone tower too. Now, we get to work making all the mayhem and devastation we can to keep Mahog happy."

"I hope this works," Rela said.

"If it doesn't, we're both unpleasantly dead."

"I wonder where we go when we die," Rela said.

He looked at her in surprise. "What?"

"Demons and monsters from beyond, if they die here, are never seen in their hell dimensions again. I've never heard of a vampire appearing in Hell."

"No, nor have I heard of any werewolf," Stan admitted.

"Funny, the humans think something like me would have more of the answers, but regardless of the fact I'm undead, I have no more idea of the afterlife than they do."

"Guess we better put the experience off for as long as we can,'" Stan said.

Rela laughed. "You sound like a human."

"I think of myself as one," Stan replied. "One that becomes a wolf at need or during the full moon. But is that really so different?"

She looked at him.

"I guess so," he said.

"I'm not a human, nor feel like one, and yet… the friendship and companionship of my young friends means a lot to me."

"Any boyfriends?" Stan asked.

"Occasionally," she said. "But that gets complicated. A lover demands more than a friend. My appearance tends to keep older men at bay, and the young boys, well they're only interested in sex and so few can be trusted with secrets."

"Now you sound like a human," Stan said.

She shook her head ruefully. "Let's get this done. I have to admit, it does my vampirish heart good to commit some senseless destruction."

"It's not senseless," Stan said, getting out of the Hummer. He gathered up his arsonist's kit from the back. "This place is a blight."

She looked at it. "What's wrong with a little sexual deviancy?"

"Lower property values, lower tax revenues and more crime."

Rela stared. "You really did join the Rotary club."

"Yep, and this strip mall is nothing but this dump and two abandoned storefronts. It and the Valhalla trailer park over there should do for the destruction we need. We got a couple of real bodies and your gal pals will have all those mannequins ready to go shortly."

"I see one car still here."

"Probably the owner. We'll scare him off."

With Rela carrying tins of gas, they hot-footed it over to the back of the sleaze palace. The door lock caved under Stan's boot. He allowed himself a small transformation, muzzle growing, hair filling out, ears elongating and eyes gone wolf-yellow.

Inside, amidst piles of X-rated movies and paraphernalia, a weedy man looked up as the werewolf and vampire girl plunged in.

"Roowwwrrr. Awwwoooo," Stan howled.

The man looked at them. "Oh, hey. Are you a friend of Hotdog's? We're closed and, anyway, I don't have any new were-porn."

"What!" Stan said.

"Yeah, you're with the Westies right?"

Rela sighed. "How about I handle this?" She raised her hands and her voice deepened. "Look only at me."

"Sure, babe. I like… the… school… girl… outfiiiit." The weedy man's eyes rolled up in his head. In an instant Rela was on him.

"Don't kill him," Stan said, as he liberally splattered gasoline around the place.

"Small loss if I did," she said. "However I'm going to top-up. I didn't take much in my last feeding."

"Yuck," he said. "I wouldn't put teeth in that. You don't know where it's been or what it's been doing."

"Vampires have wonderful immune systems," she said. "And I can't afford to be fussy." She extended her fangs and bit.

The pair were so preoccupied by their feeding and arson that they did not notice a tall, slender figure walk in behind them. But the sound of a sword whispering out of its sheath and the shiver of power the enchanted blade sang into the air got their attention.

Stan spun and Rela turned, her fangs still in the human.

The man facing them was young with a lean, aquiline face and ice-blue eyes blazing in judgment. He wore a black leather longcoat and, hanging on a chain on his chest was the sign of the deadliest of FOE banes, the Knights Templar. He held a sword of silver and steel. Cold flames ran up and down the blade.

Stan looked down at the gas cans in his paws and at Rela who was frozen with her fangs in the sleaze merchant. "This isn't what it looks like. Rela!"

She quickly withdrew her fangs and laid the smiling man at her feet. "Who are you?"

"I'm Simon the Templar," he said in deep voice for the whipcord body, "and you have wrought your last harm on the human world."

"Simon Templar?" Stan said.

The human winced. "Yes."

"Really?" Rela said. "As in 'da dit ta do-do do do'?"

"Go ahead," he said wearily, "I've heard every bad joke about Leslie Charteris, Roger Moore and Val Kilmer that exists."

"Listen," Stan said. "We're not evil. Well, only technically. You see we're conscientious objectors."

"Oh, please," Simon said. "Have some pride. That's pathetic. You have to have a conscience to be a conscientious objector."

"No really," Rela said. "We're sitting out the Apocalypse, hoping you guys win."

"While murdering and burning," Simon grated and charged.

Rela leapt over a shelf of porn. "He ain't dead," she shouted over her shoulder.

"But he will be unless you save him," Stan shouted. He threw a lighter at the nearest pile of gas-soaked porn and then pitched the gas cans to the back. The magazines caught instantly, but Stan was too slow throwing the last can. Simon, who'd been chasing Rela around a raised checkout counter, reversed direction, lunged and the sword slammed through the werewolf's midsection, its blade protruding a foot beyond. The Templar pulled the weapon out and raised it for an overhand cut when the gas cans blew and a sheet of flame threw him backward.

Stan and Rela raced for the front door, crashing through. The Templar recovered himself, started to chase them, then turned back to rescue the storeowner.

Stan threw the keys to Rela, who blurred over to the Hummer and started it. Stan threw open a back door and managed to climb in before collapsing from the burning wound.

Rela looked at him with frightened eyes. "You're hurt. We need to get you help."

Stan gave a sickly grin. "I don't have health insurance and the local vet doesn't do werewolves. Just pull over near the Valhalla trailer park. I have first aid stuff in the back and werewolves are tough. We get over whatever doesn't kill us."

She gave him a dubious look and drove. "It's not far enough from that Templar to suit me."

"He doesn't know where we're going and we don't have a choice. Mahog will be here before you know it."

They bumped over the railroad tracks and roared in the direction of the Valhalla trailer park.

Rela ran in through the trailer park's entrance, staggering as she went. A crowd of people stood there arguing with the manager, a bearded man wearing a torn t-shirt. They broke off to stare suspiciously at the weaving girl.

"Hey, are you stoned?" one man called.

"Idiot," a woman snapped. "She's wearing a uniform from St. Lucia's."

"Haw," the man returned. "You think they don't get stoned over there."

"Run," Rela shouted. "Run. A train's derailed… toxic gas." She pointed to the tower of smoke from the burning porn shop. Also lying in the street were the bodies Stan had stolen from the morgue.

"What?" the manager began.

Rela moaned and toppled over. To her surprise two men leapt from the porch and caught her before she could hit the ground. She began gasping loudly, painfully for breath. "Save yourselves…."

"Call 911," a woman screamed.

"The phone's out," the manager shouted. "Who's got a cell?"

"Can't get a signal!" several people answered at once.

"No time," Rela coughed out. "Save yourselves. I'm already –" She arched her back in paroxysm and slumped. Since she actually was the undead, it was convincing. Her eyes stared sightlessly into infinity; her body was breathless and slack.

"Oh my God," a woman screamed.

"She's cold as ice," the man holding her by the shoulders announced. "She's done for."

"We've got to get out of here," someone shouted. "Get your families." People began to run, spreading panic.

To Rela's surprise the two men holding her began to lift her.

"Tom, Bill," a woman said. "It's no good. Leave her be, the poor child's gone."

"We can't leave her like this, Grams," one replied.

"Lay her on the porch," Grams said. "It's all we have time for. Jesus will understand. Get your own kids."

Rela was suddenly glad she could lie like the dead, or Grandma would have had her in tears. The men laid Rela down gently and took off.

Chester Moltrie, also known as "Chester the Molester," chewed his mustache as he stepped out of the decrepit trailer at the back of the Valhalla Trailer Park. He saw the last cars speeding out of the main road. "What the fuck?" he wondered. "Where's everybody going? What was all that noise about?"

"What do you care?" his partner called from inside. "Come on, man, I got a ton of meth I'm cooking here. Close the fucking door."

"Ok, Gomer. Just wanted to make sure the cops weren't coming."

"Quit calling me Gomer, you damn wetback. If you could keep your freaking hands off the underage skirts around here, we'd have less trouble. I want to get this load done and maybe get out of town. Radio says there's a lot of weird shit going on."

Chester shrugged. "It ain't got anything to do with us." He went back in and put a loaded 12 gauge against the door, just in case he was wrong.

Stan waited until the crowd of panicked renters had bolted from Valhalla in everything that could and would roll. He scrambled out and picked up the bodies he'd earlier snuck onto the roadway and tossed them back in the Hummer. Then he ran up to Rela, lying dead and waxen on the porch.

"Snap out of it," he said. "They've all bolted."

She looked up at him. "Stan, you're bleeding again."

He grimaced. "Damn enchanted blades. The wounds don't heal easy, even on a werewolf. Thank God we'll have most of a full moon. Come on. We've got to get fires started in the unoccupied units."

"I'll go get the girls and the mannequins," Rela said. She lifted off into the darkening sky.

"Never thought I'd be envious of a vampire," he sighed, watching her flit off, quick as a sparrow.

Mahog the Magnificent had fought for FOE for as long as there had been good and evil. He'd also taken one too many hard knocks to the cranium from the humans and the Atlanteans and other ancient species before them that had vanished in the folds of interdimensional space. Mahog was prone to bouts of irrational rage followed by confusion and frequent naps. Had it not been for a succubus sister-in-law, he'd have been "retired" a long time ago. Unlike young demons, which were frequently served up live, no one wanted to eat old demons, who were usually simply ploughed under in lieu of a gold watch.

Fenis had groaned in horror when he learned Mahog had been given command of the Sector. The old demon's frontal assaults on ancient human strongholds in the last Sha'Daa had turned the tide of many a battle, for the humans. Fenis had decided to give the ancient demon a tour of the least dangerous area of their Sector, avoiding the SAC base at Omaha, the new FBI field training academy and a hidden fortress of the SMOF (Secret Masters of Firc), which contained wizards and paladins. What, he'd thought could possibly go wrong at East Baumfuche?

That was before the outbreak of pacifism, desertion and cowardice had taken out his local forces. Still, from the preliminary reports a hellbat had brought him, his choice of missing the SAC base attack had been a good one. The horde of wargs and other lesser demons were being introduced to 30mm chain gunfire from helicopter gunships with appalling results.

If only he could get the demon through East Baumfuche and off to Omaha, where things were going somewhat better, he, Fenis, might be able to find a nice hole to hide out in until the victory celebration or until the pell-mell retreat allowed him to sneak off to his private cover in the Bahamas.

"Faster," Mahog bellowed from the back of the chariot. Fenis cracked a whip over the two wargs pulling the burnished old and red chariot. Both of them farted in reprisal, something that could bring tears to the eyes of even a demon. "Could this day get any worse?" he muttered. He turned off the side road and into East Baumfuche's run down 3rd Ward. Between urban blight and recession, it had looked pretty devastated before, but Fenis was pleased to see that Stan had managed to set fire to a lot of cars and a strip mall blazed cheerily. Bodies lay strewn about, though it seemed rigor mortis had affected almost all of them as limbs pointed in all directions.

"Nice work, eh, General?"

"Hah," Mahog roared. "You call this a slaughter? Look at those bodies. They're still mostly intact. Where was the suffering, the horror, the disembowelment? You know how I feel about a good disembowelment!"

"I've heard," Fenis nodded weakly.

"That's the problem with modern evil! Ignoring the fundamentals."

"Not like in your day, sir."

"Damn straight. Keep moving. I want to finish touring this shithole before I move on to Omaha."

Ahead lay a trailer park. A faded sign said, "Valhalla." Underneath it someone had written, "I'd always thought it would be more." A half-dozen wrecks, some obviously dating from the 50s, had been loaded with trash and burned along with some trailers. To Fenis' horror, he noticed that the bodies liberally sprinkled over the area were mannequins. The area was festooned with fashionable size 2 dead.

The chariot rolled into the back where they found Stan and Rela near two corpses. Fenis could tell looking at them that they weren't fresh, but at least they were real. The werewolf was leaning against a tree, a blood-soaked bandage wrapped around his chest. He looked pale and battered.

The two stared up at the demon standing in the back of the chariot.

"Greetings, Wolf and Vampire," Mahog rumbled. "I am your commanding officer. How goes the battle?"

The werewolf started to answer, then began coughing.

"It goes well, Honored Sir." the small vampire said. "We have slaughtered. We have burned and pillaged."

Mahog glared down at Stan. "What happened to you?"

Stan met his eyes. "The Forces of Light are putting up a quite a struggle. There are Templars in the area. I think they got the Westies Pack. They sprang on us when Rela was feeding on a human. Got me before we beat them off."

"Templars," Mahog said, his red eyes scanning the area, "good fighters, those. Gad, I'd like to get my teeth into one.

"Speaking of getting my teeth into something," Mahog climbed down from the chariot. What do you say to some fresh human?"

He reached down and picked up a human corpse. "Bah, this is ice-cold. It's days dead."

"He was one of the first we killed?" Rela chirped. But Mahog was striding past her, heading further into the park.

"Wait, General," Fenis said desperately. "There could be Templars."

"Stop, please," Rela added.

"Shit," Stan said, standing. "The jig is up."

Mahog plucked mannequins from the trees and the ground. "What is this treachery? These aren't bodies. What are you cowards and traitors trying to pull?"

"That's all for me," Fenis said, pulling a large caliber revolver from his satchel. "You two enjoy your disembowelment." He put the pistol to his temple and fired. Demon and pistol thumped to the ground together.

Stan made an abortive step toward the gun and Mahog stamped a foot down on it, smashing it into the earth.

"What the fuck is going on out here?" a human voice called. From the rearmost trailer, a scraggly, tattooed man, toting a shotgun and wearing a brown, leather vest. leaned out.

Mahog turned toward him. The human froze, then let a loose a shot that stung the demon.

"Rrrarrrrrgh" Mahog bellowed. "I'll be back for you two. First I'll show you how we do it Old School."

Chester backed up screaming and firing as the twelve-foot-tall horror raced toward him.

"What is it? Cops?" Gomer yelled from the back room, grabbing up a submachine gun. He spotted the oncoming demon.

Mahog the Magnificent charged into the blazing fire of the meth-cookers, then right into the meth lab. He splintered the wood of the trailer as well as the propane tank. A sheet of flame from the exploding meth lab turned into a tornado of fire and sent pieces of trailer, Mahog, Chester and Gomer in long high arcs over the area.

The Wargs pulling the chariot decided they'd had enough and raced out of the trailer park into the path of an oncoming semi. There was a horrendous squealing of brakes and the crunching of metal, wood and warg.

"We've got to get out of here," Rela said. She reached down and flung Fenis into the same fire consuming his master, then helped Stan back to his Hummer, passing a wrecked semi covered with warg parts.

"Where to?" he asked.

"My crypt is nearer than your bar," Rela added. "We should be safe there."

They drove like mad, Stan barely hanging onto consciousness until they got to the better suburbs.

"Oh, no," Rela said.

Stan struggled to focus. He saw a small, arts and crafts-style home on fire. Smoke poured out of the upper windows.

"My coffin, my stuff," Rela wailed.

"Call the fire depart–… crap." said Stan, remembering he'd lured them out of harms way.

"Quick," Rela said. "Into the garage. I have a hose and fire extinguisher."

They ran in through the back door of the garage. A figure inside the doorway slammed the door behind them. He slashed at Stan, who fell over a lawnmower and crashed to the floor.

"You again," Rela said

Simon the Templar struck Rela with flat of the enchanted blade. The blow wasn't mortal, but it flung the vampire to the ground next to the prostrate werewolf.

Stan tried to reach Rela, but the exertion finished the werewolf, his eyes rolled up in his head and he collapsed. Rela crawled over to Stan, putting herself between him and the Templar.

The sight of a vampire protecting a werewolf seemed to confuse the Templar. He brought his blade up but the movement was hesitant, without force or conviction.

"What does this mean?" he demanded.

"It means that we are no more all alike than you are," she said. "We've turned our back on FOE. Maybe we aren't FOL, but we don't deserve to die."

"You live off the blood of the living."

"Everything draws life from something else. I've learned not to kill save in self-defense."

"You have an elastic definition of that," Simon replied. "We have files on you Rela. You have slain humans."

"Rapists and muggers," she replied. "Who would have preyed on me or on what they thought I was, a helpless girl. In wiser days you humans thinned those packs out. Now you're all so concerned about their upbringing and whether mommy was nice enough to them before they started serial killing."

He gestured with the sword. "And the wolf?"

"Stan Wozniak is the name," Stan growled, surprising Rela. "My family's been werewolves from time out of mind. We control it pretty well."

"Not always so. Again there are files on you."

"Yeah, I werewolfed a little in Iraq. Uncle Sam was paying me and so what? Your beef with me is that I killed Republican Guards? That was what the Marines do. Semper Fi. I just ate em after. But I'm an old wolf now and I run a bar. Farmers lose sheep and cattle occasionally but not children or wives. So again, what's your beef with us?"

"I've never spoken so long with FOEs before," he said, almost as if to himself. "This is unsettling. Perhaps the old master was right and such conversation is dangerous."

"So's thinking for yourself," Stan shot back.

"I'm sorry," Simon said. "Truly sorry. It does seem as if you lured that demon to his destruction and tried to save the town, but I cannot chance your lying to me."

"And if we're telling the truth?" Rela managed. The pain in her side from the glancing blow of the magic weapon was growing.

"Then I will have a great penance to make. And you will both have paid for those lives of humans that you did take. Whether in a good cause or not, they were humans."

A door banged open behind Simon and Candace raced in. "Hey, you," she shouted, "leave them alone."

Simon raised a palm to her. "Stay back. I hate this too now. But it must be done."

Candace slipped between them and Simon. The Templar faced her but drew his sword away from her. Simon's back was to the door as Michelle and Barbara made their stealthy way in.

"Girl, get out of the way. You're only making this harder."

"Well," Candace said, as Michelle picked up a nearby lamp. "Speaking of making things harder." She whipped off her sweater. "Get a load of these."

Rela's last sight was of Candace flashing her impressive artillery at the bemused Templar as Michelle swung the lamp at his head.

The world came back slowly to Rela, a blurry world of shadows now filled with a horrible growling snarl. A pain throbbed in her side where she'd been struck down.

Am I in Hell? she wondered.

The shadows resolved, but she was no wiser. She appeared to be in a very tacky room, with fish and dead animals on the walls, beanbags and other overstuffed furniture and a very large TV. It might be Hell.

Slowly she turned her head, fearing it might come off if she moved faster. The growling came from Stan. The werewolf was a sorry sight, bandaged in shreds of shirt and pants, lying on his back, mouth open, snoring in a way that probably meant sleep apnea.

"You're alive!" a voice cried.

The sound went though Rela's head like a knife.

"Well, as much as you were before," Michelle said. Rela recognized her three friends standing around the couch, looking down at her anxiously.

"Honestly," Barbara said, her voice trembling. "We thought you were done for, but Mr. Wozniak said you weren't and to get you underground."

"This isn't my crypt," Rela said.

"No," Stan said. The werewolf opened a bleary eye to look at her. "Sorry, the fire the Templar set got your place."

"The Templar!" Rela said, sitting up slowly with all three girls trying to assist her. "What happened? Surely you three couldn't overcome him."

"No," Michelle said, "though Candace nearly did."

"These things are power," Candace said, throwing out her chest.

"Anyway," Michelle continued, "he sensed my attack at the last second and ducked the lamp. But with the three of us standing over you two and begging for your lives, well, he was kind of helpless. He didn't want to believe you were good, or anyway, not evil, but I guess he lacked the conviction to do anything with us opposing him. He's down at the Motel 8. Says he's going to keep an eye on things for a while. I don't think we have to worry about him."

"Well, maybe Candace does," Barbara giggled.

"Rela, are you going to be OK without your coffin?" Michelle asked.

Rela sighed. "I like a nice coffin. They're snug, but I don't need to rest in one. I do need some place safe from the sun. I will be too weak to daywalk for quite a while."

"Stay here," Stan said. "My den is underground."

"You," she said, "a werewolf, would take me in?"

"I'm not so big on rules and we made a good team. From what the girls tell me, the Apocalypse is going the humans' way, though there have been a lot of casualties. We may need each other and these girls to survive in this new world."

She looked around. "Could we redecorate?"

Stan snorted a laugh. "Gad, first thing any female wants, redo the cave. Sure." His head fell back on the pillow.

Rela looked up at the girls. "We're still friends?"

"BFFs," Michelle said, with a thumbs-up. Barbara and Candace nodded.

"Then I hate to ask but, Candace, you are the biggest and strongest. Could I perhaps…?"

Candace sighed. "Ok, but on the neck this time."

To: Commanding Officer Sector 112, Area 14.

From Rela Aisah, surviving officer, Forces of Evil, North American, Midwest, small town operations unit 1349.

Regret to report a disastrous engagement with the Forces of Light. The enemy attacked with overwhelming numbers and by surprise on the first morning of operations. Commanding Sector General Mahog and his adjutant Fenis were killed in mortal combat with Knights Templar unexpectedly appearing on the scene. All other member of FOE locally are missing and presumed dead, other than myself and werewolf, S. Wozniak, who was wounded with a Templar sword. I am unable to continue offensive operations on my own, as my crypt has been destroyed, and the Templars remain in the area. I will attempt to hold here until relieved.

If no relief possible, please consider this area as lost to FOE. Better luck next Sha'Daa.

Sincerely
Rela Aisah
Vampire Commanding East Baumfuche

*　　*　　*

INTERLUDE ONE

Astraea, former Libyan Goddess and holder of the scales of justice, torn and discarded from the fabric of her people's spiritual hierarchy, hovered without form or purpose amidst the earth's ethers for century upon century. Until that fateful time, on a cold winter's night early in the sixteenth century A.D., she came upon a terrible scene, the aftermath of an attack, a dying slave beside her slain Welsh master, amidst the refuse and filth of a back alleyway in Dublin, Ireland.

Bleeding her soul, the fallen slave girl sensed the goddess's presence, and heard a voice. *Accept me and I will grant you justice.*

"And after that?" The dying girl whispered.

A long, long life…of your own choosing.

"I accept."

*   *   *

CHAPTER TWO: ASYLUM

by John D. Manning

"Asylum seekers are not looking for asylum, just for a good place to live."
Loesje – Dutch fictional character, Active and International Girl, b. 1983

Lillian Eldridge hated Austin. It was cold and two-faced. The citizens waxed sympathetic to the homeless. They made a great liberal show – caring, feeding, and sheltering the poor for the five o'clock news. When the cameras went dark and the recorders switched off, however, the true and the ugly emerged. Women gripped their purses closer, tighter. People gave a wider berth. And, the disdainful looks and shouting began.

"Get away from my club/store/shop before I call the cops!" "Go take a bath!" "Get a job!" "Don't give her money. She'll spend it on drugs. She'll just buy booze." "Hey, Lady, I got five bucks here! What'll ya do fer me?"

Austin was no better than any other city she'd passed through during her eight plus years on the street. True, it had less winter; fewer cold, rainy days. If you weren't one of the pretty people or a cause célèbre, however, it sucked.

Lillian had not planned to be a panhandler. It was the final pooling of a cascade of events – dominos crashing one into another as they defined the shape of her ruin.

The first tile was the divorce.

She'd been married for eleven years, three months, and twenty-seven days. The union was acrimonious from the start. Fortunately, they'd had no children. After the divorce she considered retaking her maiden name, Bahr. Since it wasn't part of the original divorce proceedings she would have to file separately. The paperwork seemed insurmountable, not to mention costly, so she remained Lillian Eldridge.

Clack-clack – the sound of tiles falling against one another.

Her job was the next casualty as the cascade gained speed. The benefits she received while she looked for work covered the mortgage – or the food – or other day-to-day needs. It came nowhere near covering them all. The shortfall grew, and with it the feelings of despair and worthlessness.

Clack-clack-clack.

One day, after traveling by bus across town for yet another fruitless interview, Lillian arrived home to see a Constable's vehicle parked in her driveway. She stopped on the walk to her front door. The uniformed officer approached and handed her a folded document. She barely heard his pro-forma sympathy. She only saw his stern countenance and stony resolution as he told her she had seventy-two hours to vacate the house; that the bank had foreclosed.

Lillian had few options. Since both parents were dead, her sister, Marta, took her in. A little over four months was all it lasted before the muffled arguments between her sister and brother-in-law late at night behind closed bedroom doors convinced her she'd worn her welcome thin. She had a younger sister somewhere south, but no way to contact her. When the tensions neared the breaking point she told her sister she'd found Candice on the internet, that she had an apartment in Austin, Texas, and that she was willing to share with Lillian for a while. She lied, but Marta accepted the tale with relief and a wan smile. Marta gave her the money for a bus ticket and a little extra. Lillian would always see the relief in the woman's eyes as she did so. A part of Lillian hated Marta for that, but she hated herself more for feeling that way.

Ironically, she did find Candice during one of her stays in Austin. The weather was cool and drizzly enough to generate sympathy from the drivers passing by, especially the college kids. She'd collected a lot more than usual. Feeling good, she went to one of the shelters, took a shower, and washed her hair. She decided to treat herself to a sit down dinner for a change. Afterward she wandered Austin's famous Sixth Street District. The primal sounds and driving rhythms of heavy metal music pulled at her from the dark interior of one of the clubs. Without thinking, she stepped inside. On the tiny, claustrophobic stage was a band. The cheap sign on the wall identified them as Hell's Archangels. A young woman stood center stage in front of the band, the colored lights playing across her platinum hair, her tattooed left arm stretching toward the ceiling as she growled into a microphone. There was no mistaking the attitude in that voice or that stance. It was her sister Candice. Lillian watched until the bouncer asked her for the five dollar cover charge. She shook her head and withdrew onto the crowded street. It was the only time she'd seen her. They never spoke. She often wondered how different things might have been had she paid the cover and waited for her sister to take a break. No. Her life had changed too much – she had changed too much. She had no desire to burden Candi with her own misery.

It was a crossroads, an intersection of two country roads passing through a copse of trees. It was unremarkable, although it did seem to some that the oaks and willows crowded close to both trails. The noonday sun exerted little warmth over the juncture. A cool breeze blew across it from the north, affirming the lingering presence of winter in this part of Central Texas. The chilliness would pass, and soon. Winter was a fleeting and sporadic visitor this far south.

James Paxton sat on the hood of his three-year-old black Ford Expedition and stared down the gentle slope to the crossroad below. In the back seat lay his books on magic and hoodoo; witchcraft and Cabalistic rituals. A large wooden box painted black and covered with colorful sigils lay in the rear compartment. Inside were candles and bronze candelabra; a brass censor and an iron charcoal brazier, vials of oils and packets of powders.

Something was coming, and coming soon. It started as a whisper, a mere echo in his brain as he studied his magic. As his knowledge and ability grew, the idea filled him. It grew. It spread – a single dark word that resonated in his mind and stalked through his dreams: Sha'Daa! He didn't know what it meant, but it was a glowing ember in his brain. It pushed at him. It ate and gnawed at him.

Sha'Daa.

Higher up the hill to James' left, in the northwest portion created by the crossroad, stood a SOLD sign. He'd purchased the entire one hundred and forty-three wooded, brush-laden acres – all four parcels surrounding the intersection. If all went well with his ritual tonight, he would build an ashram on that site, a secret temple for the dark gods he worshipped, although ostensibly it would be a place of sanctuary – an asylum – for the homeless he planned to attract. He would spread the word through the media, of course, but also through the hidden, secret ways used by the down-and-out.

Paxton was no altruist. He had no interest in the comfort or conditions of his fellow man. They had only one thing he needed: mental energy. Every human being – every functioning human brain – was a living dynamo. Religious leaders and politicians the world over knew this and used it. He planned to do the same. There were a few ways to those he needed – the ones he wanted.

He could be ordained and start his own church. The credentials were easy enough to obtain in this age of the internet and web sites. The problem with that, however, was that it took time to attract a following; time he did not have.

He could go a less legitimate route and start a cult. There were always disaffected, disenchanted people willing to follow anyone who seemed to have an answer. That solution had some issues, though. James doubted he had the charisma to pull it off, knowing he was no Adolf Hitler or Jim Jones or David Koresh, able to inspire people to follow him, lemming-like, into the Abyss. There was always the chance, too, that the authorities might figure that he was up to something and shut him down just as he was about to reach the apex of his plan.

No, the best way was simply to gather people by playing to their wants and needs. Then, when the time was right, he would gather them together and harness their unsuspecting minds.

First, he had to harness a focus, a nexus of power – traditionally, a crossroads.

James slid from the hood, his shoes crunching on the dirt and gravel. He stretched, his arms stiff, his fingers spread wide above his shining, shaven head. Hyperaware from a lengthy fast, he stepped lightly toward the crossroads. He watched his lengthening shadow point him to that node of magic, that gateway to power. His skin tingled as he drew near. An electric tang danced in his nostrils, crackled in his hair. So much power pulsed around him he felt he must burst if he did not harness it. He had never felt so alive before a ritual. When dusk deepened into night, he would return to the junction with his paraphernalia. He would cast the circle and call the Dark Ones and bind them to him and order them to do his will.

And, they would obey.

The afternoon sun blasted the intersection as Lillian worked the traffic for money. The heat bounced mirror-like from the concrete sidewalk. Blistering exhaust gases assaulted her legs as she carried her sign past the idling cars. Heat and light reflected back at her from the tinted windows shut tightly against the heat. Cold air teased her each time someone lowered the glass to hand her money.

Behind her the light changed. She didn't need to see it. She heard the deepening rumble as the vehicles surged forward. She lowered her sign and turned back toward the corner to wait for the next cycle of impatient motorists.

She stopped.

A man – tall and lean and wearing a khaki trench coat, despite the heat, and a fedora hat – sat on top of the concrete barrier that divided the sidewalk from the eight-lane highway fifty feet below. His right leg was bent, his knee pointed at her as his foot dangled. In his outstretched hand was a bottle of water.

Even from twenty feet she could see the beads of condensation glistening on the outside, calling her to its coldness. As if to reassure her, the man smiled. A shiny gold tooth marred an otherwise perfect smile.

"Take a drink, Lillian, before the sun heats it up," he said. Although he didn't shout, his melodic voice carried over the roaring engines.

"Do I know you?" She shaded her eyes with her hand but could not make out his face beneath the shadow of the hat's brim.

"Name's Johnny," the man replied. "Some call me the Salesman. Johnny will do, if it's all right with you."

"What do you want? I don't have any money." Lillian looked left and right, searching for escape routes. Left was down to the freeway; right led through four lanes of rush hour traffic. The only way out was behind her. Not good. She'd heard tell of panhandlers getting mugged by people who thought beggars somehow had a lot of money. She glanced back at Johnny. She sensed no threat.

He looked intently at her, his eyes squinted almost shut. "I happen to know you have fifty-three dollars and seventy-seven cents in your left front pocket," he finally said.

She took a faltering step back. "How do you know that?"

Johnny shrugged. "It doesn't matter," he replied with a smile. "I don't want your money. No, you're going to need that and more in a little while."

"If you don't want my money…."

"I want to make a trade."

"A trade?" She laughed. "For what? I don't have anything but a shopping cart with my bedroll in it. And the bedroll ain't worth trading. I'm homeless. I live on the street. I sleep under the bridge downtown or in the woods. What could I possibly have that you'd want?"

Johnny laughed. "Relax. I'm not the devil out looking for souls, although I wouldn't doubt he's somewhere near. No, all I want is that necklace, that Saint Jude's medallion."

Lillian's hand went to her throat as if to be sure the chain was still looped around her neck. "Why would you want this? My mom gave it to me. She said he was the patron saint of lost causes. I've certainly been one of those over the years."

"Are you Catholic?" Johnny shook his head as he reached inside his trench coat. As he did, things around them became vague, muffled, as if the two of them were in some kind of bubble. "I need the medallion – rather, someone else will need it – somewhere soon. In exchange, I'm offering you these."

He pulled two bracelets from his pocket. Her breath stopped. She was no expert, but to her, they looked like gold; slave bracelets, and real gold, not ten karat crap. He held them out to her. She reached for them, nearly dropping them from the unexpected weight. Each bracelet had three black crystals – one at the wrist, one at the back of the hand, and one in the finger ring. The yellow metal had a greasy feel. They looked as if they had been exposed to high heat recently. She looked more closely at the chains connecting the three parts. The designs looked like faces….

She screamed, dropped them both to the sidewalk, and took two quick steps back. They were faces and they were moving. That was bad enough. She could have sworn, however, that one of them was Candi's face. Why had someone carved Candi's likeness in gold? She looked up at Johnny, but refused to approach the bracelets.

Johnny looked at her. "I'm sure you heard about the fire the other night. The one at the Red River Lounge."

"The one where all those people died?"

Johnny nodded. "The same. There was a band playing on the stage."

Lillian shook her head slowly from side to side in negation, denial. "No. Don't say it." Her voice was barely a whisper.

"It was a heavy metal band…."

A little louder. "No."

"…called 'Hells' Archangels'."

"No."

"Your sister was the lead singer."

"No!" She screamed and fell to her knees. Her hands went to her face as she bent over. "No, no, no, no, no." Her voice dropped to a whisper as her body rocked forward and backward.

"Lillian." He spoke softly, but her head snapped back as if he'd dealt her an uppercut. Her wide open eyes fixed on him. Her cheeks were wet.

"Candi," she sob-whispered. She sniffed, and then wiped her forearm across her face.

"Do we have a trade?" Johnny asked softly.

"W-what?"

"The necklace?" He held his hands out toward her. His left was empty, palm up, waiting. The right held the bracelets, the heavy yellow chains dangling from either side.

As if in a trance, Lillian grasped the chain that looped around her neck and lifted it over her head. The silver medallion tickled as it slid over her skin. She felt her hair fall against her shoulders and back as she passed it across to him. A brief shudder – a shiver of loss – passed through her as the chain slipped from her hand. He caught it and slipped it into his trench coat as he handed her the bracelets. She looked down at them.

"Brother Paxton." Johnny whispered, yet the words drove deep into her brain. "Asylum. Four days."

She blinked rapidly three times and then looked up. Questions lay poised just behind her lips. There was no one there. Had she imagined him? She looked down at the bracelets. Candi's face looked back at her. Her features were twisted, frozen in an expression of agony and terror, but there was no mistaking who it was. The bracelets were real. Candi's face was real. She reached her right hand to her throat. The necklace was gone.

He had to be real, too. Either that or the heat had finally baked her mind.

She rose to her feet and walked to the corner. The bottle of water – still beaded with condensation – stood on the concrete barrier where the stranger had sat moments before. She picked it up, unscrewed the cap, and took a deep drink. Icy pain spiked behind her forehead, but she swallowed one more time before capping the bottle and setting it back on the concrete. Suddenly, she was again aware of the traffic, the heat, and one other thing. She felt a new and pressing urgency to find a place called Asylum. There was someone she was supposed to meet and something she needed to do – and soon.

James Paxton – now Brother Paxton to the flock of homeless who called the ashram Asylum – slipped the curtain to one side and looked out at the gathering crowd. A simple torii – a Shinto gate – stood downhill from the motorhome. Beyond the torii lay the crossroads. A small wooden dais rose from the center of the intersection. Jet black candle stands, each one four feet tall, stood at the cardinal points. Ebony-colored candles six inches across and twelve inches high rested unlit atop each. Despite the rapidly-fading light, he could see that all his paraphernalia was in place on the center altar.

He watched for a few more minutes as the homeless drifted down to the intersection. From inside the trailer the scene resembled a George Romero film – zombies shuffling across the open field. By twos and threes they settled onto the curved benches that surrounded the crossroads. A select few maintained order, ensuring that each row was full before any sat on the next one back.

James nodded to himself as he let the curtain fall back into place. He knew they couldn't care less about the ceremony soon to take place. He provided the food. He gave them shelter. He protected them from the law. This was sanctuary. Asylum. They would humor him by attending. They were happy that he never preached sin and damnation. No one tried to take their drugs or alcohol away from them.

He smiled. Soon it wouldn't matter who was on the hooch or the smoke or the rock. He would be the capacitor to drain all of their batteries. Once the gates were opened, they would feed the new masters.

Sha'Daa!

James glanced at his watch. It was time. He slipped it off and placed it on a nearby table. One last adjustment to his black satin robe, a smoothing of hair long gone, and through the door into the sultry summer night. He looked up. The solstice moon shone the faintest sliver – almost a new moon. He smiled. A dark night for dark work.

Lillian squirmed on the bench's hard wooden surface. She looked around at the people crowding in around her. The pews, if that's what they were, were curved and circled around the crossroads with only the intersecting roads breaking the rings. Everyone seated faced the raised platform in the center. It was almost like theater in the round.

Church in the round? She thought and giggled. Although she'd never witnessed any services during her two days here, that didn't mean there wasn't a religious underpinning to the whole asylum set up. She shifted, still trying to get comfortable. The homespun robe she and the others were issued scratched her skin as the long, full sleeves brushed her arms. Although she didn't know why all of them had to wear them, Lillian was grateful for the way the sleeves draped, concealing the bracelets.

She had managed to get an end seat – just to the left of center and facing the front of the dais. Next to her sat a young woman with straight black hair. Lillian could look directly at Brother Paxton while he delivered his sermon or whatever it was he planned to do on this hot, dark, sticky June evening. Why did it have to be at midnight? She was tempted to skip the service and go back to her tent, but the instructions were clear: Any who failed to attend would be banished from the ashram. What the hell. It was a small price to pay for three hots and a cot.

She tried to remember why she was here in the first place. She barely remembered Johnny. His instructions seemed no more than an unvocalized compulsion. Her arms tingled beneath the bracelets. Although distracting, it was more of a tickle than an irritation. She fidgeted. Sweat trickled down her back between her shoulder blades. She wanted to rub against something to push the irritating drop into the gown's fabric, but the benches were backless. She briefly considered having the woman sitting next to her scratch her back, then decided to grit her teeth and bear it.

As one, the crowd gasped. Like ebony smoke, Brother Paxton materialized on the dais. His black robe made him a darker spot in the gathering gloom. He stood, head bowed, hands crossed below his stomach. Long moments passed as he remained silent. Overhead a distant jet rumbled westward, its lights winking against the dark sky – white, red, and green stars seeking out their places in the firmament. Crickets chirruped in the high grasses and trees. A breeze soughed through the branches and grew silent. The crickets ceased their chorus.

Brother Paxton slowly raised his head as he stretched his arms outward and upward. A long, slender sword stretched its silvery tongue from his right hand. A scepter – an ankh wrought in gold and lapis lazuli – extended from his left. His head continued back until his eyes stared straight up at the midnight sky.

"Om ahd dha hashan, Ablis odalai Asmoday visjiah demodus ki lachma Amidaos, mentahitme Dejio lahsma odai pujilio mansasa, et debissa hashana!" The words rumbled from Paxton's throat like boulders rubbing together in a rockslide.

Lillian looked around. All eyes were riveted to the figure on the dais. No one moved. None fidgeted. She looked back.

"Man-i-o-ka-ape Vinilamasastis, Malachasias, Pinichia, et Amonastias Briedes: et asas remikanciatos ferenaptsa, be-ah-fah afale, Sedae et ayetdi tephiretho Melocanehe: et maytabaanu perphila Melocnehe et me Ja-hila-mala!"

The acrid tang of ozone filled the air. Lillian looked up. Heavy black clouds suddenly appeared. They tumbled and boiled as they crowded closer together. A rising wind pushed down from them carrying with it the stench of rotten eggs, tidal flats, and suppurating meat. She felt her gorge rise in her throat, but managed to push it back down.

A jagged light formed in the deepening blackness. Too enduring to be lightning, it grew and stretched and widened over the dais where Brother Paxton continued to scream ancient, incomprehensible words at the angry sky. Greenish-white light sparked from the crowd and streaked to Paxton, through him, changing to an intense blue-white stream that darted toward the jagged rent in the clouds. It hit the underbelly of the tumbling blackness and spread through it with the intense glare of a welding torch. Wide fissures opened up, releasing a stream of horrific beings riding impossible mounts.

Leading the charge was a three-headed being on a dragon. One head was that of a bull, one a man, and one a ram. A serpentine tail stretched behind it. The human head opened its mouth and a long tongue of flame shot forward. In its right hand it carried a lance with a banner streaming from it, flapping in the wind. Rows of infernal creatures followed behind, maintaining formation as they streaked earthward.

The creature lowered its lance and the army surged forward, passing around the leader and descending upon the crowd. Screams of terror and agony filled the air as the demonic horde rode through the people like a harvester through a wheat field. Lillian dove beneath the bench as several beings thundered past. Something thudded on the ground next to her. She looked to her right. The dark-haired woman who had shared the bench stared back at her, eyes impossibly wide, mouth twisted into a rictus. The jagged stump of her neck oozed blood into the ground.

Lillian screamed.

The scream was cut short as a sudden calm passed over and through her. The bracelets thrummed against her arms. Although the stench of death and blood filled her nostrils, she took a deep breath and pushed herself to her feet. The three-headed being sat dragon-back before her. She straightened.

"Who dares to stand before a King of Hell's minions?"

"We do." Like an outsider, Lillian watched and listened as a voice not entirely her own passed over lips she no longer controlled.

"I see only one."

Lillian raised her arms. The sleeves fell back against her shoulders. The bracelets glowed. "We are many. And, we say you are not welcome here. We deny you passage. Begone, Unclean Spirit. Return to your dismal realm. You will not triumph this Sha'Daa!"

Uncertainty clouded his face. Behind him, the carnage and rampage paused.

"Who are you to gainsay me?"

"We are the unjustly slain! This is our world. We banish you from it."

"I shall not be denied!" He roared and lowered his lance. The dragon stepped forward. The lance's tip pushed through Lillian's chest and emerged between her shoulder blades where moments before an errant bead of sweat made her squirm.

As the last breath flowed past her lips, she smiled and brought her hands forward, her arms parallel to the spear. White light flowed in twisting streams, faces of those who died at the night club. As the streams wound about the seated figure they pushed him from the back of the dragon. A wail of despair swept through the ranks of the creatures as, one-by-one and then in groups, they found themselves pulled back toward the yawning fissure.

One of the streams separated and stood above the fallen king.

"Depart and trouble this realm no more. Your role in Sha'Daa is at an end."

The king glared, and then clambered aboard the dragon. "I shall return," he swore.

"At that time another will be waiting to deny you."

The dragon spread its wings and rose into the night sky. As the king returned to the fissure, it closed behind him. The sky calmed. The slivered moon shone wanly over the carnage below.

"Candi?"

The figure turned and nodded. "Lil."

"I don't understand."

"Nor do I, Sis."

"But…"

The figure shrugged. "It seems we both had a role in this play."

"But…"

Candi extended her hand. "There is nothing left to question. We are finished here. Take my hand."

"Where are we going?"

"To a place where we can rest and relax and catch up on gossip."

She took her sister's hand and watched as the world around them faded.

"In local news, police are still baffled by the apparent cult-style mass suicide outside of Jasper's Crossing last night. Although they are not releasing any details, it appears that a number of followers of Brother James Paxton, as well as the cult leader and his staff, were found dead around the crossroads. We have a crew on the scene, and as soon as we know more, we will pass it along to you.

"In a similar story from…"

A tall, thin man wearing a tan trench coat and a neatly-creased fedora shook his head and turned away from the big screen TV on the department store wall. He felt the chains of the bracelet shift in his pocket. He stepped into the river of pedestrians moving past the shops and vanished.

*　*　*

<h1 style="text-align:center">INTERLUDE TWO</h1>

"Now?" Ashley asked. "It's happening right now?"

Johnny shrugged. "An hour, more or less. My trades are into full swing."

Ashley was visibly shaken. But her professional side took over and she quickly rounded up the items from Johnny's list and placed it all in a large burlap sack that the salesman slung over his shoulder.

Johnny frowned for a moment. "You look a little hesitant, young lady."

Ashley smiled. "On the contrary. Now that I know the stakes, my bargaining position just skyrocketed for the next forty-seven hours."

Johnny tipped his fedora and quickly exited through the front door.

The flow of foot traffic continued to increase and Ashley quickly had Barrax phone in a few favors to double security. With this many sticky fingers wandering the floors it was going to be a nightmare keeping an eye on things.

A short six-limbed form dressed in an Altarian space-suit dropped a large, leathery egg on the counter.

A loud, mechanical hiss erupted from the square helmet's voice-box-translator.

"I want to pawn my son."

"Yeah," Ashley said, "I've heard that one before."

*   *   *

CHAPTER THREE: HUNTER'S RUN

by Arthur Sanchez

Susa stood high on the granite outcropping and sniffed the wind. His broad flat snout flared as he took in the many scents of this world – and there were many scents. If he were not one of the best of the Ul-Alutha he might have been overwhelmed by it. Lesser trackers have had their minds destroyed from the sensory assault of a world so *full* of life. But Susa knew how to focus. He knew how to peel away the layers of information, ignoring the inconsequential ones, till he found the scent he was looking for. Digging his claws deep into the stone, he hoisted himself up onto his massive hind legs as a cool breeze filtered through the forest and stirred the sensitive fur on his face. Yes, he thought, his prey was near.

The man tried to mask his scent with pine needles and animal dung but the distinctive metallic tang of his flesh could still be detected. It was a stupid choice – fleeing into this mountainous forest. The man would have done better fleeing into one of the human cities. The smells of so many humans packed together would have slowed Susa down but there would also have been casualties. That the man cared about such things was disappointing. If the Firsts had not ordered this man's death, Susa would have never considered him worth tracking. But the Firsts had been very specific in their instructions: "Do not let him escape you."

The ceremony had been in another world, in another reality. The demon hordes were amassing for the Sha'Daa, and the Firsts, walking on their hind legs and dressed in crimson robes, were reading portents and signs in the entrails of slaves. High over the obsidian plains of Harob, on an outcropping of pure crystal, the high ones prepared for the breach in reality. 10,000 years they'd waited. 10,000 years they'd planned. And the day was now here. So when the signs soured and the blood curdled upon the stone altar, the ripples of concern could be felt throughout the assembled horde. That's when the call for the best of the best, the most relentless, the most successful of the all trackers was issued. Susa was summoned.

Beside the disemboweled corpse of a human slave they showed him the artifact. It was a simple stone carving of a man, kneeling as if in prayer, with his arms crossed over his chest. The First Ones fretted and fussed over the carving. They cursed and cast spells over it. In the end, they declared it dangerous. A single man, they warned, could halt the Sha'Daa. The last of his kind, and with powers he did not even know he possessed, he could tip the scales of fate in favor of the humans. That could not be. So Susa was told that he would have from the start of the Summer Solstice till the moment the sun was highest in the sky to kill the man. That was when the demons would cross and the man could not be allowed to meet them. To aid Susa in his mission they cut a slit in his forehead and inserted the stone carving beneath his skin. Now all his senses were locked in on this man. They would be bound together till one of them was dead.

But the man had sensed him coming. How? Who knew? Perhaps it was magic. Perhaps that is why the First Ones wanted him dead. Regardless, the instant Susa arrived in the world the man had known it and the chase was on.

Susa leapt off the stone outcropping and landed in the middle of a clearing. His broad paws sank deep into the muddy soil. He liked this place. He liked the forest that made concealing himself so simple. He liked the stones and boulders that jutted out of the soil like the bones of some ancient beast. He liked how the mountains clawed at the sky and tore at the clouds. And he liked the name of the land – Adirondacks. It was a demon name. He had no idea how the humans had come to learn of it but Susa took it to be a good omen. "Hunter's Run" suited a tracker.

Sniffing the air once again, Susa took off at a brisk trot. The hunt had gone on far longer than it should have. It was already way past dawn and the man still breathed. But some allowance had to be made for the man being in his own territory. The man knew this land and how to use it to his advantage. That fact had led Susa to a realization. After hours of pursuit and two near misses, the erratic course the man had taken with its countless crisscrossing and seemingly irrational backtracking now appeared purposeful. The man was trying to remain within a few miles of his starting point. It was as if he was afraid to leave this area. To prove it to himself, Susa raked his claws across the trunk of a large pine tree. The gouges were deep and the tree immediately began to bleed sap.

Susa then went to a gap in the underbrush that would have been the natural point of departure for the man. Animals prefer not to disturb their environment – especially if being hunted. It's wiser to use a natural gap in the underbrush than to trample your way through the plants leaving telltale signs of your passage. Sure enough, a brief examination of the gap revealed several disturbed pebbles. Something had passed this way recently and had kicked them up. Further examination revealed the partial imprint of a boot heel. This was human prey and not one of the many animals that lived in this forest. Better yet, it was his target. The boot heel had a distinctive notch cut into it and Susa had learned back at the target's den that his boot had that notch. Focusing on the occasional imprint in the mud, Susa pursued the man.

Not surprisingly, after fifteen minutes, Susa found himself standing in the same field beside the same tree. The only reason Susa could think of for this behavior was that the man was trying to waste time, to extend the chase. Did the man know that the First Ones wanted him dead before high noon? Susa dismissed the thought. How could a mere man know of such things? It did not matter. The man would not live to see the sun reach its zenith. Now that he knew the game, Susa stopped following the scent trail. Instead, he launched himself through the underbrush and cut west across the dense forest. It no longer mattered who saw the path he took. The man had repeatedly looped back in order to retrace his steps. Susa would catch the man on his return trip and end this hunt.

Susa shambled through the forest with remarkable speed, his pulse quickening with the thought that he'd catch up to his target soon. So it was with a bit of surprise that he came upon a clearing full of humans. So far the prey had avoided population centers. Why then did he choose to come here? Susa sniffed the air. The man was near but the air now hung heavy with the scents of other humans. He entered the clearing swinging his head from side to side, attempting to tease free the one thread of information that mattered to him.

He was halfway across a paved lot filled with overheated metal boxes when the air was pierced by a shrill, high-pitched, scream. "Look, Mama, a bear!"

Susa would have ignored both the scream and the shout had either contained even a modest amount of fear, but neither had. He turned his massive head toward a wooden structure he took to be a human temple or trading post. A small child was standing by the entrance and she was jumping up and down with excitement.

"A bear!" she screamed. "It's a bear!"

Other humans began to emerge from the structure and there was a sign hanging above the entrance that declared that this was the Adirondak Loj. The First Ones had given Susa the ability to understand symbols but despite being able to read the words they were meaningless to him. What did mean something to him was the fact that he was certain that his prey was within the structure. The building did not appear to be a fortress. The walls would be easy to breach. They had windows on the ground level and no one formidable guarded the entryways.

"Quick, Myrtle, take my picture," a voice called out.

Susa turned to spot a bowlegged, overweight, male human running towards him. He did not appear to be attacking, so he was of no concern.

"Don't get too close," an equally round female called after him. She'd swathed herself in clothes dyed in garish and conflicting colors. They neither complemented her natural coloring nor helped her blend with her surroundings. If anything, they'd made her stand out as a natural target for predators. Susa wondered if her flesh was poisonous. Poisonous creatures often advertised that fact with garish colors.

"Don't worry, I'll be fine," the male called back.

"Harold," the woman screamed, "it's a wild animal. It could take your head off."

"You've been watching too much Animal Planet," the man countered. "Look, I'll make friends with it." Something struck Susa on the side of the head. "There, I gave it half of my candy bar. Now we're friends, ain't we big fella?" Susa stared down at the food offering. It smelled sweet and fatty.

"You like that, huh, big fella? You want some more?" The man held out more of the candy bar.

When the man got within reach, Susa did the obvious thing. He lashed out with a paw and decapitated the fool. There was a satisfying look of surprise on the man's face just as his head rolled off his shoulders and blood squirted ten feet into the air from the severed neck. The headless corpse continued walking a few steps until it fell down, quivering uncontrollably. After a suitable pause the air was split with new screams, all of them filled with terror. Susa was pleased.

Moving quickly lest his prey hear the commotion and take off again, Susa charged the building the humans had branded the Loj. Humans scattered before him and one even tried to prevent his entry by standing in the doorway and waving his arms and shouting. As if putting on a display of ferocity might dissuade him from his mission. Susa took great pleasure in running the man down and crushing his skull beneath one of his paws.

Susa hesitated at the entranceway. So far the prey had chosen to avoid him and run. However, his scent was heavy within the building. This was not the first time he'd been here in the last few hours. Why? Was this where he'd chosen to stand and fight? Had he discovered his special ability and was he now prepared to use it? Susa moved into the building cautiously.

The interior of the building was cool and dark. Susa's eyes adjusted quickly to gloom. Several humans were fleeing out an entrance on the far side of the room, but none were his target. There were tables and chairs scattered throughout the interior of the room. Pictures hung along the walls of scenic locations around the area. Susa recognized some of the mountaintops, as he'd been crossing them just this morning. Someone had been eating in here. The remains of the meal had been trampled in their rush to escape. From what he could see it had been better food than what that man had offered Susa outside. Susa was glad he'd killed the man. Slaves that made inferior offerings deserved to die.

Moving slowly Susa allowed the prey's scent to flow over his entire olfactory nerve. The man was close, enticingly close. That's when he heard them. Around the corner of one wall he could make out the voices of two humans having a conversation. Susa's ears perked right up. How odd. He'd just cleared out this entire building by sending individuals running in terror from every exit, but these two were calm enough to be holding a conversation. Susa silently moved to the edge of the wall. Angling his head so just one eye was exposed, he peered around the corner at the humans.

There were two human males standing there. One was his target. Despite having never seen the man before Susa still recognized him for what he was. The stone artifact in his forehead ensured that. Susa, however, was not very impressed by him. The man was of average height for a human, thin, tan-colored skin with long, black, hair braided into a single thick chord that fell down the center of his back. Susa could tell that he was past his prime from the silver strands that shot through the braided hair. Dressed in simple working clothes, the man had no weapons, no armaments, not even a spiked tail of which to speak. Yet he was a threat?

Directly in front of the man was a second human male. This one was tall and thin, with most of his body encased in an animal skin that had been tailored to fit his frame and hide his limbs. He wore a head covering that, in sunlight, would have shaded his face and hidden his features. Indoors, away from sunlight, the covering seemed more like an adornment than a necessity. This second male was intensely staring at Susa's prey. He was holding out his right hand with the palm up and in his left hand he held some sort of container up for the prey to see. He appeared to be trying to negotiate a trade. There was nothing extraordinary about this human, yet everything about this individual made the fur on Susa's neck stand on end. Susa risked pushing the tip of his nose past the edge of the wall to get a sniff of the cloaked man but he got nothing. That was, of course, impossible. Everything had a scent – from the varnished wood floors to the worn entryways that bore the residue of hundreds of hands pushing open the doors, to his target's fear and desperation-soaked shirt. Everything, except this man, had a scent.

"Do we have a trade?" the tall man asked of Susa's prey. He stared so intently at the man that he seemed to be trying to will him to comply.

The man hesitated. Then he nodded. "Yes, we do." He then drew out a leather pouch that hung around his neck by a string. It had lain hidden beneath his shirt. He opened it and drew out a small animal bone. He contemplated it for a second before handing it to the tall man who handed over the container. The tall man then stepped back, slipped the bone into his pocket and tipped his hat to the prey. He then did something that made Susa's blood freeze. Having concluded his transaction, he turned, looked straight at Susa as if he'd always known he was there, and smiled. A gold tooth gleamed in that smile. Susa roared and charged forward. The Salesman had been a creature of myth and legend, a story told to every demon to frighten the unwary. He was not supposed to be flesh and blood and here trading with Susa's prey.

To his prey's credit, the man did not hesitate to turn and dive through one of the low windows. Glass and wood shattered as he landed outside, rolled onto on his feet, and began running. Susa skidded to a halt in front of the window, confident that the man could not escape him. He turned to confront The Salesman only to find the man gone. Not a surprise. Legend spoke of his ability to come and go as he pleased. Susa turned back to the broken window and leapt through it. He had a mission to complete.

His prey was barely down the dirt road when Susa hit the ground. Extending his claws he dug deep into the earth and propelled himself after the man. The man ran screaming and waving his arms and as he reached the end of the road he veered left into an open field. Madness, Susa observed, often comes to those who are not prepared to die. He adjusted his path so that he could cut through the trees and catch the man just as he reached the center of the field.

After all was said and done, it was pathetically easy. Susa had five times the speed of his human prey. As he barreled down on the man he felt a great satisfaction in proving his worthiness. The First Ones had entrusted this task to him and now he was about to ensure that their confidence in him was not mistaken. The man, in his hysteria, had not even noticed that Susa was no longer following but instead was about to blindside him. Susa had debated barreling into the man and trampling him to death but decided against that. The sun was already too high in the sky. They were minutes from the crossing and even trampled the man might live long enough to cast a spell or utter a curse. Susa had no idea what power he possessed but he knew he could not give the man the slightest opportunity to use it. He would decapitate the man the moment he reached him. He could present the head to the First Ones upon their arrival. Their gratitude at his service should be considerable.

To his surprise the man stopped in the middle of the field. He had his back to Susa and appeared to be doubled over in pain. Susa smiled. The end had come and only now had the full extent of his desperation become apparent to him. Susa reached out with a paw. He'll make it quick. The deathblow would –

The man ducked low under Susa's extended arm as he spun on his heel and cast a handful of reddish powder into Susa's face. Susa involuntarily sucked in the powder and before he could blink his mind exploded in agony. His senses were on fire! Susa crashed to the ground and buried his snout in the mud. He tried desperately to rub the sensation out with dirt, and when that failed, raked his face with his claws in an attempt to dig the powder out. But nothing helped. His mind, overwhelmed by the sensations, sent conflicting messages to his muscles. His limbs jerked and shuddered as even the most basic of commands, like get up and walk, were scrambled beyond recognition. A lesser Ul-Alutha would have lost consciousness, but Susa was able to detach enough of his mind from the pain to be able to observe what was happening. The man now stood over him with a satisfied look on his face. Susa wanted to rip it off his skull.

"Gotcha," the man whispered. He held up the container the Salesman had given him and upended it to show that it was empty. "Freshly ground Ghost Peppers," he said. "It's one of the hottest chili peppers on the planet and my eyes are tearing just standing next to you. I can only imagine what a fistful of this would do to one whose senses are as superb as yours." Susa wanted desperately to show him the agony he was feeling.

The man knelt down and reached out to Susa's face and for an instant the demon thought the man might try to pet him. Instead, the man reached up to where the First Ones had cut into his forehead, pulled back the skin, and retrieved the stone artifact.

"Legend said you would bring this to me," the man said with awe in his voice. "I never believed it. Who believes the stories his grandfather tells him?" He stared down at the little stone man with the crossed arms. He then reached up to his own face and for the first time Susa saw that the man had things dangling from his earlobes. From his right ear he retrieved a small granite disk. He laid it on one of the arms of the stone statue. Susa suddenly felt a surge of power course through the air.

"10,000 years ago my people wandered this land," the man said to him. "They watched the skies and learned from the world around them." He then reached up to his left ear and retrieved an obsidian shard. It was shaped like a spear. He laid it across the statue's other arm. The surge of power in the field was now doubled. This is what the First Ones must have feared.

"When your kind first appeared, they overran my people and there was much death and destruction," the man explained. Susa tried to get up but his limbs would not respond. He'd hoped the effect of the chili pepper would wane but instead he felt it seeping deeper into his system. His throat was swelling and he was finding it hard to breathe. It was as if his body was trying to cut itself off from the poison but in doing so was causing its own destruction.

"But then a hunter recalled that on the night that the demons first appeared a star had fallen from the sky. The people had taken that falling star as a sign of the dark days to come, but the hunter pointed out that where that star had landed, no demons were to be found. The people searched, many were killed, but when they found that star they found the hunter's word to be true. The demons could not approach it, could not pass it. It was a wall they could not breach. The people made this from it – to honor the hunter." The man held up the little statue and Susa could see that what had looked like a man in prayer was now a man holding a shield and a spear. His kneeling stance had not been one of reverence but of defense, a pose meant to ward off attack.

"But in the final battle," the man continued, "the one that closed this world to your kind, the statue was destroyed and the pieces scattered. We were only able to retrieve these two," he indicated the spear and the shield, "but broken they were useless. Prophecy, however, promised that the statue would be made whole when it was needed again. Who knew that it would be a demon who would make it happen?"

The man turned and placed the statue on the ground. He said a prayer over it and Susa could feel the power in it surge. It poured out of the little stone man like a geyser erupting from the ground and flooded the air around them. To Susa it felt as if something had landed on his chest and was pressing against his heart. His eyesight began to dim and he knew he was done. Done in by a small statue he himself had carried into this world.

The man wandered into what was left of his vision. "I bet you're wondering why I'm telling you all this." Susa would have preferred to die in silence. He cared little for legends. "It is because this is the story of how we remember and because there is nobody else who would understand this story. We," he indicated the two of them, "are the last of our kinds." He then shrugged his shoulders. "At least, we soon will be." Susa's eyes went wide. He must warn the others but try as he might he could not even move his head.

The man sat down next to Susa's head in order to remain within his vision. "Do you know what a Hunter's Run is?" Susa tried to move a paw, a claw, anything to strike the man down. "It's a trap. It's where hunters drive prey so that they will have nowhere else to go. That is what Adirondacks means," he said. "It is an ancient word for an ancient plan. The statue creates a barrier. The demons create a portal. When the demons attempt to cross the portal they will encounter the barrier. They will not be able to pass it but they will not stop trying to pass it. The demons in front will be crushed by the press of the demons in the rear and they will continue till they have all trampled each other to death."

The man looked up into the sky with anticipation and Susa joined him. It was almost high noon. His heart was slowing and his breath was failing. His death was imminent and there was nothing he could do to prevent it. He was the best of the Ul-Alutha. He was the most relentless of all trackers. He had found his prey and in doing so had delivered the stone statue to the one man in the universe who could use it. The irony, if nothing else, did not escape him. Though, with his last thoughts fading, Susa could only wish that it had.

*   *   *

INTERLUDE THREE

It took Ashley/Astraea four years to track down the men who murdered her master and nearly ended her own life. The last detestable creature dropped at her feet, his throat cut by a vicious dagger on a country road outside of the west coast town of Dingle, Ireland. He was kicked into a roadside ditch to disappear from sight.

Walking away from this drama, having cleaned her hands on some wet grass, Ashley slowly roused as if from a dream.

She suddenly knew, on some deep level, that her former tormenters were no more. How they had passed, how Astraea had brought about their end, no images sprang to mind. But all that knowledge seemed unimportant at the moment, for Ashley now felt she was free. Free from her vow of revenge. Free of hate. Free from the terror that had accosted her and so dramatically altered her life.

But what now? Ashley's deific conscience whispered in her mind. What purpose will you embrace?

Ashley looked back upon the village of Dingle that she had remembered entering, but not actually leaving. Its people were a microcosm of the world at large, some friendly, some outgoing, and just as many distrustful and suspicious and even prejudiced and hateful toward foreigners, especially those of Asian or African descent. Still, Ashley felt a strange kinship to this village, and the ancient standing stones that marked a portion of its perimeter.

"I think," Ashley said, "I think I will make my home here."

And what will we do?

"We'll run a store… a shop," Ashley said.

*   *   *

CHAPTER FOUR: FALL FROM GRACE

by Jeff Barnes

"Pride, the first peer and president of hell."
— Daniel Defoe

Tommy's family was having a yard sale.

A pallid, thin man, dark eyes shaded by a hat, walked into the yard. He was wearing a dark suit and overcoat entirely too heavy for the weather. The strange man spent some time looking through the boxes. He stopped at one of the boxes with Tommy's cast-off toys and picked up a figure of some kind of ant-man beast and brought it over to her.

"Ma'am, my name is Johnny. I'm a salesman specializing in… curios. You have a fine collection. However, I'm interested in this particular item. Would you consider parting with it?"

"Hi, I'm Madeline. You really want that thing? I'll be happy to give it to you for a dollar."

"How very kind of you, Madeline. Could you perchance apprise me of its provenance?" Johnny stuck his hand into his coat pocket and started rummaging around.

Madeline had to tear her eyes away because it looked like half his arm was in the pocket. "Provenance? Well, it was my son's. I have no idea where he got it. That thing creeps me out. I almost threw it away, but I decided to stick it in the yard sale on a whim."

"Ah, here we are. How fortuitous for us both that you acted upon that impulse." Johnny pulled his arm out of his pocket with a silver dollar in his fingers. He rolled it across the back of his hand into Madeline's outstretched palm.

"Wow, I always wished I could do that…. Wait a minute. This is a real silver dollar. I can't accept this!"

"Shouldn't all silver dollars be real my lady? I hate it so when the fake ones vanish without warning. They are as bad as the second sock in the dryer. I want to visit the dimension that sucks socks. They owe me! At any rate, a deal was made and the deal done. Could I trouble you with one minor request?"

"I suppose. Do you need a restroom, or a glass of water?"

"No, nothing so intrusive. I would merely like to ask your son about this item if he is available."

"Sure, just a moment. Tommy, come out here for a minute please!"

A couple minutes later a ten-year-old Tommy came out of the house onto the lawn. "What is it Mom? I paused the game, but I need to get back in there."

"This man, Johnny, wants to ask you about your action figure."

Tommy saw Messy Fleas in Johnny's hand. "Oh that thing. Messy Fleas. I'm glad we're getting rid of it."

"Tommy, when did you get, uh, Messy Fleas?" Johnny asked.

"I'm not sure," Tommy frowned.

Johnny's dark eyes grew large in front of Tommy. The little boy suddenly felt like he was falling into the endless pools of darkness that were the Salesman's pupils.

"I think…," Tommy whispered, "I think it was about three years ago…."

Mephistopheles was among the mightiest of the scouts who would prepare the way for the horde at Sha'Daa, but he wasn't content to be among the mightiest. He wanted to be acknowledged the mightiest and breach the doorway first, ready to inflict pain and terror upon the weak humans on the other side. There was one obstacle in his way: Sarshoth, leader of the scouts. Sarshoth had defeated all challengers so quickly that all were afraid to challenge his position.

Mephistopheles examined himself critically. A seeming mix of ant and human, he stood seven feet tall at the head and over twelve feet long in the body. The chitin that covered him could shrug off most blades and projectiles with ease, showing few nicks or dings from previous fights. His upper body had cutting claws, able to sheer through steel like tin foil. Grasping claws jutted out under the cutting claws, able to perform delicate tasks when needed. His head bore human features with the exception of questing antennae jutting from the forehead. Mephistopheles knew what was in that head would give him victory over Sarshoth.

Mephistopheles had witnessed all of Sarshoth's duels. He was snake-like with arms that folded back against his body when not needed. His scaly hide was well armored, but the two keys to his victories were the hinged fangs in his mouth that released a toxin almost instantly lethal and the fantastic speed that rendered him nearly invisible when used to full effect. Within the confines of the challenge ring Sarshoth could launch an attack so fast that his opponent was thrashing in death throes on the ground before the bell stopped vibrating. Mephistopheles had seen those fangs easily penetrate armor nearly as tough as his own.

Mephistopheles saw his servant had finished applying the oil. He strode from his enclosure, shouting, "Sarshoth, I, Mephistopheles challenge you for leadership of the scouts. Meet me in the challenge ring, Worm!" Noise levels increased as word was passed and demons crawled, scuttled, and flapped to find places to witness the challenge.

Mephistopheles had just taken his place in the ring when he heard words that sounded as though they were formed from a high-pitched steam kettle. "You dare to disturb me at my rest, bug? You have grown weary of life!"

Sarshoth paused at the other end of the arena to examine Mephistopheles. "You think to best me by waking me and facing me dressed in oil? You think perhaps my fangs will miss because I am not fully awake, or that they will glance off because of a bit of oil? Clever, but futile. I accept your challenge. I have been too long without a kill." Sarshoth pulled himself into a tight coil, prepared to end the fight immediately as he always had in the past.

Mephistopheles suppressed a smile. He had released hormones into his brain and body as Sarshoth spoke. As Sarshoth coiled, Mephistopheles completely emptied his reserves and felt everything slow around him and heat began to build. His body and mind quickened. He carefully kept his movements very slow to appear normal and felt satisfaction that Sarshoth had fallen for his misdirection. He stood tall and waited for the gong.

As the gong began to sound Mephistopheles pulled his main body to the ground and bent his torso completely backward so his upper body was lying on top of his lower body. This left his claws up and he watched Sarshoth sail over him in slow motion, going for a center mass hit as he always had in the past. With a cutting claw, Mephistopheles cut one of the extended fangs from Sarshoth's mouth and with his grasping claw turned it over and stabbed it into the belly that was flying over him.

Mephistopheles turned as he heard the thump of the body into the ground and saw Sarshoth thrashing in slow motion. As he had suspected, Sarshoth was resistant to his own poison, but not immune. Mephistopheles leapt and pinned the body to the ground just behind the head. He carefully reached around and pried the mouth open, cut the second fang free, then drove it through the snake head beneath him.

He leapt free and watched the death throes of his foe. Stunned silence around the ring seemed to stretch for minutes. Mephistopheles knew that the event had taken place in less than three seconds in objective time. Now he had to get away to cool or internal heat from the hormones would roast him in his chitin. He had scouted a pond that would be sufficient for the task a couple miles from the edge of the fortification. He was gone before the silence turned to cheering.

The water steamed around him as he immersed himself in it. His thinking became muddled and his mind drifted. Mephistopheles let the smile he had suppressed earlier sharpen. As his mind drifted he became aware of other minds around him. He jerked his eyes opened and prepared to defend himself, but no one was nearby. As he became more alert, the minds he had touched disappeared. Curious, he verified that no source of harm was near and he settled back into the pond, putting himself into a light trance. Again he let his mind drift and once again felt minds around him. He let them wash over him and realized that these were humans! As he felt their thoughts flow through him he realized that these insipid minds belonged to sheep, lambs to the slaughter when the gate was opened. The thought of the blood and terror to come sent shivers of delight through his body. One mind speared through the insipid crowd like a jolt of adrenaline.

I hate Vivian. I hate her, I hate her, I hate her. Drown her in mud. Cut her. Burn her. Tear her apart and watch her insides go everywhere. Feed her to the dog. I hate hate hate hate.

The hatred was intoxicating. Weakened, but recovering, Mephistopheles could not resist reaching out to these beautiful, hateful thoughts. After a moment of resistance, he felt contact with the other.

Hatred, rage, these are good things, my child. They make you powerful.

Mephistopheles felt the mind pause in surprise. He fed back some of the raw emotional energy to the other mind. Rage is powerful. Vivian is weak. What you feel is right. Vivian must die at your hand. It is the way this must end.

The rekindled rage on the other end was euphoric. This was a feeling Mephistopheles did not want to lose, could not stand to lose. He devoted more power to the link to strengthen it. As he did so, Mephistopheles was struck by the strength of the link. This place was a weak spot in the barrier between the dimensions. Even in his weakened state, Mephistopheles might be able to pierce the barrier if he could use the mind on the other side as an anchor to draw himself through. He would be able to cross over before a gateway opened and establish himself as the rightful overlord before any of the others could cross over through an open gateway during Sha'Daa. The thoughts of the chaos created by his own hand served to heighten the euphoria generated by the contact with the other side. He almost smiled for a second time at the thought of the rest of his brood breaching the gate to find nothing remaining for them to do, but there was work to be done.

You must act on these feelings. This is the path to true power. I can help. Working together we destroy Vivian.

She needs to die! I want it to be bad and gross. I need to do it. The mind resumed its raging fury.

I can help you if you allow. I can come to you. Together we will give Vivian the ending she so richly deserves.

Who are you? How can you help me? I hate Vivian. I want her to die. I want to kill her.

I am Mephistopheles. With your help I can come to you and together we can kill Vivian in the most beautifully horrible way you and I can imagine.

Maffis…Messy…whatever. You can come here and help? Help me to kill Vivian?

Yes, I can. The hatred you feel gives me strength. If you let me bind myself to you I can use that hatred to pull myself through the dimension separating us. Then together we can bring Vivian to the gruesome end she so justly deserves.

We're going to kill her? Tonight?

Yes we will. As soon as you agree to let me bind myself to you, we can work together to bring me to you. Then Vivian will experience unimaginable pain. Her death will be a work of art.

I like art. What should I do?

You don't need to do anything. I will bind my will to yours and use that to pull myself to you. Trust me. Let me be your servant in the destruction of Vivian.

There was a long pause, then a firm, Okay.

Excitement stirred within him. Mephistopheles poured power into the connection. He located the firm core of the mind and wrapped his own mind around it, melding himself to it, creating an anchor within its desire. He then devoted his power and concentration to using the bond to pull himself to the mind on the other side, toward the hatred and deep desire for revenge that drugged him. It was excruciating and sublime, as though he were being squeezed and shredded and enmeshed with that sweet hungering rage. He continued to pour power into the pull and felt the resistance suddenly give way as he fell to a hard surface on the other side of the barrier. Eyes closed, he was elated by his success. He had expended a lot of power breaching the barrier, but that would return. He was in the world of humanity before any of the others. He reveled in his future of blood and terror.

"Ow, what did you do? That hurt in my head a little!" A momentary pause, then, "You're kind of ugly, but kind of cool too Mefes…Messi…I'll call you Messy Fleas! My name is Tommy, Tommy Carter."

The voice was a cold shock to Me… Messy Fleas. In horror he realized that the new name had become his own. His eyes flew open and he looked… up… at a boy of about six. Messy Fleas' mind reeled. He was a shrunken shadow of himself. He fought off an urge to… cry… throw things. If he were in his former realm he would have been maiming and killing. He thought perhaps the trip had tired him… that he needed … a nap? What?! His kind didn't sleep! What was going on here? He was the mighty Me… Messy Fleas. A cloak of despair settled over Messy Fleas as his new identity wrapped around his psyche.

"So Messy Fleas, what are we going to do to that evil little thing Vivian?"

The hatred reenergized Messy Fleas, renewed his feeling of power and strength. With proper guidance, Messy Fleas would regain his former power and stature as Tommy grew into his potential. Messy Fleas felt his mood swing.

"Vivian. Where is Vivian Tommy? I want to show you the great things we can do, Tommy."

"She's in Sandy's room. She's my little sister."

"Vivian is your little sister? Excellent! This will be so cool!" Messy Fleas felt refreshed as the hatred flowed through the room, though he wondered a bit at his own use of words. Maybe he was just adapting to this time and place.

"Yuck, that's gross! Sandy is my sister. Vivian is her stupid doll."

"Vivian is a doll? We're going to kill a doll?" Messy Fleas fought a sudden return of despair. Perhaps this wasn't so bad. It could be the first step of turning Tommy into the creature Messy Fleas needed him to be.

"Yes! Because of Vivian I got sent to bed without getting to watch Super Friends. I want her to die!"

Messy Fleas' mind reeled again. "What is Super Friends?"

"You don't know Super Friends? Everyone knows Super Friends!"

Messy Fleas looked into Tommy's eyes with dark intensity, bringing the conversation back on track. "Okay, so Vivian is Sandy's doll. Vivian must die. We will kill her now. Vivian will never again get in the way of what you want."

"Yay, Messy Fleas! You're my friend! Let's kill her right now!"

"Vivian is in the room with Sandy?"

"Yes, she sleeps with her every night. She is such a baby!"

"Okay, you sneak out to the back porch and I'll get Vivian. I'll see you there in a couple minutes."

Messy Fleas left the room and crossed the hallway to the next door. He quietly cracked it open and looked in. The parents' room. He should have asked Tommy which room Sandy was in. He sighed and crept down the hall to the next door. Bathroom, dammit! Across the hall and a moment later he had the next door cracked. Even in the dark he could see a room so pink he worried his eyes would bleed. He crept into the room and approached the bed. He could hear the even breathing of someone asleep. He wasn't tall enough to see who lay there, so he approached the corner and climbed up the bed post. He found a little girl snuggled into the covers with a doll clutched in her arms. Her thumb was planted firmly in her mouth. The cuteness of the scene combined with the pink room made Messy Fleas a bit queasy. He needed to get through this quickly before he did some impromptu redecorating with his stomach contents.

Messy Fleas approached the girl and laid his grasping claw on her brow, commanding her into deeper sleep. She moved restlessly then settled down. Slowly and gently Messy Fleas removed the doll from her arms. Sandy whimpered once and settled back into sleep without waking. The doll was as big as Messy Fleas so he draped her over his middle segment and dropped quietly to the floor. As he settled the doll in place, Messy Fleas noticed that his powerfully armored chitin had become soft and flexible. He had to remind himself of his potential for the future to stave off the depression that threatened him.

He hesitated, listening for signs of movement. He heard Tommy sneaking not so quietly down the stairs, but no other noises out of the ordinary. He went through the door, closed it quietly behind him, and scuttled down the stairs to meet Tommy at the back door. Messy Fleas felt a spike of anger as Tommy snickered to see Vivian riding Messy Fleas like a weird little horse as he unlocked the door and they went onto the deck in the back.

Messy Fleas put the doll down and Tommy snarled. "Let's do it right here! Vivian has to die now!"

"Shhh….You need to whisper Tommy. In your room I could shield our voices from being heard outside its walls, but I can't do that outside. We don't want to wake your parents."

"Okay," Tommy whispered. "You said it would be gross. What are we going to do?"

"You watch while I take care of this. You'll be very happy with the result. Stay here. I need to gather some supplies. I'll be right back." Messy Fleas spent a few minutes in the yard gathering some items to help his work before returning to the deck and the doll.

As Tommy watched, Messy Fleas studied the doll for a moment before going into action. First he used his claws to shred the doll's pajamas. He placed the shredded cloth haphazardly around the doll. From the corner of his eye he saw Tommy practically quaking with excitement. Then Messy Fleas sliced open the arms and legs of the doll with his cutting claws. He used sticks artfully placed to look like shattered bones poking through the skin. Then he slit open the cloth belly. He pinned the cloth 'skin' open with pebbles. He carefully sculpted the fiberfill insides to look like entrails spilling from inside the cavity. He wrapped one loop of fiberfill gut tightly around the doll's neck. Now came the harder part. He used energy to mold the soft plastic face of the doll. He caused the glass eyes to look down into the gaping cavity and the mouth to open in a silent scream. For a final touch he partially scalped the doll and re-formed the plastic underneath to look like skull bone. He stepped back and looked on his work with satisfaction.

Tommy excitedly clapped once before remembering about the noise. He was bouncing up and down as he patted Messy Fleas. "You did it! That is awesome! It's so gross! She will never bother us again. You're the best, Messy Fleas!"

Messy Fleas felt the atmosphere around them and was satisfied that no weather would disturb his work. He laid a minor repulsion on the doll to make sure that no animals would disturb it. The repulsion would also heighten the impact when the doll was found in the morning. Tommy and Messy Fleas returned to Tommy's room where Tommy babbled on happily for some time before finally dropping off to sleep.

Messy Fleas relaxed and restored his energy. He found himself examining his soft body and tiny claws, but forced himself to stop before a whimper could escape. He turned to making plans for how he would mold and shape his young protégé into the person that would restore Messy Fleas to his former power and glory, followed by preparation for the arrival of his brood. Tommy was his ticket to dominating the humans here. When Sha'Daa arrived and his brood finally opened a gate here, Messy Fleas would take great pleasure in accepting their obeisance. His dark fantasy kept his mind off the catastrophe that had befallen him as the sun came up and the rest of the family began to move about the house.

Messy Fleas froze as the door cracked open. The mother poked her head inside and saw Tommy asleep. She turned her head back and said, "He's still asleep. I'll get breakfast started. We can wake him when it's ready."

From the hallway a deeper, slightly sleep-blurred voice said, "Okay Sweetie. I'll check Sandy."

Messy Fleas' sharp ears picked up a sleepy voice saying, "Morning, Daddy."

"Good morning, Sweetheart. Did you sleep well?"

"I had a scary dream, Daddy. But it's okay 'cause Vivian…Vivian? Where's Vivian, Daddy?"

"I don't know Sweetie. I don't see her in the room. Did you leave her downstairs last night?"

"No, Daddy. I went to sleep with her and now she's gone. And I had a bad dream. I'm scared, Daddy," the voice trembled.

"It's okay Sweetie, we'll find her. Come help me look."

"Okay."

Messy Fleas heard the covers rustle as the man picked up the girl and the floor creaked as he walked through the hall and down the stairs. Minor sounds of movement drifted through the house as father and child looked for Vivian.

Messy Fleas jumped onto the bed and shook Tommy. "Wake up, wake up. They are going to find Vivian soon. You don't want to miss this do you?"

Tommy woke up groggily, wiping the sleep away from his eyes. "Wha…Oh!" He sat up and heard his father walking around downstairs. Then they heard the slap of his feet on the linoleum of the kitchen floor. The sound paused for a moment. They heard a gasp.

Tommy's father said "Baby, don't loo…." The silent house was shattered by a scream.

"Vivian. Somebody killed my Vivian," followed by body-shaking sobs of pure grief. The sobs became muffled as her father pulled her head into his chest.

They heard the sound of her mother running across the floor to join them. There was a gasp and a shocked, "Who would do something like that?" Then, "Sweetie? Daddy's going to take you back up to bed and stay with you. We'll take care of Vivian, okay Sweetheart?"

Tommy heard his father coming up the stairs and he moved to his door and opened it. Over his shoulder, Messy Fleas saw the father come into view with Sandy in his arms, sobbing so hard that her little body was heaving in his arms. He could see the side of Sandy's face awash in tears and snot. The father looked helpless and full of grief. He spotted Tommy looking out of his doorway. "Tommy, go back into your room and play. Maybe we can go to the zoo tomorrow instead. We have to help Sandy now. If you need us, call us. Maybe later on we'll go to McDonalds."

Tommy backed into his room and left the door cracked. He looked shocked.

Messy Fleas felt a troubling change in the emotion coming through their bond and strove to rekindle the fire that had so suddenly dimmed. "That was great! Did you see that? Pure pain. See, I told you we would do it right! Even your mother and father are in shock. This is just the beginning. As a team we will rule this land by the time you're twenty. When my brood arrives they are in for…."

"Shut up Messy Fleas! I wanted to kill Vivian, not to hurt my little sister. I love Sandy even if she is a rat sometimes. And now I won't get to go to the zoo, either! You don't talk any more. No more!"

Messy Fleas opened his mouth to calm Tommy down when he found that no sound would come out. He tried to whisper, to shout, but nothing came out but air. Damn, he thought. Subservience in the thrice-damned binding!

Messy Fleas started to panic, but he remembered their mind link. He reached out with his mind and felt Tommy. He felt grief and guilt in Tommy's mind. He projected calm and spoke through the link. Tommy, be calm, be happy. This is what we wanted. This is why we came together, why you brought me here. Please let me talk again.

No! I said be quiet! You're not my friend anymore. You're bad. I don't want to hear you talk in my head anymore either! You stop that now! No talking to me in any way, and I don't want you listening to my head either!

With deepening horror, Messy Fleas felt a wall slam down around his mind pinning it within the bounds of his own head. In his rising panic he started to race around the room, running, stomping, and knocking into things to try to get Tommy's attention. Some rational part of his mind recognized it as a temper tantrum as he jumped onto Tommy's dresser to be at eye level with Tommy. He saw Tommy, now lying in his bed, crying quietly. Wild in the silence beyond his own mind, he ran across the dresser to jump on the bed. Tommy must release him. He must understand. One of his thrashing legs caught Tommy's red truck as he moved to leap to the bed. It fell to the floor in a clatter and a wheel broke off.

Tommy sat up in the bed and saw the broken toy. He looked at Messy Fleas and the tears were joined by a look of pure five-year-old fury. "Messy Fleas, you don't move, you don't talk, you don't do anything ever again! You're very bad and I don't ever want to play with you again!"

In stunned horror, Messy Fleas felt his body lock in place. He had reared back to leap to the bed when the order came. He felt himself topple forward and off the dresser to the floor. The view tumbled as Tommy picked him up and threw him into the back of his cluttered closet.

A short time later he heard the muffled voice of Tommy's father from the hallway. "I picked it all up and threw it away. She must have left it outside last night where some neighborhood kids found it and decided to get creative. I wish we had some way to find out what kid or kids did this. They need a serious sit-down with their parents. They need counseling."

Then the bedroom door opened and he heard Tommy's mother come in. "Oh Sweetie, don't cry. Sandy has had a bad scare and lost her best friend. We will help her find another best friend. It'll be all right Sweet Pea."

Messy Fleas heard Tommy's sniffles smothered as his mother hugged him. After a time he heard her lay Tommy down to sleep and Messy Fleas felt optimistic. Tommy would get past this and learn from it. Tommy would lift the geas from him and they would get back on the road to domination. But hope faded as days, then weeks, passed. Toys and racks and gloves and piles of stuff that Tommy didn't want or use anymore buried Messy Fleas in the closet. He settled into despair. His downfall was complete.

Tommy shivered suddenly, his eyes quickly refocusing.

"Yeah Messy Fleas," Tommy said. "He had some other name but I couldn't pronounce it so I called him Messy Fleas. He liked it. I don't know when I got it. A long time ago when I was a baby."

"I see." Johnny said. "Since I am taking possession of Messy Fleas it only seems fair that you give him to me willingly."

"Yeah, whatever. You can have him. Can I go back in now Mom?"

"Tommy, if you'll help me with an oath of transfer, I will trade you a nice item in return. Perhaps a NASCAR collectible car?" Johnny the Salesman rummaged once again in his pocket, smiled and pulled out a die cast car.

"Wow, that's Dale Junior's car, and he's signed it!" Tommy turned to his mother. "Oh please, Mom, can I do this? I want that car! It's perfect!"

Madeline looked at Johnny skeptically. "What is it you want my son to do?"

"Ma'am, it is only a simple oath, transferring this figure into my keeping. Nothing more than words, but they have value to me, and I consider this a very fair trade." Johnny's wide smile winked gold in the sunshine. "I only do it with children – so I am sure they won't feel cheated."

Madeline looked at Johnny like he was more than a bit crazy and was less than thrilled about the crazy man giving her son a toy, but she saw the longing in Tommy's eyes, and the sooner she could get this nutcase out of her yard… "Okay."

"Thank you, my lady." Johnny turned to Tommy. "Okay, all you need to do is say these words. 'I give Messy Fleas to Johnny the Salesman completely and unconditionally, now and forever.'"

Tommy repeated the words and smiled as Johnny dropped the car into his hand. "Thanks, mister! Can I go back in now, Mom? I want to call Cory and tell him what I got today."

Madeline turned to watch Tommy run to the house without waiting for an answer. Smiling, she turned back to Johnny. "Thank…" The strange dark man was nowhere to be seen. Madeline felt creeped-out all over again, but she forgot about it as a car pulled up in front of the yard with potential customers.

Messy Fleas had learned to live with despair. He accepted that he would be no more than a forgotten toy, especially when he was put out for sale today, and now this. He had felt his despair and humiliation deepen in the cold grasp of the dreaded hand that pulled him from the box. Now he was the property of the legendary power of The Sha'Daa.

His fall was complete as he dropped, endlessly, into bottomless darkness to join the mass of strange and esoteric objects that inhabited the vast, terrifying space that was Johnny the Salesman's coat pocket….

INTERLUDE FOUR

Ashley bit her lower lip and poked her head into one of the side rooms. A mix of human teenagers and hell-spawn were engaged in a boisterous game of Dungeons and Dragons. On closer examination she could see that the odds and repercussions of this strange competition were much higher than mere pride. An unusual amount of precious jewels and silver and gold coins lay strewn across the large folding card table.

"Nobody said anything about wealth changing hands back here," Ashley shouted.

One teenage boy, primped up in full Goth attire with blue, spiked hair and a metal studded dog collar around his neck spoke up. "We'll cut you in for ten percent."

"The house gets twenty-five percent or you all walk now, Turbo."

The table fell silent for a few tense seconds, and then everyone acquiesced with snort, grunt, hiss, and growl.

Ashley turned around. Back in the main display room Johnny was standing next to a glass-topped counter by the front door.

"Your entrepreneurial spirit never ceases to amaze me, Ashley," Johnny said.

Ashley frowned. Though it had only been a few hours since she had last seen the salesman, there was a cloud of weariness upon his angular face.

"And something tells me you're not just here to say hello," Ashley said.

"Perhaps my amorous side needs attention, my dear," Johnny said. "Have you ever noticed how the two of us never seem to have a date, engagement, or tryst on a Saturday night? Perhaps this is kismet?"

Ashley snorted and walked up to the front counter to smile at her oldest customer, and, strangely enough, closest living friend… at least, she thought he was living.

"I hit on you for three hundred years, tall, dark, and handsome," Ashley said. "Why do I get the vibe that this is the last time in all of existence I could get you to escort me to Dingle's annual ice cream social?"

"Wise and beautiful as always," Johnny said. "I have something you might find of interest."

And without further ado Johnny reached into his trench coat and pulled out a cunningly crafted contraption made of fire-pinned gears, gold and silver casing, and spinning crystals. "I do believe you have been looking for one of these for quite some time."

Ashley held back a gasp, and then ran her hands over the ancient Greek device.

"And you guarantee that it…" she replied.

"…was created by Posidonius himself," Johnny said, "with three times as many moving parts as the Antikythera mechanism."

"Is it true that it's real function is that of a fate weaver… a calculator of broad probabilities along the alignment of the stars?" she asked.

"In a word," Johnny said, "yes."

"What do you want in return for this?" Ashley asked.

Johnny tossed a piece of ancient parchment with a long list written on it. Ashley's eyes went wide.

"You're raping my inventory, old man," Ashley said.

"This device is worth ten times that list," Johnny said, "and watch it with the hate words."

With a wide smirk Ashley snapped up both the trade list and the πρόγνωση mechanism. "I'll be right back."

A loud crash sounded from one of the side rooms and Ashley nodded at security. The Dungeons and Dragons group had switched over to a ferociously competitive tournament of Magic The Gathering. So far only a couple of broken limbs and a minor concussion had resulted, but things could always get worse.

Turbo's loud nasal voice exulted from the card game.

"Take that hoser! A shadowmage infiltrator can't be blocked except by artifact creatures and/or black creatures. In your face."

This was answered by a monstrous howl that set the chandeliers rattling.

"Get over yourself, Gronk," Turbo said. "I told you before we started I had a killer deck."

*　*　*

CHAPTER FIVE: LIFEGUARD

by Michael H. Hanson

"From a proud tower in the town, Death looks gigantically down."
-- Edgar Allan Poe

The sun crested the distant fence of giant spruce trees. The small wisps of morning fog that hugged the camp's shoreline every morning flared to a beautiful white brilliance.

A moment later the glorious spectacle was over.

He was like a king, all this for his pleasure only.

Humid sunlight washed down over the sleeping camp. In another twenty minutes the camp director would wake up and ring the large bronze bell that sat in the center of the sleeping cabins like an invulnerable and ageless watchdog.

Time for a dip.

He stripped off his bright blue T-shirt and ran out along the white, metal pier, then leaped headfirst into the clear mountain lake in a long shallow dive. Cool, tingling bubbles streamed upward along his sleek smooth muscles. The shock of the sudden immersion kicked his heart into first gear as his momentum carried him into the deep shadowy reaches of the lake. This was his perfect moment of the day.

All of the sounds of above-lake life were now muffled, and the Lifeguard felt safe and secure as the water pressure increased and hugged him tightly. In another moment he entered a thriving patch of ten-foot-long lake weed on the lake bottom. Though he could never quite feel the underwater current himself, the lake weed always rippled and parted around him like living tendrils, occasionally lapping at his sides. Red Cross lifeguard classes had always taught him that such patches of underwater growth were inherently dangerous, and had taken the lives of many experienced swimmers. But the Lifeguard didn't care. Somehow, for some reason, he felt an affinity with the lake's eerie swaying denizens.

Three minutes later he quickly broke through the lake surface gasping for air. The morning dip was always refreshing.

The Lifeguard smiled, revealing a perfect set of long, shiny white teeth. The bell started ringing around his fifth lap. It was time for breakfast.

"Sha'Daa," a voice seemed to whisper. The Lifeguard spun around, but no one was in sight. Shrugging, he jogged back to his cabin. Several small, black squirrels scurried out of his path and then resumed their daily nut gathering. His campers were still asleep. Or so he thought.

"Surprise! Happy Birthday!" The entire cabin screamed in unison after jumping up from a series of feigned snores. All eight kids tackled the Lifeguard to the floor and commenced to give him his twenty-six birthday tickles.

"Okay, okay, you got me," he laughed. "Now chill out. We gotta get set for breakfast!"

Reluctantly, after two squealing renditions of 'Happy Birthday To You,' the Lifeguard was able to hustle the twelve-year-old kids into the bathroom. He turned to his counselor bunkmate with a sardonic grin.

"How'd you find out about today, Jim?" he asked.

"Why," Jim laughed, "I broke into the nurse's files, how else? God knows I'd like to break into more than that, though!"

They both laughed and the Lifeguard slapped Jim on the back. Along with the other counselors he was more than aware of Jim's hopeless dalliances with the camp's attractive young nurse.

The Lifeguard had no doubt he could score with the naive bitch had he half the inclination, but he of course said nothing of the kind to Jim.

"How easily your kind bruises," the Lifeguard mused, at Jim's retreating back, while quickly stripping out of his wet swimming trunks and digging a clean white towel out of the pinewood footlocker at the foot of his bed. The three urinals and two toilets in the back of the cabin started to flush in a staccato of gurgling voices.

"David you little pig, pick up your toilet paper!" Jim suddenly yelled out. "Oh Christ what a mess!" he continued. "I'm gonna call you the toilet paper man from now on, David!" This last statement was answered with laughter throughout the entire cabin.

A picture of a thick shag rug suddenly filled the Lifeguard's mind. He frowned as the mental image resolved into sharper detail.

He was eight years old. He would run home from school, quickly remove his sneakers and pull his socks three quarters off his feet and pretend they were diving fins like those Jacque Cousteau wore on TV. He would "swim" around his living room's shag rug always aware of the danger of sharks, the bends, and running out of oxygen. In his mind, he saw the deepness of the ocean, felt the comforting pressure of hundreds of feet of water overhead, and frolicked amid the sea life....

The Lifeguard sat on the edge of his bed, oblivious to the strange looks his fellow counselor Jim and eight assigned campers were giving him. A slightly reverent smile was plastered on his face.

It was his 12th birthday. As custom demanded he told his homeroom a tale of his past. Sitting in his sixth grade class, having told his classmates all about his rug scuba diving, the other kids were snickering.

"Strong desires to return to the comfort of the womb!" the teacher expounded to a giggling and hypertensive gang of children. "Compulsive paranoia over the fear of bedwetting," she added sarcastically.

He had been the laughing stock of his class for over a week.

The Lifeguard snapped out of his unpleasant reverie at the sound of the breakfast bell, with a startled and painful tensing of his shoulders. He noticed with some surprise that Jim and the rest of the cabin's inhabitants had already left on their way to the dining hall.

The Lifeguard checked his watch and realized he had only five minutes to shower, shampoo, shave, and dress for breakfast. He finished skillfully with a whole two minutes to spare and realized, bemusedly, that his four-year hitch in the Navy had not been a complete waste.

As he was toweling off his wet hair, the Lifeguard caught a glimpse of himself in the body length mirror on the rear wall of the cabin. He examined his physique with a dispassionate eye.

Lean, muscular, a six-foot-two male in his mid-twenties, his skin sported a Hollywood tan and his hair, almost black during the non-summer months, had been bleached a light, golden bronze from constant exposure to the sun.

His eyes were a soft green and surrounded by long, thick lashes. His chin was a small brick of manly solidity and his lips were thick and sensual. All in all, he wore the clichéd pose of a Lifeguard very well.

The cabin door swung shut quickly, making a shushing sound that seemed to echo that strange word he had imagined earlier. "Sha'Daa."

The entire camp (three hundred boys from ages eight to sixteen, and one hundred and fifteen counselors) filed into the dining hall. The main dining space was one large open room, filled with forty circular oak wood tables. The Lifeguard quickly spied out an un-chaperoned group and made his move.

As a member of the waterfront staff he was required to sit at a different table every other day. He returned a chorus of "Happy Birthdays" with half the dining hall before sitting down with his assigned ten campers. The Lifeguard sat back to enjoy a fine meal of pancakes, French toast, sausage, bacon, coffee and orange juice.

The laughter and chatter of campers and counselors echoed freely throughout the hall. Upon sitting down, the Lifeguard had automatically turned on his trademark smile and dived, once again, into an alien world of upper-middle and upper class mores and sensibilities.

"Did yuh hear? Abraham's dad got him a new CD and a motorbike for his birthday!" one handsome, black-haired youth from Manhattan spouted out enthusiastically. "That's so RAD man!" he added with a dazzling grin.

"Screw that!" the red haired youth to the Lifeguard's left replied. "I'm getting the next generation iPad with a shit-load of apps this September. Would you believe it? It's to help me in school!"

"No way!" the black haired kid answered. "Your old man fell for that crap?"

The Lifeguard took in the barrage of affluence and one-upmanship among these eleven year olds with a relaxed smile and a few approving nods. He was safe. He knew they had accepted him. In a manner of speaking he had already begun his entry into this foreign world of wealth and upward mobility. The Lifeguard knew his camouflage of good looks, indifferent smiles and stylish clothes endeared him to every kid in the camp. He would finish college in another year and then use one of his contacts, possibly the parents of one of these rich brats, to smooth his way into a more suitable and comfortable lifestyle.

The Lifeguard swept his eyes around the dining hall. He knew that most of the other camp counselors, younger college students with only half of his own ambition, would never draw the praise and admiration from the kids that he did. He was unique. Special.

The Lifeguard finished his breakfast and then instructed his campers, amid a chorus of groans and mimicked heart attacks, to start stacking their dishes in the center of the table. In a few minutes the cooking staff would stop at each table and pile the morning's dirty dishes onto several large carts and dolly the refuse out through the kitchen's large, swinging double doors.

A squeal of anger; the Lifeguard turned his head and spotted a crying, outraged camper whose head was covered with milk and cereal. His table-mates were laughing like banshees.

The bathroom door was being forced open. He was standing naked and wet with a towel in his hands, just out of the shower. His brothers were snapping Polaroids. The photos circulated his elementary school, and he was laughed at for a week. When the taunting became unbearable he would hide within his mind, deep down in a cold dark place of safety….

The Lifeguard shook his head and noticed that people were starting to leave the dining hall. The kids at his table were staring at him strangely. He smiled, stood up, and headed out to start his day.

The Lifeguard's job was to sit on the elevated, white watchtower, next to the waterfront's gate entrance, and supervise the checking of campers and staff into and out of the swimming and boating docks. He had a plastic-covered, cardboard map of the two waterfront facilities that he always carried with him. Every time a waterfront instructor entered the area with a class the Lifeguard would take his grease pencil, count heads, and draw the tallied number of people over the map space they were training in.

If any one of the kids in that particular group left the waterfront, he had to erase the original number and draw in the new tally. The same was done for the boating division, with the exception that instead of circling the numbers he would draw the shapes of canoes, rowboats and sailboats around them.

On an active day there would be over two dozen half-smeared numbers plastered over the face of his laminated map. The Lifeguard prided himself on the fact that he had never had a discrepancy between his map's figures and the body count made during the buddy checks given every ten minutes. The kids were safe under his care. Adults were another matter.

The Lifeguard was different, almost separate, from the rest of the waterfront staff. There were swimming instructors, life-saving instructors, canoeing, rowing and sailing instructors. In fact, there were even waterski and windsurfing instructors. There was, however, only one Lifeguard. The Lifeguard. The waterfront director may have technically been in charge of overseeing the camp's lakeside operation, but it was the Lifeguard who actually coordinated the placement and safety of all campers and staff in the waterfront via his laminated map.

I'm the only Director around here, the Lifeguard thought atop his lofty tower.

The day streamed by in a haze of pounding sunlight, shrill whistles, an occasional cut toe and the ever present, though highly unlikely, expectation of a miss count on his map. The five o'clock bell rang and the Lifeguard climbed down the twenty-five foot tower.

During the free swim in the late afternoon, the Lifeguard relinquished his aerial post to the waterfront director so he could help patrol the swimming docks. Throughout the day only about one hundred campers ever used the waterfront at one time. During free swim, however, the entire camp was allowed access to the beachfront and deepwater swimming area out by the floating raft. On a hot day there would be upwards of three to four hundred people in the water at one time.

It was an unusually hot day.

The Lifeguard climbed down from the tower and walked toward the swimming area. A flicker of movement from within the dock house caught his attention. Nobody was supposed to be in there.

The Lifeguard entered the tall white shack that was filled with oars, paddles, PFD's, and yards of line. Standing in the far corner was the shadowy figure of a man.

"You realize this is private property," the Lifeguard said, "Salesman."

The man the Lifeguard spoke to was roughly six and a half feet tall, with dark hair, medium complexioned skin, clean-cut with a hawkish nose. Belying the warm weather the intruder wore a dark suit, leather shoes, black trench coat and fedora.

"Johnny doesn't think you like his candy," the Salesman said. "Is this true, Mark?"

The Lifeguard frowned for a moment. How did this enigmatic drug dealer always seem to know what he was thinking or doing?

"Yeah, well," The Lifeguard retorted, "I traded you for meth, crack, coke, and X. Those friggin' pills you gave me were Clonazapam, Risperdal, and fucking Zyprexa. What the fuck? I told you I needed uppers. Stuff to keep me going. Not this goddamn psycho shit."

"How did you find out?" the Salesman asked.

"I've got a brain, bogeyman," the Lifeguard said, "and a few minutes on Google and Wikipedia will answer any questions."

The Lifeguard had been furious when he'd matched the pills via shape, color, and markings the night before. It was bad enough the variety of trade goods this dealer demanded for his wares (handmade camper lanyards, a half dozen PFD's, two lifeguard whistles, a canoe paddle, and a box of camp postcards), but his smug confidence always made the hair on the back of the Lifeguard's neck stand up.

The Salesman stepped forward, slowly, his large hands by his sides. His mouth broke into what should have been a disarming smile filled with bright white teeth, but a shiny gold left lateral incisor offset this intent.

"Johnny is only trying to help you, Mark," the Salesman said. "I apologize for the subterfuge, but you are not well. You need help. Something terrible is going to happen. Something… that should not be for another ten thousand years. But you… you are special… and sick. Please. Take these."

Johnny tossed a small prescription bottle at the Lifeguard's feet.

A quick glance showed it was Seroquel, the treatment for schizophrenia.

The Lifeguard looked back up and locked eyes with The Salesman. The strange man in the dark trench coat had unusual black eyes, dark pupils that seemed bottomless. The Lifeguard could not look away.

"Please," the Salesman said, "this is my last chance to help you. I've thousands of trades to attend to. I can't wait here any longer."

A loud burst of children's laughter from the dock broke the spell.

"Fuck you," the Lifeguard said and kicked the bottle away into a dusty corner. "I don't know what your game is, buddy, but…."

The Lifeguard did a double take. The Salesman was no longer there.

The waterfront director wanted the Lifeguard patrolling the swimming docks during free swim because he was the strongest and fastest swimmer among the entire twenty-five person waterfront staff. The Lifeguard picked up a ten-foot-long, hollow bamboo rescue pole from inside the waterfront shed and strode quickly out onto the pier. His nylon shorts made a faint swishing sound over and over again, a continuous whisper repeating one word endlessly. "Sha'Daa."

The Lifeguard glanced around and made a quick head-count of the twelve other waterfront staff members on the docks. This did not include the two staff members out on the raft.

Julie, a handsome and shapely blonde from the University of Miami, smiled and waved a brief welcome to the Lifeguard as he walked out onto the farthest arm of the dock. The Lifeguard liked her. Julie was always using him as a model for her life-saving students.

"We're hitting Riley's tonight," Julie dimpled. "Why don't you cut out early and ride in with me?"

Julie was wearing a skimpy, light blue skin suit that high-lighted her eyes and showed off her hourglass physique. She lightly pressed her hip against the Lifeguard's thigh and placed her left hand demurely over her stomach. He glanced down and examined this maneuver much like a scientist would look over the outline of a specific breed of bacteria.

"We'll see," the Lifeguard smiled back. "I don't know if I can get out of bunk assignment or not."

It was a good ploy. Julie always fell for it.

"Okay," she replied, obviously disappointed. "I'll keep my fingers crossed!"

But not your legs, the Lifeguard thought smugly. You'd pin me into your boring, middle-class social life with all the excitement of an enema.

She turned and went to her assigned station. The lifeguard had his eyes on other prey this summer. Specifically, the rich widowed mother of a young camper from Jamaica.

Parents' weekend was only ten days away and he didn't need any bleeding heart sentimentalist mooning over him when the Jamaica bitch needed attending. He had to do something about Julie. She was becoming quite a nuisance.

A little too much alcohol, he thought. Some rough bed-play, a couple insults. That'll take care of it. He briefly sketched the scenario in his mind before returning to his duties. He'd have Julie fitted into her niche by the end of the evening.

The Lifeguard didn't have a stationary spot like the others. The waterfront director liked to keep him constantly moving among the permanently stationed waterfront staff during free swim. It helped keep them on their toes knowing that the Lifeguard was looking over their shoulders.

The Lifeguard smiled back at Julie and just as quickly pointed his safety pole in the direction of a couple of fifteen-year old campers who were wrestling in the deeper water out by the raft. The campers were struggling just under the raft's diving board and so were out of sight of the two raft watchers above. Julie blew a hair-raising screech on her whistle and pointed out the two delinquents to the raft staff.

The sun was starting to sink behind the forested mountain range on the opposite side of the lake.

The resulting grayish-black shadows rippled quickly toward the camp's waterfront.

Laughter exploded from a couple of campers playing water basketball directly in front of him.

The Lifeguard looked down.

An eight-year-old camper, clutching a water basketball, cried fiercely as two older campers pushed him into the deeper swimming area. The lifeguard recognized the younger camper immediately. It was Chris Rosenthal, a beginner who could not swim.

Julie, seeing the direction of the Lifeguard's gaze, leaped into the deeper end of the dock and quickly pulled Chris into shore.

The two older pranksters smirked up at the Lifeguard, daring him to chastise them.

His parents took them all to the Jersey Shore for his sixth birthday. He was on top of his Dad's inflatable rubber mattress, his two brothers dog paddling their way out to the roped off border of the swimming area.

He looked up and smiled at the crystal clarity of the shiny, blue sky. There wasn't a single cloud in the heavens. Suddenly, without any warning, both of his brothers pushed the mattress forward so that it floated up against the buoy rope that marked the farthest boundary of the swimming area.

The water here was over ten feet deep. He didn't know how to swim.

He stared in white-faced shock as his two giggling brothers rapidly swam back to the shore. And just as suddenly a riptide current practically flung his little raft out over the buoy rope and rapidly out to sea. He had moved over one hundred yards before his paralysis broke and he started screaming for help. But it was too late. The roar of the surf drowned him out.

He was found three days later by the U.S. Coast Guard, fully catatonic and desperately clutching his deflated air mattress that seemed to have anchored itself upon an eight-foot diameter mass of seaweed and barnacles.

Surrounded by constantly circling sharks, his living and slowly disintegrating green island was spotted 65 miles from shore.

Exactly one year after this trauma, his catatonia broke, and he awoke to the world with no memory of even having gone to the beach that day. Until now.

A shrill whistle sucked his mind back into the present. Julie, standing with her back turned in his direction, had just cautioned two campers for wrestling in the water. They were the same two kids that had played their little prank on Chris Rosenthal.

"Alone," his mind echoed hollowly.

Intense nausea.

The image of both of his brothers' leering faces burned in his mind. The sound of their laughter echoed in his ears. And an ebony wave of surfacing horror loomed darkly over his soul.

A voice spoke in his mind, something reptilian and sickening.

"The portal at the bottom of this lake has granted our voice passage," it said wordlessly. "We have seen your power. Long buried until now. You need only employ it, today, now. It is the time of The Sha'Daa. All things are possible. Remember what they did to you...."

And then, the Lifeguard's sanity, padded and nurtured and protected by a dozen years of control and tedium and routine, shattered.

The Lifeguard strode to the far side of the Intermediate dock and looked down into the shadowy waters of the lake with two soulless eyes.

"We are not powerful enough to break through this cycle," the eerie voices said, "but you can be our proxy. Love us, Mark. We will never betray you.... Love The Sha'Daa...."

And then, the bubbling darkness of his shredded subconscious vomited forth an unending mass of slithering dark snakelike horrors that crawled rampantly through his mind.

And as this apocalypse tore and slithered through the Lifeguard's thundering synapses, freshwater weeds, as long and slimy as fifteen foot snakes, broke free from the deep lake's bottom and undulated toward the shore.

The Lifeguard then turned to look back upon the many happy campers, and he saw they were all alike, for each and every one of them now wore the face of his brothers, his leering, laughing, terrible brothers.

Somewhere, far away, Julie screamed as dozens of children were simultaneously engulfed by lake weed and pulled under the water to thrash about and drown in terror.

And all the while, ignoring this horror, one single coherent thought surfaced above the miasma of dark, slithering madness that was now the Lifeguard's mind.

There are more beaches left in the world, Lifeguard. So very many.

*   *   *

INTERLUDE FIVE

Ashley's first two hundred years in the town of Dingle, Ireland were probably her most difficult. With the blessing of the African avatar of justice streaming through her veins and arteries, the former slave quickly found herself mastering the local economy and becoming a shrewd shop owner.

This did not come without a price.

A single woman and former slave of Nigerian/Arab descent, in the fifteen hundreds was not a legally recognized landowner in this small Gaelic community. However, a reputation as an apothecary and mid-wife unexcelled, with additional rumors of being a witch you should not cross, Ashley found herself in a comfortable position of security and mild wealth after her first fifty years.

Realizing that she was not aging, Ashley created a series of disguises, which she would use to convince the townspeople that she was both mother and daughter at her small shop. When the time seemed appropriate, Ashley faked her own death, becoming her own daughter in everyone's eyes, keeping her mother's name as a sign of respect. This was a shadow play she would carry out every seventy or so years to keep her immorality a secret.

Still, there were always men, some important, some mere vagrants, who thought she was a helpless woman ripe for the picking. Many a night came when they would arrive at her shop in groups of three or four to ransack, or steal, or worse. And each time this happened, the most horrible of shrieks might be heard coming from her shop near the midnight hour, but the next morning no sign of any struggle could be seen. And the only note of something strange were the whispered rumors of young men gone missing, possibly waylaid by the British Navy.

*   *   *

CHAPTER SIX: DUST

by Sarah Wagner

For centuries, Matong's body was little more than dust, motes designed to watch, learn, and wait. Her motes bore witness to the greatest achievements and the greatest atrocities of the humans, who thought the earth belonged to them. Her people were far away, waiting for her to open the gate so they could storm through and claim the earth for themselves.

Matong thought of the Urichresh as her people, not because she was one of them, but because they had brought her into existence, given her life and purpose. Whether it was magic or science, she did not care. For them, she scattered herself to the winds to learn from the enemy and watch for the signs that would tell her when the time was right.

When the first sign appeared, the disappearance of a small star in the northern sky, Matong sang to the wind, calling all her pieces back to herself. Even as she sang, she knew it would take a century or more to be made whole again. Plenty of time to do her duty to her creators. She was nothing if not patient.

Every speck that rejoined her brought with it a wealth of memories, all they had seen and learned on their great journey. Some of the oldest memories were degraded beyond repair, but they weren't important. The enemy as they once were did not matter to the Urichresh's plans, and so did not matter to Matong.

After a quarter of that century, enough of her had returned to allow her movement. It had been so long since she'd done anything more than roll about in her sheltered stone grotto that every sensation was new again. Every caress of the wind sent a thrill through her. The sudden rise of a storm, the thrum of electrical charge reminding her that her creators had given her life beyond data collection and the unique ability to open the great door.

The last sign came and went, marking one Earth year to the night when all things would align just so and allow Matong to open the door for the Urichresh at last. She waited six months more, until she could not wait for her last motes. They knew where to go if they did not find her in the little hollow. As patient as she was, Matong was anxious to begin the journey south to the temple that had been erected around the great door. Using the memories of her pieces, she shaped herself into the form of a slender, young, dark-haired woman. Her outermost motes had to simulate simple clothing that wouldn't look out of place when laid beside her most recent memories of the enemy.

Those same recent memories said there was a house a few miles to the south. There, an old woman lived alone. It wasn't the ideal target for her, the woman was too old and not likely to have the kind of things Matong would need to reach her destination. Though Brazil was closer to Nevada than it had once been, given the innovations of the enemy, it would require things Matong had no access to, things like money and a passport. She couldn't trust the wind, as fickle as it was, to get her where she needed to be in time. The wind still hadn't returned all of her pieces yet, and it'd had a hundred years to do it in.

During the long walk to the old woman's house, Matong practiced with her new form, stretching her new arms and legs, wiggling slender fingers and toes. Her voice sounded nothing like the enemy's voice. The sounds that came from her new mouth were more like sandpaper rubbing over stone than the sweet melodies of the human voice. If she whispered low and quiet, she could almost pass for human. Almost. Unless she wanted to risk being discovered, she needed to find a better way to communicate. Her motes had memories of a language that wasn't spoken, two of them. One written on paper and the other using symbols made by the hands. Matong absorbed every memory she could find on both writing and sign language. One of her motes had spent several years floating around a school for the deaf and brought back with it the memories of all those visible words. The majority of the enemy did not speak this way, but enough did to facilitate enough communication to get where she needed to go. In fact, if she interpreted the data correctly, she would be pitied and largely ignored. That worked in her favor.

When the old woman's house finally came into view, Matong shivered with anticipation. Her first interaction with the enemy would be a great test of her own skill and the skill of her creators, the Urichresh, as well. Had they created her perfectly enough to succeed?

The sun-bleached, wind-worn blue siding needed paint, but the house itself was in relatively good shape. The windows sparkled in the sunlight, the covered porch free of dust and grime, and a well-used broom stood beside the front door. Matong made her way up the porch steps to the door and lifted her hand to knock.

She didn't get the chance. The woman, who was older than the memory of her, opened the door, her mouth gaping in a surprised O.

"Goodness! You frightened me!"

The woman peered out toward the road, looking for something. Her rheumy eyes narrowed slightly in a look that Matong's motes told her was suspicious.

Quickly, Matong began to sign. It didn't matter if the woman understood, only that it was believable. "Help me," she signed, "my car broke down and I'm lost."

"Oh dear." The woman's eyes changed, the suspicion giving way to pity. Her wrinkled face softened. "I'm afraid I don't understand you. I don't even know anyone who can translate."

Matong waited, patiently inspecting the woman, feeling a surge of victory as the woman opened the door and motioned for Matong to follow her inside. Matong stepped into the house, the mechanically-cooled air kissing her motes, sending a rippling tingle through her. The old woman led her into the kitchen, took a notebook and pen from beside the phone and set them on the table. Matong glanced at the pen but made no move to take it.

Matong scattered. As the woman screamed, millions of motes shoved themselves into her mouth, down into her cancer blackened lungs, packing every inch of space, pushing the air out and away until breathing was impossible and her heart gave out. Certain of her victory, Matong evacuated the woman's body, rejoining herself in the shape of the old woman. She searched the house, finding what she wanted in a bedroom in the back. Matong dressed in one of the simple dresses she found there, her pieces adjusting and readjusting until every wrinkle, every silver hair, every layer of fat was an exact match to the old woman.

She searched the house thoroughly, shoving money in the wallet she'd found and leaving everything else. Matong did not find what she needed most – a passport. She'd have to find someone else.

With some effort, Matong dragged the woman to the basement and rolled her down the stairs. Making sure no one would immediately realize she was dead was important. It wouldn't be the end of the world if she were caught, but there was no point in letting the enemy know. She could be anyone, anything.

Taking the woman's keys, she let herself out of the house and walked to the carport where a small, mildew-green Impala sat under a layer of dust. She could see no one, so she didn't have to worry about moving like the woman. Her gait still needed work. The car itself was easy to figure out. It was a machine, created by the enemy as a slave. What passed for Matong's heart broke a little when she realized the car had no consciousness, no will of its own. It was not, in fact, anything like her. She was no slave. She was a subject, a creation, perhaps a savior.

Pulling out of the driveway, she spotted the old woman's neighbor peering through the front window and waved. It was good. She'd been seen driving away. It would give her more time before anyone went to check on the woman. She drove, listening to the radio and finding herself enthralled by the music, especially the music by a band called Journey. One of her motes had floated through one of their concerts, been inhaled by a man named Neal who played the guitar, and breathed out again at an after party with a recording of the entire performance committed to its memory. Perhaps she could convince the Urichresh to have mercy on those who created such amazing sounds.

About a hundred and seventy miles later, the car sputtered, shuddered, and died. She searched through the memories and realized she hadn't given any sort of thought to gas. It didn't matter. She didn't have time to drive all the way to Brazil and she still needed to find a passport.

Leaving the car in the middle of the highway, Matong began walking. She took care not to move too fast or with too much grace. She was supposed to be an old woman after all. Twenty minutes later, someone stopped on the side of the road. The car's flashing lights and black and white paint marked it as a police car. Matong knew it would be better for her not to kill him. A missing police officer would be noticed long before a senile old woman. She needed an enemy who wouldn't be missed to get her to Brazil.

The police officer was a tall man. He adjusted his snug uniform, pulling his gun belt up tight under his shelf of a belly. Before he could approach, Matong began signing, allowing her fingers to be frantic. "Help me. I ran out of gas."

The officer cursed and reached back into his car to grab a notebook. Matong winced. Understanding the premise of written language was one thing. Actually doing it legibly and believably was something else. She'd do her best, but, if she had to kill the man, she had to kill him. One less enemy for the Urichresh to face.

When he handed her the notepad and pen, Matong forced her hands to tremble slightly as she wrote out exactly what she had signed. It wasn't perfect by any stretch, it was shaky and amateur. She poised herself to attack.

The man took the pad and read what she'd written. He smiled then, muttering through clenched teeth, "You shouldn't even be driving, lady." Then, he motioned for her to get in his car. The officer shut the door when she'd situated herself, walked around and climbed in the driver's seat. He drove her back to the Chevy, poured some gas from a red container into it and sent her on her way.

The car started right up and Matong headed on down the highway with the officer's car right behind her. She'd drawn too much attention now and would have to ditch the Impala somewhere soon. The old woman's form would work for a while, but it wasn't very comfortable and it certainly wasn't pretty. She knew what pretty looked like, thanks to her motes, and the old grandmother wasn't.

She pulled off the highway at the next exit, watching as the police car followed her all the way to the gas station. Instead of getting out of the car, Matong rolled the window down when the officer approached again. She pulled money from the stolen wallet, handing the man a twenty dollar bill and signing, "Thank you."

The officer went into the station, talked to the clerk for a moment while he paid, and then took the time and trouble to put gas in the Impala for her. She was glad then that she hadn't killed him. Even if he didn't think little old women should be driving, he was respectful and polite. Good qualities. She hoped he had a good life to enjoy for the last days before the Urichresh came to exterminate them all.

When they got back on the highway, she was glad to see the officer's car go in a different direction at last. She drove on for another hour or so before taking an exit that didn't look too heavily populated, but had a truck stop, its lights the brightest point for miles. She wouldn't take a new identity from the same place she left the car. The enemy wasn't stupid. If she wasn't careful, one of them might figure out the creator's plan and she couldn't afford that. If she failed, she would never get to meet the Urichresh and every single mote of her being wanted to look on the faces of the creators and bask in their praise.

She pulled the Impala into the lot and parked it far away from the building, tucked into shadows. She left everything with the old woman's name on it under the passenger seat of the car. The dress she'd taken wouldn't work on a smaller form, so Matong pulled it off and threw it in the backseat. Her shape changed, something smaller, more in line with what she knew to be pretty, but not so pretty as to be noticed. Her motes shifted color, wrapped around other motes until her new, younger figure was solid and clothed in jeans and a plain red t-shirt.

Making her way through the parking lot, Matong took careful note of all the vehicles parked there. Her motes' memories told her a long-distance trucker might be her best mark to get to a big city, one full of identities that might actually have a passport. There were two options for travel: doing something called hitchhiking or stowing away inside one of the trucks. As much as she liked her new form, she knew it was better to be unseen from this point to the next.

She unformed and stuffed herself through the cracks in the back of one of the large trucks. It was full of boxes. She would ride here, where no one was likely to check, or if they did, would only wonder where the dust came from.

Time passed. The truck moved and stopped and moved and stopped. At each stop, Matong sent a mote out to see where they were. She needed a city, somewhere with enough people that her hunt for the right paperwork wouldn't be difficult. At some point, she realized it would be easier to find an airport and stow away on a plane the same way she stowed away on the truck, but she did not want to waste time being flown all over the world in the hopes of finding Brazil by accident.

It wasn't until the fifth stop that the truck arrived in a place where Matong felt certain she could find what she needed, a young woman with a passport and money. How hard could it be to find one in a city of at least fifty thousand people? She couldn't immediately identify the town, but her motes told her she was surely in Texas somewhere. Given the closeness to the Mexican border, surely passports were commonplace.

She cast a net of her motes, sending them to find her the right mark while she waited on top of the highest building in the town, nestled in the steeple of a white church dedicated to the god of the humans. She wondered while she waited if her gods would expect such things from her when they had conquered Earth.

Near dark, three of her motes returned with promising potential marks. Of the three, the young travel agent looked the most promising. As a travel agent, her mote assured her, she would have all the proper paperwork, plus she was young and pretty. Not as pretty as Matong wanted to be, but pretty enough. She would only use that form to get where she needed to be, and she could take any form once she was in Brazil.

In the darkness, Matong and her motes crept through the town toward the woman's home. She took form in the shadows, gathering herself back into the form of the old woman. This mark would certainly open the door to an old woman in distress, especially one with a disability.

It took only a moment for the woman to open the door and, once Matong began to sign, she ushered her inside. "I'm sorry, I don't understand sign language. I have a notebook though. What happened?"

Matong didn't bother writing anything down. The moment the slim blonde turned away, Matong unformed, swarming over the woman, pushing her motes into every open point of entry. The woman struggled and, from the doorway, a scream caught Matong's attention. A man, slightly younger than the woman, with similar facial features and the same blonde hair and blue eyes gaped, fear and fury at war on his face. Matong pulled out of the travel agent, leaving her sprawled on the floor, gasping for breath. She rushed toward the man who was already running away, throwing the door open and fleeing into the night. She wasn't fast enough to catch him.

Thinking quickly, Matong shut the door and turned back to the travel agent, finishing the job she'd begun as quickly as she could. Wrapping the body in her motes, she maneuvered it down the hall and into the garage where a black Honda waited. Matong reached into the driver's side and popped the trunk, walking the body like a puppet to the back and into the trunk. She covered it with a blanket and shut the trunk, carefully molding herself into the young woman's form.

She ran back into the house, searching for the woman's purse. Her ID said her name was Angela Bennett. Matong practiced for a moment, saying Angela Bennett in as quiet a whisper as she could manage. A few moments later, the police began pounding on the door. Careful to look upset, she rushed to open the door. "Thank God!"

Two officers in blue uniforms stood there, the young man just behind them. "Ma'am? Is everything all right?"

Matong shook her head, holding one hand to her throat. "A man attacked me. So fast. Don't remember much. I think he choked me."

"Can you tell me what he looked like?" the shorter of the two men asked, a notepad and pen in hand to take down the details. In raspy, low whispers, Matong made up a story about an old man in need of a telephone. She watched the young man as she spoke, registering his suspicion. She answered the officer's questions, followed them as they searched the house, allowed them to take pictures of her gradually darkening "bruises", and refused their offers of medical care. The invasion of police seemed to take hours. The young man, apparently Angela's younger brother, gave quite a different story about what happened, but Matong wasn't worried. She could tell by the policemen's reactions that they didn't believe him, just as the young Bennett boy didn't believe her. He knew something was wrong.

Rather than stay there with her, Bennett turned to leave with the officers. That was very telling. She was good enough to fool strangers, but not family. She hadn't expected to need to be. Luck kept her from being discovered, from anyone believing Bennett for a moment.

"If you think of anything else, let us know. We're just a phone call away, Ma'am."

Matong nodded and whispered, "Thank you." Watching them leave, she knew she didn't have much time. Bennett would be back as soon as he thought he figured out a way around her attack. It wouldn't matter. She'd be long gone by the time he returned.

With no care to the state of the house, Matong searched quickly and thoroughly for the passport. It was in the desk, along with several other documents that might be important: birth certificate and social security card. With those in hand, she pulled a suitcase out of the closet and dumped clothes into it. The clothes themselves didn't matter. They were merely props. A woman didn't travel the globe without a suitcase.

Searching the woman's purse, she found three credit cards and cheered silently. Following the instructions of her ever-observant motes, she logged onto the internet using the woman's laptop and ordered her tickets that way. All she had to do was make it to the airport and get on the right plane. After that it would be, as the enemy said, cake.

Matong loaded the suitcase and her purse in the passenger side of the Honda. She'd take the body with her. As long as Bennett didn't find it until she was out of the airport in Brazil, there would be nothing anyone could do to stop her. She smiled, not constraining her motes and allowing them to spread the grin wider over her features than would have been possible if she were human.

As she pulled out of the garage, she noticed a white truck where there hadn't been one before. For a moment, she was concerned, but it was a neighborhood where people lived. Surely it was simply a matter of someone coming home or coming to visit. Nothing she needed to worry about at all.

Her certainty shrank when the truck began to follow her. It shrank further when it stayed behind her onto I-35 and all the way to the airport. In her wavering confidence, Matong separated twenty of her motes and sent them away, to gather information on the car and report back to her. The truck finally took a different turn in the parking lot. While she went to long term parking, the truck veered into the short term lot.

After unloading the car, she locked it and threw the keys under the car. Matong took her luggage and printed copy of the ticket and made her way to the terminal. A shuttle took her from the long term lot to where she would need to check her bag. She went inside rather than doing it curbside because she was more likely to find someone who could sign there and she didn't want to keep testing her inhuman voice. The cops believed her only because she told them she'd been strangled. She couldn't be discovered so close to success.

At the desk, it took a few minutes, but a translator was indeed found and Matong was able to check her bag and get everything lined up for the flight. It would be a long flight, but she was so close to victory that it was starting to effect her mood. Nothing could upset her now. After so very long, a few more days would be like nothing and yet be the longest days she'd spent in her existence.

She wandered the airport for a time, watching everything and everyone. Just before it was time to board, five of the motes she'd sent after the truck appeared and nestled into her hair. Their most recent memories were quite disturbing to Matong. The driver of the truck turned out to be the brother, the young Mr. Bennett. When he'd parked in the short term lot, he'd done it only so he could watch her and find out what plane she would be on. He made no move to follow her into the airport, keeping a very long distance to remain unseen. Only after she'd checked in did he come up to the counter and talk to the woman who'd checked her bag. He gave them a story about how she dropped her book and could they get it to her. He told them he was her brother, even showed his ID, but they wouldn't let him follow her. Instead one of the ladies took the book and told him she'd be certain to get it to her on the plane and not to worry. "Because it's just such a long trip to Brazil." The stupid woman had told him where she was going!

A flight attendant tapped her on the shoulder, interrupting Matong's search of the motes' memories and signed to her. "It's time to board. Follow me please."

Matong had little choice but to do exactly that, no matter how furious she was. She could not fall apart in the middle of the airport, there was no way she could kill them all. The flight attendant ushered her onto the plane, allowing her to board a few minutes early because they assumed she could not hear and Matong did nothing to dissuade them. Matong situated herself in her aisle seat, trying to keep calm as she called up more memories.

Just outside the airport, he'd met a man. This man she knew. The Urichresh had told her about the Salesman. She was not to touch him, speak to him, or be seen by him if she could help it. If there was a way for her to be defeated, this Johnny would know it and have it to offer for trade. That he was speaking to Bennett could only mean bad things for her.

"I can help you." Johnny smiled at Bennett, his gold tooth glinting in the fluorescent lights of the airport's entryway.

"Excuse me?" Bennett hadn't understood what the Salesman meant, his voice filled with confusion.

"The woman you are following. I know where she's going."

"Yeah, me too. She's headed for Brazil." Bennett shrugged and shook his head. "That's a big country. Once she's there, I'll never find her again."

"Not so." Johnny reached into the pocket of his trench coat. "As it happens, I have a map here that shows where she's going. But, Brazil is a really long way away and you aren't really prepared for something like this, so I understand if you don't want it."

"How? How do you know where she's going?"

"Let's just say that I have access to some... sensitive ... information." Johnny shrugged his narrow shoulders and grinned mischievously.

"And you'd be willing to give that information to me?" Bennett's voice was full of suspicion. Matong could not see his face because her motes had been firmly affixed to the front of his shirt or in his hair.

"No. I am a Salesman. I'd be willing to sell you this information for a price, say the rabbit's foot in your pocket."

"Dude, are you insane?" Bennett's voice rose, the pitch indicative of hysteria.

"Perhaps. But then, I'm not the one who has been seeing monsters, am I?" Johnny grinned and pulled a map from inside his coat. "So, do we have a deal?"

Bennett pulled a bright green rabbit's foot on a chain out of his pocket. "I've carried this since Afghanistan. I've never gone anywhere without it."

"Well, those are the terms and I have more to do than just stand here talking to you, so you'd best decide quickly."

"I owe it to Angie." He laid the rabbit's foot in Johnny's palm and took the map, opening it up to inspect it. Johnny had circled the area where the temple sat, marking its entrance with a tiny red X. "Even knowing where she, it, whatever is, I don't think that's going to be enough to do the job. It's not like I can shoot the thing, is it?"

"No. It isn't. What else do you have on you right now?" Johnny's eyes narrowed.

"A couple of dollars, some change, my keys, a pocket knife." Bennett emptied his pockets onto the hood of his truck.

"What about that watch?"

"This? It's not worth anything. It's just a regular watch." Bennett took it off and added it to the pile on the hood.

"Here's what I'm offering. You give me that watch and the knife and I'll give you this box." Johnny held up a military style box, olive green with caution labels on the outside.

"What the hell is that?" Bennett asked.

"A prototype. The Japanese have been working on this for a long time. It's an electromagnetic pulse gun."

"You think that'll stop it?" Bennett reached for the box. "For this to even have an effect… you're telling me this thing is a machine?"

"It will slow her down enough for you to do what needs done. When you use it, make sure it's somewhere sheltered, where she can't scatter too far. You don't have a lot of time, just about a month and a half to prepare. Get there and get it done. Don't be late. Good luck, my friend." He lifted his fedora and grinned before he disappeared.

Matong seethed, ignoring the other passengers that boarded the plane. The Salesman's finger always seemed to fall on the human side of the scales. Anything Bennett did wouldn't matter. She was invincible. But the word Afghanistan bothered her. That meant Bennett was likely a member of some armed forces. It wouldn't be wise to underestimate him.

The flight attendant came to her just before takeoff and handed her a book with a note on the cover. "Your brother brought this to the desk. You'd forgotten it."

Matong signed a quick thank you and waited until the attendant walked away before opening it. On the title page, Bennett had written a very special inscription just for her. "I don't know what you are or what you're after, but I will stop you. That is a promise. You messed with the wrong Marine's sister."

The flight lasted just under eleven hours. Matong fidgeted and half tried to watch the movie playing on the screen. No one offered her headphones because, of course, they believed she was deaf. It was never boring though, as Matong spent her time daydreaming about meeting her creators and plotting obstacles for Bennett.

After she made her way through customs, getting Angela's passport stamped in a country the woman would never see, she stepped out of the airport into a very different kind of world. Here, a woman's form was a disadvantage. She figured that out very quickly, watching the men looking at her with a different kind of interest than she wanted. When she was certain she wouldn't be seen, Matong slipped into a shadowy alley and allowed her motes to shift and recolor. Shorter, more muscular, and male, this form was not to her taste. Why she decided she was female when she was not given a gender, she didn't know, but she didn't want to think of herself as neutral. The female form was more appealing to her, less bulky and with fewer appendages to manage.

Matong made her way through the streets of Rio, looking for a vehicle she could take, whether she had to kill for it or not. What she found was a motorcycle. The punk kid that had been riding it wasn't able to breathe through her dust either and she left him in an alley, and sped away on his pretty, black machine. With a new set of wheels, Matong could be anyone she wanted again. She chose a very plain, featureless form as, when she rode exposed, it took a great deal more effort to keep all her motes together and she couldn't afford to expend energy on maintaining a specific form.

She knew the way to the deep jungle without giving it much thought, as if the temple was calling her home. Or perhaps the Urichresh were waiting on the other side, beckoning her to them. When she reached the point where the jungle became too thick to ride through, she left the bike and transformed again, choosing a jaguar for its speed and agility.

Days turned to weeks and Matong lost track of time. Her only concern was getting to the temple before the stars were quite right. She knew she didn't have many days left. She had no need for sleep, moving through the bright hours and the dark hours as if they were the same, the pull of the temple growing stronger.

The temple was practically buried in flowering vines and trees, not tall, nor grand, just a jut of stone and a cave entry to mark it. Matong looked to the sky and figured she had two days to wait and prepare before it was time to open the great door inside. She busied herself clearing away some of the vegetation and creating a path from the entry to the temple to a small clearing where the Urichresh could gather and prepare for the great war.

On the afternoon of the day of the opening, Matong heard the whir of helicopter blades and stiffened. She did not want to usher her creators into a world already prepared for battle. Dispersing herself, Matong floated on the air, pushing herself high enough to see. The chopper landed in a different clearing than the one she'd prepared about an hour's hike away. To her great relief, the chopper did not stay. A single figure got off the helicopter before it lifted back into the sky and flew away.

For a moment, she couldn't believe it. Bennett, had followed her all this way to do what? Destroy what couldn't be destroyed? She readied herself and waited for him, taking on the form of one of the native tribesmen. Bennett wouldn't know that the natives avoided the area around the temple. She chose not to worry about the box the Salesman had traded to him. Matong knew what machines were – brainless servants – and she was not a machine. All the things machines lacked, Matong had in plenty.

She waited for him, patiently sweeping the area before the temple with a bundle of tree fronds. When he approached, she stopped to look at him. He wore fatigues meant for the desert, not the jungle, Bennett's eyes, ears, nose and mouth covered by a strange apparatus that Matong's motes called scuba gear. That limited his air supply, limited the time he could take to try and best her. At most, considering they were on the surface, he'd have an hour to try and defeat her before he ran out of air and would have to remove the equipment. In his right hand, he carried a long machete, useful for cutting through thick brush, but what would be a killing blow to most would pass right through her. It was an hour she could spare, but not too much more than that. Once the sun set, the first lock would disengage and allow Matong access to the great door.

Matong shifted her form back to that of the travel agent, smiling when fury flashed in Bennett's blue eyes. He ran awkwardly toward her, swinging his machete, trying to say something she couldn't understand through the mask and tubing. Maybe it was a curse as he realized his weapon would not harm her. A few motes separated, searched the man for any opening in his gear, but found nothing. There was no sign of the Salesman's box either.

Dropping the guise of his sister, Matong took the form of her creators, the Urichresh, squat bipeds with thick bodies and muscular arms, black spikes protruding from their wrists, shoulders, knees, and back. He jumped back. His fear sent a thrill through her. "You should not have come here." She no longer cared if she looked or sounded human. This enemy would not live long enough to tell anyone anything. Matong rushed toward him, knocking him to the ground. He flailed beneath her as she struggled to make her form solid enough to take his blade from him.

Bennett swung the blade blindly, just trying to keep her away, trying to keep her from growing solid enough to do him damage. Matong dropped her form entirely, dropping to the earth like so much dust. She stayed like that for a long time, waiting, watching. He stepped away from her, light glinting from the dog tag laced into his boot, giving her a chance to read what was written on the heels of them, "O-POS," in thick black letters on both boots. Matong's motes explained about blood types and meat tags. She would make sure she left the boots unharmed, let whatever remained of the Bennett family know what happened to their soldier.

As the sun slipped down beneath the horizon, a great shuddering groan echoed from within the temple. Bennett jumped, whirling toward the entrance to the cave, machete over his head, prepared to battle anything that might step out of the darkness. Matong had no more time to play with her victim. The time had finally arrived for her to fulfill the very purpose for which she was created.

She gathered herself together quickly, silently, behind Bennett's back and rushed him, lifting him up into the air and slamming him against the rock. He could be the first victory for the Urichresh when they marched through the great door in all their glory. Bennett would be her offering to them as she presented them their new world.

She took form again, not as any of her stolen identities, but as the woman she envisioned herself to be, exotic, the epitome of beauty in the world that had been hers for so long. Slim figure with ample curves, her tanned skin covered by little more than decorated gauze, black hair flowing loose to her waist, and bright green eyes.

Navigating through the temple would have been difficult if her chosen form were her true form. The tunnels were made by and for a people that preferred to walk on four legs rather than two, and there had been some subsidence over the years. It was remarkable how much of the structure remained unchanged given the invading vines, animals, and certainly humans who had been wandering it for centuries.

It took some time to reach the hidden center of the temple, a deep cavern that held the great door. Low but nearly thirty feet wide with deep carvings on the stone, niches and holes leading to the complex dimensional locks inside. The carvings were nothing of Earth, but from the land of the Urichresh, detailed marks that Matong alone understood. It was the language of her birth, the language of her creators.

"Open the way for victory and glory shall be yours."

She touched the words and smiled as she freed her motes to spread through the door. The great door shuddered at her touch, as her motes filled the empty places of the locks and disengaged them. Matong pulled herself back together, into the form of the Urichresh.

As the great door moved, Matong couldn't keep still, each of her motes dancing with anticipation. The door moved fully out of her way. Matong howled. There were no Urichresh waiting to greet her, only a vast expanse of emptiness. Sun-bleached bones littered the stone road beyond the door, piles of spike-boned Urichresh, long dead, nearly glowed in the light of their blue moon. The air smelled heavy, stank of sulfur and sand. Far to the south, at the very edges of her vision, a ruined city lay like ancient gravestones, teetering on their foundations, crumbling away beneath the wear of exposure. Gone. They were all gone.

Matong screamed, a violent, aching scream, her motes rising together in a small funnel of whipping dust. Alone. Lost. Her purpose for existing no longer valid. Fueled by desperation and anger, she spun faster, pulling foreign sands and stones into her funnel, growing bigger, stronger as she did so. Her wind sucked the door closed again, sandblasting its face free of the symbols and complex locks, grinding it clean.

"Something go wrong with your plan?"

Matong spun around to see Bennett, her rage growing, focusing. "It doesn't matter. I'll do what they did not survive to do. I will break all of you. Every single one. I will claim this planet for myself in their name. This isn't your world anymore."

Only as he lifted a strange contraption that looked like a battery with a tiny satellite dish welded to its side did she realize that something was different about him. He wasn't wearing his mask anymore and he had not only the device in his hands but a belt with blocks and blocks of white clay and black wires attached to long metal cylinders jammed into the clay.

"A bomb? You bring a bomb to what? Trap me? I am dust, you fool." She shook her head and charged at him again.

"You're a machine." Bennett pressed a button on the box.

A great wave passed through Matong. Motes fell away, dead, dying, or twitching in confusion. She couldn't communicate with them; she received nothing but gibberish. All that remained of her was her centermost self, motes shielded from harm by so many millions of others. Reduced to a mass the size of a cockroach, her scream of shock and misery was little more than an unheard squeak as Bennett stepped beyond her to what remained of the great door.

Matong watched as he took off his belt and tucked it into a small natural depression above the great door. Not that it mattered. There was no one on the other side of the door to wait for it to open again. She hadn't failed, they had. Her creators had abandoned her, forgotten her. But she had been victorious. Bennett would not stand in the way of that. Her victory would be complete.

With new purpose, she skittered across the floor, up Bennett's leg, separating and spreading out, all her remaining motes headed for the man's nose. They gathered together again in the back of his throat, binding together across this airway. Matong sealed his airway off, cut off his air supply. Bennett cut her down, tried to destroy her, and now was going to blow up her temple, the only evidence of her home. Only she was allowed to do that. Matong did not enjoy killing. Except this once. She would relish this once.

As Bennett struggled to breathe, Matong tightened her seal on his airway. Laughing with what little voice she had as he jammed his fingers down his throat trying to dislodge her. He gagged, but nothing could breach her seal. Nothing could move her. What little she had left of herself cheered as Bennett's body collapsed, but she did not release him.

The explosion gave her no choice. It broke him, pulled him away from her, scattered all her motes, alive and dead, into the debris, out into the night. Matong let the explosion take her, separate her from the rest of herself. She would not call for what little of her remained functional. Someday, the few motes left would forget they'd ever had a purpose. Someday, even she might. Until then, she'd let the wind take her. She'd float until she didn't care that she'd outlived her gods, her creators. She'd fly until she'd forgotten the Urichresh completely, forgotten what it had been like to be whole.

*   *   *

INTERLUDE SIX

It was eight hours after Johnny's surprise announcement, and business was somehow even busier, the flow of foot traffic nearly overwhelming.

"How much for the pig-sticker?" a customer asked.

Ashley looked down into the bloodshot eyes of an anorexic, punk rocker with spiked, green hair. She turned to regard what she was pointing at. High on the wall near the ceiling, in a glass fronted wood case was a long, ancient, iron-shafted Carthaginian throwing spear. Ashley turned back around.

"I want it," the punk said.

"Display only," Ashley said. "We've got a nice Peruvian Atlatl on the wall behind you."

The girl tossed a large wad of euros onto the counter, pointedly, "No, that spear."

"Sorry," Ashley shrugged. "There ain't enough money in the world, kid."

Seeing the sudden glare in the girl's eyes as she pocketed her cash, Ashley nodded to Barrax, her seven-foot-tall Masai head of security, who immediately escorted the protesting pale chick toward the front door and outside with a shove.

"Customer relations is into full swing I see," Johnny said.

Ashley looked up and smiled, "Oh, I can't wait to see what you have for me now."

"I was here first," a German-accented voice rang out.

Ashley looked around in confusion and then leaned forward over the counter. A grizzled looking dwarf, dressed in shorts, sneakers, and a Beatles t-shirt was holding a large gunnysack in his big hands.

"Rump," Ashley laughed, "don't tell me…. Gold twine?"

The dwarf tossed his heavy bag up onto the counter. Ashley opened it.

"Platinum," he said. "Oh, and hi, Johnny. Been awhile."

"That crystal loom still working out?" Johnny asked.

"Oh yeah," Rump said. "Best trade I ever made with you."

"So," Ashley said.

"Pawn," Rump said. "I need rubies and sapphires, stat."

It took Ashley five minutes to complete the transaction. Afterwards, Rump smiled, bowed, and disappeared in a burst of foul-smelling smoke.

"So, Johnny," she said, "the world still seems to exist all around us."

"Would you believe it?" he said. "Ten hours and humanity is holding their own. Can't say how long that will last, my dear."

Johnny reached into his coat and pulled out a plastic-sheathed comic book.

"Hmmmm… Action Comics number one," Ashley said, "mint condition. Very nice, but, I was hoping to be blown away."

"Autographed by Jerry Siegel and Joe Shuster," Johnny said.

Ashley's jaw dropped.

Ten minutes later Johnny left the shop with a lovely, framed, Monet under his arm.

Ashley walked up to the front bay window. She peered out from behind the pawnshop's large, multi-colored, art nouveau neon sign that read The Right to Pawn Possessions is the Right to be Free.

The streets of Dingle looked peaceful enough, but she knew that all hell was right now attempting to break out across the planet.

The Tuatha De Danann guardians trapped in the ancient Celtic standing stones surrounding the village should protect us from the largest of invaders. Astraea spoke in Ashley's mind. And you can trust that the shop's four cornerstones that we smuggled from the Greek ruins of the temple of Themis on Sicily, will ward off most middling demon lords.

"But if any of the fighter castes break through…" Ashley whispered.

Then things might get interesting…

*   *   *

CHAPTER SEVEN: DOOR 790

by Diane Arrelle

All right, I've been stuck in this basement since the turn of the century and not the last one at that, he mused and took a sip from the flask he didn't even bother to hide any more.

"I've been trapped in this damned human form, eating this damned human food, acting so damned human I even answer to my human name without giving it a thought," he said, surprising himself by vocalizing what he should have been thinking. "Wow, really human way too long!"

Taking another swig, he sighed, another human gesture he'd picked up since he started breathing air. One blessed mistake and he was damned to this plane of existence waiting for the Sha'Daa to finally occur again so he could redeem himself.

"Ahem."

He looked up from the pile of unsorted mail in front of him. "Yeah?" he growled, then noticed the tall, thin man standing in front of the counter. "Oh, it's you."

The man smiled without humor, the gold tooth glinting in the dim overhead lights. His gaunt face was half masked by the felt fedora and his body was hidden behind a long, dark trenchcoat.

"Yep, it's me. Worried?" He bent closer and studied the nameplate. "Damon Fuchupp."

"Funny, Johnny, you know my real name, you know who I am."

The man tipped his fedora, "Well, Mr. ah, Mr. Fuchupp, I have no idea what you are talking about. I just came down here to tell you that I plan to stay at the hotel for a few days and if any mail comes in, I'll be in room 690. Odd, a post office buried in the basement of an old resort hotel, still active long after it has stopped being necessary."

The postman, presently the human, Damon Fuchupp snarled and said in a whisper, "Better watch out for more than letters, Johnny."

The man known as the Salesman smiled, a real smile this time, the tooth shining brightly. "Or what, you'll go postal on me? Remember, room 690." His smile broadened. "A clever and appropriate name change for the duration. Did you pick it yourself?"

The demon started to retort but the Salesman was gone. Discovering that he had drained his flask, he hung up the 'Out to Lunch' sign and wandered down the long twisting corridors of the basement. The halls turned without warning and split off into branches. They seemed to be endless, which they were, half of this earth and half of another. But tomorrow night when he opened the door, the halls of this hotel would lead straight to hell. He absently rubbed the metal key in his pocket and felt calm and at peace. He held the key that would open that portal. All he had to do was wait a little longer and then he'd do the job, correctly this time, and his purgatory here on this world would be ended.

He found himself outside the doorway to the dark, narrow stairs leading to the indoor pool. He trudged down, barely fitting. The body he'd been assigned was soft and flabby, the bad human body of a more than middle-aged man who looked like he'd been stuck behind a postal desk for a century. Once at the bottom, the steps widened to reveal the glistening, beckoning pool.

Funny, a demon of his rank wasn't supposed to be fond of water, but as a human he delighted in the feel of it. He glanced around, saw he was alone, which wasn't surprising since so few guests at the inn could ever find this place, and stripped off all his clothes. Waddling down the steps into the pool, he let the heated water slowly cover his miniscule balls and pencil-stub penis. Of all the humiliations that befell him when he had been cast out of Hell, the loss of his magnificently, grotesquely, humongous genitals hurt him the most. He reached down at least ten times a day to scratch at them, through decade after decade of being condemned here, and each time he did so he was momentarily shocked to find two marbles and a nub.

But they were now covered by the water, and he was submerged up to his neck. He relaxed, and started to doggie paddle about, a wondrous experience to him because demons didn't float in water. They sank like a stone.

The water at the other end of the pool began bubbling and churning and joy started bubbling and churning within him. It was almost time. Surely this was a sign!

The joy sank to the bottom of his toes, as a head, a human head, burst out of the water and smiled at him. "Hey, Dude, how's it hanging?"

Obviously the other swimmer hadn't been swimming underwater with his eyes open to ask that question. "Fine, just fine," the demon Damon Fuchupp replied and covered his inadequate manhood with his hand. Shame – such a human emotion. Hades, he had to get out of this prison, out of this skin, out of this world. "I wish to heaven I could get out of this place!" he mumbled and stood waiting for this foolish human to leave him alone. The moment of relaxation and meditation about the coming holocaust had been ruined by this human intrusion and now all he wanted to do was get dressed and return to his mailroom.

The young man, more a boy than adult, bobbed up and down at his end of the pool. "Isn't this just the greatest place in the world? My parents discovered this inn years ago when they'd been lost in a thunderstorm in the Catskills. Can you just imagine the thunder booming, the lightning flashing and the place just appears on the side of the road? Now, like, this place is a family tradition. I'm working here, at the concierge desk."

The demon nodded, wondering how long the kid would talk.

"And, like, it seems normal enough and all, but do you know they're missing a room on the top two floors. Yeah really! When I walk up there, everything appears the same on every floor but it isn't. The top two floors don't have room 90, but all the other floors do. Only nobody else seems to see it and when I asked about it, nobody seems to know what I'm talking about. Freakin' eerie."

He smiled at the demon, and continued talking in an endless stream of gibberish. "Anyway so here we are, like the only two people in this entire labyrinth of a bottom floor and we both discovered this pool even deeper down than the basement and it's warm and clean and perfect. Freakin' creepy but amaz-ing!"

He stopped, ducked under the water and surfaced. "Yo dude, like you don't have any clothes on. Freakin' great! I'm

Mark. I started working here last month. Hard to believe that it's already summer. Why the solstice is soon, and I read that —"

A flash of fire leaped from the demon's eyes and incinerated the verbose bellboy, boiling the water around him and turning that incessant blathering into screams.

The smile that had spread across the demon's face faded to agony, as he realized that in human form he had no powers at all and the boy continued to prattle.

"Anyway, it was nice to meet you, Dude. Later," Mark said, and got out of the water and walked into the dressing room calling back, "by the way, I didn't catch your name."

The demon thought for a second and figured Mark could be useful, a nice first sacrifice to the hell-horde after he opened the gateway tomorrow night. "Damon," he said and smiled. "Glad to meet you. I'm the postmaster at the inn. Stop by later."

He watched the kid disappear, quickly climbed out of the pool, and dressed in a rush before he had to see him again.

Back in the mailroom, which was his penance for rushing through the rift in the worlds that randomly opened from time to time, he picked up a pile of mail and stared at it. Damned humans and their banal correspondences. He opened the first letter and read it. It was a large business plan that was here for the man in 208. The guy came here every summer with his wife and kids.

He stared at it and stared at it, waiting for some sign that his powers were returning, but nothing happened, not even a tiny wisp of smoke, so he took out his lighter and set the corner of the document aflame. He grinned as the word 'Urgent' turned black and crumbled to ash.

The next letter he picked up was from the wife of the guy here for two weeks with his girlfriend. He read it over twice trying to decide what to do. The wife who thought he came here every June for a religious retreat with his male coworkers decided to surprise him this year and visit for the weekend. "Decisions, decisions," he muttered. "What to do." He really respected the guy for the elaborate set-up he had going here. Surely it would reserve the guy a space in hell. If he destroyed the letter, the jig would be up, and that would be a shame. But if he let the man know his wife was coming, then it let a decade of deceit safely continue.

"What the hell," he declared. "I'm done here, don't need this entertainment anymore." And he set that letter on fire as well.

The third letter was for room 690. Odd, there was no room 690. Just like 790 didn't exist, neither did 690. But 790 did exist on the other side. Damon knew 690 had no other side and yet it was Johnny's room. Is that how that sly shifty no-good son-of-a… son-of-a… son-of-a-whatever traveled? Damon shrugged it off and opened the letter. Fallen Demon: Couldn't resist reading my mail could you? Meet me at the bar after closing. I think I have a trade you'd be interested in.

He knew it was from Johnny. What was he pulling? Damon wondered as he burned that letter as well. Heaven would have to turn hot as hell for him to show up and deal with that wild card.

"Oh, like wow, you're the postman!"

Damon looked up and groaned.

Mark stood there grinning like a human. "Like, do you work for the postal service or the hotel?"

Damon sighed; it was getting to be a habit lately. "Neither. What do you want?"

"Just wandering. This place is amazing. You know how I was telling you about room 790 not being there at all? Well, I found this old key earlier and it had the room number on it. I knew it couldn't be real or anything because all the doors here have those electronic card keys, but I went up to the seventh floor and I swear, man, I swear I saw a door shimmer just for a second on the blank wall right between 788 and 792 even though there isn't room for a broom closet between the rooms. Weird, huh?"

The fallen demon didn't hear anything the kid said after he heard the key wasn't in his pocket anymore. His hand flew to the pocket and of course found it empty, as empty as he felt inside when he realized that the Sha'Daa was less then 36 hours away and he'd fucked up again. That key did more than just open the gateway to hell. It opened his path to hellish redemption.

"Let me see it!" His hand was shaking as he held it out.

Mark shrugged. "Sure. Come upstairs and I'll show you. Funny thing when I walked past where 690 should have been, it shimmered too. Bet both rooms work on the same keys."

"Really?" Damon said, his voice dripping with hunger and scheming. The kid was slight, a swimmer's body. Probably strong too.

But flabby middle-aged body or not, he was still a demon deep down and he could kill the kid with one hand. If only he'd had his powers he could make the kid's organs burst, but for now he'd settle for snapping his scrawny neck.

He closed up the post office and allowed Mark to lead the way to the elevator. Stupid, careless, old fool echoed through his brain over and over. In his rush to squeeze through and make the first kill when the rift opened last century, a common enough occurrence as rifts happened randomly and allowed a little hell on earth from time to time, he'd carelessly let the portal slam shut behind him, stopping the rest of the demons from crossing over. A mistake he'd been paying for for the past century, and now he'd carelessly dropped the key… it probably fell out of his pocket when he'd stripped to swim.

First they got off on the 6th floor and as they walked past 688 an ever so slight shimmer appeared at the corner of his vision. "See it?" Mark asked.

"See what?"

"The door, 690."

"Nope," he lied.

"All right, I'll show you 790. You can't miss that one."

They took to the stairs going up one flight. Mark ran two steps at a time, while Damon felt himself gasping for air as he slowly climbed upward.

"OK, now watch!" Mark exclaimed and stopped between the two rooms. "Wow! It's got more form now."

"Of course it does," Damon said, so low the kid couldn't hear him. "The Sha'Daa is getting nearer, stronger."

He stood directly behind the young man and reached out to get his neck in a strangle hold and break it. As his fingers closed in to wrap around it, a flash of light exploded in his head and Damon found himself flat out on the ground. The kid was leaning over him.

"What happened?"

Kid shook his head, "Dunno, you must have tripped."

"The light, didn't you see it?"

"Light?"

Then the demon saw the rolled up comic book-sized magazine in Mark's back pocket. He felt a sinking sensation.

"What's that?" he asked, pointing.

"Funny thing. It's a book of runes to protect me from evil."

He already knew but asked anyway, "Really? Where'd you buy that?"

"Traded with a tall, creepy dude came up to me yesterday morning."

He couldn't help but ask. "Traded for what?"

"The key to room 690. I had to look for it but it was just stuck in the bottom of a drawer at the front desk. I figured no one would miss it; after all, it was metal and useless just like the one for 790. And I thought a book of magic incantations would be fun when me and the rest of the staff held our weekly D and D game night."

The demon just nodded, a feeling of hopelessness starting to eat away at his world. "I see."

"Yeah he gave me this book of protective spells and a box of waterproof markers. The whole gang of us had a ball drawing the spells all over ourselves last night. Made it a drinking game. I lost so I have the most drawings."

Damon suddenly remembered the drawings he had taken for ridiculous tattoos on the kid's body when he got out of the pool.

Protected! No wondered he'd been knocked on his ass.

"Well, Mark," he said, "I better go to my room and rest after that fall."

"If you're all right to make it yourself," Mark called.

Damon waved in a friendly manner and thought, please give me enough power to just set his hair ablaze.

He needed that key but that creep Johnny had made sure he couldn't touch the damned kid. He changed out of his uniform and after a few hours of cable porno, went to the bar to meet Johnny. It couldn't hurt to see what he wanted.

Sure enough, Johnny was sitting in the dark, deserted bar nursing a drink he must have poured himself. "Scotch, Demon?" he asked, and pointed to the bottle on the table and the second tumbler.

Damon poured himself a glassful and asked, "What do you want from me? We both know it's happening tonight and I know you only trade to give us trouble. What could you possibly trade with me?"

Johnny held up a key that shone slightly in the dim backlighting.

The demon grabbed it from his hand and clutched it to his chest, relief filling him up and replacing the growing dread that had been creeping into him since earlier in the afternoon.

"Come on you know the rules – a trade," Johnny said in a low growl. "Let's keep this on the up and up."

"What?" Damon asked.

"I want a 'Canceled' stamp from the post office."

Damon laughed, "You want the rubber stamper I use to cancel the postage when it comes in? That archaic piece of junk I haven't had to use in years? Sure!"

They went down to the post office and Damon gave Johnny the stamper. "Done?"

"One thing: that key is for 690. I'll be leaving in a few minutes. Got a ton of trades to do in the next 22 hours. Before you start laying useless curses on me, the key does hold power."

"What kind?"

"The powers of good and evil. The 'how's and 'why's are for you to figure out."

Damon looked at the key in his hand and mumbled curses. That SOB Johnny; always on the wrong side. "Say…" he began but he was alone.

Three o'clock in the morning and he found himself wandering the halls. By midnight, the Sha'Daa was a go and he had to decide what to do with the wrong key. He went up to the 6th floor and stood between 688 and 692. The door to 690 shimmered brightly but when he tried to touch the key to it, long ropes of shocking light, like jolts of electricity shot toward him. Obviously, he was not allowed to open the door.

He went upstairs to room 790 and held the key up as he stood where 790 would appear. The door shimmered and wavered for him but he wasn't sure the key would work enough to open the portal at midnight. And if it could, why would Johnny have traded it with him?

"I gotta get my key back," he snarled and thought about Mark and all his protective markings. "I bet he'll trade with me when I show him my key does the same thing. Humans are so gullible, show them a trinket and they'll always want it."

He waited for morning and looked for the kid. When he couldn't find Mark anywhere, he finally asked the other staffers, people he'd never bother with normally.

"Day off," one of the nameless, faceless workers told him. "Said he'd be back after dinner. Had some errands to run."

Damon sat behind his counter all day, not bothering to do anything but drink. He knew that no matter how drunk he got, he'd be fine the minute the portal opened and he reverted back to his true form. The hours ticked by like decades. Time crawled as he waited to catch sight of his new buddy, Mark. Maybe he'd eat him as soon as he became himself again and not sacrifice him to the horde. There would be plenty of others to kill – like every soul in this hotel to start with. And then, of course, the entire world. Humanity would be done this time. And he was going to do his part to guarantee it.

Finally daylight began to fade and, being the longest day of the year, the Sha'Daa was mere hours away. Asking around for Mark, he was told that the kid was down in the pool for his daily swim.

Damon rushed down, suddenly aware of the passing minutes. As time had dragged endlessly toward infinity earlier, it felt like it was hurtling away from him now.

He ran down the narrow stairs to the pool and found Mark in the deep end near the diving board. "Hey, Mark! How you doing?"

"Fine, Dude, just fine. Couldn't be better. You know I took my key upstairs and the doorway is getting more distinct, almost like it's turning into a real door."

"Come out of the water for a minute, Mark," Damon called. "Wanna talk to you."

Mark grinned. "What about?"

"That key."

Mark swam over to the side and pulled himself up out of the water in a fluid, graceful motion. "Look it's my swim time; I gotta practice like every day to stay in form and keep my scholarship. I'm going to the Olympics next year."

"You'll be rotting in hell, next year," Damon whispered with a smile and walked over to the kid still covered in magical markings. "Look I dropped that key. It's been mine since I started working here and it brings, me, you know, luck."

"Oh wow, man, like a lucky charm!" Mark said and walked to the diving board. He casually bounced on it as he added, "well, okay, I'll give it to you in a couple of days after I see what happens with those shimmering doors."

Damon held up the key to 690. "Here, trade me for this one. I was upstairs earlier and this key caused the doors to appear, too. I just want my lucky key back. I really like the number 790."

Mark frowned for a second, then grinned again. "Sure why not?" He took the metal key from the pocket of his swim trunks then started jumping on the board, higher and higher until Damon couldn't believe the height the kid achieved. After about six jumps, Mark bent his body into a jackknife and slid into the water with hardly a ripple. He surfaced and moved to the side and got out again. "God, this is my environment!" he said. "I wish I spent all my time in the water, don't you?"

Damon ground his teeth together. Was the kid wasting time on purpose? Could he know something? "Nope, like it on dry land just fine, now the key?"

"Oops, I dropped it. It's on the bottom of the pool. Let me show you."

Damon couldn't believe what was going on. The kid was definitely playing him. Yes, he decided, he'd kill Mark as soon as he could. He walked to the edge, but Mark grabbed his arm, "No, you gotta stand on the board and look down. It's right under the diving board – straight down."

Damon snarled, frustration building up until he felt like he could erupt out of his damned human body. But he knew he couldn't. He was stuck this way until the Sha'Daa freed him. He yearned to scream at the kid, tell him to fuck off, let him know he was an all-powerful demon. But he needed that key more than anything else in this and every universe and he couldn't swim well enough to dive down and get it. So he played along, letting the knowledge that Mark was doomed carry him.

He stood on the edge of the diving board, wondering what the kid had in mind. What's the worst that could happen? The kid could push him in and he'd doggie paddle to the shallow end and then find a way to murder the punk, protective spells be cursed.

As he stared into the water, looking downward, he started to make out some shapes but Mark shouted. "Oh wait, here it is!"

Damon looked away from the pool and at the young man who had silently moved up on the board directly behind him. "The key," he said to Mark, baring his teeth in a primitive gesture. "Give me the key, now!"

Mark gasped, stepped back, then held out the metal key. "Hey man, like calm down, I was only fooling around. Here it is."

Damon reached out and to his shock Mark swung something at him striking his outstretched hand. As it connected with his palm, searing pain hit him at impact and traveled rapidly up his arm.

He looked at the mere mortal who had struck him and gasped.

Mark had stamped Damon's hand with the stamper from the earlier trade and it was cancelling the spell over him. Energy suddenly started running though his veins; power like he hadn't felt in a century rushed though him. Bat wings sprouted from his back and tusk-like fangs grew from his teeth. He was redeemed and saved. He was becoming himself once again, a demon to be feared by all. And somehow this stupid little mortal had caused it to happen. Boy, did Johnny screw up this time!

He looked at the clock. Less than an hour to go and now he could open the door as he should be, a full demon. Everything was perfect except his hand still burned. He watched as it blackened, swelling and cracking down to the bone. "What have you done to me?"

Mark stood his ground, the spells on his skin glowing against the evil filling the room. "Washed the stamp in Holy Water like the man in the hat told me. He said you were a real demon and that I needed to stop you. And, like wow, he was right."

Spells or no spells, Damon glowered menacingly at Mark, knowing he was going to rip the scrawny human into pieces.

"And then the man told me to do this," Mark shouted and started jumping on the board, sending vibrations through Damon who was still standing at the edge.

Fury finally made Damon react and his good hand landed a glancing blow to the kid, knocking Mark off the side of the diving board onto the concrete floor.

The full impact of the strike was deflected by the powerful spells covering Mark and, as the kid screamed and toppled, the backlash of the runes' protection slammed back at Damon, knocking him off the already quivering board. He fell backward into the water, one arm flailing and the other weak and useless at his side.

The demon once called Damon on this lousy plane of existence struggled to rise up, tried to paddle his arm, but suddenly remembered he was a demon once again and sank down ten feet to the bottom of the pool. Mark, who had somehow gotten to his feet, steered Damon's leaden body, jabbing at him from above using the long pool-cleaning pole.

The demon suddenly realized what was happening. The shape he had glimpsed earlier when looking into the water was a large pentagram drawn on the floor of the pool with those waterproof markers. Mark had directed his body to land in the center. He was trapped – trapped at the bottom, unable to swim away, unable to move from the lines that held him. He was going to miss the Sha'Daa and his absence would be noted, especially when the portal remained closed. He wished he could still breathe air and put himself out of the agony of defeat, but he was now a full demon once again and didn't use air.

Hopelessly he watched his arm sizzle and blacken. He didn't know if the holy water was powerful enough to travel his entire body and kill him, but he really hoped it was and would before others from the Sha'Daa found him like this and decided on a new and better punishment.

*   *   *

INTERLUDE SEVEN

Though mostly a thriving business throughout the majority of the pawnshop's five-hundred-year history, Ashley went through a ten-year bout of decreasing revenues that left her flat broke by the end of 1851. Hundreds of years of accumulated wealth and pawn stock had been sacrificed for a greater good: The Irish Famine.

As word of Ashley's munificence spread among the homeless poor of Ireland, dozens, then hundreds, then thousands came begging for food at the shop's back alley doorway. Ashley spent thousands of pounds on all manner of supplies for the starving: bread, soup, fresh vegetables, slaughtered chickens, pigs, and beef, but the toll of the potato blight had afflicted millions, and her actions were but a flimsy bandage on a massive, fatal wound.

Ashley would never forget the An Gorta Mor, or Great Hunger, the death of millions, and the emigration of hundreds of thousands of Ireland's people, never to return. It took her decades to build the business back up to its former glory, but her memories of suffering remained sharp, and her anonymous annual donations to world charities were always lavish.

* * *

CHAPTER EIGHT: BLOODSTONE

by Gustavo Bondoni

Thin rock, and beyond, the unmistakable smell of humans – unwashed, dirty, and acrid – all of the things that made humans so easy to recognize. Grenntak placed his face right up against the rock, savoring what little of the people's essence came through the paper-thin sheet.

"Yes," he breathed. "This is the place where I want to come through. There are men here, many men, and they are near despair, closer to death than to life. They will listen."

He looked back at his troupe of demons. Most of them huddled near the shining rift, as if unwilling to let go of the safety it represented. The world they came from held little for them, but it was a known quantity. There was safety in numbers there and, if one stayed in the horde, sheer statistics would probably keep you alive for years, decades, maybe centuries. The tiny demons of the lower castes were not smart enough to imagine a world where food was limitless and life-force could be had with just a little effort.

He would change all that. Some of the insignificant, misshapen creatures that arrived with him would return to their barren hell nearly as large as Grenntak himself, and then they could stand tall, and live off the inconsequential herds of lesser creatures. Grenntak would gain power as well.

But, would it be enough to get him ascendancy? It would if they managed to find the crystal key.

"Stand back now. They come. If you harm any of them without my consent, I will tear you to shreds."

As his minions scrambled to get out of reach, a point of metal broke through the thin stone from the far side. It hung there a moment as if undecided about what to do next, and then, with a side-to-side tug, it was pulled slowly back. A thin beam of flickering light came through the hole it had made, and the lesser demons moved still closer to the portal. They didn't need light to see because theirs was a lightless world, but they were just smart enough to know that anything new was potentially dangerous.

Voices drifted in behind the light, and Grenntak stopped to savor them. It had been ten thousand years since he'd last heard those tones. The voices were as weak and powerless as they'd been then, but still made the power rage within him. Well did he remember that the last time he'd listened to humans, he'd come through the portal among the ranks of the pitiful deformed creatures he now commanded, but he'd returned stronger, gorged on the life energies of the men he'd taken. The only thing that had kept him from even more power was the fact that he hadn't succeeded in liberating the crystal key and opening the portal that would have allowed him true freedom to roam the surface, and he'd had to content himself with the limited range allowed by the rift.

This time he would not fail.

The humans on the other side were in conference. "We've broken into some kind of open shaft," one of the voices said. The language seemed to have changed since the last time, but it made no difference to the demon. He didn't need to worry about languages.

"What's on the other side?"

"We can't see. There is no light there. We need to open it further to get our light in."

"Leave it. There might be gas caught in there. If it gets onto our lamps, we'll all be killed."

"If there was gas in there, you'd be dead already." This was a new voice, much stronger than the rest. It was a voice that held power – pitiful, nearly nonexistent power in demon terms, but much more power than the inadequate threads of the other humans – and Grenntak knew that this would be the human he'd have to negotiate with initially. He also knew that this human would be his own personal prize. No matter what happened, he would be the one to consume this prize.

"Now get back to work, you shit-stained monkeys!" shouted the voice.

Grenntak heard the sound of a whip striking a soft body followed by whimpers and yelps. Even his minions stepped forward a half-step. This world might be unfamiliar, but violence made them feel at home. Food that couldn't defend itself always made the weakest demons take notice.

The metallic point hit the rock again, dislodging another piece of the wall. A second pick impacted beside it, and the weak blows continued until, aided by a quick kick from Grenntak's taloned leg, the whole sheet of rock collapsed upon itself.

This was the critical moment. His demons, pitiful though they were, had their instructions. The only question was whether they would obey. Would they be smart enough to know that the imaginary dangers that faced them in the human world could never compare to the certainty of slow, painful destruction at his hands if they balked?

Grenntak knew his future for the next ten thousand years hung in the balance. Rage rose within him as his minions hesitated, but he had to contain himself. He couldn't go on a rampage and destroy the humans – not yet anyway, not when there was so much more to gain.

One of the demons closest to Grenntak moved forward, scurrying into the wider shaft. Perhaps he felt the larger demon's rage; perhaps he was just smarter than the rest. Whatever the case, the floodgates opened, and a misshapen tide of small bodies flowed out among the humans and behind them.

Grenntak heard the humans' shocked exclamations, savored their fear, felt them flinch, as a group, away from the shaft they'd opened. He heard the movement as the confused humans tried to escape down the same shaft they'd dug. But soon enough, they found their way blocked by the massed bodies of demons. There was nowhere to go, and they milled around in the half-light. Grenntak smelled the panic rising inside them. They were herd creatures, likely to stampede, but still he waited. Only when the fear was at a fever pitch did he show himself.

"Greetings," he said.

Unlike that of the pitiful humans, his voice held power. Dust fell from the roof of the mine and supporting timbers shook. In one corner, a small landslide closed a side passage.

The humans moved away from him as one. Only the demons at their backs kept them from breaking and running at that very moment.

"I am Grenntak," he told them. "And from this moment forward, I am your master."

The silence following this proclamation allowed the demon to look over his conquest. This lot made his own puny army look like a division of demon lords. They were weak, infirm, too young or too old. He could tell that some of them wouldn't live much longer, while others might live for years, but would be useless as anything other than ballast.

A young boy in the front rank fell to his knees and pressed his head against the ground. He was quickly followed by another, and then a third. Soon, only two men were standing: a bull of a man with skin like polished ebony who held a whip like he meant to use it on Grenntak himself, and a wizened human who seemed to be a collection of bones with skin stretched around them, and looked somehow familiar. Grenntak ignored the old man he was probably too deaf or senile to have received the full coercive force of demonic voice – and concentrated on the other. "And why do you not acknowledge me? Do you mean to challenge my right? I am your master!" He put all the contempt at his disposal into the tone.

The big man took a step backward but held himself together, and Grenntak was impressed. The human's fellows, sensing the demon's anger, were pressing into the rock and whimpering, begging for mercy in piteous whimpers; this man stood – not particularly tall, and not particularly strong in demon terms – but he stood. Perhaps he was more than just a lackey with a whip.

"What have you to say for yourself?" Grenntak asked. He lowered the intensity, sensing that this one might be more useful if he were allowed the illusion of choice.

The man tried to speak: once, twice. He stuttered again but finally managed to get the words out. "I am the foreman of this shaft. I don't know what you are, but you can't just come here and move me aside." On finishing his speech, the man seemed shocked by his own words, but the demon didn't give him a chance to take them back.

"And how would you stop me?" Grenntak immediately smelled the other man's anger. The human actually took a step forward and raised his whip. The demon laughed, causing another fall of dust from the roof. "You are a brave one, that much can't be denied. If you help me to find the crystal key, you shall have a reward beyond your imagining."

"What is the crystal key?" the man asked. It was obvious that he wasn't convinced, but greed shone like a beacon from his eyes. Grenntak fed on the energy that the man emanated, draining his essence even as he fed the fire of his hope.

"It is a stone that reflects light like no other. It is a matrix of pure energy made solid by the same forces that hold the dimensions apart. It is the key that will allow us to enter this world." He paused for effect. "It is buried somewhere in this area. Help us find it, and I will give you whatever you ask of me," Grenntak lied.

Even so, the man, far from exulting, seemed taken aback. "A crystal matrix? What color is it?"

"It is pure energy in crystal form. It has no color."

"Then we shall never find it. This is a diamond mine."

Diamonds? Grenntak didn't know what they were, but he looked more closely at the walls. Within a few yards into the rock, he could see dozens, hundreds of impurities: crystals of near-perfect matrix. Of course, none of them were as flawless as the key itself, but each would take a few seconds to inspect, and the clock was ticking. They only had forty-eight hours to find it, open the portal, and find enough humans to feed on. If they failed, they would return to their own world without any additional strength – to face demons who'd been more successful in their allotted time. It would not go well for them.

The tribesmen who'd bested the demons on Grenntak's prior incursion into this dimension had chosen their hiding place well. They'd seemed frail and inconsequential, but they'd had powerful magic – and powerful spirits – on their side.

And then Grenntak remembered who the other man who'd seemed immune to the power of his voice reminded him of. He was the very image of one of those savages who'd so roundly beaten them back. The demon turned, ready to make him feel the full force of demonic rage.

But the old man was gone.

"You're not as old as you look."

Boima stopped dead in his tracks. No one had used this shaft for over a dozen years, and everyone who knew of its existence had long since perished, either from the brutality of the slavers or from the dangers of the mine itself. The man in his path should not have been there at all. Boima tried to edge away, but it was immediately apparent that the man's long legs would make flight useless. "And what is it to you?"

The man unshuttered an old-style lantern and stood silhouetted in the glow of the lamp. He was completely out of place, dressed in a long coat and a hat unlike any Boima had ever seen. Gold glinted in his mouth as he spoke. Even if the stranger's skin had been as dark as his own, Boima would have known that the man was from far away. He reminded the miner of the men who would sometimes come into the camp to trade with the warlord, men from afar who wanted what the land gave, and were willing to pay for it with guns for the warlord's armies.

"I need an elder. Well, I don't really need one, but you do. Your race does."

"The Gola? We have been under the heels of the warlords for so long that I'm not all that certain that we are a race any longer."

"I'm not talking about the Gola. The race that needs an elder is humanity itself."

"I am not an elder."

"I think you are. Are you not the leader of your tribesmen in this mine?"

Boima spat. "Any fool could lead this rabble."

"There are any number of fools in this mine – and yet none of them truly lead. But you do."

"I am just a cripple, a man who didn't have the courage to fight back when the slavers cut off his hand."

"You traded your hand for your life. It seems a fair bargain," the tall man said.

"I traded away my pride. Now I live without it. There is no life there."

"Perhaps you are more important than you think. I believe I can make a more significant trade with you."

"I have nothing left to barter."

"What's in the pouch around your neck, then?"

"Nothing I'd give to a dark spirit."

"I am not always a dark spirit."

"Then what are you?"

The tall man shrugged. "The name's Johnny. But I think you don't really have time to chat any more. You're about to have company."

The sound of small bodies scurrying toward them from the main shaft reached Boima's ears and he hurried forward. The man, Johnny, simply melted into the shadows and let him pass.

The human had been here, Grenntak was sure of it. The small side passage was the only escape from the main shaft. The problem was that none of the demons had seen the old man escape – and some had paid for that oversight with their pitiful lives. He couldn't sense the old man in any way. It was, perhaps, understandable that the psychic presence of a single human among so many might be impossible to detect, but it was inconceivable that the smell of a man would have disappeared from the floor. The demon began to sense that something else was amiss.

Plus, there was another sense, an energy that hinted at something stronger. Grenntak thought he knew what it represented, but if his suspicions were well-grounded, he also knew that the spirit the energy belonged to would be unable to interfere directly. Nevertheless, its presence was disquieting.

He paused to get his bearings. The humans had come up behind him, spurred on by the troupe of smaller demons, who were still wary of coming within arm's length of the demon lord.

As Grenntak calmed down, he realized that there was little sense in having all of them scurry down the shaft after the human. "You," he pointed to one of the demons at random. "Go find the missing human. Bring him back or don't bother to return." It scurried off into the darkness. The large demon faced the humans. The one who had spoken earlier was in the front rank. "Will you help me? If we are successful, you will be rewarded."

"What is the price?" one man said.

"Price?"

"There is always a price. What will we sacrifice for helping the Jinna?"

'Jinna' was not a word he'd heard before, but Grenntak saw many of the humans making warding signs with their fingers. One even spat at his own feet. He assumed that was the human name for demons. "You will be betraying your own kind. But the rewards will be well worth the cost."

Grenntak half expected the humans to attack him, in a futile attempt to defend their race, but most didn't seem to realize what was going on – or even to care.

One man, emaciated but still seemingly strong, said, "Our tribe is all locked inside these mines, and we're probably the lucky ones." Others assented.

Grenntak turned to the man who'd spoken, a man whose face, crisscrossed with scars, had nowhere near the luster of the man with the whip, the dark skin looking more grey than black. "Why do you say that?"

The man took a step back and hid his features. "Ask the foreman," was all he managed before terror turned him mute.

"Why does he say that?" Grenntak inquired of the man with the whip.

"He is unhappy because he is weak. The strong rule the weak. It is the same here as it is everywhere."

Ah, so there were factions among the humans. Interesting. "In that case, let me rephrase my original offer. If you don't help me, I won't kill you myself. I'll let them do it. I think taking away your whip ought to be enough."

The tall man laughed. "They wouldn't dare come near me, even if I were tied to a tree."

But Grenntak had seen the hatred in the eyes of the other men. He'd seen some of them – men he'd thought were beyond caring about worldly events – look up from their despondency when the possibility of violence was discussed. Some even edged imperceptibly toward the big man. He took a decision. "I think they'd kill you even without being tied to a tree. In fact, all they'd really need would be to see you suddenly helpless."

With a single lightning motion, Grenntak stepped forward, reached out with both hands at once and took the big man's wrists in his hand. Then he pulled downward hard. He felt the man's shoulders leave their sockets, felt the energy from the pain fill the air, and delighted in sucking it in. He paused only long enough to look into the man's wide-open eyes before he began pulling again. He felt the tendons tear, saw the flesh rip. Only after the demon dropped the useless arms to the ground into twin pools of blood did the man realize what had been done to him. He began screaming.

But it was too late. Even before Grenntak was fully out of the way, the other men, the ones who'd seemed so domesticated just moments before, attacked.

In their weakened state, they took a long time to kill their former overlord. Finally, someone recovered a pick and drove it into the man's forehead and left it there as the rest tore the body to bloody gobbets.

Grenntak savored every moment of it, feeling the death energy pouring into his own body, feeding his own power.

If one single human could create that much power, then he would be unstoppable.

But they had to find that key.

Boima stopped to catch his breath. He'd heard the screaming hours before, but it still haunted him. The desperate cries of someone being subjected to forces beyond human endurance had seemed to emanate mere meters down the corridor, and they seemed to feed upon themselves – the echoes feeding back into the original sound – so that no matter how far he ran down the shaft, they only seemed to come nearer.

The anemic beam of his helmet light, which he'd turned on because the passages, despite his twenty-eight years in the mines, had become unfamiliar, barely gave any illumination. All it would really do, if worse came to worst, was give away his position.

"You've got a little time," a voice out of the darkness told him. "Why don't you rest, and let's see if we can do a little business."

Boima's heart nearly stopped, but he wasn't really surprised when a tall figure stepped into the yellow light. A sparkle showed the position of the man's gold tooth.

"How is it you speak Gola?" Boima asked.

The tall man chuckled, his completely inappropriate hat bobbing in the darkness. "One picks things up over time."

"No Europeans speak Gola. There are hardly any Gola left in the world, and no one bothers to speak to us. Even the slavers force us to learn their own tongues." Boima spat.

"The Gola are a lot more important than people know, and besides, I'm not European," Johnny replied. "You don't really have enough time to discuss linguistics right now."

A deep weariness came over Boima, as if the weight of the entire planet had suddenly dropped onto his shoulders. "You said you wanted to trade something."

"Yes, I have something you need."

"How could you possibly know what I need?"

"Let's just say that I have a different perspective on things. Now, what do you have that you can trade for it?"

"Nothing you'd want. I don't suppose the helmet light would do you any good?"

"I think you probably need that more than I do. Now, I believe you mentioned that you're carrying some bones in that pouch hanging from your neck?"

"These are the bones of my right hand. They cut it off when I was fifteen, because I tried to escape. Back then, I still thought it was my right to live free. I traded these bones for my life, and I don't think anything you can give me short of some type of heavy weaponry would be worth giving them up for. And I can see that you're not carrying any heavy weapons."

"I have this." The man thrust his arm into the beam of light, and showed Boima something delicate: wire frames and glass.

Despite the harsh conditions and lack of contact with the outer world that came with being a slave miner in Liberia, Boima had seen eyeglasses before. They were worn by some of the traders that came to the camp, and also by the leader of some hard-looking men with yellow hair so light it almost looked white, who'd fought alongside the warlord for a few months. Those glasses had eventually gone to Fat Fromba, the guard who almost never moved from his shack. As far as Boima could tell, the obese man didn't need them, but he'd taken a liking to the things and the mercenary had just shrugged and given them away.

And now this man wanted him to trade his very pride and shame for a small pair. "I can see well enough without them. I cannot read more than my name in any event. I just have to stay ahead of the things chasing me."

"These are special glasses," the man replied. A small amount of strain seemed to be entering his voice. "You need these because they will help you make a choice, a very important choice."

"If I need them so badly, and if I'm so important, then why don't you just give them to me?"

"That would take much too long to explain. Do you care for humanity? You've seen that thing. You can make a difference, the way your ancestors did before. If you don't accept this trade, that demon will be loose upon the world. Do you want that?"

Boima knew the man spoke the truth. But was he willing to do anything at all for the world? After all, the world had done nothing for him. He'd been taken prisoner and used like a farm animal for his entire adult life – and for some time before it. He owed it nothing.

But was there a higher order? Perhaps this way his life would actually count for something. Perhaps his ancestors would receive him with pride instead of disdain, if he managed to continue the work of the spirits. And he knew, without knowing how, that this tall man with the golden tooth was on the side of the spirits.

"Take my shame," Boima told him. He placed the softly rattling bag in Johnny's hand before gripping the spectacles.

"I take the token of a man who should be proud," Johnny replied. "Now go!"

Boima placed the spectacles on his nose, and was surprised by the sudden light. He could see deep into the walls, identifying countless glittering sprinkles, which the years had taught him to hate.

Diamonds.

"Hurry, now. You need to go!"

Boima stumbled on, memories decades old guiding him into passages long abandoned in which he'd once toiled away the days.

Grenntak fumed. Each minute that passed convinced him more strongly that the old man knew what they were looking for, and that he was running because he had the crystal key. There was no other explanation for the man's determination to stay ahead.

They'd been very near to trapping him more than once, the tantalizing smell of human sweat hovering sweetly in the immobile mine air. But every single time, the man had managed to scurry out of their grip, slipping into an unsuspected side passage or between a couple of boulders that looked to seal off the exit. And each of these escapes, narrow though they were, had gained the bastard several minutes, and the hours had turned into a day.

There were no more humans with them. Each, in his turn, had tired from the relentless chase, and collapsed. Malnourishment and beatings had made them weak, but that gained them no respite. Grenntak had devoured one out of every two that had fallen, and given the others to those of his followers who could shoulder aside the rest.

This had made him strong, larger than ever before, but it also slowed them down. There were places where his newfound size caused certain complications. His shoulders rubbed against the sides of the passage, and he had to crawl forward at times like a Hrunnic.

But he felt strong enough to chew through the rock if necessary and angry enough to attempt it. Already, the interference of this meddling human, probably a guardian set by the tribe that had thwarted them all those centuries ago, had cost them twenty-four precious hours. Even if they caught up to him that very instant, half of the profit would be ruined.

To make matters worse, nothing seemed to indicate that the old man would be caught as easily as that. They'd just reached a fork in the passageway, and the man's scent was not present in either. Perhaps some spirit was shielding it. Or – and this had proven more likely – perhaps he'd shuffled down some unnoticed side passage.

Grenntak bellowed in rage, and stone fell from the ceiling.

Boima stared. What faced him, embedded about a hand's width in the wall made the pain from his sore feet fade to nothing, and made him understand, why the demons were after him.

They thought he had this.

It made the diamonds he'd passed, the millions of stones that could be polished to absolute perfection, look like rat droppings in mud. This stone was perfect. Even though the spectacles were showing it to him through a layer of rock, it was still obvious that it couldn't be matched by anything else in the world.

His fascination lasted for just a few moments. The realization hit him that there was no way he could get through even a thin sheet of rock before they descended on him. And this was more than just a thin sheet. He had to leave the stone where it was.

But that wasn't all.

Boima suddenly understood what the trade with the strange specter had really been about. He hadn't traded a set of old bones for a set of spectacles. He'd traded everything those old bones represented – his pride, his shame, his very life – for the chance to make something of his existence.

Boima knew that if he continued down the passageway he was following, he would probably escape. The demons would likely stop chasing him now that they had what they wanted. He was just a worthless old man, after all.

But he'd made a deal, a deal to do what he could to protect humanity, and that meant that he couldn't allow the demons to catch him.

The only alternative he saw was to return to the intersection he'd passed a few moments before and choose the other path. This far into the old mines he couldn't recall which way was better, but he knew that he wouldn't be able to make up the lost time. And furthermore, he had to make certain that the demons followed him without pausing to investigate this side passage. He would have to give himself away – in a manner that the demons would find irresistible.

Boima sighed. He would not survive, after all.

"You've led us on a merry chase, human. You have my respect."

The old man, looking up from where he'd collapsed, said nothing. Grenntak realized that his eyes weren't really as old as the rest of his body.

"Are you going to give it up, or will I have to tear your body apart to get it? I have only a single hour to enjoy its fruit, so I am in no mood to be patient."

Grenntak exulted. It wouldn't be everything he'd dreamed of, wouldn't allow him to dominate the other lords, but at least he would have an hour of time to rampage on the surface. It would be enough for most of his needs, and would make the next ten thousand years much more pleasant than the last.

"A single hour?" The old man seemed puzzled.

"Yes, then I must return to my own dimension."

Again the man seemed to frown – he probably had no idea what a dimension was – but then he burst into laughter. He went on for almost a minute, a precious minute, but Grenntak was curious enough that he didn't launch straight into the man. "Why do you laugh?"

This time, the effect of demonic voice worked on the half-dead wretch. He answered immediately. "I laugh because I know at which moment you became certain that you had me."

Became certain? A ball of fury began to form in Grenntak's bosom. He was in no mood to play games. "Are you referring to the intersection where you cut yourself on that rock? You left droplets of blood from then on. You were easy to follow."

"Yes. How long ago would you say that was?"

"Three, maybe four hours. Like I said, I respect your resourcefulness. But there is no more time for this." Grenntak took a step forward. "Give it to me."

"If you return to that intersection, and take the other path, you will find it."

Return…. Three hours or more?

Grenntak bellowed again, louder, longer, the sound of immortal fury and frustration.

It brought the entire roof of the shaft down on their heads, but Grenntak was beyond caring for a few more tons of loose rock – and the immense sound itself had already sent Boima into the welcoming arms of the spirits of his ancestors.

*   *   *

INTERLUDE EIGHT

"Pawn, sell, trade, or sacrifice?" Ashley asked.

"Sanctuary," the faerie begged.

Ashley looked up in surprise. Facing her across the counter was a hovering four-foot-tall woman of delicate build and sporting large flapping butterfly wings from her naked back.

"What's the deal?" Ashley asked.

Panting and crying green tears, the faerie pressed tight to the counter.

"My name is Llewellyn," she said. "My tribe was just massacred in the Doulough Valley."

Llewellyn held up a silver necklace from which hung a shiny emerald the size of a chicken egg.

"I carry our genetic legacy. I am the last of the Anjanas," Llewellyn said. "If I am killed, all is lost."

Ashley bit her lip then called Barrax over.

"Put her in one of the guest rooms downstairs," Ashley whisered. "I want a guard on the door and keep it quiet."

"So your shop has become an embassy unto itself, eh?" Johnny spoke.

Ashley spun around and smirked.

"My place, my rules," Ashley said.

"Diplomatic immunity from the Sha'Daa could carry a heavy price," Johnny said as he laid a small, ornate treasure box on the counter before him. "Be careful that your own welfare does not become part of the cost."

"So is it the contents or the box itself that you're bartering?" Ashley asked.

"Clever girl," Johnny said, "the curiosity of Pandora and the skepticism of H. L. Mencken. Trust me. Look inside."

Frowning, Ashley slowly lifted the lid. A splash of golden light washed across her face and her eyes went wide. Johnny tossed a small piece of torn parchment next to the box. Six items were scrawled across it, in blood.

"We happy?" Johnny asked.

"Yeah, we happy." Ashley said.

"You have got to be shitting me," a shrill female voice rang out from the other side of the main floor. "You resold my body? I was given forty-five days for the pawn. It's only been thirty-five."

"Well, we left messages on your cell phone account every day for a week, ma'am," Ashley's middle-aged and balding emloyee, Frank said. "It's not like we didn't try to reach you."

"Look at me," she squealed. Frank did and pursed his lips as he contemplated the free-floating and admittedly shapely spectral female apparition that hovered before him.

"I need a body," she wailed.

"We've got a male teenage zombie on ice," Frank said. "You can take it on loan until we track your corpse down."

The angry apparition hovered forward, her spectral nose half intersecting Frank's bulbous schnozz, "Do I look like a hermaphrodite, buster?"

*   *   *

CHAPTER NINE: SILVER AND IRON

by Leona Wisoker

Vacation. And how sweet it was, and how hard Leanne had worked for these precious few days alone with her darling Mazoe.

Early summer lay hot and dry across already browning lawns. Water restrictions had been put in place early this year, and the neighbors on both sides hadn't stopped bitching for three solid weeks about the death of their precious, chemically-treated former perfection.

Leanne smiled and smiled every time she saw her own lush, green, weed-infested lawn – the one her HOA routinely made clucking noises over, right up until this time of year, when they mysteriously shut up for a few weeks.

And summer solstice began tomorrow; the solstice. The promised solstice. The one Leanne had been waiting for and working toward for nearly ten thousand years.

She was ready.

Truly, it was a perfect time for a vacation.

Of all the times she'd lived through, Leanne thought, this had to be the best. Health insurance! They fought over health insurance! That hadn't even been a twinkle in the sky when Leanne had been born. Car insurance. Real estate insurance. It was incredible. She'd made a tidy bundle off the various aspects over the years, more than almost any other enterprise she'd tried her hand at. The numbers involved were simply staggering, and the regulations only now getting to the point where they might have a chance at spotting her manipulations of their systems.

Humans were so gullible, especially her darling Mazoe, a prime example of a once-proud line gone to complete rot.

Leanne regarded her with a certain amount of pride; she'd had a hand in shaping Mazoe's life, after all. Everything according to plan. But she did feel a tiny twinge at the thought of losing that sleek body and ready laughter, even if the body came from nearly anorectic dieting and the laughter came from a naive misunderstanding of the world.

Only a twinge, though.

Mazoe rolled over as Leanne watched, exposing her bare back and legs to the summer rays. Even without the privacy fence, Mazoe probably would have sunbathed nude. It was just her way. And Leanne certainly didn't complain about it.

"Leanne," Mazoe murmured, then propped her chin on her crossed arms and grinned up at Leanne. "You look delicious. Is it almost time for lunch?"

Leanne smiled and knelt beside Mazoe. She ran her palm gently down the knobs of Mazoe's spine, enjoying the feel of soft, warm flesh. "I'm going to make you wait," she said. "I'm going to make you eat some real food first, love. You're too skinny."

"You always say that." Mazoe moved her arms and laid her face flat, her words ending in a smothered mumble.

"I don't want to feel like I'll break you with a hug." Leanne slid her hand up Mazoe's back and scrubbed her fingers through the girl's short hair.

"You won't!" Mazoe turned her head to glare at Leanne, squinting. "And I'm not hungry."

Mazoe was never hungry. "Eat something for me anyway. Please. More than a leaf of lettuce this time."

The girl sighed and rolled to her side. "Why does this matter so much to you, Leanne?"

"Because I love you, you silly nit," Leanne said lightly. "And while you may not see it yourself, you're outstandingly beautiful, and you don't need to have all your bones sticking out like a starving horse for that to stay true."

She tickled Mazoe's sensitive stomach before the girl could say anything. The resulting wrestling match was entertaining, but Leanne regretfully wrapped it up long before Mazoe wanted to stop.

"I'm serious," Leanne said, as Mazoe, breathing hard, resumed her face-down spot on the lounger. "You need to eat, Mazoe."

"You'd really still love me if I topped a hundred pounds?"

Leanne smiled with centuries of practice and said, "Of course I would. I love you for your mind, not your body."

Mazoe flattened her face against the chair for a few moments, then sighed deeply and propped herself up on her elbows. Leanne tried not to stare. Mazoe could be a peculiar mix of brazen and self-conscious at times.

"How about a… a sandwich, then? Hummus and mes-clun and that fabulous cheese you brought home the other day. What's it called?"

"Havarti."

"Yeah, that." Mazoe smiled and wiggled her shoulders a little, giving Leanne tacit permission to leer. So Leanne leered, just to see Mazoe smile.

"Coming right up, love," Leanne said, well pleased, and went back into the house. Hummus and mesclun! Well, it was a start, and more than Mazoe had been willing to eat at one sitting before. And really, after tonight it wouldn't matter, but Leanne had been a perfectionist for a very long time. It bothered her a little that she wouldn't get to see Mazoe develop into a normal-shaped human. The girl had so much potential…

That only bothered Leanne a little, and only for a moment, though. Then she discovered the hummus had mold growing on it, and the tahini was so close to empty as to be absurd.

The downside to not having a regular housekeeper had never been so apparent. Leanne swore, searched through the cupboards hopefully for a few minutes, then swore again. She leaned back against the counter, tugging at her lip and consid-ering, this close to the Sha'Daa, she hated the thought of leaving Mazoe alone. Anything could happen if she wasn't around to protect her darling, and she would need Mazoe tonight.

There were other things for Mazoe to eat, and Leanne was fairly sure she could talk the skinny twit into doing so; but… this was Mazoe's last day on earth. Her last day of life, although she didn't know it yet. Leanne had sworn to herself to give Mazoe absolutely anything within reason today, as her secret reward for the part she would play tonight.

A trip to the store wouldn't take very long.

Leanne went back out to the pool and knelt beside Mazoe. Rubbing her back gently with one hand, using the other to steady herself, she said, "I have to run and get supplies for your sandwich, sweetie. Do you want anything while I'm out?"

"Actually, yeah." Behind the smoked glasses, Mazoe's eyes stayed shut. "If I'm going to break my diet, I may as well bomb it out of the water. I used to really love Reese's Cups when I was a kid. Do you think you could bring me one of those?"

"Absolutely." Leanne leaned down and kissed Mazoe's shoulder. "I'm so proud of you. I'll be right back. You stay put and don't answer the door without me here, all right?"

"Mmnrrph." Mazoe yawned and buried her forehead against her arms. "More danger of a sunburn," she said, the words muffled against the mat.

"Not with the amount of sunscreen you slather on, sweetie."

Mazoe loved to lie out in the sun, but for some reason had no interest in a tan; seemed to prefer her delicate white skin to stay that way. Again, Leanne didn't argue the point.

"'zacly."

"Oh." Leanne smiled at the unexpected cleverness and patted the girl's bony shoulder, then stood. "Be right back."

There was an accident at the loop-around, of course; and another out on the main road just before the turnoff to the grocery store. And then the tahini wasn't the brand she wanted, and the clerk rang it up at the wrong price and tried to tell her she'd been the one to make a mistake. Involving the manager would have taken too long, and – again – it really didn't matter any longer.

Leanne decided she would pay the stupid clerk a visit tonight, though. Not long after midnight, to be sure nobody else got to him first. He'd given her attitude before, enough to be high on her hit list.

She grinned as she walked out into the bright summer sunshine, feeling the chill of the grocery store sloughing off her skin. Hit list. How appropriate a term. She vaguely regretted that more of the humans who'd offended or insulted her over the years couldn't suffer in the coming apocalypse of their world; but at least she'd done her level best to ensure they suffered during their brief lives.

Jerry Falwell had been particularly satisfying in that respect.

The accidents had been cleared away by the time she went back through. To her relief, only scatters of broken glass remained to mark where fire trucks and ambulances and gawkers had filled the two areas. She grinned again, amused at the irrelevancy of broken glass and spilled blood, rather like spilled milk, in the face of what was coming tonight.

Tonight. Tonight. Tonight. It rang like a song through Leanne's whole body. She couldn't stay angry about anything for long these days, not with the final summer solstice just hours away.

Tonight she'd lose Mazoe – the thought of which hurt, for a moment, rather more than she'd expected it to. But the Sha'Daa was more important than any human could possibly be. It was family. Her cousins waited beyond that barrier, victims of an ancient betrayal that drove the fae from the mortal realm. They'd suffered the close company of demons for millennia. Enough was enough. Leanne had sworn to free them, had done far blacker deeds than sacrificing a lover for the cause.

Mazoe was – mostly – human. More than likely, the other blood that fluttered through her veins, the incredibly distant kinship they shared, untraceable by any mortal, was behind Leanne's ridiculous attraction to the girl. But attraction was always trumped by duty: she had to free her kin from the realm they'd been trapped in by that bastard who'd fathered Mazoe's distant ancestors.

Had Arthur known he was shutting away the fae along with the demons? It was likely. It had solved a number of difficult issues he'd been facing at the time. And of course, as the victor he'd been able to slant the historical accounts however he wanted. The persistence of Arthurian legends showing him as a hero generally irritated Leann. And the nonsense about Merlin and Nimue! Well, it just went to show how gullible humans could be.

When Leann pulled into her driveway, a strange flutter ran through her stomach. At first she thought it was more of the nervous anticipation she'd been struggling not to show all day, but this had a darker tone to it. A familiar feel. After a moment, she placed it. Something else powerful had passed this way recently, a creature even older than herself. Not fae – that would have set the gold lights across the ceiling of her garage blinking brightly, and they remained still and dark as she pulled into the bay. But something wicked this way came... or had come.

Too close. Far too close, and at the worst possible time. She left the supplies in the car and almost ran out to the pool to check on Mazoe. She was still sunning herself placidly and showed no sign of having moved an inch, was probably even asleep, in fact, as she gave no reaction to Leanne's hurried arrival.

Leanne sighed and went back to the car for the tahini. As she made fresh hummus and built Mazoe a sandwich, she wondered if she'd been imagining things; but centuries of experience warned her against making that mistake. She'd stayed alive through a drastically changed world by never ignoring her gut.

But right now it was time to feed Mazoe's gut. She finished the sandwich, cut it carefully into quarters, set the candy on the edge of an oversized white plate, then carried it all out to the pool.

Mazoe had moved this time, to stretch out on a poolside lounger beside a low glass table, in the shade and busily texting away. Leanne repressed a growl of annoyance and kept her tone light as she put the sandwich down on the table. "I thought we agreed no cell phones during our vacation?"

"Oh…yeah. This was…" Mazoe hesitated, just a fraction, her eyes flicking to the screen and back up to Leanne's face. "It was an emergency call."

"To whom?" Instant suspicion flared through Leanne.

"No, from… an old friend of the family needed to talk to me for a minute. It's done now." Her thumbs stopped moving; she set the phone aside, smiling at Leanne. "I won't pick the phone up again, I promise. Ooh, that sandwich looks good. And huge. Do you think you might help me finish it?"

"Of course." Making her eat the whole thing would only end in Mazoe getting sick, and that would completely ruin the day and possibly even make tonight more difficult. "Anyone I know?"

"No," Mazoe said. "I haven't seen or heard from him in years myself. Not sure how he got this number."

The last part sounded true, but Leanne knew what Mazoe sounded like when she lied. Everything else she'd said – and the "family friend" part – was utter fabrication. "What was the emergency? 'Personal?'" Mazoe said, and took a bite of the sandwich. "Mmm. Wow. That is really good."

Leanne hesitated, wanting to push; but Mazoe rarely clammed up, and when she did she didn't take being pressed well. And how important, anyway, could a few minutes of texting be? She shrugged and lifted a sandwich segment to her own mouth, agreeing with Mazoe. This batch of hummus had come out really well. Adding orange juice had been a fantastic moment of inspiration.

She wondered if she would still be able to cook after the Sha'Daa arrived. It didn't seem likely, but then again, some demons had strange tastes. She'd even heard of vegetarian demons, but that was probably just a fad reflected over from the human realm. So she might find a job as a cook…. She shook her head, silently laughing at herself. Thinking of jobs, on the eve of the Sha'Daa! She'd been among humans too long.

It was definitely time for a vacation.

"Hey," Mazoe said, "do we still have any of that lemonade?"

"Oh – I'm sorry, sweetie. I forgot all about a drink." Leanne went back into the kitchen. When she returned, Mazoe gulped down half the glass of lemonade, then proceeded to chatter amiably, around small bites of her sandwich, about everything from the temperature to the curtains she was thinking about replacing in the spare bedroom.

Leanne watched and listened, mildly bemused, and ate her half of the sandwich without really paying attention to the taste. She wondered if Mazoe had taken something, or if the sudden animation came from something related to that mysterious text message.

As she washed the last of the sandwich down with the last of the lemonade, Leanne found herself yawning. The combination of heat and the strain of preparing for tonight was making her dreadfully sleepy. She needed a nap, but not until she found out what the message had been.

"Gotta go potty," Mazoe announced brightly, and took herself and the dishes into the house.

As the curtains over the sliding doors swayed shut behind the girl, Leanne reached for Mazoe's cell phone.

The texts had been deleted. All of them. The entire history, even the cutesy love notes they'd sent each other in the beginning, the ones Mazoe had insisted she'd always keep. That really bothered Leanne, but she had no way to remark on it without admitting she'd been snooping; and this was not the day to pick a fight with Mazoe.

She put the cell phone exactly where it had been and leaned back in the lounger, unaccountably drowsy.

Just a little nap. That was all she needed. And midnight was more than eight hours away yet – plenty of time to arrange the final ritual.

Plenty of time.

She dreamed, as she sometimes did, of a vague and shadowy form looming over her; of a blast of intense heat searing her into a charred and melting blob. She awoke shaking and nauseous; gulped down some water from the glass Mazoe had thoughtfully set next to the lounger, then sprawled back, asleep again nearly at once.

The next dream had the same shadowy form, but this time it resolved into a tall man in a long trenchcoat, his slender limbs almost lost in the seemingly overlarge folds. Then he spread his arms wide, the fabric spread into wings, and he screeched in an alien language. The words trailed off into manic laughter, and she saw a glint of gold among his teeth. His next words came through clearly. "Iron and silver, iron and silver, iron and silver!"

She awoke again, trembling violently this time, and sat up, curling into a tight, arms-around-knees bundle. It had to be the imminence of the Sha'Daa causing the nightmares. She'd been warned strange things would begin to happen as the veil stretched thinner and thinner.

And of course, iron and silver, being her only weaknesses, would appear in nightmares; but who the hells was the creature in the trenchcoat? She couldn't recall ever seeing or hearing anything about a creature like that before. It hadn't been human, she felt certain of that.

At last she dismissed it as the product of an overworked imagination and reached for the glass of water, draining it the rest of the way dry. A few moments later she was asleep again.

Candlelight flickered, bringing a ghostly illumination to the basement studio. The wall frescoes of cavorting fae seemed almost to move in the shifting light, and the shadows all danced just where Leanne had wanted them to.

She refilled their wineglasses and handed Mazoe hers, grinning. "Here's to a year together, love," she said. "Happy anniversary."

Mazoe's pale eyebrows drew down into a puzzled frown. "A year?" she said. "But we met on the…"

"We met during last year's summer solstice," Leanne explained, resisting the impulse to roll her eyes. "That doesn't follow calendar dates."

"Oh. Really? I mean, I remembered that it was summer, but what's the solstice?" Mazoe sipped her wine, her big blue eyes innocent. She'd repainted her nails while Leanne napped. Usually she went with bright red, but this time she'd chosen a thick, glittery silver polish. Leanne couldn't remember ever having seen Mazoe wear this one before. She rather liked it, although it had globbed a bit and seemed to weigh Mazoe's hands down somehow.

"The beginning of summer," Leanne said, "longest day of the year."

"Oh. Really? How do they figure those out? And who does the figuring, anyway? Scientists or astrologers?"

Leanne bit her tongue for a moment before answering. "Has to do with the tilt of the planet on its axis," she said. "And it's our anniversary, love, let's not spend it talking about this, hmm? "Okay," Mazoe said readily. "What do you want to talk about, then?"

"Well," Leanne said with studied casualness, "I would really love to have you pose for me tonight." She'd been trying to talk Mazoe into doing that for months, but gently; just as a lead-in to tonight's push. "I promise I won't draw your face or hang them in the gallery."

Mazoe drank some more wine, eyes downcast as she considered. At last she nodded. "Okay," she said. "As a special present to you, just for tonight. Okay."

Leanne breathed deeply with relief; she'd expected it to be harder than this. "Thank you," she said.

"Can I talk while you draw me, since you're not drawing my face?"

"Of course." Leanne could tune out Mazoe's mindless chatter easily enough, but decided to start out with an idle question of her own, to be sure the conversation stayed light and trivial. "Where did you get that nail polish, by the way?"

"Oh… someone gave it to me a few days ago. It looked interesting. Kind of strange, though, the guy wouldn't take money. He wanted my earrings in exchange.""Which ones?" Leanne paused to frown at Mazoe.

"The kitty-cat ones."

"The ones I gave you last month?"

"Uhm… yeah." Mazoe shrugged. "They were awful heavy, and they gave me a headache to wear. I didn't think you'd mind."

Leanne shook her head and went back to working, obscurely hurt at how readily Mazoe had given away a gift. Heavy or not, the earrings had been expensive – antiques, in fact, elaborate hoops set with a strange black stone carved in the shape of a sleeping cat. They'd fascinated Leanne as soon as she'd seen them, and had looked fabulous against Mazoe's pale skin.

But it didn't really matter now. In less than an hour, earrings and nail polish wouldn't matter a damn bit.

"Okay, where do you want me?" Mazoe set the wine glass aside and stood, already pulling her loose shirt off.

Astounded by Mazoe's unusual compliance, Leanne pointed to the table she'd set up toward one end of the basement studio. "Stretch out on that," she said, "face up. Just like you're going to sleep on your back."

"That doesn't sound like very much fun to draw," Mazoe commented. Pulling down her shorts and lacy thong, she kicked them aside to join her shirt.

"I'll ask you to move after I get the easel set up," Leanne said. "I don't want you to feel strained while you wait for me. Do you want a blanket?"

"No, the room's really warm. It's usually really cold down here, but tonight it's like you have the heat on or something. Ooh, and it's even warmer right over here by the table. How nice. Did you install a heater under here?"

"No," Leanne said hastily, before Mazoe could flip the covering cloth out of the way to look beneath the table. "No, it's just warm in here tonight."

She picked up Mazoe's half-empty wineglass and surreptitiously dropped in a tiny, colorless gel tablet. Her hand around the glass hid the brief silvery sparkling as it dissolved.

"Here, love. Finish your wine while I move the easel into position, then stretch out."

Mazoe accepted the glass readily, her legs swinging, kicking back against the cloth and pushing it back into the empty space below the table. Leanne dragged the easel into position, well back from the table – not smart, being too close to the portal when it opened. The demons might not be paying complete attention to the distinction between allies and enemies in the first few moments.

Leanne's easel had a few built-in tricks to compensate for that, and the arrangements she'd made over the years made it a certainty that an old ally of hers would be first through the portal. If that failed, she still had a few other tricks in reserve.

She'd been planning this a long time. Had even turned it into a role-playing game a few times, to see what flaws a group of the best gamers she could find would discover in her plans. They'd been unexpectedly interesting companions, and had given her some astoundingly good insight; as had a group of writers whom she'd actually managed to coax into applying themselves to the same scenario.

The writers had even made some money off their work. She didn't mind, and a few of the stories had been entertaining. It had helped seal her plans to perfection; that was all that really mattered.

Dragging herself back to the moment, she pushed the easel into the spot she'd long ago chosen and matched it with a high metal stool. Mazoe's glass was empty, and she was already looking sleepy. Good.

The clock on the wall read 11:35, the green glow a sullen presence above and behind the table. Altar, Leanne reminded herself. She'd done the research, and a solid stone block was only tradition, not necessity. A sturdy table with carefully drilled drain-troughs hidden under a black cloth did just as well.

The stability of a stone block was most useful when the sacrifice was screaming and thrashing about; but Mazoe lay back placid and unaware of anything the least bit wrong. In a few moments she would be asleep, and in twenty-five more minutes, a rack of spikes would crash down out of the elaborately decorated ceiling, precisely onto the table. The drain-troughs would allow the blood to flow down to fill the symbol etched deeply into the floor.

The blood – and not any blood – the blood of Mazoe Smith. Such a common last name for a descendant of a king and a witch. Such an unremarkable last name for someone whose blood was more valuable for opening the Sha'Daa than that of a hundred ordinary humans.

Such a shame Mazoe was too dim to dig into her own family tree. It might have saved her life. But then Leanne herself would have lost her place within the ranks of the Sha'Daa; so that thought didn't trouble her overly much.

"Hey, Leanne?" Mazoe said around a yawn. "This heat is making me awfully tired. I feel like I might go to sleep. That would ruin your portrait of me, wouldn't it? Maybe I better sit up." She propped herself up on her elbows, clearly struggling to manage even that much.

"Nooo," Leanne said reassuringly. "It'll take me a while to get set up. There's a lot of pastels and pencils to arrange. You know how picky I am. You just relax. I'll wake you up when I want you to move, how's that?"

The clock said 11:40.

"You're being so nice to me tonight," Mazoe said drowsily. She didn't move from her propped-up position. "You're normally more impatient than this."

Leanne rattled trays of colored pencils about for the appearance of the thing. "Yes, well, you deserve it, sweetie. You're a really special person."

"Yeah," Mazoe said. "I guess I am. Do you know, I don't think I ever told you this, but I did this genealogy project a while back?"

Leanne's blood froze. Her hands stilled; the pencils went quiet. "Oh?"

"Yeah, and I talked to my grandmother, and you know, she said some really weird things. I guess I was in grade school at the time. She said, get this, that there was this big secret I wasn't to tell anyone. She got carted off to a mental hospital, of course, a few years later." Mazoe fell silent again, breathing deeply.

Leanne tore her eyes away from what that did to Mazoe's silhouette and blinked hard. "So what was the big secret?"

"Oh, what? I didn't say?"

11:45. "No."

"Oh. Well, it was something about how I was a direct descendant of King Arthur and the sister of Morgan le Fay. That's why I'm named Mazoe, after the sister of Morgan le Fay. Funny, huh? Talk about a crackpot grandma."

Leanne forced her voice to stay steady. "Yeah, that's funny." She went back to rattling pencils.

"Leanne?"

She tried not to snap this time and almost made it. "Yes?"

"I think I'd really like to make love to you."

Leanne looked at the clock: 11:47. Now? She almost screeched. With passable calm, she said instead, "Aw, sweetie, let me draw you first. You know the mood drawing puts me into. It'll be so much better that way."

"Oh… all right. But can I have a hug, then? Please?"

"Sure." There was plenty of time for that, and the drug should be knocking Mazoe out any second now. Leanne set the pencils aside and approached the table.

Mazoe's arms wrapped around her in a surprisingly strong embrace considering the drug even now walloping through her system. "Love you," she murmured into Leanne's ear. Her fingernails dug into Leanne's back as though in a moment of passion. Leanne winced, figuring the spasm came from the drug finally kicking in. But the spasm didn't ease. Mazoe's nails slid into Leanne's back like a set of tiny knives.

"Jesus!" Leanne exclaimed, trying to break free. "Mazoe, hey, that hurts!"

"Good," Mazoe said, and let go, shoving Leanne away from her. Leanne stumbled back, too astonished to be afraid. Even when her legs went out from under her and she sprawled on the thinly-carpeted floor, she felt nothing but bewilderment. It was like having a pet Pomeranian bite you.

"Mazoe, what the hell!" She could feel blood trickling down her back. The clock read 11:50. In the distance, tornado warning sirens began to wail.

Mazoe smiled and slid down from the table. "Exactly," she said. "You know, I told them you wouldn't really do it. I told them you loved me enough to turn around at the last minute. I was wrong, apparently – Leanan. Leanan Sidhe. Doesn't take much powdered silver and cold-forged iron to lay you out, looks like; I only put an eighth teaspoon into your sandwich and your water combined, and what little came in that special fingernail polish was enough."

She held up her hands; the nails had broken off clean at the fingertips, meaning the tips were still buried in Leanne's back. No wonder it hurt like blazes.

Leanne tried to get up. Her body wouldn't obey her.

"You're a moron, Leanne," Mazoe said, squatting beside her. "Smart in some ways, dumb in others. Did you really think that there wouldn't be people working across the ages to stop people – excuse me, faeries – like you from bringing about the Sha'Daa? My family has been passing down the lore since the day Mazoe le Fay gave birth to the daughter of King Arthur. Each generation has been extensively trained in what to watch for and what to do when the day came. Oh, and how to act really stupid, too. That helps, especially in modern America."

Leanne rolled her eyes to look at the clock. 11:55, and the drop of the spiked grating was wired in to that particular clock. Five minutes. Less than five minutes.

"Mazoe," she whispered, but couldn't think of anything else to say. "My family," she said after what seemed hours. "My family, Mazoe. I had to."

"Yeah, whatever," Mazoe muttered, but Leanne caught just a hint of moisture glittering in the girl's eyes for just a moment. "You've earned what you're getting."

"I know," Leanne said, surprised at herself for making the admission. But somehow, right at the moment, relatives she'd never seen before seemed less important than this young girl, her beautiful lover, who was in the process of killing her. The room felt almost scorchingly hot around her. Four and a half minutes, maybe less, before the grate crashed down. Maybe her own blood would work, and her death could serve as both penance and prize. "Put me on the table, Mazoe, and then run. It's the only way for you to survive."

The sirens wailed with idiot, broken-hearted-child persistence.

"I fully intended to," Mazoe said, grinning, and hoisted Leanne over her shoulder in a fireman's carry, revealing more surprising strength. "But it's not going to do what you think."

The table slammed up under Leanne's back; Mazoe wasn't making any attempt to be gentle.

"Remember that text earlier?" Mazoe said. "That was from a really weird guy named Johnny. He's been, well, not a friend of the family, but he's been popping up to trade items with us for generations now. They always seem like pointless things, but they turn out useful within days if not hours. Yesterday I gave him the earrings for the fingernail polish. I traded him a sandwich today, while you were gone, for the bag of metal powder. It's an old family heirloom that got mislaid somewhere along the way. Johnny returned it to me."

Leanne moaned as another wave of agony racked her entire body.

Mazoe kept talking. "A week ago, I gave him your high-heeled green shoes in return for a piece of information I've been after for years and couldn't find. I told him to only send it when I really needed it, and, between his showing up three times in one week and his sending me that message today, told me this would be the solstice we've both been waiting for."

Leanne shut her eyes, somehow knowing what the fatal piece of information would be: her own heritage. Whoever this Johnny was, he definitely wasn't human.

"You see, love –" Mazoe's voice was dripping with irony as she arranged Leanne's limbs.

Leanne moaned again, in part from the spiky aches swirling through her but mainly from the shattering suspicion that Mazoe had never really loved her after all; that it had all been an act, the two of them dancing an elaborate game around one another. Two perfect actors engaged in the perfect scam, and Leanne would die not only a failure, but a fool who'd never really been loved by anyone.

Mazoe went on, cruel as a cat with a bird between its paws, "– now I know that you're the daughter of two of the fae left behind in the wake of the last failed Sha'Daa. Your blood is the exact same as that of the monsters waiting beyond that portal. Do you know what happens when your blood hits that pretty engraving you have drawn in the floor? Especially with all that blessed silver and iron dust I sprinkled into the lines while you were napping earlier? Really blessed, by a true holy man during the time of Morgan le Fay, back when the magic was strong in the world. My great-grandmother was pissed when that bag of powder disappeared, and here Johnny comes along to hand it back over just when I need it. Interesting guy, Johnny. You'd think he'd ask more than a peanut butter and jelly sandwich for something so priceless, but there you go."

Leanne closed her eyes and moaned. "Run," she said. "Run."

"Run, fun, go, Mazoe," a man's voice said. Leanne turned her head to the side, blinking hard to focus her eyes. "You need to go, go, go, Mazoe." He giggled.

He's shorter than in the dream, was her first, hazy thought; but then, she was on a relatively high table, so that probably skewed perception. Once Leanne adjusted her sense of proportion, he actually turned out to be taller than Mazoe, and very nearly as skinny, with almost Marine-short dark hair and demon-black eyes. His long black trenchcoat seemed ridiculously out of place beside Mazoe's lean, naked body.

"I know, Johnny," Mazoe said, and sighed. "I really did love her."

Leanne felt a shock of relief open in her chest. She let out a gasping sob and fought to speak, but the words just wouldn't emerge.

"I know, Mazoe," Johnny said, then giggled again, swaying from foot to foot. He squinted up at the ceiling. "We must go, go, though, 'zoe." He laughed, delighted as a child at his idiotic rhyme. "You have something I want?"

"Take the easel," Mazoe said, pointing. "She's been gimmicking it up. That ought to be worth something to you."

"Easel, schneizel," Johnny said, shaking his head. He pointed at the box of pencils Leanne had been rattling around. "Pretty pencils."

Mazoe snatched up the box and handed it over without protest. It disappeared into one of Johnny's voluminous pockets.

Leanne rolled her head the other way and looked up at the clock. 11:58. "Run," she said again. "Run, Mazoe."

Mazoe sighed, then said, "Goodbye, my Leanne Sidhe. I'll eat a hamburger in your honor. I've been craving one for years, did you know that? It's been sheer hell – hah." She stopped short and laughed a little. "Anyway, goodbye. I really wish you'd changed your mind."

Leanne turned her head one last time to look at Mazoe; saw Johnny open his arms wide, the black trenchcoat flaring like demonic wings. Mazoe stepped up close into his embrace. Johny's arms closed, the trenchcoat swirling into a tunnel of black, and all the candles and lights in the room went out.

Whether that was a moment of mercy from Johnny or from Mazoe, or whether the shock of the Sha'Daa arrival had caused it, Leanne never had time to figure out.

The ceiling opened. The grate crashed down, skewering Leanne firmly into place, and her blood began to flow into the by now red-hot portal beneath her.

Leanne's last thoughts, just before the fire blazed her into nearly instant ash, were a mixture of despair at how badly she'd failed – and delight that for once in her life, someone had truly cared about her. In a rare moment of real selflessness, she hoped that Mazoe would enjoy her vacation with Johnny instead....

The explosion took out two blocks of chemically treated perfection in all directions and did about twice as much damage on the other side of the portal. The portal itself, seared by blessed silver, blessed iron, and fae blood, comprehensively glued itself shut. It would never be used again.

*　*　*

INTERLUDE NINE

It was during a short vacation trip to London in 1888 that Ashley read a newspaper account of the newly dubbed Jack the Ripper. Her goddess avatar of justice suddenly demanded instant ascendancy. Ashley blacked out.

Three days later she awoke in the countryside, in a small estate's gazebo, beside the eviscerated remains of some well-dressed gentleman.

He was the murderer of prostitutes in the White Chapel district. Astraea spoke in Ashley's mind. I judged him guilty.

Ashley looked down at her own hands, covered in dried blood.

"But… I don't…" Ashley muttered.

Enough. He sent away his servants until the midday. You can wash up in that nearby stream. Our carriage is resting by a rear gate to this estate.

Ashley, still in mild shock, stumbled to the tributary.

Judging the value of your daily business activities, and killing the occasional midnight thug or gang boss back in Dingle, has become somewhat of a bore for me, Ashley. I needed a distraction. And now, I think I have found a hobby to keep me busy on the odd weekend… during a month or two in the course of each year.

"This isn't the first time… you… we… we've killed before, is it?" Ashley asked, dropping to her knees and splashing her hands in the river. "I cannot remember what happened to my attackers we tracked down hundreds of years ago… but I feel… I feel they received a dark judgment."

Yes. I have until now shielded your mind from all such violent events… but you should know the truth. I only harmed those who hurt you or wanted to do you great evil. They will not be missed. Now. You have training ahead of you, Ashley. There are many martial skills I need to teach you. The guilty of these isles, those who prey on the innocent and weak, they have a new enemy… and we will be their judge, jury, and executioner.

*   *   *

CHAPTER TEN: GLOOM

by Michael Griffiths

An upturned grimace looked like a gash in his wrinkled face, formed when he reflected on the mistakes the others of his kind were making. Warwick had always been ridiculed and abused, his classmates, co-workers, even his family. He hated them all. Humanity had turned their back on him and he had found a way to return the favor.

"Fools, you pushed me straight into the darkness and there I stayed, until it became my lover." Warwick had been talking to himself for years. Ever since the first time his mother had locked him in the closet.

His fingers wrung together. Like the rest of him, the flesh of his hands hung in damp folds. These wrinkles were not the simple marks of aging, but something far fouler. A corpse soaking in a lake for a week could begin to describe it.

Thoughts of his appearance rarely lingered in Warwick's mind.

It was but a small price to pay for the Bestows he had received and now the day of deliverance was upon him. The

Sha'Daa. When he opened his gateway to hell it would become a tidal wave of malign energy and he would surf its crest. "Those others are fools. Either they try to crash a gate into the middle of a city, where there's no limit to the people around that could stop them, or they fall back to the desolate and the wild, where there isn't enough available on which the Infernals can feed."

His eyes pierced through the trees just enough to see the city twinkling below. "By the time my gatelings reach their dinner, it will be too late for anyone to stop them."

Lost in his own thoughts, he walked to the side of the Mogollon Rim. A place where pine trees covered its edge and, two thousand feet below, a desert stretched over the five miles to Sedona. "Pompous, spoiled, wealthy pukes. You had to live in the middle of all this beauty. Now you will pay for moving into a vortex, you misguided life-flushers."

There was a sound behind him.

He turned in no great haste.

Giggler stood ten feet away grinning like an idiot.

"Have you done the scouting as I ordered?"

"Yes, of course." A giggle escaped his lips, sounding more like the hiss of a wounded snake. "There are four different groups of campers within easy grabbing range. Twenty-nine in all," he managed to get out before his speech was overtaken by another string of giggling.

"One of the numbers of death. Nicely done. Gather the others, have them gather their Six.

"What of the other Six, my master?"

"I will check their cages myself. Once we have begun, nothing will be able to stand in our way. First the Infernals will feed through our pets. Then, when they gain the strength to enter this sad, backward world, their real meal waits below."

This time Warwick joined Giggler in his compulsive laughter.

David lingered beyond the edge of the light created by the roaring campfire. Some of his best friends gathered around the crackling blaze. He would join them shortly, but something had gotten his attention. It was a subtle feeling – a taint of ill wind or a sound of distress.

Marco was getting another ale from his cooler. After retrieving it, his considerable height caused him to duck under a low-lying branch, which stretched away from the towering Ponderosa Pine. Seeing David, Marco approached.

"What is it? You look torqued."

David rubbed his hand through his half beard, before adjusting his 'Cthulhu on Campus' cap. "Not sure. I thought I heard something."

"Like what?" Marco asked, while lighting up a smoke. His lighter flared into the darkness, illuminating his clean shaven face for a moment.

"Maybe it has just been too long since we got out of the city for one of our SCA exercises, but the woods feel weird to-night. I'm getting a strange vibe, like a predator just got lucky."

"Whatever," Jerome said, over his shoulder, while he got ready to pee on a young Juniper. The firelight reflected off his glasses when he returned to his pressing business. "So many people are camping around the rim tonight, no cougar or anything is within five miles of here."

"Remember that time we saw a puma up here with Mums?" his sister called out to him. "What are you... oh my

God! Do you have to piss ten feet away from me? You're so gross." Like her brother, Bella had skin the color of hot cocoa, but while Jerome kept his hair even shorter than Marco, Bella's puffy lengths were big enough to use as a weapon.

His moment of introspection long gone, David returned to his seat beside his girlfriend Loni. His arm swept under her long curls and he gave her a quick kiss on the cheek. More friends joined in the laughter of another joke and he smiled. Uno had sparked up a joint with a few other buddies making some food around the camp tables.

"It's so nice to be up here again," she said with a smile.

"Yeah, but it isn't going to be all fun and games. We should try to crash early tonight. We need to go through those drills again tomorrow if we are going to have any chance beating that damn pike wall team."

"Don't you think we have a strong team ourselves?" she asked, while brushing a stray strand of chocolate colored hair behind her ear.

"Yeah, I do. We're all strong, tough fighters in our own way, but what we need to do is act like a team. We aren't going to be able to fight through a pike wall at the Warrior Games if we all go rogue and try to do everything our own way."

He grew tense. There it was again. The odd taste, like a sticky coating of grime on his tongue. And just the hint of a howl. After favoring Loni with a distracted smile, he double-checked that his old sword remained at his side.

He had been working on the Viking-style blade every chance he had gotten during the camping trip. It was an older blade, which he had found amongst his grandfather's stored stuff after he passed away last winter. David's grandfather had brought back a crate of odd items when he returned from The

War to End All Wars. After taking another pull of ale, he strapped his dagger to his hip. If some rabid animal lurked out there, he wanted to be ready for it.

The fire sent lazy sparks into the night sky. They glowed, their short lives winking out quickly. David tipped back his ale and got lost in a story Jerome was telling the ring of friends. After taking another sip, the malingering presence faded from his thoughts. He loved it out here.

The six cages had been brought to the forest floor and placed in a rough circle around the steaming pewter cauldron. The cauldron was surrounded by a roaring fire of rotten wood, which sent large plums of rancid smoke into the darkness. Within the impossibly large cauldron, a thick grey paste bubbled and popped. The stench left even the caged beasts wide-eyed and cautious.

A Power lanced through him. Warwick's body buzzed with untapped energy. "I feel the call of the Six." For once the Giggler stayed silent. "Summon your brothers. We are about to wreak havoc on this world."

Soon each of the six Glooms stood before one of the cages. Once they tasted the foul essence that seeped from War-wick and his minions, the snarling monsters drew back, whimpering in the corner of their cells.

Their tattered gray robes tossed in the wind, until it was hard to determine where they ended and the thin mist which spread its tendrils through the trees began. Each of the Glooms had a part of the Bestow to recite and the twisted words of the Abyss shook the forest. When they finished, their eyes trans-formed into a glowing dull red and they hissed and moaned as the spell continued. Warwick took a step forward and drew a large mason jar from inside his undulating robe.

Six squirming crawfish fought for space within the container. Each man in turn drew out a jar filled with six thrashing creatures.

Warwick's voice boomed into the valley and across the cliffs as his dark soul drew on the mana of Sedona, even while it embraced the upcoming Apocalypse storm that was the Sha'Daa.

"On this, the most unholy of nights, we call out to thee, Sha'Daa. Wash over us with your might. Strengthen yourself as your servants feed. And prepare yourself for the true meal to follow."

"We become the…"

Each Gloom uttered, "Six," in a hollow voice. "Holding the Six," they thrust their mason jars over their heads. "That are surrounded by the Six." From within their cage, the shadowed beasts roared.

"As one, we summon thee, Sha'Daa, and bid you to feed!"

The Glooms threw their jars into the cauldron where they broke and sunk to the bottom.

"Now quickly," Warwick hissed, "we don't have much time." Turning toward the Giggler, "since you said there are only four groups of campers in this area that means you need to send your bats north in search of more prey. And you, Wad, need to send your wasps south. The rest of you send your minions toward those that were unlucky enough to camp this close to us."

His speech over, they returned their gaze to the cauldron. At first, he feared the worst – had something gone wrong? Then the first hairy leg of a bloated spider forced its way out of the clinging pus. The head of a giant assassin bug followed. Soon all six types of vermin were pushing their way free and crawling, creeping, and flying toward their Gloom master.

"Be off, our children. Feed, and as you feed, so will the Infernals until they have the strength to once again enter this world and reclaim it as their own!"

This time David knew he had heard something. There it was again.

He stood up and gazed out into the darkness past the coolers.

Loni touched his arm. "What's wrong?"

"I hear something. It sounds big."

Then they all heard it. A snapping crashing sound quickly rose from being subliminal to undeniable. David bolted out of his seat and the others quickly copied him. Whatever it might be, it came straight for the campsite.

"Get some lights over here!" he shouted.

Uno and Bella were quick to comply. The narrow beams jarred and bounced through the shadows. He saw something, something big, and there was more than one of them. His jaw dropped, and he almost let go of the sword he did not even know he held, when they finally came into view.

At first, he thought the animals were somehow giant reptiles, but then he saw the pinchers. They each had huge arms like a scorpion or a lobster. But these things had aquatic tails. "Are those things crawdads?" Jerome asked.

"I don't care what they are! I'm getting my gun!" Marco cried out.

"Me too," Ken yelled.

David knew it would still take them some time to dig out their firearms and the damn things were almost upon them.

Without thinking, he grabbed the largest cooler and lifted it over his head and then sent it at them. A shrill cry erupted from one of the beasts. It only broke off one claw, but it did slow their charge and threw the creatures into chaos.

Terry ran up to him. "That's my cooler, man. What the hell are you doing?" he screamed.

"We're getting attacked by some type of crazy animal!"

"Oh bullshit, what the fu–… Oh holy hell!"

A crawfish, easily as long as a man, had crawled onto the cooler and its pincher took Terry in the neck. Terry did not have time to scream, and before David could react; his face was sprayed with blood as the claw cut halfway through Terry's neck. It stopped only long enough to decapitate Terry and then, with a screech, came at David. Stabbing forward with his sword he managed to keep the thing at bay, but his blade could not penetrate the beast's exoskeleton.

Uno had grabbed a shovel and tossed scoops of burning coals into their multi-eyed faces. This did little to damage them, but slowed down the creatures' advance. Several fell into eating Terry, but David had his own problems as the one fighting him sent a series of snapping assaults his way, while trying to bowl him over. He had been forced to retreat to the edge of the flames and fought to keep the thing's elongated claws at bay.

Loni screamed for help as she used a camping chair to keep another back. Shots rang out on the other side, but both the manic crawfish and the spreading fire separated Loni from most of the group.

"Go for the eyes," he shouted, through gritted teeth, as he managed to draw his dagger. Using it to block a claw, he dove in close and stabbed at the top of the thing's twisted face. It took two tries and the giant crawdad's claw snapped an inch from his head, but on his second stab the tip of his sword passed through the thing's eye into whatever sad excuse for a brain it had.

David dashed over to help Loni. He came up behind the thing, so he reversed the grip of his sword and stabbed down with it two handed. This time he managed to pierce the shell. "Help me get it into the fire!" With a grunt and a shove, he used his sword like a lever, and with a push from Loni's chair, they rolled the beast into the flames where it crackled and fought until its shell turned red.

He made a move to help his friends, but the guns had done the work killing the other four; but not before several of his crew had been injured. Wiping the blood from his face, he tried to catch his breath. When he opened his mouth to speak, screams to the north started to reverberate through the forest and made a shiver run up his spine.

Once the cauldron had vomited its empowered creations into the forest, Warwick had his minions stoke the bonfire into impossible heights. Sparks flew, catching other trees and scrubs ablaze. Warwick could have cared less. This once beautiful vortex of mana would be destroyed, stripped bare.

The Infernals would need to feed.

He yelled at his man-slaves, "Keep feeding the flames, my brothers!" He laughed and tossed a jerry-can of gasoline onto the blaze. It exploded wildly, sending ash and flames in all directions.

"Come, my brothers. We need to prepare the Loomers. The ritual has begun. They will help ensure nothing stops us until it is complete."

From out of the bowels of the wood, he could now hear the screaming of the innocent... if there really were such things these days. Sounds of gunfire were less appealing, but at least he knew his little creations were finding their prey.

"The forest catches fire, my master," Giggler said, making no attempt to hide his namesake.

"Let it burn. It will all burn."

"X'lent, I like fires. Big fires."

"And you aren't the only one."

"What the hell just happened?" Ken yelled, while his trembling fingers dropped more bullets onto the forest floor than he was able to load into his pistol.

"Shut up and help me bind Janet's ankle," Bella cried.

David grabbed Marco and Jerome and pulled them aside. Uno saw the gathering and David was pleased when his old friend joined them.

A horribly long tortured wail trailed off. "Okay, something crazy is going on."

"Yeah," Uno said, for some reason smiling. "That was kinda fun. It's like we somehow ended up in some bad 50s horror movie."

"Terry just died, man." Jerome said, while adjusting his glasses.

"Yeah, sorry." Uno's face lost its smile, but the man still hovered with nervous energy. "That part sucks."

"But we did okay, mostly because I think we've always been the lunatic fringe, and since most of us grew up in south Phoenix or Boston. Besides," the firelight played over David's face creating a dance of light and shadow, "we have been training to fight like a team and we did well. I never thought we'd have to do it for real.

"But from the sounds of things, there're others out there not faring as well."

"What're you saying?" Marco asked, while loading more shells into his shotgun.

"We need to help those people. They're in serious trouble." Marco just nodded. David turned toward Uno and Jerome. "Jerome, it looks like your sis is doing first aid. See who would need to stay back."

"And me?"

"Uno, you see who wants to go help rescue the other campers."

"What about Terry?" Marco asked. "Some of us aren't in too good shape and I don't just mean physically."

"Not much we can do for him. Those who aren't going off with us to help the other campers can watch his body or maybe take some of the cars and just get the hell out of here."

"Since when did you get all GI-commando anyway?"

"A friend of mine was killed by two pitbulls in Boston. They were owned by some gang bangers. I might have been able to save him, but I just ran. I swore if something like that ever happened again, I wouldn't run the next time."

"How old were you?" Marco asked.

"Fourteen, but it doesn't matter. We just need to grab whatever weapons we can scrounge up. Steve was going hunting tomorrow; make sure he brings his rifle."

"You were only fourteen, man. Don't be too hard on yourself." There was a moment of silence between them. Marco broke it. "I brought a sledge hammer to help split wood. I'll go get that too."

Marco took off to gather gear. Loni and Ken were helping Bella with first aid and for a moment, he was alone, but that did not last long.

Someone was walking out of the shadows. His fedora had been knocked off-center by a stray branch and the thin man's overcoat looked way too warm to be wearing on a June night.

"You're David, right?"

"How the hell would you know that?"

"Please believe me: I might be the last thing you see not of hell this night." He paused for a moment and lit up a hand rolled cigarette. Smoke curved around the edges of his hidden face. "My name is Johnny, also known as the Salesman. I'm a bit busy tonight, so if you'll allow me to get to the meat of the matter. I couldn't help hearing your set of… obstacles and was wondering if you would be interested in a trade."

"What the hell are you talking about?" David took a step closer to the man. "Do you know anything about what's happened? You aren't releasing these insane animals are you?"

The man held up his hands. "I can tell you that I'm not your enemy, if that helps. I assure you that people are in danger and they will need your help." There was just enough light to illuminate the smile peeking out of the shadow of his fedora. "Now I had mentioned a trade."

"Do you have something that could help us?"

"I'd like to think so." His hands moved like twisting spiders in the dark.

"I don't really have much on me, but if you have something that could help us deal with this insanity, I wouldn't turn it down. But if you want us to help some people why can't you just give it to us?"

"Trading is more fun, don't you think? Besides you're the one that spoke about rescuing others. I merely agreed that they could use your help. Now, I might have a great use for that multi-tool you have there on your belt."

"This, why this? I got this as a bonus for surviving Y2K. I–"

"You are facing the real thing this time, David. The Sha'Daa is your world's Apocalypse."

"And what is the Sha'Daa? Mister did you get hit on the head or something? You aren't making much sense."

"Let's just say that the Sha'Daa is something that has been planned for a while. It will hurt many people and I doubt a man like you would like it."

Johnny only nodded. "If you know so much about it, why can't you just give us what you have that could help? Why does it have to be a trade? And why are you lurking outside of our camp?"

He straightened his overcoat with a cough. "I don't lurk. I'm always right where I need to be and I can tell where I need to be because I'm already there."

David took a step back and eyed the odd man. "But, I do have something that could help you. However, I also happen to need a few things for my own... agenda."

"Okay... but this is all crazy."

"Crazier than being attacked by crawfish the size of alligators?"

David stared at the man, who had grown quiet. The fire played a game of light and shadow over his ominous form. "So what do you want to trade?"

He could just see the hint of a grin. "It would be no fun if I told you first."

"Oh, what the hell, I'll try my luck. I suppose we could use all the help we can get. But if I find out that you have something to do with my friend Terry being killed, you'll pray that the cops reach you in time," David said, while removing the multi-tool. "I just hope you aren't going to trade me a spatula or something."

"Don't ever say the Salesman let you down. Johnny's my name and sometimes being lucky helps, but this can help more," he said, while tossing a fist sized object to David.

He almost dropped it which would have been very bad, seeing how it was a grenade. It looked a bit old and rusty. David guessed it could have been some left over relic from WWII, but he was no expert. His eyes moved back up and he was about to ask a question, until he saw that Johnny was gone.

When the forest fire continued to grow, Warwick organized the removal of the Loomers to the stone lip of the rim. He cursed the delay, but the Loomers were important. Nothing must interfere.

Their powerful canine bodies shook the cages and foam flew from their squared, meaty mouths. They would be ready and up for the task.

"Amazing what one can do with a few dogs from the pound, aye Giggler?"

"Yes, but will we even need them? Our Sixes will claim the lives of everyone in a sixty-mile radius."

"You are undoubtedly correct, my loud friend, but the Sha'Daa is only once every 10,000 years. To be born before one of these blessed horrors becomes not just a duty, but an obligation. Nothing must stand in our way. We have planned so long, so perfectly."

He petted a cage and the Loomer whined and drew away. "These Loomers hate everything that lives, but fear us. As soon as they leave our presence they will kill anything in their path. In some ways, our little pets are the real first wave of the Apocalypse."

Giggler kept giggling until the Loomer's howls mixed with his laughter. And together they watched the forest burn.

Tending the wounded and getting them on their way back to civilization during the middle of the night, especially with all the insanity brewing, did not make much sense. It also did not make much sense to sit back and listen to the screams echoing through the forest and not do anything to help. So David had his friends who had volunteered to help get ready and they headed out a few hours before dawn. Once they did leave, David and his friends were in trouble almost from the start.

"What's that?" Marco asked, as the howling rose in pitch and echoed through the forest. He leaned his sledgehammer against a tree for a moment and pointed his shotgun toward the echoing sounds.

"Damn, don't look at me," Jerome said. "I'm still trying to wrap my head around those giant bloated ticks we just fought."

"Maybe it was good they were bloated," Uno said. "It slowed them down and when you hit one – those explosions were sickhouse."

Bella had her hands on his narrow hips. "Yeah, but what do you suppose they had just been feeding on? Do you think it was maybe those campers we heard screaming, you freak?"

David broke in. "At this point, I'm not sure if any of us know what to think. We just have to see what's happening to these other campsites and maybe do what we can."

"Why are we stuck being the rescue squad again?" Jerome asked.

"Because we are the only ones these people got. We're fifty miles from the nearest phone. If we don't help these other campers no one will. I'm not sure about you guys, but I don't feel like sitting around melting butter for a giant crayfish fry, while the sounds of people screaming echo through these woods."

He got a few nods. Everyone had joined the group because they wanted to help. He still felt a little unsure about having Loni along, but she insisted she felt safer with him. Ken was in the rear, with his pistol, guarding their trail and David had also managed to convince both Glen and Steve to come along and flesh out their numbers.

Glen was still whining about his bite. It had been nasty, but Marco had hit the damn thing with a sledgehammer before it had done too much damage. "Oh man, I think I'm leaking pus or something. I hope I don't get that Rocky Mountain tick thing. Is this part of The Rockies? It isn't, is it?"

"Shut up. I think I hear something," David said.

Then it came again, the rustling of leaves like something big and awkward was crashing through the bushes toward them.

"Is it more of those damn crawdads?" Jerome yelled. "Bella make sure you stay behind me."

"No, I think it's something else." David said. Steve fired a few shots from his hunting rifle and then they were on them, long colorful insects with scarlet bodies highlighted with gray and near four feet in length. The most disturbing part was their hanging deflated proboscises. They were the size of his arm and in the dancing light; he saw that the flopping ends were covered in blood.

There seemed to be only three. Marco blasted one to pieces with his shotgun, but with the others, bullets pierced their hides, but failed to slow them down. One came at David and again he was able to do little more than keep it at bay with his Viking sword.

Its nasty snout whipped at him, but could not grasp the long blade without injuring itself. Marco took a step forward and blasted the one David fought into flying bits of shell. The others were finally slowing the last one down when something dropped from the trees onto Steve. The gun fell from his hands and his body went limp and then began to convulse on the forest floor.

"One of those damn bugs has him," Uno yelled, as he started to try to hit the thing off Steve with an axe. The others were still finishing off the third beetle. David, Marco, and Loni rushed over to help, but it was too late. Steve was not moving.

The men finished off the bugs, but Loni shook her head. "It must have had some kind of poison. His heart stopped."

"Damn, this is insane!" David cursed.

"That doesn't even start to describe this," Marco said, once again reloading his shotgun.

"Yeah," Jerome burst in. "How can this be happening? Giant bugs and shit. It just isn't possible. Maybe we should just get out of here."

"We probably should," David said. "And we will once we can get those other campers we heard back to our site. Besides, now I'm in the revenge business.

"Yeah, if any of these others are even still left," Ken mumbled.

David poked at one of the more intact beetles with the tip of his sword. "I'd swear these look like giant Assassin bugs. If they were, that would explain the poison."

"Do you think someone could be making this happen on purpose?" Loni asked. "Like some kind of experiment or something."

"Not much out here in the way of buildings to be hiding a lab," Uno said. "I've driven my jeep all over through here and –"

"Hey wait," David interrupted. "What's that glow over there? Is that a forest fire?"

"It sure looks like it," Ken called out.

"Either some fire got out of control when some campers were attacked, or some asshole crazy enough to make giant bugs has lit the forest on fire too. Either way I say we check it out." David paused for a moment. "I swear that howling seems to be coming from that direction. Come on!"

No one argued and the group of friends followed him toward the glow.

The gunshots disturbed him.

Just when he thought that their vermin had finished the job, the gunfire would start up again. And it was closer this time.

"And they said I was wasting my time with these Loomers," Warwick grumbled to himself. "We'll see who laughs longest."

"To the tops of their cages, all of you!"

They hastened to comply. Once everyone was in their places, Warwick nodded and they pulled the cord that released the gate to their cage. The war beasts snarled and raced away from their vicious masters, seeking soft flesh.

"Just as I planned. Nothing will stop us. Everything is going perfectly."

The Giggler only laughed and the others kept their thoughts private.

Sometimes Warwick wondered if the other Glooms were even worthy to share this with him.

In the distance, the howling became intensified. They had caught a scent. Warwick hopped to the ground and called over his shoulder. "Throw the cages into the flames, we will soon live in a world where such things need not be imprisoned and our darkness will rule the Earth!"

A wind had picked up. It blew toward the south and had shifted the fire. Smoke owned the forest and at times the group could barely breathe. Loni had the worst of it and suffered from long coughing fits.

"Look," Marco said while pointing. "I think the fire has moved. We might be able to pass through here." Then, without waiting for the others, he started to enter the burnt forest. After a moment of hesitation, they followed him. Fires still burned on every side of them, but most of the brush had been cleared away. The ravaged forest was free enough of the fires that moving carefully through the area was just possible.

Soon their trip became a journey through Hell. Fires pressed in on every side and spit sparks at them. The heat from the ground began to seep through their boots. They needed no light to move through the fiery landscape, for the woods glowed a sick pulsing orange. Footsteps kicked up coals and soon disturbed ash competed with the billowing smoke for the right to choke them.

David joined Marco at the front of the struggling group and chopped a burning branch from their path. A small hill rose before them. Fires churned out smoke and he started to wonder if they should turn back, when he heard a savage growl, followed by a howling that sounded far too close. More howling answered the first call. Whatever was making the calls was heading their way.

"Where is that thing?" Marco snarled. His face was so dark with soot that it nearly matched his leather biker jacket.

David yelled, "Come on! Something really bad is headed our way."

Looking around the burning pines, he saw that one place was about as good as another, but he had the group retreat behind a large fallen tree.

Then they came.

At first, they moved so quickly that he could barely make out what they were. Canines, yes, but how could they be so large? Their bodies were a sleek, wet black and as they moved, he saw that they not only possessed the speed of horses, but also their size. As before, they were six in number.

The campers opened up with their hunting rifles, but something was wrong. Few bullets were finding their target. It was as if the beasts were part shadow or mists. Some hit, but others passed harmlessly through.

"Just fire at the one in the middle" he yelled. "We need to kill some of them before they can get to us. Try one at a time!"

Another shotgun blast hit home and the one in the center dropped, but it was too late, for the rest were on them.

He heard what might have been a scream from Ken, but then soon lost track of everything other than trying to just keep himself and Loni alive.

One had easily leapt the tree and turned to face them. David did not hesitate and hacked the dog-beast in the shoulder. Its growling jaws sprayed foam, but he was pleased to see the sword had cut deep and the thing did bleed.

Then it was on him. Its fangs almost snapped his face off. David stabbed forward and caught the monster in the neck. It tried to lunge forward, but only drove the sword deeper into its throat, and Loni smashed a burned log over its head. It whined, but Loni smashed it again and again until it pulled free of the sword. David took this chance to get a two-fisted grip of his blade. Then, with a long lunge forward, he swiped his sword out in a huge arc, going low.

The beast howled when its front leg was severed.

Glen was on the ground before him with a dog-thing snout buried in his guts. He was not even screaming any more.

With an angry yell, David charged forward and brought his weapon down like an executioner's axe. The blow cut half-way through the beast's neck and it bled its life onto the glowing pine needles.

Marco had lost his shotgun and was raging through the re-maining dogs with his sledge hammer, but then, even as David watched, one of the last hounds bit Marco's left arm and started to thrash its head back and forth. Marco screamed as he tried to hit the beast away.

David lunged forward taking the thing deep in the chest, but it still would not let go. He stabbed it again and again. Finally it turned on David with its bloody mouth agape and he drove the sword into its offered throat. It sunk so deep that David thought the thing would bite his hand off, but it died just inches before that could happen.

He jerked his sword free but found that his remaining friends had finished the rest of the pack.

Marco's arm was a bloody ruin and he hurried to try to help his friend. "I'm done man. You have to finish this." His teeth clenched as he continued. "Whoever is behind this shit, needs to be taken out"

"You'll make it, buddy. Come on."

"Maybe I will, maybe I won't, but here." He thrust his shotgun toward him and began to fumble with his pockets. "I got shells in there. Take them, finish this." He shifted his position while David tried to bind his wounds. "Don't worry, I'm not going to roll over and die, and I don't want burn to death either."

David took in the rest of the group. Both he and Loni were uninjured and it seemed that Jerome made it through all right. Uno was still standing even though he had taken a nasty wound to the shoulder. Ken was gone. His mangled body lay not too far from Glen's. Bella was also injured and had blood running down her face.

"Jerome, how's your sister?"

"She smashed her head against a tree when one of those bastards charged into her."

"Do what you can to help her, because she needs to get ready to help Marco back to camp." Standing up, he cocked the shotgun loudly. "The rest of you gear up. We aren't done here. Before, I just wanted to help rescue the other campers. But now, after what has happened to our friends, I'm not leaving until we finish this and I can tell you one thing, whoever is behind this is going to be made to pay!"

Warwick had not been pleased hearing the gunfire so close to them, but it had not lasted long and he knew that whatever survived their vermin would be no match for his mighty Loomers.

He contemplated sending a brace of men to check, but then thought better of it. Even if the Loomers were overcome, no humans would be a match for the Glooms' mystical strength.

Yes, the Glooms will remain at the site. We can play the defensive card. Besides, it won't be long now.

I sense them coming.

Bella and Marco had tended each other's wounds after she shook off the effect of being slammed into a tree. "Let's go, the wind is shifting," Bella said, standing painfully as a new bank of thick smoke rolled toward their part of the damaged forest. "We need to get back to our camp."

Heaving the sledge hammer over his good shoulder, Marco said, "I'm not heading back. I'm going to help them."

"Are you nuts? You're torn to shit and I'm not that much better."

"I'm feeling better now that you've bound my arm."

"Bullshit. Why did you say we were heading back and then change your mind?"

Marco looked around at the smoldering forest for a minute then puffed out his chest with a long breath. "They're going to need our help. If something happens to them and I could have helped, I wouldn't want to live anyway."

She stared at him for a long moment before heaving out a breath of her own. "All right let's go. I shouldn't be leaving my brother anyway. Mums would kill me."

"So you are coming, too?"

"Are you hearing deprived? Let's whip their asses."

Warwick's head jerked, as gunfire exploded in the night, flashes of light marked the humans' assault. Bullets cut down Dicco, the youngest of his Gloom', before the attackers could be stopped. The others dove for cover, but Warwick took a more extreme approach and created a wall of thick fog between the humans and his sacred site. The shooting continued, but the suicidal campers were all but blind.

These fools are going to ruin everything unless I stop them. One of the men burst through the wall of fog and opened up with his hunting rifle. "Take that you – what the fuck are you things?"

Another of his Glooms died before Warwick uttered the arcane words that set off his most powerful Bestow: Flesh to Mist. He cackled, when the gunman screamed and dropped the rifle as his flesh dissolved from his bones and joined the surrounding mists.

"Uno, get out of here!" This second man only had a pistol, but it was enough to keep Warwick's followers pinned behind trees. Warwick let forth a scream of curses when yet a third figure appeared, a woman this time.

"Stop her," he shouted. But it was too late. She had already grabbed the fallen rifle. Seconds later, she was firing and even Warwick was forced to take cover.

A twisted grin spread over his wizened face. The bitch's gun clicked empty. Soon the pistol followed.

"At them!" he shouted. "Strip the flesh from their bones!" His three remaining allies started to give chase, for the humans had wisely chosen to run. "Hold, Giggler. Stay with me. Those two will easily be a match for those three unarmed fools."

The ground beneath him shook and he felt the first titanic rumble.

"They draw near."

Giggler was crossing the clearing, which held the bubbling cauldron and heading toward Warwick. A longer tremor hit the rim. It would not be long now.

Then another man was dashing out of the fog and heading toward the Cauldron. The Giggler turned just in time to see the man before a shotgun blast took him in the chest.

"By the abyss, six thousand curses upon your head!" Warwick shouted. Once again his hand thrust forward and his corrupt Bestow struck this new man. The trespasser cried out in pain, and Warwick could see the look of terror on the man's face when first his clothes and than his flesh dispersed.

Warwick took a step forward. "Your matter is reverting to its base form." Another rumble struck, knocking over tables and spilling his supplies.

"You sick freak! What're you trying to do?"

The largest tremor yet hit them and Warwick was surprised to see the man retain his footing.

"Only bring forth the Apocalypse and destroy everything you hold dear."

He walked closer to where the man quivered in agony. "Painful isn't it, having your body dispersed into molecules."

"Does it hurt as much as this?" He heard someone cry out and then a tremendous impact send him stumbling back, even as he his ribs snapped in several places.

Warwick was quite surprised to see a man, who was so wounded he could barely stay standing, drawing back a sledge hammer for another attack. "Imbecile, why would you think you could be a match for me?"

He sidestepped the blow easily and lashed forward with his sickle striking the man in the gut. With a gasp, the human dropped the hammer and fell to his knees. But, before Wivalynn could soak in his victory, his eyes grew wide with panic, for the first man was racing toward the sacred cauldron.

Giggler, even in his wounded state, went to grab the fallen shotgun. But another woman appeared and kicked him in the jaw. "No, I don't think so, baby." Turning toward her ally, she yelled, "Finish it, David!"

Another giant tremor rocked them. Warwick laughed. "Ha, why am I worried? There is nothing they can do to stop the ceremony now. Wait, what does he have?"

The explosion rocked the forest. Somehow the Infernals intensified the effects. For the force of the blast sent Warwick tumbling through the air. He realized too late that he had been near the end of the rim and his fall didn't stop for a very long time.

It took him nearly a week to recover to the point where Warwick had the strength to climb up the cliff and return to the rim. He had fallen a good thirty feet and had rolled a hundred more. Search parties sought to find him, but even wounded, it was a small matter for him to avoid their detection.

He might not have survived if he had not been able to call upon the aid of the Giggler's bats. They had followed his commands and gathered mice for him to eat raw. Water was a harder issue, but he had survived drinking drops of the precious liquid off their damp fur.

The authorities had long since left what was once his sacred site. The goal he had worked on each day for half his life.

His feet stirred up ash and exposed a red shotgun casing. He picked it up and crushed it in his hand. He would have his satisfaction. Those people would be found and made to pay. In the distance, he heard a radio blaring.

The hunt begins anew.

* * *

INTERLUDE TEN

Ashley chugged a large beer stein filled with coffee. No cream or sugar. Fatigue was beginning to hit her.

One full day into the Sha'Daa and the customers were taking on a desperate and downright wacky cast. This latest loser just wouldn't give up.

"I swear on me mother's grave," a thin voice rang out, "these are the authentic socks o'Turin."

"And you've got the provenance to back up this baloney, Mister Brian Finn?" Ashley asked.

"Well, uhhhhh…" the diminutive Leprechaun murmured while going through the motions of checking his various tiny pockets. "I had the Pope's personal certificate of authenticity in hand when a large dog, uh, mugged me on the way here, yes, snatched it right out of me hands he did. The scurvy mutt ate it. Uh huh. Now enough of this nonsense, damn it! I want me blessed talismans back, the ones I pawned yesterday, and I want 'em now. We got a trade or not, sugar-britches?"

Ashley rolled her eyes and signaled Barrax to pick up the doll-sized swindler (and his foul-smelling gym socks) and escort him to the front door.

Brian managed one final epitaph before being shoved out the mail slot.

"…always shafted for me lucky charms!"

"Things okay downstairs?" Ashley asked.

"Okay?" Barrax frowned, "if you consider two hundred specters, aliens, demon draft dodgers, uncommitted djinns, and a troop of self-declared conscientious-objector golems all demanding political asylum and free booze, then yeah, things are peachy."

Barrax shouldered his way through the crowded shop to break up a half dozen fist-fights that had erupted over Turbo's latest game of chance in the side room, an unbelievably high stakes round of Parchisi.

"Wow. Quite the rave you've got going," Johnny said.

Ashley wiped her brow and smiled. "The AC is over-loaded, I haven't had a break in eight hours, my safe is full, and my stock room is half depleted. There's a moral in there some-where, but I'm just too damned tired to find it."

Johnny placed a bright red, fist-sized jewelry container on the counter.

"If you're proposing, be warned," Ashley said. "Seventy-five years of celibacy has turned me into one ultra-horny bitch. I can't guarantee you'd survive our wedding night."

"It's not a ring," Johnny said.

Ashley sighed and lifted the lid. A smile split her face.

"It can't be," Ashley said.

"Yep," Johnny replied, "courtesy of the Secret Squadron. Mint condition; working cipher dial and complementary photo of the big man himself."

Ashley slowly lifted the brass badge to eye level and began reciting in a reverent tone, "On a mountaintop high above a large city stands the headquarters of a man devoted to the cause of freedom and justice, a war hero who has never stopped fighting against his country's enemies, a private citizen who is dedicating his life to the struggle against evil men everywhere…"

"Captain Midnight," Johnny said.

Ashley smiled at Johnny, "I've never seen your headquarters, Salesman."

"If we survive the day, who knows…" Johnny replied. "Now, here's my short list."

*   *   *

CHAPTER ELEVEN: DOUBLE CROSS

by Paul Barrett

Azrol stood in the upper depths of hell, dressed in his best killing loincloth, and impatiently awaited the summons. He had been dreaming of this moment ever since he was an imp sitting on his spawner's knee, hearing the stories of glory and destruction. Hatched only 5,352 years ago, he had not existed during the last great Sha'Daa. He knew nothing of the world above save what he had been taught in his "Know Your Enemy" lessons, the barriers between the planes too strong for him to learn anything firsthand.

But now, the ancient walls were crumbling again, the Sha'Daa weakening them, and Azrol caught the smell of human souls, sweet and mouth-watering. He longed to taste the flesh and drink the blood. The anticipation of hearing for himself the screams so often described to him had him bouncing from foot to foot. The thought of the rape and pillage he would be privy to made him stiffen to the point of pain.

After so long waiting for this unholy event, the prospect of more delay made Azrol want to shriek in frustration. A messenger imp walked too close. Azrol grabbed it and flung it against a stalagmite. It squealed in pain and dashed into a pool of lava to get away.

Others had already gone forth, those bigger and older than him. Even some in his own crèche had already crossed, laughing with glee and taunting him as they left. But he would show them all. He might be smaller and weaker than the others, but he had more cunning. He'd done extra studies while his fellow students were busy setting each other on fire. He would kill more humans than any of them, and in ways to inspire so much terror that the name of Azrol would be whispered in fear even unto the next Sha'Daa. He would be a legend in both Earth and Hell.

If only he would get the Satan-damned summons.

It started slow, a tingling in his chest he almost dismissed as nervousness. But as it grew stronger he recognized the call. Sha'Daa, it said, the word rolling through his horned head and reverberating through his body. Sha'Daa. The word reached him in demonic voices, rattling his bones and singing through his teeth. Then the tug began. Ephemeral hands reached down and wrapped around his torso. Human-shaped hands, which he found odd until he decided they must be a phantasm of the tormented souls that would soon fall to his claws. The hands lifted him from hell's rocky soil and he shrieked in joy. At last, the Sha'Daa was upon him and he would bask in blood.

He slammed into the barrier, the separation of hell and Earth, and it parted like soft skin. He slipped through as easily as his teeth would rend a liver. He gnashed those tusks in eagerness, ready to taste such delights. His vision blurred, colors going soft, the constant soothing smell of brimstone replaced by a cloying scent. Azrol didn't know this aroma, and tried to ignore it despite its attempts to make him ill. He wanted nothing to ruin this day.

A bang, loud as the scream of Asmodeus, struck his head like a crushing hammer, blinded him with white light. He yelped. Azrol expected the Sha'Daa to be many things. Painful wasn't one of them. He clutched at his head, willing the ache to go away.

Wonder of Baal, it did. The throbbing disappeared and he could see again. He was standing on Earth. No more than ten feet away stood two teen males, their mouths agape as they stared at him. Azrol smiled. His first kills. He had heard child meat was especially tender. He salivated as he envisioned biting into their succulent flesh. He stepped toward them.

And slammed into an invisible wall that crunched his nose. He stumbled backward at the pain and fell on his ass.

"Holy shit, it worked," one of the teens said. Azrol rubbed his nose, stood up, and took a moment to assess his situation closely. He was in a living room. That much he guessed by the large-screen TV, game console, and furniture. The curtains were drawn, so Azrol didn't know if it was day or night. But the candles, at least a hundred, black and red, provided both warm yellow light and the sickly scent he had noticed earlier. The hardwood floor looked old, light-colored and spotted except for where Azrol stood. There it was a dark rectangular patch, as if a carpet had protected it from the sun for many years. It was clean except for the pentagram drawn in chicken blood.

Pentagram? Unholy Satan, it couldn't be. He looked at the boys. They were both dressed in black. One of them actually had on a robe and pointed hat. The other wore a Cruxshadows shirt, a gold ring through his nose and another in his lip. They were both decorated with eyeliner, worn thick.

Azrol reached toward the boys and his hand again hit the invisible barrier. I'll be saved, he thought. The greatest event of my lifetime is upon us and I've been trapped in a fucking summoning circle by a pair of Goth dickheads.

He didn't panic. He could get out of this. Humans were stupid. That's what he had been taught. The number of people who could actually summon an imp, much less an actual demon, was rare enough to be counted on two hands. These jerk-offs weren't on the list. They were no older than he, relatively speaking. Azrol couldn't summon a human to hell. He doubted these two could manage the reverse. This was all some sort of strange mistake.

"I didn't really think you could do it," the one who hadn't spoken before said. His voice was nasal and irritated Azrol the moment he heard it.

"I told you," the one wearing the ridiculous robe said. His voice was deeper, rich, almost pleasant. That irritated Azrol even more. "During the summer solstice the wall between the planes is weak. Summoning is a breeze."

The child's comment stunned Azrol more than running into the pentagram wall had, but it made perfect sense. The Sha'Daa was in effect. This idiot child had the luck of the savior. He had picked the one time in ten thousand years he could have actually succeeded at his insanity. And Azrol had been the one unlucky enough to be snagged. That pissed him off.

He had to get free. There were people to kill, starting with the twits in front of him. They might be fortunate, but that didn't mean they were brave. He stood to his full seven foot height, his horns gouging into the ceiling, and roared with heartfelt fury. "Who dares to summon Azrol the Mighty? You shall now face the wrath of all hell!"

The boys shrank back, much to Azrol's pleasure, and their already pale skin grew lighter. Azrol caught the smell of urine.

The summoner's friend had lost control of his bladder and his dark pants turned even darker.

Azrol continued. "Know that your life is forfeit if you do not immediately remove the circle. I shall wear your intestines as a girdle and your balls as earrings. If you want to live, break the pentagram."

The wimpier one move forward, his head bowed, and Azrol thought the threats were going to work. His claws flexed. As soon as the barrier went down, he would paint the walls with these kids' blood.

But then the robed one stepped up and stopped his companion. "Don't listen to him. He… dude, did you piss your pants?"

The other boy mumbled, his head still down.

"He can't do anything to us as long as the pentagram isn't broken. All he can do is scream and ruin my parents' ceiling. And who cares about that? After they're dead and we're rich, we'll get a place far away from this crappy town. Go change, dude. The smell is making me sick."

Azrol's pointed ears perked up at the boy's words. The boy wanted his parents murdered. That had possibilities. Azrol could handle murdering parents. He couldn't do it because this brat commanded him to, though. He'd never hear the end of it. His crèche brothers would give him all sorts of heaven if they found out.

The robed boy stepped forward. "Demon, summoned by the power of darkness, tell me your name."

Azrol shrugged. No harm in that. "Azrol."

The boy laughed. "Azrol? More like asshole. I can't believe you would actually tell me your true name."

"Oh, but you compelled me to," Azrol said, rolling his eyes. "Besides, who said I told you the truth?"

The boy's brown eyes narrowed, and Azrol was impressed. The kid actually looked like he could murder someone. "I command you, in the name of the Prince of Darkness, to reveal to me your true name."

Azrol tried to ignore the command. He tried with all his might. But as soon as the boy's words finished, Azrol's guts twisted, a hammer pounded on his head, and his nerves danced the Macarena throughout his skin. Even his toenails hurt. He lasted all of three seconds. "Okay, that is the truth. My name is Azrol."

The pain disappeared and Azrol wanted to faint from the relief. He staggered but forced himself to remain standing. He wouldn't give this little prick the satisfaction of falling again.

"That's better." The boy giggled, grating against Azrol's ears like brimstone. "My own minion. This is so fucking cool." He straightened up and looked at Azrol. "Now, you –" he stopped as a high-pitched, two-note sound that was so pleasant it made Azrol want to pull out his tusks rang through the room.

"Christ," the boy said, and Azrol flinched. "Who could that be?" He took a step toward Azrol and smiled. "Don't go anywhere." He laughed at his own joke as he walked out of the room.

I am so going to rip your limbs off and feed them to you, Azrol thought. But first, he had to figure a way out of the pentagram. Intimidation wasn't going to work. He had to come up with something.

The other boy walked back in and Azrol smiled. The kid had changed his black pants for a pair of jeans, ruining his stupid Goth look. They rode large on him, so they obviously belonged to sorcerer boy. As he stepped in, he hitched them up and looked around, obviously surprised to be in the room alone with a seven-foot-tall demon.

Somewhere in the direction the pointed hat had gone, Azrol heard a door open and a voice, deeper than the kid's, spoke. A flash of heat brushed through Azrol and he shivered. Something about that voice bode ill. He suddenly wanted to be anywhere but this living room.

Relax, he told himself. Probably just a Jehovah's Witness. That's enough to give anyone the shivers. "What's your name?" he asked. The boy looked ready to faint so Azrol kept his voice soft. He couldn't get information from someone unconscious.

"Carl," the boy answered, his high voice quivering.

"First demon, Carl?"

The boy nodded.

"Having second thoughts?"

The boy glanced toward the direction of the voices, then back to Azrol. He nodded again.

Azrol smiled. The boy took a step back and grew paler. Humans were so faint-hearted. "What's your friend's name?"

"Rich... uh, Ricky."

"So, what's the deal? You and Ricky fags?"

Carl looked up at Azrol. The demon didn't think it possible, but the boy went paler. "What?"

"It's a simple question. You two playing wild stallions with each other? Got your own little Gothback Mountain going on here?"

Carl glanced over his shoulder. Azrol could still hear voices. They sounded argumentative, and Azrol again felt the flash of heat sear over him. As a demon, the only thing he feared was other demons, but he didn't want to meet whoever was at the door.

"Why would you think that?" Carl asked as he turned back to Azrol.

"No judgment here. But a guy talks about killing his parents, taking their cash, then both of you running away to live together, what's a demon supposed to think?"

"Well, that's not the case." Carl looked at the floor. "We're not lovers."

The slamming of the front door indicated the end to Azrol's alone time with his new friend. "Hey Carl?" Azrol said. The boy looked up. "Don't worry. Your secret's safe with me."

Carl became a bed sheet; his pupils grew to a size that almost obscured his blue eyes. He stumbled back and sat on the couch. Ricky walked in, saw the situation, and immediately ran to his friend. "What's wrong?"

"Nothing," Carl said. He stuck his head between his knees and took deep breaths.

Ricky looked at Azrol. "What have you done to him?"

"Nothing, Ricky. We were just having a little conversation."

"You told him my name?"

"He told me his name too. Didn't you, Carl? Our conversation was very informative."

Ricky walked up to within inches of the pentagram. He looked ridiculous in his robe and pointed hat, but Azrol couldn't fault his bravery. "I command you, in the name of the Prince of Darkness, do not speak to Carl again. You talk only to me."

A jolt of electricity started at Azrol's center and ran through his body, tingling his fingers, toes, and horn tips. He looked at Carl, thought about saying something, and felt a warning throb in his head. He looked back at Ricky. Oh, I owe you so much pain, you little shit. "Don't worry, I won't. I already found out everything I needed to know."

Ricky looked wary a moment, then nodded. "I command you, in the name of the Prince of Darkness, to kill my parents."

Azrol struggled again, even though he knew it was useless. Every sinew in his body burned with the urge to destroy Richard and Amanda Lovestone, Ricky's parents. He saw their faces floating before him and longed to rip their skin away and expose the skull beneath. He wanted to eviscerate them. Longed to eviscerate them. It's what he did. He would gladly do it. But it chapped his ass that he had to do it because this twerp made him.

Then he realized the sooner he did it, the sooner he would be free. The summons fulfilled, he would return to hell and could be sent back to join in the slaughter. He could even come back to Ricky and take him on a slow dance with some razor blades and alcohol. The Sha'Daa had just started, so there was plenty of time. Still a chance to make his mark. He might take some guff and a few lashings for getting trapped in this ridiculous situation, but he could still show the Unholy Trinity that Azrol was a demon who could get things done. He could eat a little shit for a few minutes to revel in what would be his ultimate victory. He looked at Ricky's eyes, brown and large beneath their eyeliner. "Fine. I will do as your command. Where are they? Upstairs?"

"What are you, an idiot? You think I could summon a demon in my living room if my parents were still at home? They're at work."

Azrol almost laughed out loud. Satan was watching over him. He still had a chance to escape this with his dignity intact. All he had to do was wrangle his way out of the pentagram before Richard and Amanda came home. After he killed their son, he might stay and kill them anyway. But if he did, it would be because he wanted to, not because he was compelled to. All he had to do was make good an escape. He started with a lie. "Okay, we'll have to wait until they get home."

"What? No! Go kill them at work."

"I can't."

"I command –"

"That won't do you any good," Azrol said, glad demons didn't sweat. This was a make or break moment. "This pentagram is tied to the house. In order for me to leave here, you'd have to break the pentagram." He offered the boy a big, toothy grin. "Feel free to do that if you want."

Ricky took a step back, his long face uncertain for the first time. "Is that true?" He looked at Carl. "Is that true?"

"I don't know," Carl said. "This was all your idea. What did the book say?"

"It wasn't real specific." He looked back at Azrol and the determination came back to his face. "Can't hurt to try. I command you –"

"But it will hurt," Azrol said. "It will hurt badly. If you command me, the strain of me trying to go against the confines of the pentagram will destroy it. Then I'll be free to carry on with the whole pulling out your entrails, et cetera." He brought up the power to immolate his skin and glowered at Ricky. "By all means, command me."

"This was such a bad idea," Carl wailed. He stood and pushed himself against the wall as far as possible. "I told you we should have just used an axe."

The light of the flames from Azrol danced on Ricky's face, which had adopted a petulant frown. "Fine, we'll wait for them to come home."

"And when is that?" Azrol asked, still flaming, voice low.

Ricky glanced at the cable box, with its glowing green clock. "Another hour and a half, at least."

Azrol doused the flames and used all his demonic will to keep his relief from showing. Plenty of time to get the circle broken. He could already almost taste the marrow he would be sucking out of Ricky's leg bone. "So what do you want to do? Maybe we should talk about mine and Carl's conversation."

"Who was at the door?" Carl asked, and Azrol delighted in the panic he saw in the boy's face.

"Some weird dude who wore a stupid looking hat." As he talked, Ricky flopped on to the suede couch and took off his own stupid looking hat. It didn't surprise Azrol when a mass of unwashed, stringy black hair fell out.

"What did he want?"

"It was really strange."

"Stranger than us standing here with a demon in your parents' living room?"

"Maybe," Ricky said. "He wanted my shoestring. Said he needed it for someone. Said he'd trade me this." From the pocket in his robe, Ricky pulled out a splinter of wood, perhaps three inches long and thick as a pencil, tapered at one end to a point. "I did it just to get rid of the weirdo."

Something tugged at Azrol's mind, a warning, but he ignored it. "That's nice, but let's talk about other things." He looked at Carl and saw the pleading in the boy's blue eyes. He was in torment, waiting for Azrol to spill his secret. Azrol found he enjoyed watching the boy suffer. More fun to let him swing a little longer. "Why do you want to kill your parents?"

"Because they suck."

Azrol laughed, a deep, booming chuckle. "You summon a demon to kill your parents, pretty much guaranteeing you an express ticket to hell, and your best reason is because 'they suck'? Wow. How exactly do they suck?"

"They won't buy me a car. They won't give me anything I want. They have all this money and I get nothing."

"So you're basically a selfish little shit?"

Ricky sat up on the couch. "What's it to you?"

"Nothing. I just find your stupidity and egotism amusing." He turned to Carl and started to speak, but the warning thrum in his teeth stopped him. He eyed Ricky. "What about your friend? Think he cares about going to hell?"

Carl pushed away from the wall. "I'm going to hell?"

"You're not going to hell."

"Of course he is," Azrol said. "He assisted you in summoning me. Pretty big taint on the soul."

"I don't want to go to hell."

Ricky stood. "You're not."

"I don't want either of us to go to hell."

Azrol grinned, both at his chance and the room's tension. "I can help with that. Let me go now, release me from your command, and you'll be safe."

"You're lying," Ricky said. "Demons lie. We let you go and you'll kill us."

Azrol held up three fingers on his right hand. "Scouts honor."

"Boy Scouts go to hell?" Carl asked.

"No, but we have a few troop leaders down there who got a little too friendly. This is your last chance. Let me go."

Ricky clenched his hands, still holding the splinter. "No. I've come this far, I'm not backing down now."

"Please Ricky, let's run away. We can leave now and let your parents deal with this. I'll steal some money from my parents. If we don't kill yours, maybe we'll still go to heaven."

"Maybe Carl should tell you why he doesn't want you to go to hell."

"He's my best friend," Carl said, the panic back in his eyes.

"I think it's more than that. You should ask him, Ricky."

Ricky looked at his friend. "What's he talking about?"

Carl's eyes darted around the room, focusing on anything but his friend. "Nothing. He's a demon, remember? We didn't talk about anything."

"You're a bad liar. You always have been. You're my best friend, dude. You can tell me."

"Oh, he wants to be more than a best friend."

"What does he mean?"

"Tell him, Carl." Azrol flinched at the spike in his head.

"No."

"Tell him." The spike went deeper, but he pushed past the pain. "Tell him or I will."

"Tell me what?"

"Your best friend Carl wants to fu –"

"I love you!" Carl shouted, his voice ragged as the confession tore from him. Azrol feasted on the agony. "I love you." The tears started, and it was all the demon could do to not clap. He had to let it play out and hope things worked in his favor. "I've loved you ever since sixth grade. I'm sorry."

Ricky's expression went flat. "Don't say that."

Azrol shook with glee.

Carl talked to the floor as tears speckled the hardwood. "Why do you think I let you get away with your crazy shit? Torturing the animals, beating up the other kids, stealing. That's not me. That's you. But I can't help it. I love you."

"It's not true. This asshole is making you say it."

"No," Azrol said with a smile. "I think it's your asshole that's making him say it."

Ricky stormed up to the circle. Azrol watched as the boy's robes came tantalizingly close to the chalk lines, but didn't pass over. "I command you to shut up. I don't know what you did or said to confuse Carl, but my best friend is not some dick-smoking fag."

"No, he's not," Carl said.

Ricky turned around. Carl stood there, head up, eyes bright. Tears had smeared the eyeliner, turning him into Alice Cooper on a bad day, but he looked more composed than Azrol had seen him. "He's not a fag," Carl repeated. "But he is a homosexual."

Azrol couldn't see Ricky's face, but his shoulders tensed under the robe and his head tilted. "Then you don't have to worry about summoning a demon. You're already going to hell for being a cocksucker."

"Don't say that."

"It's true. Fags burn."

"Please don't say that."

"We're both going to hell. And I'm going to stomp the shit out of you every day for being a goddamn ass –"

"SHUT UP!" Carl screamed. He ran at Ricky and shoved him in the chest. The boy's hands flew up as he stepped back, tripped over his robe, and fell through the circle.

Freedom. Azrol felt it like a breath of fresh brimstone. The pressing weight of the pentagram disappeared in a flash.

And Ricky lay at his feet like a piece of sushi before a cat.

The boy barely had time to scream. Azrol reached down with his clawed hands, latched onto Ricky's arms, lifted him, and sank his teeth into the top of the would-be sorcerer's skull. A delightful crunch greeted his ears as the wine-red blood and succulent brains filled his mouth. His teeth met and he chewed, savoring his first victim. Shivers of pleasure racked him. He heard a scream and was dimly aware of Carl watching the death of his former best friend. Azrol lifted the body and took another bite, removing the rest of the head. Blood from the neck gushed onto his chest, but he was too busy relishing the soft eyeballs and tough but delicious tongue. He would have been ashamed to have his crèche brothers see him, but he actually drooled on himself as he chewed, so intense was the experience.

The blood quickly stopped flowing from the body and Azrol soon swallowed the last of Ricky's head. He opened his eyes and looked at Carl, who stood rooted with tears and shallow breathing. The front of his recently donned jeans had darkened.

"Satan, kid. You must have the bladder of a weasel."

Carl hitched his breath but said nothing. He looked on the verge of shutting down. Something shifted inside Azrol. He actually felt sorry for the brat. This hadn't been his doing. He had come along for love – a disgusting emotion, but one appallingly common among humans. Azrol was still going to eat the boy, but he didn't have to be a dick about it.

"Hey Carl, you're not going to hell." Azrol found a chunk of flesh stuck in his back teeth and prodded it with his tongue. It remained lodged.

The boy swallowed, appeared about to throw up, and swallowed again. "Is Ricky in hell?"

Azrol closed his eyes. He concentrated, his tongue still picking at the wedged gobbet. They already had the little magician pinned down with pitchforks and branding irons. "Oh, yes," Azrol said.

Carl's shoulders tensed and he backed up until he hit the couch. "You said I helped him, so…"

"I lied," Azrol said, taking a step forward. "Demons do that. But in this case I'm telling the truth. You're not going to hell. You don't have the taint."

"But I'm gay."

"So?"

"Homosexuals don't go to hell?"

"Sure they do. But not because they're homosexual." Azrol took another step forward. "I'm going to eat you now. Say hi to Saint Peter."

To his credit, Carl didn't run or scream. He closed his eyes. "Make it quick."

Something on the floor caught the demon's eye. He looked down and saw the splinter of wood that had fallen from Ricky's hand. He probed at the stuck meat again. The splinter would make the perfect implement to extract it. Azrol smiled. At least the dead kid had proved useful for something. He picked the splinter up and wedged it into the offending area.

A vision came to him in rapid glimpses. Christ lying on the cross. Fragments of wood shattered from the back side as the nails broke through. A man in a cloak picking up a shard. The same man in a fedora handing the shard to Ricky.

The warning that had tried to get Azrol's attention came back to him, but it was too late. "Salesman," he said as blinding white pain whickered through his jaw and radiated down his body. "You tricky son of a –"

He felt himself turn into a pile of dust.

The rest was silence.

*　　*　　*

INTERLUDE ELEVEN

The Pawn Shop had hosted many social gatherings over the years, but perhaps none held more ramifications in its outcome than a secret soiree held Easter eve of nineteen-fifteen for the headquarters staff of the Irish Volunteers.

At the midnight hour, Ashley carried several flasks of whiskey into the shop's side room, which had been decorated and set up as a Victorian lounge for the event. Cross-arguments between her eight guests had commenced the moment they'd arrived.

Eoin MacNeill, Patrick Pearse, Joseph Plunkett, Bulmer Hobson, Thomas MacDough, Eamonn Ceannt, J. J. O'Connell, and Michael Collins plotted a dozen plans and schemes for home rule, cutting each other off in mid-sentence, and vociferously voicing why each of their own plans was the only plausible avenue for ultimate success.

During a brief moment shared to quaff spirits and refill pipes with tobacco, Collins strolled over to Ashley, who was preparing plates of cheese, grapes, and biscuits.

"Your reputation is well earned," Collins said in fluent Gaelic, "milady. Your beauty is barely surpassed by your generosity. Yet…"

"… yet why is a woman of obvious African descent so well-versed in the history of Eire," Ashley replied with a purer and more regionally accented version of the blessed tongue, "so well respected by the shadow societies of this island, and so willing to help you lads start a war that may result in the death of thousands of innocent Irish?"

Collins looked toward the group that had renewed their arguments, then back at Ashley.

"I'm technically not a member of the headquarters staff," Collins said, "and am here as a barely-tolerated observer… a mere lad of twenty-five. I return to England tomorrow."

"You're telling me my secrets are safe with you, Michael?"

Collins laughed, "Fair enough, Milady."

Ashley frowned then smiled. "A number of you are good Christians, and I hoped that the symbolism of this day might temper your understandable bloodlust with a reminder of the nature of true sacrifice."

"It has been said that his rising does not change this world about us," Collins said, "and it is the fact of his ascension that gives us the spiritual power to do this work and make the needed sacrifices."

"Did not Matthew tell us," Ashley replied, "that You have heard that it was said, 'Love your neighbor and hate your enemy.' But I tell you: Love your enemies and pray for those who persecute you'?"

"You acknowledge the justice of revolution," Collins said, "but not the cost."

"I know the price of freedom, Michael," Ashley said, "and I've dealt with its consequences."

"Michael," Hobson yelled, "quit flirting with the dark lass and bring us some victuals."

Collins eyes narrowed for a moment, "You are as wise as you are beautiful, Milady." He bowed his head slightly, relieved Ashley of her trays, then finished with the parting words, "and you have won me over with your argument. Easter is indeed a potent symbol."

*   *   *

CHAPTER TWELVE: THE BOKOR

by Richard Groller

*"To fear death, my friends, is only to think our-
selves wise, without being wise: for it is to think
that we know what we do not know. For anything
that men can tell, death may be the greatest good
that can happen to them…"*
— Socrates

A frazzled Joe Campari was surprised when he received a
phone call where the caller ID said Voodoo Museum, New
Orleans. "Now what?" he said out loud. He'd had enough pressure from the Archdiocese and the miracle seekers that wanted
more insight into his vision. He hoped this was a wrong number,
picked up the receiver and said, "Hello."

A voice from the past with a distinctive French accent sent
a cold shiver down his spine. "Bonjour, Joseph, this is René,
from Haiti. Do you still have the ouanga I gave you?"

"René – my God, it is good to hear from you after all these
years. Truthfully, no. My late wife thought it unseemly for a

Catholic man to keep a voodoo talisman and it was 'lost' during a move to our new house years ago. Do I need it?"

René answered gravely, "I believe you do."

Joe was hesitant, "Well, maybe – you call at an interesting time."

René's voice was firm, "I know. Joseph, when I helped you in Haiti, the death loa sent me to you in a dream. He sends me now to you again, to stand against the Sha'Daa. Do you know of this Sha'Daa? I do not."

"I wish I didn't. The vision I had has caused me nothing but grief since it appeared to me. If the vision is true, a terrible thing will occur to the world and soon, on the summer solstice. I just don't know what to believe any more."

"Then believe me when I tell you the death loa sent me to find you again. So… you are on furlough, I am in the United States, and we have much to discuss. Can you come to the bayou?"

When Joe finally spoke, he said, "Where do I need to go?"

I lay my phone down to begin this new chapter in my life, for you see, this is an ancient story of the lesser of two evils triumphing on the side of good – a devil's bargain, for the enemy of my enemy is my friend. I should know, for I am evil. I am a Bokor. This tale began back in Haiti, when I was known by my birth name, René Dumouchel and was working for the Duvalier regime in their Intelligence and Security apparatus. Papa Doc Duvalier ruled as the dictator of Haiti from 1957 to 1971. His private army, the tonton macoutes, followed his every command – they had no choice.

I remember the first time my Colonel marched a squad of his troops off the roof of a three story building to impress a CIA operative by proving his men would obey his orders without question, even unto death. The operative was visibly shaken. Of course the American did not know they were already dead.

When I first met Joe Campari, decades ago in Haiti, he had been a young history teacher from a Catholic High School in Brooklyn. Joe had gone to Haiti as part of a Catholic Relief effort to help the devastated poor after Hurricane Flora. He had volunteered to help distribute supplies and minister to the sick and injured, using his training as a medic from the Army Reserve.

I was told in a fever dream to find him, a pasty-faced white man wearing a newly minted medal of St. Martin de Porres, patron Saint of mulattos and loa of Baron Kriminel. I found Joe Campari walking the streets of Port-au-Prince and seeking the needy among the storm refugees, oblivious to the undead around him, craving salt to keep their decay at bay.

For Haiti is still the wellspring of zombies. But, there are zombis and then there are zombies. Zombis were once people of free will, who involuntarily underwent zombification by a bokor such as me, via the use of a deadening potion containing the poison of the puffer fish. This potion makes the drinker appear to be dead and thus he is buried, tying up loose ends. The bokor then simply returns for the "corpse" and forces it to do as he wills. The victim is given datura, to keep him in a detached state, and so becomes a mindless automaton. The "Manchurian Candidate" got nothing on the sorcerers or houngan of vodoun – our old school ways render our charges incapable of remembering the past, unable to recognize loved ones, and doomed to a life of toil doing the bidding of the zombie master.

But these living dead do need upkeep, for the victim is alive, so having a state apparatus to support this type of labor with no union representative is useful. I did this for the regime and worse. I was a priest who knew even darker paths beyond the sensible world, the world hidden beneath and above – the world of the spirit. I had the necromantic skills of the reanimator. From the grave, from dead bodies whose souls have departed, I could conjure undead life, to be controlled by my will – true zombies. This made me very useful.

Most folks in Haiti knew to steer clear of shambling work gangs, especially those under the control of the tonton macoutes. Joe had carelessly gotten separated from his co-workers, and was just trying to be a good Christian, but when he started checking the vitals on some particularly sickly individuals uninvited, he was in for a rude awakening. My intervention saved him from a quick and unceremonious death by machete. He was spooked, shaking, and utterly thankful.

The dream spirit didn't tell me why to seek out this man of the First World, but I knew better than to question the loa of death. I surreptitiously gave the zombie handlers my special "salts" for their charges' daily upkeep, since they were degrading rapidly in the aftermath of the storm. Then I scurried him off for his "safety."

We ran a mile or so for good measure, to get the adrenaline flowing and to put some distance between us and "them." We stopped at a small bistro I knew, and I ordered us some fish and rum. Joe was buzzing like a bee and effusive with his questions. I explained to him gently that when in other countries, even those as poor and impoverished as ours, one must not upset the local gendarmes in the pursuit of their business, saying to him, sotto voce, "It could be very bad for one's health, if you get my drift."

I knew this man cared, truly. In my youthful ambition, I had followed the left hand path to power; easier it is to destroy than to take time to create. As a priest I can appreciate the good in others. I gave him a gris-gris amulet of protection and took him safely back to his people. We exchanged information and I told him if I ever came to America I would look him up.

I began to question and re-think my evil ways. The loa had guided me to a being of light, one who freely gave when he was not expected to, to those in dire need. I came to realize how corrupt the regime had become and to feel ashamed for what I had helped it to accomplish in the oppression of its own people, and I began to undermine the regime from within. Soon my machinations were discovered and I was forced to flee my homeland.

Eight years later, with the fall of "Papa Doc," I was a refugee, under an assumed name, with a price on my head from the regime's followers for my assistance in his fall and accusations of crimes against humanity for my complicity with the regime. Damned either way, I fled to the bayou country of Louisiana, where the climate, culture and language suited me and I could blend in without too much trouble.

My nature had changed and I decided to atone for my sins by setting up a small church deep in the bayou. And deep in such an insular community, there is plenty of room to hide from the prying eyes of the authorities – in my case Interpol and the remnants of the tonton macoutes.

That is how I came to America, hiding in plain sight, by opening my little church and becoming the shepherd of a small flock of Santeria on a tiny island of connected cypress hummocks in the bayou. Church lit by candlelight. No electricity except for an old gasoline-driven Honda generator when needed. No phones. No computers. Quiet transportation by skipjack, courtesy of a five-horsepower motor. A simpler life, austere, in tune with the Grand Bois, the loa of the forest. I achieved a modicum of peace and for the first time in my life I was happy.

For over twenty years as the shepherd of my flock, I protected them and defended them. My new name was Jean Dubois, the Elder of the House of Ghede, but everyone knew me as Papa Jean or Papa Ghede.

Pater Familias of the congregation, the love and care of my Vodoun family was the most important consideration of my life. One's blessings come through the community, and one should be willing to give back to the community for there are no solitaires in Vodoun – only people separated geographically from their elders and their house.

Decades passed, and this strange history slowly morphed into distant, poorly regarded memories, and occasionally troubled dreams.

Only a fool believes the past is inviolate, and without fangs…

The death loa visited my dreams, dreams of a terrible foreboding, of evil rising, rising from the swamp to devour my people. Baron Samedi whispered that the evil had a name – Sha'Daa. I knew nothing of this strange sounding name. I decided, against my better judgment, to venture from the safety of the bayou and go to New Orleans, to find out what the nature of this evil was. I went to see the curator of the Voodoo Museum on Bourbon Street, to see if he had ever heard of such a thing in all the lore of the Vodoun.

He had not but offered to send me to a seer who might help me scry the meaning. I took her information. He also said we could try using his computer and could search the Internet for the information. I was unfamiliar with these modern tools, but told him to go ahead. He uncovered links to two articles.

The first was one about a defrocked Byzantine Rite arch-bishop who was claiming the end of the world was near and had been committed to an asylum, shouting "The Sha'Daa is coming!"

The second was an article about a Catholic high school principal in New York City who claimed to have had a revelation while at Mass about the end of time and the coming of the "Sha'Daa," upon seeing a weeping statue of St. Martin de Porres. The New York Archdiocese was investigating the "sign" for authenticity, and many faithful were flocking to the Church to see the miraculous statue. The principal is on indefinite leave until the matter is fully investigated. His name was Joe Campari, a name from my old life.

I knew it was dangerous to me personally to reach out to people from my past life, but I could make no other decision than to protect my Vodouisants. I must keep my promise made all those years ago, and look up my old acquaintance from a dream quest. That was my undoing, for no good deed goes unpunished.

I met Joe at the Voodoo Museum on Bourbon Street. We entered the building, and Joe said gravely, "René, I have a bad feeling about all of this. It's nearly the summer solstice and I truly fear for my very soul."

"Joseph, I know you feel obligated to me, but don't. Just know that by my dream and by your vision, the spirits mean to tell us that we are truly compelled to act."

A very strange man sauntered up to us, a tall white man in blackface to give himself the appearance of a Negro. He had a bright gold tooth and absurdly wore a trench coat in the humidity of the New Orleans summer. Mardi Gras is in the spring, but he was dressed up as Baron Samedi, with a silk top hat on his head, a cigar in his mouth, and a metal flask etched with Bacardi 151 on it in his left hand. On top of the blackface he wore the semblance of a skull, as well as a black tuxedo, dark glasses, and cotton plugs in his nostrils in the manner of a Haitian corpse.

I immediately recognized him as a being not quite human. Before I could speak, he shot me a look that froze me mid-step, then put his finger to his lips to silence me. I turned to Joe and silently mouthed, "Do whatever he says."

The Baron Samedi trickster smiled at Joe with a gleam in his eye and a glint off his gold incisor. "So traveler, you want to do some business? I have interesting wares I could trade with one such as you, the perfect souvenir for one in your state of grace. Come, let us make a trade." From his trench coat he pulled a black candle with twine wrapped around its middle. Pressed in red wax on its underside were the initials "BK". "I will trade you this light – it will guide you when things become darkest – for that St. Martin de Porres medal you are wearing around your neck."

BK, I thought, Baron Kriminel. What is this trickster up to?

Joe replied to the Baron, "This old thing? It is an inexpensive medal, easy enough to replace. But I have worn it for many decades. Why would you want this?"

Baron Samedi continued, "this Dominican Brother, this patron Saint of mixed-race people – he is a young saint, his spirit renewed and strong, canonized only in 1962. He is a spirit of the times. Each of the loa of Vodoun is associated with a particular Roman Catholic saint. St. Martin is associated with Baron Kriminel, a very fearful spirit of the Vodoun religion. He too is a death loa of the House of Ghede, like me. He is invoked to pronounce swift judgment – a condemned man, frightful and terrifying. When the hour is darkest, he will give you strength."

Joe saw the pleading in my eyes and wistfully opened the lobster-claw clasp and handed him the medal. The Baron handed him the candle and let out a laugh – joyous and sinister at the same time. He walked out into the street, stopped, and with a wink of the eye, tossed Joe the flask of rum. Then he bowed and disappeared into the chaos of Rue Bourbon.

It was late afternoon, and the skipjack quietly pulled up to the small, wooden dock at the edge of the cypress hummock that had been my home for so many years. Activity in the swamp en route had been strangely animated, as if all creatures great and small knew there was a horror coming, and so had begun to flee.

During the long ride, Joe had told me all he knew of the Sha'Daa, and now he was very quiet and contemplative. Living in New York City and pushing a desk, he had not aged well. Sweat poured profusely from every inch of skin in the bayou humidity, and the spare tire he carried around his gut did not help. For my age, I am trim and my skin leathery and tough from the world of living close to the Grand Bois.

The door to the small tool shed at the end of the dock was ajar. A freshly severed hand clung to the door handle. My immediate reaction was fear that the tonton macoutes had finally come to exact their vengeance. Joe's immediate reaction was to vomit. One look inside the shed revealed my .30-06 and shotgun were missing, along with a five-gallon can of gasoline. Four bang-sticks and two detachable-head harpoons and a few break-away pole snares for trapping alligators were untouched. The wall cabinet still held the .22 caliber pistol for dispatching snared alligators, a handful of flares and a couple of sticks of dynamite. I had already retrieved my Bowie knife and machete from the skipjack, and had my ever-present old .32 caliber revolver in my pocket.

We grabbed what was useful and quickly covered the hundred meters through the dry land in the fen to the edge of the hamlet. Much of the hidden hamlet in the cypress hammock was gone. Not that the hamlet was big to begin with. Ten extended families in all, eleven including myself: a big communal kitchen with a chicken coop and vegetable garden, a one room school that doubled as a nursery, the church, and individual shanties for the families. The shanties formed a circle around the hamlet's three center buildings. Five of the shanties had been flattened. The most substantial structure was the Santeria Church I had built with my own two hands and where I lived. It was gone – swallowed by the bayou. A sinkhole had opened beneath it. Perfectly. No room for the doors to open. Only deep enough to cover the roof by a foot. This was the devil's work.

The Sha'Daa had begun and I was not there to defend my people. I turned to Joe and said, "In Haiti we have a saying – every houngan is the head of his own house. Well, I have failed my house – it is dead."

Just then I heard a scream and a gunshot from the nursery. We ran and I could not believe what I saw next. Gilled and scaly humanoids, about seven feet tall, with webbed fingers and razor sharp claws, muscular, with glistening skin. One gillman lay on his back with half his face blown off a few feet from a nursery window. Four more were lumbering towards the building.

I yelled in Creole into the nursery, "Don't shoot. We'll take care of these creatures." Then I turned to Joe, "You were in the military. I assume you can use this?" and handed him my .32. I gathered the bang sticks and ran for the nearest monster. The first one seemed surprised at my audacity and took a broad swipe at my chest with its claws. It missed and I shoved the bang stick into its chest dead center. The shotgun blast rocked it back ten feet, dead before it hit the ground. The others then turned in my direction. Joe made a carefully aimed head shot and took down one. I ran to the one closest to the building and zigzagged in front of it. It swiped at me twice, turned and tried to grab me as I dodged past it. I ducked low, then came up behind it. The bang-stick connected with the back of its skull and the skull was gone. Joe took another aimed shot and finished the other gillman.

Maman Brigitte opened the door and we hurried in. The nursery/school held survivors – thirty children, three of the younger mothers, and Maman Brigitte, the teacher. The nursery was a big square building with one door, two windows and a fireplace.

Mama Brigitte was visibly relieved. "The first creature just walked into the hamlet. Pierre had just come back from hunting wild boar, and he killed it with his compound bow. That thing, it scared the bejesus out of us. We had never seen anything like it. Pierre banged on the mess triangle to summon the others, and all the men and some of the women went to the church to see what was going on. They went inside to talk about what it was and then the building just fell away.

"I knew this was very bad juju. I gathered everyone that was left and went to the nursery. I then sent five of the young mothers to go find some weapons and get some gasoline for the generator."

Maman let out a tearful moan, "Papa, only three came back! I am so sorry."

I looked around and saw they had retrieved the goods from the dockside shed. I gave Maman a hug and said, "Maman, you did good. Papa Ghede is home now. Go take care of the babies."

Now was a good time to use that portable Honda generator we had bought for emergencies and special occasions. The school had a few spot lights and a fan. Joe and I set up the fan indoors to cool the children and the spots to give us a view of likely routes of ingress to the three openings of the building. I retrieved my .32 and left Joe with the rifle and Maman with the shotgun. I then took the other women and the three oldest teenage children with me to the communal kitchen. There they gathered food as I searched for more weapons. Knives and cleavers might come in handy. Then I saw a few rolls of chicken wire and got an idea. I also grabbed an old pump insecticide sprayer, empty bottles, soap and oil.

When we got back, I put the teenage children on watch at the windows and doors and put the women to work feeding the children. Joe and I placed some low wooden boxes about ten feet out around the windows and the door. On top of these we laid the chicken wire as a hasty barrier. About two feet above the chicken wire, I erected a single strand wire that I pulled from the vegetable garden. It was an electrified wire we used to keep pests out of the garden. The Honda might provide sufficient power to make the creatures think twice. Our next task was the construction of Molotov cocktails laced with soap – napalm. After assembling a dozen of these, my thoughts turned to reconnoitering the perimeter, to see what had been forgotten.

Joe and I walked the perimeter until we spotted the enemy, more of the creatures rushing the nursery. Joe was very accurate with the 30-06, and took several out at the edge of our vision. We raced to the corner of the nursery nearest the church, to see several gillmen standing in the water on the roof of the chrurch and tearing at it with their claws. The wood shingles were easily torn through. Then they stopped, stooped over and fished a body out of the water. They lifted it up like it was nothing, threw it onto dry ground, and proceeded to eviscerate it with long slashes of their webbed hands. Then they dug in their claws, and began to eat.

We finished them off with a few shots. I said rhetorically to Joe, "How many more will come before the night is over and we are overwhelmed? How are we to defend the babies from these monsters?" This was an epiphany for me. I knew now I must once again serve the loa with both hands, as they say. We walked back to where we had dropped the harpoons and pole snares, and retrieved them. "Joe, you must trust me on this. Please stand guard but ask no questions."

I began fishing the bodies out of the Santeria Church I had built with the rope snares, and laying them in a line along the edge of the building, twenty bodies in all. Once they were all positioned, I stripped down. I lit one of the flares we had brought with us during our perimeter patrol, and dove in, straight for my quarters. I found my box of supplies, grabbed my ritual implements and swam for the surface, ready to begin my dark task.

Joe looked relieved when I broke the surface, but his relief soon turned to agitation.

"Joseph," I said gravely, "I never told you this before. There is no easy way to say this. I am a Bokor. It is my intention to reanimate the dead among my people to save the living."

He looked me straight in the eye, *"things aren't fucking weird enough already?"* As he went to storm off, about a half dozen gillmen emerged from the darkness from multiple directions, probably smelling the corpse smorgasbord I had laid out for them. I pulled my .32 and Joe raised the rifle, and we stood back to back picking them off. Joe stopped the two in his line of sight. I dropped two more. More came at us from the side. I pushed Joe out of the way as I dropped, rolled and pulled out my machete. One accidentally tackled the other. While they were both down, I decapitated the one on top from behind with the machete. The one on the bottom lashed out with his claw and cut my chest. Blood flowed and flesh hung, as I was knocked on my back. The gillman loomed over me while Joe fired point blank with the 30-06 and the creature collapsed. He helped me up, then grabbed my shirt and tore it up to make a field dressing. He still had the flask of 151 and emptied its searing contents onto my chest, then wrapped my shirt around my chest to try and slow the bleeding. I pulled out my .32 and reloaded. Then he looked me again in the eye and said, "If you can raise the dead, do it!"

Joe stood guard, as I pulled the salts and the incenses and the oils from my kit, and began to summon the death loa. I had already made a personalized gris-gris for each one of my flock, a small, leather pouch now tied around their lifeless necks. Inside the pouches were stones and engravings specially tailored to each wearer. Tears ran down my face as I sprinkled the pouches with blessed water and the dark incantation was recited. Shingles from the church's roof served as the altar, and on it sat a burning black candle. Baron Samedi would exact a great toll from me, but I would gladly pay the price for my Vodouisants.

I worked quickly. More than once shots rang out from the 30-06 while I kept working. The night was getting darker – clouds began to roll in and blocked out the stars. Soon the first body stood up, eyes open once again, incapable of expression. Yet I felt them reproach me, for disturbing the sleep of the dead. Soon twenty undead stood before me – puffy, bloated, drowning victims, all from my flock. I failed them twice. Once in life, and now in death, disturbing their holy sleep.

Joe looked terrified. I thought he might shit himself then and there, but he soldiered on. I sent Joe back to the nursery to collect all the knives, cleavers, machetes, and hatchets. He returned with a gunny sack full. I distributed them to my army of darkness and sent Joe back to guard the nursery. Then I took them to the dock area to meet any enemy that dared emerge from the water.

The clouds broke and the beach was bathed in the light of the summer solstice full moon. I looked out and saw many of the fishlike heads emerging from the water. My twenty zombies were arranged in a ragged line, with cleavers and machetes raised, waiting for the onslaught, staring, unseeing, unafraid. The gillmen came in waves. Zombies hacked off limbs. Gillmen slashed open the zombies. Intestines spilled onto the beach. The sand became slippery with gore, and the stench would have turned any normal man's stomach. I am no ordinary man by any stretch of the imagination, so this stench to me was only a reminder of a dark day's work from long ago. And I am sure the gillmen found it savory. But the zombies did not fall. Blows that would have killed a living man were absorbed by flesh already dead. I stayed in the rear and shot any gillman that penetrated the line.

Some men are great warriors that experience time as slowing down during battle. I on the other hand experienced cognitive dissonance from the sheer quiet The sound of battle is normally fraught with shouts and screams of terror and rage. But my zombies were silent, and so were the gillmen. The only sounds were the thuds of falling bodies and the muted slash of steel rending flesh and bone. And my occasional gunshot, which kept me focused.

The first three waves of gillmen lay dead on the beach. The fourth wave changed tactics. The gillmen came in hunched over, almost crawling. As they drew near, they lunged, tackling the zombies' legs and bringing them down. The zombies thrashed and slashed and grappled and bit chunks out of gillmen. The gillmen did the same. The final wave of gillmen came in from behind and attacked the prone undead, slashing at necks and legs. In the end, the zombies were either reduced to immobile ineffectiveness or finally inanimate. But the gillmen's numbers went from over a hundred to a dozen or so I began the short trek back to the nursery, firing all the way.

The gillmen surrounded the nursery, a demonic ring around the rosey, with a slow inexorable death march. The women provided cover from inside with the 30-06, the shotgun and the .22.

Joe took the three teenagers outside with the makeshift napalm grenades. They had better arms for throwing than he, so he lit a flare and began lighting the weapons and telling them where to target. They threw long beyond the makeshift barrier and set many to flame. Four bottles each on three sides broke the lines, but still they came. Then they hit the chicken wire and as they went to climb over, hit the electrified wire. They crackled and fell back stunned. But the ones coming from the blind side were not so encumbered. They hit the rear wall and began beating on it with their claws. Some crawled beneath the hot wire. The perimeter had been breached.

The teenagers fled inside, followed by Joe, who barricaded the door. The banging grew louder. A gillman's face appeared at the window on each side. A teenager on each side struck. The last two bang sticks did their grisly work. Then the lights dimmed, flickered, and went out. The littlest ones began to scream and cry, "Please, please turn on the light."

Joe remembered the candle he still had in his pocket from the strange man in New Orleans. He lit a match to it. The light lit the room like a flare, but didn't burn hot. Joe hit the floor and began to convulse. The children screamed more, and the women tried to help him.

Maman Brigitte said, "No. Let him be." He thrashed on the floor and then suddenly stopped – eyes wide open, crazed, his face like a skull. He stood up and moved like an avatar of death. He began to shout obscenities at the gillmen, to spit at them through the window. He grabbed a table, lifted it up and blocked one of the windows, wedging it tightly with incredible strength. He grabbed another table and wedged it against the door. He tore open a box of candles, lit them with his candle and said to the children, "Pray for a good death." Then he took the black candle, a machete and the gunny sack we had brought from the shed and jumped through the open window.

Maman Brigitte turned to the children. "Don't be afraid. He is possessed by Baron Kriminel. The loa have come to protect you."

When I arrived, with a half dozen gillmen still on my heels, the scene of carnage was horrific. Joe was dancing like a dervish, his machete slashing and hacking as he moved, fluid, faster than gillmen could move to catch him.

He danced to the generator and found the half-empty five-gallon can of gasoline. From the sack he pulled an empty three-liter plastic bottle, and filled it with gasoline from the can, attaching the mister from the insecticide can with duct tape. Then he began his dervish dance again, slashing and spraying the gillmen as he shouted obscenities at them in a deep nasal unearthly voice. He returned to retrieve the gas can, then went to the back of the building where a crowd of some thirty gillmen were about to collapse the fireplace. He poured nails and stones into the can, and duct taped the dynamite to the can. Then he lit another flare and tossed the can into the center of mass of the gillmen. The makeshift claymore did its dirty work. Blood and gillman body parts were everywhere, and a section of the chimney did collapse and crush many of the hapless monsters.

I was reeling now from loss of blood and fatigue. I crawled up a cypress tree, figuring I could fire safely from a perch above the melee at whatever approached the nursery, and be able to shoot down on any gillmen that tried to follow me up.

I watched as Joe ran for the kitchen. When he returned, he had all the chickens from the chicken coop before him, several dozen, under his command. He sprayed them with gasoline. The grim realization hit me that Joe was possessed by Baron Kriminel. Now I understood the candle the mysterious trader had given him. I was both sad and elated. Baron Kriminel calls for the sacrifice of chickens doused in gasoline and set alight. It appeals to his cruel nature and appeases his dark urges.

The candle pulsed and sputtered and sent tendrils of flame in every direction to all the chickens; they screamed as they ignited. But the flaming birds did his bidding, and each made a fiery beeline for a gillman who had also been sprayed with petrol. The field was bright with burning bodies.

Gunshots rang out until my revolver ran out of ammo, and my machete became my weapon of choice. When I buried that in the skull of a tree climbing gillman, I was left with my Bowie knife. I felt dazed and exhausted. Yet still I watched as Baron Kriminel's machete slashed, and still the reports of the 30-06 and the shotgun rang out from within the nursery.

Dawn broke, and not a gillman was left standing. I closed my eyes only for a moment in silent prayer to the loa, then I eased myself down from the tree. I found my pasty-faced friend from the States lying face down in cardiac arrest. I tried to give him CPR, but it was to no avail. His heart gave out.

I am a Bokor. I serve the loa with both hands. I protect my own. I pay my debts. The cleanup will be rough, but these horrified teenagers must grow up fast now. I cannot do it. I am too weak and already I feel the fever rising in my chest. I will have them drag the scores of bodies to the swamp. Rather than burn the bodies, they should become food for the alligators — an offering to the Grand Bois.

I am still the head of my own house, though a much smaller house.

I do not know why the Sha'Daa is visited upon us, but I suspect it may have been perhaps as trial and punishment for my past evil.

I thank the death loa for sending me dreams, and an avatar to save my people. I believe Baron Samedi may have forgiven me my wickedness, for none of the children were harmed. But, we will see. For now, it is well past dawn, and I must sleep.

I lie beside my dead friend and close my eyes. Perhaps Joe and I will connect one last time to wander the streets of Haiti, laughing, and drinking rum with the loa…

* * *

INTERLUDE TWELVE

Barrax lowered his shoulder-braced rail-gun. Two were-wolves, three vampires, a succubus, and four dwarves lay in various stages of dismemberment across the main pawn shop floor. The hyper-velocity, depleted uranium shells had done their job well.

"Clean this up, stat," Ashley shouted to her staff. "We're a business, not a slaughterhouse."

Johnny suddenly appeared out of nowhere. "Another attack like that and you're Fort Apache," Johnny laughed. "Oh my, oh yes, what a mess."

Ashley wiped green and blue blood off her face with a Mickey Mouse beach towel.

Johnny's face looked pale and drawn. His eyes were bugging out and he danced nervously back and forth on his long legs.

Over the centuries Ashley had seen these weird, unexplained intervals of near madness overtake The Salesman, but now it was most assuredly rubbing her the wrong way.

"Always nice to know my friends are near in times of need," Ashley spat.

Johnny frowned, regaining a moment of composure. "You of all people know my limitations, shop owner. I am forbidden from directly interfering in the course of The Sha'Daa."

"Words," Ashley said, "mere words. Tell me, did you ever actually *try*?"

Johnny's eyes seemed to glaze over for a few seconds, and his face took on an even ghastlier cast.

"Yes, my dear," Johnny said in a voice that chilled Ashley's intestines. "Many millennia ago, I chose to break this scripture… and my punishment was… all-consuming…"

Ashley gulped and then picked up the strange gold necklace with white-gold, triangular pendant Johnny had placed upon her counter.

"Jewelry?" Ashley asked.

"But no ordinary trinket, Ashley," Johnny laughed. "Oh ho, no no, not at all."

"Then what?" Ashley asked.

"It has been known by many names and many games," Johnny snickered. "The Agimat, or Bertud, or Anting-Anting…"

Ashley gasped. "The stories… are they true?"

"Yes," Johnny nodded, "but be warned. The strength of its powers are unpredictable, and they will only work for the course of a few minutes, after which it will forever turn into a simple clump of jewelry… until it changes hands, once again, hee hee hee……"

"And what of my display do you want for this?" Ashley asked.

"That which is unseen," Johnny said. "Oh yes indeed, that which you have hidden, and which you prize for the darkest and most complex reasons…. I want the slave chains your long dead master placed on you, mere minutes before he was murdered, ah ha ha ha ha…"

Ashley's eyes went wide and her hands began to shake. She looked down at the Agimat and realized that Johnny was indeed worried for her safety. This trade was his only way of protecting her. Five hundred years flew by in her mind and there she was once again, lying on the dank ground of a Dublin back alley, her belly bleeding out after having been stabbed repeatedly. Beside her, lay Master Arwel Jepperson, his throat cut by ruffians angry over losing a large bet on a hand of cards. They had followed master and servant several blocks before cornering them in this death trap. Ashley the slave had died on that night, only to be reborn.

Ashley dropped to the floor and opened a small compartment beneath the floorboards. She placed the rusty, black ankle shackles gently upon the display counter.

Johnny snatched them up without preamble and strode to the front door. A moment before exiting he turned and locked eyes with Ashley. "I will return if I can. Be prepared. Far worse is to come this final half day." And then he was gone.

The mob of customers who had fled minutes earlier rushed back into the shop to recommence their earlier trades and pawns. Poking her head into the side room, Ashley could see Turbo and Gronk's high stakes game of backgammon had continued unabated through the recent attack. Shaking her head she returned to her work.

"Pawn, sell, trade, or sacrifice, Enuk?" Frank asked a yellow-skinned, orange tunic-wearing lizard-man.

"I want to sell my Katana," Enuk replied. "It's an ancient sword and worth at least ten thousand pounds, gold or sterling."

Frank squinted his eyes for a moment and then chuckled. "Not likely, pal."

"What's so funny," Enuk asked.

"Made in Japan," Frank said.

"Of course it's made in Japan," Enuk said. "It's a damned Katana! High- and low-carbon steel hammered and folded into a thousand layers by a Master Japanese sword-smith. The strongest, sharpest, and most dangerous bladed weapon known to man."

"No, I mean the words made in Japan are machine-stamped into the blade collar."

* * *

CHAPTER THIRTEEN: KEEPSAKE

by Mallory Makepeace

Ki Shan i Romani, Adoi san i Chovhani
"Wherever Gypsies go, There the Witches are, we
know"

Focul Viu, whose name means 'The Fire' in Roma, staggered and struggled through the knee-high snow blanketing the mountain pass. The searing cold wind against his exposed eyes and the gnawing hunger in his belly, however, barely touched his thoughts.

Shame, he thought. The shame of a homeless gypsy.

For such a man was Viu. A Romani without family was a man without a soul. A dead man. And if he should drop now never to move again, it would be as if nothing had happened.

Focul stopped for a moment to yank a small, gold, oval locket out of his jacket. Cringing in pain he opened it to reveal a tiny photo of a beautiful woman with dark hair and eyes, his fickle love… and his doom.

Viu's clan, the Apuseni, named after the Transylvanian mountain range that had been their home for over a thousand years, were most unforgiving…

The trial had been difficult but brief. Five elders of the Zamoly bloodline stood in fire-shadowed witness to Gaboriana Nagy's exclaimed innocence.

"He took me," Gaboriana cried in large tears, "against my will."

Her husband Doncsev Nagy, unusually taciturn, stated his own testimony. He had found them together by the river. When Focul realized he had been caught in the act he ran away like the craven creature he was.

Focul Viu yelled again and again. He did not attack her. He was not a ravisher. Gaboriana had seduced him.

Paid no heed, the slender seventeen-year-old slumped in the muscular arms of his captors as Klaucescu, the eldest, pronounced sentence, "Expulsion from the Apuseni. Forever."

Focul's screams cut through the crisp night air as the Tribe's Chovihano branded Viu's naked chest. The fire-heated metal burned through skin and the lad fainted from the overpowering stench of his own tortured flesh.

Upon waking he was spat upon and escorted to the nearest tree line.

"Viu. Ka jav te xenav tut."

"Te bisterdon tumare anava Focul."

And so he was cast out. Like so much debris…

It was thus that he relived the previous day's tragedy over and over, the severe cold and oozing black scar unheeded as he staggered near the end of the pass.

Bitter and hollow, Viu suddenly took notice of the remains of a large structure. Castle or church he knew not, nor did he care. Perhaps it held some shelter to extend his miserable life for a couple of more hours. Already half convinced he was a Romani spirit damned to traveling endlessly through Hell, Viu crossed a bridge-like structure of stone.

Halfway across this ruin of a bridge, he remembered the legend of the Dark Valley. For years he had heard the story told as a cautionary tale by many a gypsy grandmother to grandchild. As the tale went, a great evil was born in these parts millennia ago. And one day, it would be freed again to wreak havoc. As the legend ends, both heroes and monsters were destroyed and mankind was left to choose the path of good or evil for itself.

And the Dark Valley was supposed to be far east of the Apuseni… and Focul had traveled in just that direction for quite some time.

But it is not just a legend Focul Viu, a strange voice spoke in his mind. We have broken through many times into your world. Sometimes we conquer, and others, we are repelled.

"This is crazy," Viu said. He spun around but could see no one. Then he realized he was hearing this voice inside his own head.

Look down and you may see the breath that is our portal. It is mostly closed. We cannot penetrate into your reality during this cycle.

A single ray of silver moonlight broke through the clouds and struck a small portion of the jagged ravine below, where something sparkled in reply.

The Sha'Daa is a most holy time, Viu. Perhaps you can take advantage of it now… perhaps you will be our voice… our proxy until the next ten thousand years come to pass. Look closely, and you might see the thinnest flicker of light from our realm….

Viu was hooked, he dropped to his hands and knees and squinted his eyes for a better look.

Our portal is but a mere wormhole during this cycle. We cannot cross over. A stream of matter, less than the diameter of a molecule, might possibly make it through…. Look close Viu…

It was his undoing, for the side of the walkway was merely snow and ice that had piled up and outwards from the stone bridge, and was inherently unstable. In the space of a heartbeat his snowy shelf collapsed and Viu fell into the ravine.

The fall was not direct, nor was it merciful.

The first impact of flesh upon cliff stone occurred halfway between Viu's right kneecap and ankle. The loud snap and crunch echoed throughout his body as the compound fracture nearly removed his entire foot.

The second impact during his fall shattered four vertebrae and instantly paralyzed the lower half of his body.

Then things got worse.

The third impact bounced him like a rubber doll off a jagged chunk of rock shaped not unlike a shark's dorsal fin. Half a dozen ribs fractured. One tore through a lung and plunged into Viu's heart.

Next he skidded face down along a cracked stretch of rock that tore off his eyebrows and his nose leaving behind a long bloody swath.

Viu struck earth and rock for the last time. He hadn't even had time to start screaming aloud his agony and pain.

Viu's body flipped over upon the end of his fall, and the back of his skull smashed itself back onto the tiny mote of sparkling light.

Just as quickly as life fled the Romani's body, it flooded back in.

Focul Viu sat up straight and screamed in agony. But the pain he felt now was not that of death. It was a pain of abnormal rebirth. In shock, he became instantly aware that all of his injuries were mending. Focul suddenly felt sensation in his lower extremities. He ripped open his shirt to see the gouge above his heart was closing shut.

He reached down and felt his right leg to be whole again. His fingers ran over his sensitive face to feel the last vestiges of cartilage and skin harden into place.

He was healed.

Instinctively, Viu reached behind his head only to feel the deep cut close. He looked to the ground but could not see the tiny spot of unearthly light that had caused both disaster and miracle.

And then he knew he had been saved for some greater purpose. A cause. A mission. What it was he did not know. He only realized that now he no longer felt the cold and hunger. He no longer felt weak and helpless, but strong and… invincible.

"Nais Tuke" he murmured, thanking whatever deity had interceded in his fate.

Focul removed his gold locket for one long look, and then tossed it into the snow. He had no need of such keepsakes now.

He slid his fingers across his chest. Though his new flesh had healed from the shameful branding, the original scar, the Apuseni Weird known as Waffedi, remained, forming a startling black design that was hard, smooth, and shiny as ebonite.

It only took a moment to decide.

With long proud steps Focal Viu, a walking breathing talisman of transcendent health and vitality, strode back through the Hellish pass from which he had come.

"Te potshinen penge lajav," he vowed.

He would bring justice and honor to the Apuseni. There was a new trial to be held, and this time, Focul Viu would be Judge.

Focul started jogging and in moments it turned into an all out sprint. The Waffedi brand on his chest pulsed with a dull green light.

Minutes later he was charging over the snow as rapidly as the fastest of horses.

Jek dilo kerel but dile hai but dile keren dilimata.

"One madman makes many madmen and many madmen makes madness."

A mere twelve hours after his rebirth, Viu returned to the village.

Before entering the main clearing, though, Focul found himself facing a most unusual man dressed in garbs reflecting a foreign origin.

"Do you seek to bar me from my mission?" Focul asked.

"No," the tall man in the dark trench coat and black fedora replied in idiomatic Romanian, "it is not within my purview to alter your destiny in so coarse a manner."

"Yet here you stand," Focul said, "a sentinel at the ancient gate. A wise man would be a fool not to take note. Who are you? What is your purpose, stranger?"

"I am but a salesman, Focul Viu," the stranger said, "though I fear I have nothing to trade that you would find of value."

"My clothing tells you I am a poor man of no land or means, is that it?" Focul asked.

"No," the Salesman said, "I mean a mystical shard of unearthly matter from a long-lost hell dimension has punctured the back of your skull and grafted itself deep into your brain. This sliver of DNA is but a splinter of a once mighty race that used to frequently cross the borders of a dimensional portal between worlds… and now their legacy nestles tightly between your cerebral hemisphere and cerebellum. This fraction of a hateful alien race has altered you in ways both insidious and obtuse. You are that which should not have been, Focul Viu, a vengeful creature of dark intellect, savage imagination, and frightening strengths and recuperative powers."

"And who are you to judge my soul, Salesman?" Focul said. "Have you suffered as I have? The torture of branded flesh? Do you know the icy kiss of death? I have seen oblivion. Tasted its foul ash. And I have been reborn, and now possess a vision… a most holy one, to fulfill."

"You will never know peace, Focul," the Salesman said, "and yes, I have supped of the darkest of defeats and the most unholy of redemptions. And I can only leave you this blessing…. May your own journey be far shorter, and your regrets much less painful than those I've endured for the many millennia I have traveled this planet."

And a moment later the Salesman was gone, disappearing like a fine morning mist fallen victim to a sudden strong wind.

Focul frowned, and then put the apparition behind him. He had business to attend to.

Entering the heart of the village, Focul was rushed by a crowd of two hundred women and children. They surrounded the silent pariah, cursed his name, spat on him, and proceeded to stone him to death.

With the deed over, the villagers turned to continue on with their lives, but were stopped by Viu's otherworldly voice.

"Are you finished?" he asked. A smile formed on his bloody face. Somehow, some way, he managed to stand back up even though his body was a horrific landscape of compound fractures, blood, and torn flesh.

Mothers screamed and tried to ward off the evil eye. Most just stood there in shock as Focul Viu's wounds and injuries healed and mended in a matter of minutes.

"Well?" Focul yelled, with madness in his eyes.

The women and children fled, only to be replaced shortly by the men who had just been called back from the fields.

Doncsev Nagy was the first to rush Viu. He sprinted forward and impaled Focul with a large wicked looking scythe. Nagy spit on Viu's fallen corpse and readied to turn when he felt something on his ankle.

Viu, his hands like serpents, leapt upon Nagy, pulled himself up the larger man's terror frozen body, and gouged out both of Doncsev's eyes.

Two other village men rushed Viu from behind and stabbed him repeatedly in the back with long knives. Focul managed to stay on his feet as his wounds healed rapidly, closing like tight mouths all along his skin. Viu then took one knife from an attacker and cut the larger man's throat just before hamstringing a fourth attacker.

Viu tore off his bloody ripped shirt revealing dozens of wounds, all of them closing up and leaving behind fine yet visible scars. And with each failed wounding the ebonite Waffedi scar upon his chest would pulse with a strange green glow.

And more men arrived to test this boy, kicking him, punching him, stabbing and chopping him, and then finally dying in his reprisals, until upon a field of one hundred dead men a crowd of three hundred men stood back, terrified to confront Viu, as evidence of the lad's powers was now spilled all about their feet.

"I cannot be undone," Viu stated.

And then he ordered that the Five elders of the Zamoly bloodline be brought forward for judgment. And they were beheaded.

Next, a screaming and crying Gaboriana Nagy was dragged forward.

"Mercy," she pleaded.

"Very well," Viu said. "I will show you the mercy you allotted me."

And thus was Gaboriana's forehead fire-branded with the mark of a gypsy harlot, and her tongue cut out so she could never bear false witness against another.

And finally the tribe's Chovihano was brought before Focul.

"You would not dare kill a holy man," he spat proudly.

"You are right," Focul replied, "cut off his hands, lest he ever feel the urge to brand his weirds upon another innocent man."

And so it was done.

One day later Focul stood before a gathering of all thirty thousand of the Apuseni.

Three times assassins tried to kill him.

The first with knives.

The second by a staggering flight of arrows.

The third by several bursts from a dozen AK-47s.

As Viu's wounds miraculously healed and the would-be assassins were beheaded in his presence, the Apuseni fell to their knees and prayed to their savior with the otherworldly Waffedi brand glowing upon his naked chest.

Focul's speech was short, curt, and all-inclusive. He ended it with a promise.

"We will create," he stated humbly, "an empire of justice, a country of fairness… one great tribe."

Four hours later the Apuseni swarmed into Bucharest.

*　　*　　*

INTERLUDE THIRTEEN

It was a dreary night, late evening of June twenty-eight in 1963, when Ashley found her shop the object of sudden, unwanted attention…

Just as she was about to close up for the night, having minutes ago dismissed her staff, the Police Chief of Dingle burst through the front door, soaked from rain, with his face all puffy and red.

"We're closed, boyo," Ashley said. "You know my hours."

"Can't be helped lass," Tim said. "We have a special guest. Word of your little shop caught his interest, and so we're here on a whim."

"I don't care if the Queen of England wants to pawn the crown jewels," Ashley snarled. "I've had a long day and…"

"I apologize for intruding without notice, young lady," a strangely familiar American voice resonated, "but your goods come highly recommended."

Ashley spun around and her eyes went wide at sight of the handsome middle-aged man in his stately suit and dark brown trench coat. Standing behind him were three large, tough-looking men in black suits, all sporting sunglasses.

"Mr. President," Ashley stuttered, "of course. Please come in while I put on a fresh pot of tea."

The next three hours passed quickly as Ashley found herself and her wares under intense scrutiny by this dashing and charming scion of Eire, an intelligent, educated man with a seemingly endless series of probing and thoughtful questions.

A momentary pause occurred in their discussion, as they both stood before a lovely two-foot statuette of the Greek goddess Keres.

"Britain-Roman," Ashley said, "carved from Connemara marble during Emperor Hadrian's reign."

"Beautiful," JFK said, "and its eyes…."

It happened in a fraction of a moment, and so Ashley was the only person close enough to see. A short burst of faint scarlet light shot from the green-tinted statue's eyes and mesmerized the U.S. President for a full four seconds. One of his secret service escorts was about to step forward when the leader of the free world shook his head and then smiled at Ashley.

"You have wonders in this little shop the envy of the Smithsonian, Ashley," John said, "but I'm afraid my time is up. We are off to Dublin."

With a slight bow, and a courtly kiss on the back of Ashley's left hand, John F. Kennedy and his train of bodyguards and assistants emptied out of the pawn shop and into the rainy night.

A small tear leaked from Ashley's right eye. Keres, the Greek goddess of violent death was never wrong. JFK would be murdered, slain by an assassin's bullet, in less than five months.

*   *   *

CHAPTER FOURTEEN: "THE SAGLEK INCIDENT"

by Bruce Durham

Belaam grew aware of a drip-drip-drip of liquid, a steady, rhythmic patter of fluid. Its assault on her consciousness proved irritating and intrusive, yet her mind sensed it as strangely important. Grasping that belief, it became her focus, a guiding light used to ascend the slow path to wakefulness.

Her first sensation was of the cold, a cold that produced an avalanche of memories. It was the time of Sha'Daa and she hunted. The hunt had been good and the feeding better, her quarry proving surprisingly weak of body, offering little resistance and even less sport. Until they had banded together.

Hunted in turn, she had made a game of it, leading the human cattle across flowing ice fields and over rough, snow-crusted hills, cunningly separating and trapping each, mercilessly toying with their weak flesh in gruesome ways and leaving the mangled bodies for their brethren to find.

But eventually it all went wrong. Ice cracked, a ledge crumbled and Belaam tumbled into darkness.

Until now.

Carefully opening the outer lid of her left eye she was met with a blinding glare that reflected off vast fields of white snow and through pillars of ice. Quickly she closed it.

Confused, she remembered passing from her plane into a place of dim twilight, sunless sky, and bleak landscape, not some world of overbearing sunlight. Panic surged within her. How long had she been unconscious? What if her prey was near? The moment swiftly passed, and Belaam felt shame for allowing such cowardly thoughts. She was demon-kind. Primitive cattle were beneath her. They were to be disdained, not feared. Angry now, she forced open the outer lids of both eyes and stoically endured the intense discomfort until they had adjusted to the unnatural brightness. She slid open the inner lids and waited again.

In time she turned her head, searching out the noise source that had awakened her. A massive cone of ice hung by her left shoulder, melting under the blazing sun, its heavy drops pooling on the ground. She looked at her feet, and growled with a start. They were trapped in ice. Angrily she attempted to move the right, but found it held fast. She tried the other, and grunted with faint satisfaction as two claws shifted, the ice restraining them splitting into a spider web of cracks.

Not surprisingly she found her arms trapped, too, and wondered how she could have frozen so swiftly after her fall. Putting that thought aside for later, she flexed her arms. The right was solidly held in place. However, the left was less secure. Muscles bunching, she wrenched it free amidst the sound of shattering ice. She set to releasing the right. Ice cracked and flaked under repeated blows until it broke free. Growling in triumph, she bent over and smashed the ice constraining her feet.

Leaping from her frozen prison, Belaam paused to observe her surroundings. She had to make sense of things. How had she become trapped in ice? How much time had passed? Was the Sha'Daa close to ending? That the Sha'Daa continued she was certain. The odor of human cattle remained strong, though oddly different from what she remembered. Closing her eyes, she reached out to locate the portal, her way home.

And couldn't sense it.

Panic threatened, but she wrestled it under control. What had happened? Why had the portal vanished? She was uncertain of her fate if she remained beyond the end of Sha'Daa, but suspected she would simply cease to be. It was a mystery, but there was little she could do about it. What she did know was certain. She would see the Sha'Daa through to its end. And after that, accept the consequences.

Her nostrils flared as she inhaled, relishing the faint smell of cattle. Belaam growled content. She would hunt, and feed.

Something was wrong.

Belaam crouched on an icy knoll overlooking a series of buildings, strange buildings far removed from the primitive dwellings she remembered before her accident. They were solid structures of varying shapes and sizes, both in look and smell, or more precisely, lack of smell, and crafted from some alien material. The ground about them was artificially flat, covered in a black tar-like substance that snaked into the distance. Some kind of path leading to another village, she guessed. Evenly spaced markings decorated the substance, primarily before the largest of the buildings. Between a set of markings sat what appeared to be a metallic wagon. She wrinkled her snout, focusing on the familiar odor of cattle, and promptly ignored the strange artifact. As near as she could tell the humans resided in the large dwelling. Concentrating, separating the various smells, many of them puzzlingly unfamiliar, she determined there were at least four.

Belaam growled with contentment. She was famished. She hadn't realized the extent of her hunger until breaking free of the ice and sensing prey. And now with her quarry so agonizingly close, the greater her appetite became. She would feast well before Sha'Daa came to an end. Her clawed hand swiped at the thick drool oozing from her maw.

Slipping off the knoll's reverse slope, Belaam loped across the open ground, her clawed feet digging into the soft snow as muscular legs propelled her demonic body at an extraordinary pace. She observed neither guard nor hunting party, leading her to believe the cattle of this odd village had grown complacent, if not overly bold. Perhaps they believed her dead, and had little to fear. She growled; a low grumble of malevolence. She would show them fear.

Pausing on the edge of the blackened surface, she warily scanned for signs of movement or hints of a trap, but saw neither. A faint sound, like metal on metal, drew her attention to the large building. A door swung open. Exploding into action, she raced across the odd surface, the claws of her feet clattering loudly as she bore down on the entrance.

A figure appeared. Belaam determined it was female. The cattle halted mid-stride, her eyes wide with a shock that descended swiftly into fear. Belaam smelt the fear, and even though it heightened her hunger, she paused, sensing a difference. Instead of heavy furs, this female was clad in unusual clothing of a type completely unfamiliar. She sniffed. The garments had come from no animal, possessing an odor impossible to place.

The female cattle screamed, breaking the spell, and retreated into the building, shouting. Belaam growled and bunched her legs, lunging forward and striking the door before it closed, grunting with surprise at its extremely hard surface. The door flew open, striking the interior wall with a resounding clang. The female cattle screamed again as she was thrown from the impact to slide across the floor.

An equally startled Belaam stumbled into the dwelling and landed hard on her stomach, drawing a shocked grunt. Instinctively rolling to her feet, she briefly absorbed her surroundings, realizing they were unlike anything she had encountered before. But that was something to ponder later.

Movement and voices arose from someplace deep within the building. The female cattle splayed on the floor continued to shout and scream while backing away like some frenzied crab. Belaam bared her teeth and loped forward. Stopping before her quarry, Belaam spared a moment to relish the sheer terror emanating from the female. But when the voices grew louder, she grunted in resignation as her clawed hand lunged out to sweep across the human's exposed throat, sending the female into a gurgling paroxysm of death.

Rounding a corner, Belaam entered a long corridor and spotted two more cattle several strides away. They were male, and dressed similarly to the dead female. They had stopped at her appearance, and stood rooted in place. Suddenly one spoke and both turned, running.

Belaam grunted and followed, catching both in three long strides. A powerful sweep from her clawed hand near decapitated one of them, his blood flying in great spurts against the walls, across the ceiling and along the floor. The second she grabbed by the crown of the head, hoisting him off the ground to face her at eye level. The man's terror was exquisite, and her long, raspy tongue swept across long serrated teeth. Taking her other hand, she slowly twisted the head completely around, relishing the sound of cracking bones. She let the body drop.

Three meals now, she thought. However, she sensed one more. Prowling along the corridor, Belaam came to a strange door that was part metal and part open. She reached out. The opening had substance, solid to the touch. It was a window. Windows she was familiar with, though not on this plane. It was yet another mystery to digest. Beyond the window sat a second female. This one glared at her with a mix of defiance and fear. She was talking, though Belaam could see nor sense any other cattle in the area. Perhaps the human called upon her gods.

Growling in contentment, Belaam broke down the door and advanced. This made four. She would feed extremely well.

Satiated, Belaam wiped at the blood that covered her snout, licking the crimson liquid off her claws one at a time. Standing amidst the gutted remains of the cattle, she grew curious about the strange dwelling and set out to cautiously explore it. However, beyond simple items like beds, tables, chairs and some utensils, she could make no sense of the majority of items, and soon grew frustrated with her lack of understanding.

A voice startled her, and she cast about for its source. Her nostrils flexed, but she could neither smell nor sense anything out of the ordinary. The voice continued. Curious, Belaam tracked its source to the room where she had culled the second female. The voice appeared to emanate from a device on the wall. Growling, she grabbed it in one large hand and ripped the offensive thing free. The voice stopped. Satisfied, she tossed it into a corner.

The silence was short, as another sound caught her attention, a steadily growing noise that resembled a high-pitched windstorm swirling somewhere outside the building.

She raced for the exit, her inner eyelids closing to reduce the effect of the blinding sun, and scanned the sky. What she saw puzzled her. Sweeping into view roared some giant metal construct, some metallic bird, floating effortlessly in the cloudless sky and approaching fast.

Exposed as she was, Belaam wavered between reentering the dwelling or seeking safety in the rough, snow-covered landscape. Anger swelled at her fleeting sense of uncertainty. Shameful. Whatever approached, she would face and fight.

The construct reached the large building and hovered, casting a continuously driving wind that churned snow and dust, forcing her to retreat several steps against her will. Annoyed at giving ground, Belaam spread her muscular arms, bared serrated teeth and issued a long, deep challenge.

An opening appeared along the side of the metal bird and a figure appeared. Belaam allowed a moment of triumph. For all its strangeness, the thing was inhabited by human cattle, and cattle were weak and easy to kill. She had to bring the thing to ground.

Over the noise produced by the construct came a series of sharp cracks, causing the ground before Belaam to erupt in a spray of debris. She leaped back, puzzled. The cattle she was used to hunting were armed with primitive flint-tipped spears or leather thongs capable of slinging rocks. Belaam was no fool. She could be injured, possibly killed, even though she possessed a hide that was impervious to all but the most determined blow. But the force of this unknown weapon had penetrated the solid surface at her feet with power, and Belaam knew it posed a serious threat. It was time to digest this new danger and formulate a response.

Turning, she bolted for the snow-covered rocks as the weapon sounded again and debris kicked around her. A sudden grunt of pain tore from her muzzle as something struck her lower left leg. Staggering from its force, she managed to recover and reach the protection of the deep crevices and sharp overhangs.

Crouching in shadow, Belaam examined her leg. Whatever had struck it had passed through. Ignoring the pain, she let it be as her accelerated recuperative powers congealed the dark blood. Soon it would scab over.

Meanwhile the construct approached, and Belaam wondered if it had discerned her hiding place. But it passed overhead, traveled for a distance and then came about, following yet another path. Belaam grunted satisfaction. It couldn't find her. Leaning back, she waited, closing her multiple eyelids and allowing thoughts of home.

Eventually the noise drifted into the distance until it ceased altogether. Belaam crept from the dark shadows to examine her surroundings and immediately caught the scent of cattle. Moving carefully across the rough ground, she reached the knoll that oversaw the buildings. She was not surprised to find the metal construct settled on the black surface. At least two figures stood beside it, each holding what were probably weapons. Moments later another pair of humans hurriedly exited the large dwelling, one doubling over to spew liquid. Belaam growled softly, chuckling at the obvious sign of weakness.

The humans gathered into an animated group, gesturing and pointing in all directions. Belaam suspected they discussed a form of response. A male, for she had determined from their scent all were male, entered the construct. When he returned he swept his arm in her general direction. Three humans set out, leaving one to guard the metal bird. She decided she would circle around, kill the lone guard and destroy the construct. Then her hunt would begin in earnest.

"You really stirred the hornet's nest, you know."

Belaam swung around, growling with surprise and sweeping viciously with a clawed hand, striking nothing but air.

A male stood just beyond reach, grinning. She noted the gold tooth. Crouching, her claws flexed and her muscles tensed as she made to leap.

The male held up a hand. "I wouldn't do that."

She leapt and struck the opposite wall, the impact stunning her as she slipped to the ground.

"I told you."

Shaking to clear her head, Belaam noted the man occupied the spot she had leapt from. She gathered herself again.

The male continued to grin. "We can do this all day, you know. Now, aren't you at all curious how it is you can understand me?"

Belaam paused. He was right. In her shock and rage she had missed the obvious. She relaxed and sniffed, her muzzle crinkling with confusion. He had no scent, which explained how he managed to surprise her.

He said, "You don't remember me?"

Belaam peered closer. A distant memory of a faraway place and time came to her. "You," she growled. She swept a dismissive hand. "I did not recognize you in that ridiculous garb."

The man glanced down at his clothes: a suit and trench coat. "I rather like the outfit, if I do say so myself." He moved to a rock and sat, then motioned her to do the same. "People call me Johnny these days." He pursed his thin lips. "You've been gone a long time, you know."

The demon snorted. "Nonsense. This is the Sha'Daa. Why else would you be here?"

Johnny nodded. "A fair question. The simple answer, one I'm sure you'll find hard to believe, is this is not your Sha'Daa."

Belaam opened and closed her maw, speechless and confused.

"Is it not obvious?" he continued. "Your cattle (as you so fondly refer to them) dressed in furs and were armed with spears and slings. Their villages were of ice, rock, wood and thatch. Have you found any evidence of that here?"

Belaam gave her rendition of a shrug.

"Of course you haven't. That's because you've been frozen these past ten thousand years, from the time of the last Sha'Daa. You've awakened in a different time, a time that's populated with extremely advanced cattle. Cattle that bite back."

For the first time Belaam felt a twinge of fear. This explained why she had sensed no portal. The rift between planes allowing her passage was long closed. Baring her teeth, she grunted and jerked a clawed thumb. "They are not as dangerous as you say. I fed on four in that dwelling."

The man nodded. "Because they were unarmed and unaware of the Sha'Daa, or you. You merely killed four people occupying a far north observation post called Saglek." He raised a finger. "Now I agree, these cattle remain physically weak, but their weapons are not." He pointed at her leg. "How is that wound?"

Belaam growled.

"As I thought. One bullet caused it. Those hunting you have weapons capable of firing hundreds more. They will rip you to shreds. I've seen it happen."

Belaam pondered her situation. If she was truly stranded, she would remain alone until death claimed her. If that was the way of it, she would not die without a fight. Standing, she growled.

Johnny raised a hand, sensing her decision. "There's no reason to die needlessly. I can arrange your safe return."

Belaam slowly settled, her muzzle crinkling with sudden curiosity.

"Silver," he said.

She nodded understanding. Silver would work. It would be painful, but it would work. "You have a weapon? A blade?" she asked hopefully.

Johnny shook his head. "You forget. I am forbidden to interfere."

Belaam grunted. "Then why offer me this false hope? Small wonder they call you the Trickster."

"Now that hurt."

"And furthermore, why would you care if I live or die?"

"That's simple. This is not your Sha'Daa. You shouldn't even be here. And, well, let's just say it would be a favor for a friend."

"A friend? What friend?"

Johnny frowned. "Would you explain the reason you do what you do to a human?"

Belaam snorted. "Of course not." She lapsed into silence. The man seated before her could end her existence with the snap of his fingers. She sighed. "Point taken."

"Smart. Now, back to the blade. The deed must be done by someone other than me, and thankfully you're in luck. I can think of four candidates, at least one of whom is nearby."

Belaam resisted the urge to poke her head up and take a look. "Does he carry silver?" she asked.

The man stood. "Leave that part to me."

"Explain again why I should trust you?"

Johnny wagged his finger. "No explanations. Remember? Just call it a leap of faith. I know that's a strange concept for a demon. Now, let me talk to our candidate and convince him this is the only way to kill you."

Belaam grunted assent. "While you talk, I shall kill and feed on the others."

Johnny quickly shook his head. His voice grew stern. "No more feeding. Remember, this is not your Sha'Daa."

The demon snarled, displaying serrated teeth. "Very well, then. Bring the cattle. I shall wait." She blinked as the man simply vanished. Curious, she climbed from the safety of her hiding spot to find Johnny standing several dozen feet away, talking to an obviously surprised and agitated male. The conversation went on for several minutes, with much gesticulating and waving of hands. Finally, some kind of exchange was made. Belaam saw a long, silver knife leave Johnny's hand, but couldn't tell what was offered in return. Then, pointing directly toward her, Johnny led the human over.

They stopped before her. Belaam smelt intense fear on the male. She growled, showing her teeth.

Johnny waved an admonishing finger. "Don't spook the cattle. He's on edge as it is. He doesn't exactly trust me."

"The feeling is mutual."

"Then you both have something in common. Are you ready?"

Belaam thrust out her chest. "Make sure he strikes true."

"I will."

"I would thank you, Trickster, but it is not my way."

"I know."

The male cautiously approached. Belaam watched as Johnny indicated where to strike, and the amount of force to use. The man nervously nodded. The knife came up, paused, and sharply descended.

The pain was intense at first, but with the oncoming darkness came a sense of relief. A light appeared before her, a portal to her plane. She reached out, heard a cry of fright as the human cattle struggled to break free of her grasp. A shout of surprise from the one who now called himself Johnny, followed by his fading curse caused Belaam to growl with satisfaction. She was going home, and she had a snack.

*   *   *

INTERLUDE FOURTEEN

The main assault was far worse than Ashley could have imagined. The first wave came all too quick.

Given only a fifteen-minute warning, the pawnshop owner barricaded all doorways and stacked hastily filled sandbags up against the interior of all ground floor windows to created fortified firing positions. Only about fifty of her customers had elected to stay when she announced the evacuation, and they were all busily helping her staff prepare for hostilities.

Ashley had just sent Barrax down to the cellar to recruit any of the five hundred sanctuary tenants who were willing to help protect their protector.

Ashley pushed a stepladder up against the wall and smashed her padded elbow against the glass-fronted display case. With reverence, and using both hands, she clasped and removed the large spear, the symbol of justice among the last tribe of Africans who had worshipped Astraea.

Forty of the refugees, the most bellicose of the diverse group of separatists and neutrals, poured up from the basement and were quickly armed and positioned by Barrax by every window and doorway. Minutes later it began.

"Ashley," a voice boomed in Gaelic from outside, "your defenses are impressive, but no match for an attack of this scale. Release all of your cowards who hide below. They have betrayed their Sha'Daa masters. Do this now and you, and you alone, might be spared."

Barrax glanced out the window and blanched. "Their leader is a saurian," he said, "ummm… a big one."

"Step aside," Ashley said. She ran forward and threw a grenade out the open window, overhand, like a professional baseball player. A moment later an explosion shook the roof and was followed by a massive thud and a gargantuan growl of pain.

"Holy shit," Barrax yelled, "you just blasted one of the giant bastard's legs off. Dropped him like a redwood."

"Attack," the fallen saurian howled in agony. One hundred hell-spawn charged every window and door.

"Fire," Ashley yelled.

Arrows, javelins, Teflon coated bullets, armor piercing ammo, darts, shot, and foul language poured out of every path of ingress to the pawn shop. The attackers started dropping in twos and threes, and then by the dozens, falling over each other, and finally piling up and blocking all four ground level doors into the shop. Multicolored gore spilled all about the outside of the building, making it look like a psychedelic set piece for a Doctor Seuss movie. Five minutes after the assault began it was over, the opposing forces annihilated.

A small amount of offensive ordnance managed to penetrate the shop proper, killing two werewolves and wounding about one dozen aliens, C.H.U.D.S., and moon maidens.

"Get the wounded and dead to the basement," Ashley yelled, "and reload. No way this is all they're throwing at us."

"Yahtzee, you fat bastard," Turbo's voice echoed from the side room. "I win the whole fucking till. Come to poppa."

"You pasty little freak," Gronk's megaphone voice bellowed, ""if I ever find out you cheated, I will haunt your reincarnated ass into oblivion."

* * *

CHAPTER FIFTEEN: SOUL PROVIDER

by Jamie K. Schmidt

Salame left the crowd watching the poker game with a vague feeling of unease. Two twin brothers, both former Gods, were battling it out Texas Hold 'Em style. Roger was playing for the demons and Kenneth for the humans. Salame would have liked to have seen a greater chip lead, but they were well matched and the game seemed to go on forever. The crowd was restless and she could see things might get violent if there wasn't more drama at the table.

Of course, when Irini put itching powder on her Uncle's pants, that did liven things up, but it also stopped the game. Then there were bets as to whether Roger would kill his niece and if Kenneth would die to save her. Sometimes there was nothing more dramatic than a Friday night in Vegas.

It was a shame really that the brothers never got a chance to know the girl. Irini's mother, Talia "Aces High" Santana was a half-demon and a poker player. She bet that she could screw with Fate, but Fate buried the pot and Talia cashed out when her daughter was a few months old. Of course, Talia never told Kenneth he was a father. Salame didn't think it would have mattered, no matter how much Kenneth told himself it would have been different.

Salame raised Irini. She taught the girl a trade and how to protect herself. It was as close to a motherly instinct as Salame had.

She leaned over and kissed her major domo on the cheek.

"What was that for?" Frenchie asked.

"Do I have to have a reason to show you affection?"

He considered her question. "Usually you have ulterior motives."

"Stay at the table. Make sure Irini doesn't interfere again. Danal will kill her."

"I am not a babysitter." He sniffed, affronted.

"You are what I say you are." Salame narrowed her eyes at him, dropping the glamour so he saw the anger in her red, goat-like eyes.

Frenchie swallowed hard and looked away. "Of course, Mistress. I will keep an eye on the little whore."

"Good luck with that." Salame shook her head. Irini was a handful even before her father traded the Salesman his lucky dice for her contract. As a freelance hooker, Irini would create havoc and chaos. It almost brought a nostalgic tear to her eye for her own youth so many centuries ago.

She watched Frenchie saunter back to the table, talking to a few demons and accepting their bets. Salame felt a trill of unease down her spine. She wanted to be back in her own casino on Fremont Street, where the fighting hadn't reached yet. Taking the portal, she was beamed into her office. The glittering shine of diamonds welcomed her. Diamond Dreams Casino, where you could bet your soul that you'd wind up with your heart's desire. Salame smiled. For a price.

Demons were battling humans all over the world. But tonight in Las Vegas, things were status quo. Tourists were zip-lining down the street, spilling beer on the people below and hooting like it was the last night of the world – which it just might be. She should have felt comforted. No matter who won, her place was assured. As a half-demon, Salame had the best of both worlds. If the humans won, she would still be managing this casino. If the demons won, there would be no need to replace her. She was safe and had the luxury of watching the Armageddon from a ring side seat.

Easing herself into her plush desk chair, she switched on the cameras and searched until she found what was making her itch like an infected mosquito bite.

"I thought I sensed you, Salesman," she hissed, tuning out the background noise so she could hear his conversation. She veered the camera in to capture the fifteen-year-old hooker who was hurrying away from him.

"Irini, wait," the Salesman said. He gripped her arm and almost yanked her off her five inch heels.

"Johnny, forget it. My days of turning tricks are over. At least until I blow through this stash." Irini was young enough that her beauty was still a fragile, lovely thing, unless you looked into her deep, brown eyes.

"I want you to consider my proposal."

"What proposal? I don't see no ring. We're in Vegas, for Chrissakes on the verge of Armageddon. There's enough wedding chapels. Pick one and get me there. Or go away and let me be."

"Earth isn't safe."

Salame leaned forward eagerly. Was the Salesman admitting that the demons had the upper hand? She crossed her legs and upped the volume as her assistant, a cat demon with the most lovely, green eyes opened the door to tell her something.

"Not now," Salame ordered.

"It's not that kind of proposal," the Salesman gritted out between his teeth.

"Then I'm not interested. Too many freebies ain't good for business. Besides, I have an interview with Danal at the Galaxie tomorrow morning. I'm going to be a showgirl."

"You're too short."

"Oooh, you!" Irini wrenched her arm away and stalked up the stairs and headed for the buffet.

"All you need to do is trade me something and I can provide you with safe passage."

"I've heard that before. You can at least buy me dinner." She angled her head toward the cashier at the front of the buffet line.

"No need," said a slim man with a suit pressed so sharp it would cut, literally. He offered Irini two vouchers. "Compliments of the house."

While Irini thanked him enthusiastically, the Salesman glared up at the camera.

Salame blew a kiss.

"What is that all about, Mistress?" The cat demon said, curling around Salame. She rubbed him behind the ears.

"I don't know, but I think Zerifiah might be interested in this conversation."

"I thought you liked Irini."

"She's a good worker, but I think we may have found her niche."

"I will summon Zerifiah."

"You do that," Salame said and fiddled with the cameras and sound until she was watching the Salesman again.

"Look," Irini said, cracking a crab leg the size of the table. "You're not the boss of me no more. You gave up my contract to dear old Dad and he gave it to me. I ripped it up. I'm not leaving Earth. I'm not in the market for another pimp. I'm going to freelance it and you can shove your twenty percent."

"The world is changing. Maybe irrevocably. In less than twenty-four hours all this," he waved his hand, "could be gone. Every ten thousand years."

Irini lowered her voice and her head. "You think I don't know about the Sha'Daa? You think I didn't have demons for customers? It's triple the money. And if you let them drink your blood...."

"What about your soul?"

"How much is it worth? I ain't using it at the moment."

"I'm offering you a trip to Callisto. It's a moon of Jupiter."

"Can I breathe the air?"

"Of course, there have been special parts of it designed for Earthlings."

"Like a prison?"

"It's a very nice place. Think of it as a vacation."

"A vacation I can't leave. Unless you're going to teach me how to dimension travel."

"You don't have the bank to trade for that knowledge."

Irini seemed to think about that while jawing down on yet another crab leg. "My soul should be enough. I've got Daddy's blood. That makes me half a God, right?"

The salesman laughed. "Technically, but no one knows you exist. No one to worship means you haven't any power."

"I'm not helpless."

"Never that, Irini dear. You've always been a favorite of mine."

"Then how come you and me," she gestured with the crab leg, "never did it? Is it because I'm a whore?"

"We're all whores, Irini."

"So if you're not too good for me, why?"

"Because sex is meaningless."

"Of course it is," Irini said. "It's a biological function, like taking a shit."

The salesman closed his eyes. "This is getting us nowhere. Now, be a good girl. Trade me your soul for teleporting to safety."

"Once I'm there, how do I survive? Do they take our money?"

"You're a resourceful girl. You'll have to make your own way."

"No thanks," Irina said with a mouthful of crab.

"What do you mean, no thanks?"

She swallowed. "I mean I'll stay here. The devil you know and all. Get it?" She jabbed him with another crab leg.

Johnny snapped his fingers and the casino went dark.

"Damn him!" Salame raged as the power reset itself and the computers rebooted. She lost camera. She lost sound.

"Is there a problem, Salame?"

Salame felt the ice prickle up the back of her neck and she looked up to see Zerifiah hanging from the ceiling on a silken cord. Zerifiah was a spider demon the color of old blood. Her many eyes tracked more than the physical plane. She spun her way down to Salame's desk, her legs lithe, deadly and nimble. Poison pooled onto Salame's expense reports and the desk sizzled slightly.

"Zerifiah," Salame nodded and held her out her wrist in the traditional greeting. She managed not to flinch when the spider struck, but she couldn't resist gripping her fingers into the arms of the chair as the poison burned through her veins.

Zerifiah detached her fangs and settled her bulk in. "Tell me why you have disturbed me."

The venom made her tell the truth. "I think we can take an important soul away from the side of the Light."

"We have over 100,000 souls feeding our power to break the portal, what will one more do to the gate?"

"The salesman is trying to get her to leave Earth tonight. He seemed almost desperate for her soul."

"Indeed?" Zerifiah said. "I'll take it from here. Get the power back online. We're losing money."

"As you command," Salame whispered as her muscles spasmed once and her system was flooded with excruciating pain.

Zerifiah stroked a leg down her cheek and crawled over her to the door. In a heated shimmer, she transformed to the very model of corporate American drone. "You were delicious, as always," she said and strode out the door.

Finding the human Salame had spoken of was easy, even in the sea of humanity that pulsed through the casino. All Zerifiah had to do was scent the stench of the Salesman. She followed it to where a dejected girl sat on a folding chair, making up lies into the application she was filling out. Zerifiah looked around, but the Salesman was nowhere to be seen.

She watched as the girl stood up, squared her shoulders and handed in the clipboard with a bravado that would have cowed another human. But the desk clerk was demon and said, "Thank you. We'll be in touch."

"Don't I even get an interview?"

"We don't have any openings right now."

"But I can do anything. I'm willing to work my way up. I've got mad skills." The girl lowered her voice provocatively. "I'll do anything for a chance. Over and over again? You get me?"

When the desk clerk gaped at her unsure how to continue, Zerifiah walked up. "I'll take it from here."

"Who are you?" The girl looked up with a challenge and tossed her hair.

"I'm the owner. And you are?"

The girl switched to simper with a touch of swoon. "Oh, I'm so happy to meet you. My name is Irini Dujoie."

Zerifiah took her hand as the name registered as one of the pros that freelanced for Salame. What was Salame thinking? "And what can I do for you?"

"I want to be a dancer."

"Have you any professional experience?"

"Lots."

"Such as?"

"Broadway, the Met, you name it."

"I see." Zerifiah tilted her head. "I'm sure you're very talented."

"I get no complaints."

"Perhaps we can reach an accord. Let's go up to my office."

"Oh, sure," Irini said. "I can do girls, but it's been awhile."

"That won't be necessary."

Irini shrugged. Zerifiah led her to a hidden bank of elevators and pressed the top floor penthouse.

"Tell me a little about yourself, dear."

"Well, I'm a dancer."

"You've said that. What sets you apart from the hundreds of other dancers I get applications from?"

"I'm not afraid of demons."

Zerifiah locked gazes with her in the mirrored doors of the elevator. "And why not?"

"They're just like us. I mean superior to us," Irini finished quickly.

Zerifiah adjusted her features with a small snort. "I see."

"I figure if you guys win the war that my Dad is out there playing against my Uncle for, I'll still have a job. If you lose, I'll still have a job."

The doors opened and held for a few minutes while Zerifiah tried to regain her composure. Salame might have mentioned this was The Gambler's daughter. Holding the girl's arm gently, she guided her into the penthouse. "Your father is very talented."

"He's a hack compared to my mother."

"Your mother?" Zerifiah said, leading Irini to a padded couch.

"Talia Santana. Although you might have known her as Aces High."

Zerifiah was stunned for the second time. Salame would definitely be punished for keeping this information hidden. "Aces High" had been a luck demon who was killed for giving her powers to a lover. And now her daughter, a half demon/half god sat in her chambers looking for a job.

"I can give you your heart's desire," Zerifiah breathed, and felt the pounding of a million demons beating at the portal. It felt like her heartbeat. It was her future.

"My heart is pretty big," Irini said.

"Name your price."

"What are you offering?"

"Everything you desire, for your soul to take."

Irini got up. "Everyone seems to want a piece of that action. Johnny said you'd ask for that."

"He has his own plans and his own plots."

"He always did," Irini said.

"Ask and ye shall receive."

"I want to headline my own show."

"Done."

"I'm not finished. If the demons win the Sha'Daa, I want immunity from harm for me…"

"Done."

"And my father."

"D – err that's going to be difficult because he'll most likely be eaten by the spectators around his poker table. He's playing against us. That's not going to endear him to the victors. Wouldn't you rather save your dear old Uncle? He has his priorities straight. I'm going to make him the King of Las Vegas."

"What about Elvis?"

"He's as dead as your dear father will be."

"Not negotiable."

Zerifiah sighed. "I'll have to make a few phone calls."

"I'll wait."

"Of course you will."

Calling in a few favors, Zerifiah was able to confirm that they would shove Kenneth into a portal and transfer him into Salame's office at the conclusion of the battle, which was going on well into the night.

"Very well. You'll be a headliner and you and your wretched father will be granted immunity from the demons' wrath. Now agree to the deal and let us sign a contract."

"I'm not done."

Zerifiah shifted into her spider form.

Irini shrieked and jumped up on the couch, her heels poking holes in the leather.

"You stupid child. Hurry up for I am losing patience. I'll wrap you up and keep you as a snack and you'll be begging me to take your soul."

"If you take it under duress, it lessens the effect."

"And how do you know that?"

"The Salesman told me."

"He is an insufferable busybody."

"He also told me something else."

"I'm all ears."

"No, you're all legs."

Zerifiah pounced wrapping the legs around her and sinking her fangs into Irini's throat, injecting the venom into her veins. A stream of silk pooled from her spinneret as Zerifiah began to weave. Irini whimpered and Zerifiah unlatched from her throat. "What was that, my dear?"

"He also told me something else," Irini's eyes were closed and her voice soft and pained.

"Quickly now, soon you'll be unable to move." Zerifiah wound her silk around Irini's ankles.

"That if I traded my soul to him, he'd give me some of his immunities and protections for a brief time."

"That's a sucker's bet."

"Totally. I negotiated that if he wanted my soul he had to pony up more. I took his dumb protections, but he's also going to put in a good word for me with Danal for the new Hoofin' it with Hooters revue."

"I will kill you first," Zerifiah said and lunged again, but her fangs locked and her legs seized. Irini kicked her and rolled off the couch.

Salame was just getting feeling back in her hands when the intercom buzzed.

Mistress, you are needed in Zerifiah's penthouse."

A cold feeling of dread shuddered down her back. No one left Zerifiah's penthouse happy. In fact, most never left. "Tell Frenchie I said it was fun."

"Oh Mistress…."

Salame walked to the elevator with her head held high. She was noble – born to a human king and a demon princess. The spider might outrank her by being a pureblood, but she would never be her equal.

The doors of the elevators opened into the penthouse revealing Zerifiah on her back, those eight barbed limbs crumpled in death and Irini trying to saw through her silken binds with a champagne saber.

"Aunt Sal, can you give me a hand here. I've got an interview tomorrow and I'm going to need my legs."

*　*　*

INTERLUDE FIFTEEN

The second wave of attackers was much like the first: an awkward mix of magical earth-spawn, extraterrestrial creatures, and semi-corporeal entities. And just like the earlier charge, they favored mass attacks at all the obvious entry points to the shop. Projectile weapons of every kind unleashed pain, terror, and death in both directions.

This time several hell-spawn managed to smash their way in through the windows and kill eight defenders before being brought down.

Barrax lopped the head off an ogre with a backhanded swing of his nineteenth-century kukri knife.

Frank unloaded petrified wood shot from his sawed-off into two fearsome life-force vampires, disintegrating them in a shower of sparks.

When the fighting stopped, Ashley realized she and Barrax had suffered minor cuts that they quickly bound. Once again Ashley had her dwindling staff clear the main floor of casualties to prepare for what she felt in her gut would be an even harsher third attack.

"You plan on lending a hand some time?" Ashley whispered to herself.

Patience my dear, Astraea replied in the shop proprietor's mind. I will arise when truly needed.

This reply sent a sickening chill of foreboding through Ashley.

A moment later the distant but ever approaching rumble of hundreds of feet echoed through the surrounding streets of Dingle. Soon, every mounted or shelved item in the store rattled and shook along the walls.

"I've got a bad feeling about this," Frank said.

"Knuckle up," Ashley growled. "This is the big one."

Five hundred hell-spawn surged through the surrounding streets and charged the pawn shop.

* * *

CHAPTER SIXTEEN: TIME FOR A CHANGE

by Larry Atchley, Jr.

Billie Ray put his foot down on the accelerator of the old 66 Chevy Impala SS convertible as they rocketed down the hot, dusty Mojave desert highway on the first day of summer. The sun was high above in the sky on the longest day of the year, and the world the sun would rise upon tomorrow would be a very different one than today, if everything went according to plan.

"Woo hoo!" shouted Lita. She held her hands up in the hot dry air, and her long bleached blond hair whipped around in the wind. "We are gonna lay down some heavy tracks today, Billy Ray! Yes sir-ree, man. I feel something blowing in the wind. Feels like a change is a'coming."

"Put your damn arms down, Lita. The only thing blowing in the wind is your armpits!" Billy Ray said with a Texan drawl.

"Hey, that's no way to talk to a lady," Lita returned in her Southern California accent.

"You show me a lady and I'll talk nice to her," Billy Ray said, his thick short dark hair blew back from a receding hairline on his forehead.

"Aw, come on now, Dude, I'm just excited to get back in the studio, man. Aren't you?"

"Not if this album flops like the last one. I'm sick and tired of working my ass off, making music no one wants to buy, and playing gigs at dives for chump change," Billy Ray said.

"Don't fuck up my positive vibes with all your negative energy, Okay?" Lita said.

"Yeah, whatever. Tell your positive vibes to sell some more of our damn songs. And while you're at it tell them to get us a big label contract so we can all be filthy rich."

"It don't work like that, man. You got to channel your own positive energy in the direction of your ultimate goal. Visualize it, push yourself toward it, and it will happen. It just takes time, that's all. We all can make our own fate, choose our destiny. You just have to believe strongly enough in it to make it happen," Lita said.

"Yeah, well it sounds like you've been reading too much of that wacky Eastern meditation crap. I don't buy into that bullshit."

"Whatever, man. Just keep going through life with your mind closed, and see where it gets you," Lita replied.

Lita's got a lot of crazy ideas, Billy Ray thought, and she can't keep from running her mouth about stupid shit. But she's one hell of a musician, that's for sure. Put damn near any instrument in her hands and she can make it wail and moan like it was her lover. Otherwise, I wouldn't put up with her bullshit nonsense. Well, I won't have to put up with it for much longer. She is right about one thing though. A big change is coming, and damn soon.

Billy Ray pulled the big car into the dirt and gravel driveway of the recording studio and parked it in front of a one-story building, really just an old adobe house out in the middle of nowhere in the California desert. He saw Pete's white van parked around the side of the house.

"I hope they got the drums already set up. I hate waiting around doing nothing," Billy Ray said as he got out of the car. Lita opened up the trunk and took out an old beat up black guitar case. They walked into the house and saw Pete and Joey putting the last of Pete's drum kit together, screwing the Y bolts down on the crash and ride cymbals. Cords of sinewy muscles stood out on Pete's forearms.

"Hey guys, about time you made it! What took you so long?" Pete asked, with a Bronx accent that hadn't disappeared despite ten years of living in California, as he looked up and shook his shoulder-length, light-brown hair out of his eyes.

"We had to make a little detour so Billy Ray could pick up some equipment along the way," Lita replied.

"Sound equipment? A new amp, or what? " Joey asked, as he ran a hand through thick, dark, curly locks of hair falling almost to his waist. "Where is it? Let's take a look."

"I bet it's one of those fancy effects boards," Pete said.

"Forget about it for now. It ain't nothing like that. This is something different. I want to play around with it later, but not here. It's kind of a surprise," Billy Ray said.

A really big surprise for you boneheads, Billy Ray thought.

"Okay Billy Ray. Whatever you say, man," Joey said.

A man, in maybe his mid-thirties, with long blond hair and a full beard, walked into the room just then.

"You must be Billy Ray. I'm Kenny, the studio tech. We talked on the phone. Nice to meet you in person," he said as he offered a handshake to Billy Ray.

"Yeah, hey, nice to meet you," Billy Ray said as he shook his hand firmly but quickly. "This is Lita. She's our guitarist, and pretty much plays any other instrument we need played that these two guys can't cover. I guess you've already met Joey and Pete."

"Yep," Kenny said.

"Cool, man, awesome. So you're the dude whose gonna help us dial in our sound, right man?" Lita said.

"That's the idea," replied Kenny, who smiled at Lita.

They set up the rest of the equipment in the studio. Joey's bass guitar, Lita's six-string electric and acoustic guitars, her keyboard, and the microphone for Billy Ray. A few other instruments lay around the room; an alto saxophone, a trumpet, and a fiddle, which were all Lita's. They got down to the business of rehearsing some songs and recording a few tracks over the course of the next several hours.

"Alright, I think we need to take a break. I don't know about y'all but I'm starving!" Billy Ray finally said.

"Hell yeah, let's go eat." Joey agreed.

"I could go for some grub right about now," Pete said.

"Damn, I am hungry," Lita said. "I need to recharge my creative batteries anyway. Get away from all this electronic gear and outta this box and be free out in the wide outdoors!"

"Shit, Lita we're just going to dinner, we're not going on a camping trip or nuthin'," Billy Ray said.

"I know this really killer restaurant just a few miles up the road that has some of the best enchiladas you ever put in your mouth," Kenny said, as he shut off the studio equipment.

The five of them left the house, and Billy Ray went around to start his car while Kenny locked up.

"Hey, let's take my Chevy so we can ride in style, right boys?" Billy Ray hollered.

They all piled into the car and Billy Ray revved the engine and pealed out of the gravel driveway, spitting rocks and making a rooster-tail plume of dirt behind them. It didn't take long to reach the restaurant, located all by itself alongside the dusty highway. There were a few cars in the parking lot, but there were plenty of spaces left for the Impala SS. Billy Ray whipped into one and everyone piled out of the convertible.

An attractive redheaded young woman wearing a tight t-shirt and shorts that showed off her curves greeted them.

"Hey Kenny, how many you got with you tonight?" she asked.

"Just five of us, Darla. But give us the big booth in the corner. I think these boys want to stretch out some," Kenny said.

She seated them and passed out menus. Just as they were opening them up, in walked a tall, thin man, wearing a dark suit, long black trenchcoat and a black fedora. He looked like he'd walked right out of a Dashiell Hammett detective story. He carried a black guitar case that looked like it had seen better days, and walked up to their table.

"Well, hello there Lita. About time you came along. Time is running short tonight, you see," said the man smiling. His face was very pale and drawn, and his teeth were sparkling white, like he was some kind of toothpaste spokesperson. Except for one shiny gold incisor in place of the original tooth.

"How do you know my name? I sure think I would've remembered if I'd met the likes of you before, Mister."

"My name's Johnny. They call me The Salesman. I have something for you, Lita. I brought it here especially for you to use tonight, for a very special purpose." He set the case on the table and opened it up. When Lita saw what was inside, her eyes nearly jumped out of her head.

"Holy shit, man! That… that's not what I think it is? It has to be a replica, right?" Lita said in disbelief.

"Nope, it's the real deal. Want to pick it up?" the Salesman offered.

"Sure," Lita said as she carefully took it out of the case and examined it more closely.

"You know what you've got here man? I mean, really what you've got?" Lita asked.

"You're the guitar expert, Lita, you tell me." Johnny said with a smile.

Lita fingered the fret board and played a series of chords. It rang out with a rich resounding clear tone, perfectly in tune.

"Rickenbacker Model 325 hollow body, twelve string electric, made in 1964. That would make it valuable enough, but you see there was only one of these models made in twelve string. A custom model, for a chap from Liverpool named John Lennon. This has to either be a very good replica, or it's priceless. How did you get this? You don't just walk into a roadside diner in the middle of the desert with this. Besides, I don't have the kind of money to buy this guitar even if it's a fake, much less if it's genuine."

The tall, thin, pale man said, "I don't want your money. I want to trade it for something. You still have your lighter, Lita?"

"My lucky lighter?" Lita said, putting down the guitar, and reaching into her pocket and fingering the old worn stainless steel case of the flip-open Zippo lighter. "Yeah, I've got it. How do you know about that?"

"I know a lot of things. I know that someone else tonight needs your luck, Lita," Johnny the Salesman said.

"Lita, this guy is full of shit!" Billy Ray said. "You've had that lighter since you were a young punk teenage chick and found it by the side of the road with that money clip full of twenties. You never go anywhere without it, and you always said you'd be buried with it. You ain't giving up that lighter for nothing," Billy Ray said.

"It is my good luck charm," Lita said, turning the lighter over and over in her hand. "But that is one damn fine-sounding guitar, authentic or not."

"You need this guitar more than you need that lighter, Lita, because you're going to need to play the most important notes of your life tonight," Johnny said.

"Is there a record company scout in the diner?" Lita asked.

"No, but you're going to have to put on a very special performance later tonight," Johnny replied. "You'll know when it's the right time."

"Hey Salesman, why don't you hit the road with your phony collectable and keep your business to yourself," Billy Ray said.

Nothing this joker can do will mess with what's going to happen tonight, Billy Ray thought. I don't know what kind of game he's playing, but we both know he can't interfere with The Sha'Daa. I will open the gate, and nothing the Salesman gives Lita can change that.

"It's not your decision to make Billy Ray," Johnny said. "She has to decide for herself. I can't make you trade for the guitar, Lita. It's your choice. But we both know you want it. There's a lot depending on you, Lita – more than you know."

"Hey, dude, yeah," Lita said. "You know, I've had this feeling all day, like something big was going to happen. Like a heavy change was going down, you know? I think you might be on to something about my needing it for something special. I'll take your trade salesman. I don't care if it's a replica or not, it's a damn fine guitar."

Lita held her hand out with the lighter in it to Johnny.

"Here you go. It has brought me a lot of good luck over the years. I hope it's lucky for the next guy," she said to Johnny.

"It will be, I assure you," Johnny said, as he took the lighter and put it in his trench coat pocket.

"I must be going. Time is running short and I have much still to do. Have a good night," Johnny said as he tipped his fedora, just before he turned and walked out of the restaurant.

"Strange dude," Kenny remarked.

"What a crackpot!" Billy Ray said.

They ate a hearty meal of hot spicy enchiladas, rice, and beans and washed it down with plenty of cold beer, then piled back into the Impala. Lita put the guitar in the trunk next to the small wooden crate that Billy Ray had left there. They got back on the highway headed away from the direction to the studio.

"Hey Billy Ray, you're going the wrong way. Studio's back West," Kenny said.

"I want to show you guys this place I found out about not too far from here. I think you'll all like it," Billy Ray said.

He drove a few miles along the highway in the hot dusty Mojave desert night air, and turned down a side road, and then another, until they came to a large white dome-shaped building. A sign out front read: Integratron. Billy Ray pulled into the small parking lot, turned off the car and got out along with the others. He went around to the trunk and opened it up, taking the small wooden crate and an electric lantern which he turned on.

"I've been here before," Kenny said. "It's an acoustic sound chamber. Pretty awesome place. It amplifies sound naturally in a way no other sound room I've ever been in does. It's built on top of a powerful energy vortex. Some guy back in the fifties built it because aliens told him it would help mankind live longer, and become one with the universe or something. I didn't think they were open this late though."

"They're not," Billy Ray said. "This is a surprise visit. We're breaking into the place. I've got something special I want to show you guys, and I don't need any caretakers meddling around with me and what I need to do."

Mankind is about to become one with the universe all right, Billy Ray thought.

"Whoa, hey, I don't know about that, man," Kenny said. "You could get us all arrested if somebody found out."

"Yeah, Kenny's right," Pete said. "This is crazy."

Joey and Lita both looked at each other, worried expressions on their faces.

"What the hell are you doing, Billy Ray?" Joey asked.

"Chill out will ya!" Billy Ray said. "We're not going to get caught. Don't you guys want to see the surprise?"

There were murmurs of consent as the other four seemed resigned to the fact that they were curious enough to play along with whatever Billy Ray had in mind.

"If the sound is so good in there like Kenny says, I want to play my guitar inside it," Lita said, getting the old case out of the trunk.

"Sure, whatever, Lita," Billy Ray said. "Just stay out of my way when I'm setting this thing up," he said, motioning to the small wooden crate he was carrying by a handle screwed into the lid. He pulled some lock picks out of a small case in his pocket and fished around in the keyhole until he was able to open the door. He led them up a stairway that went to the second floor where they were standing inside a large wooden dome shaped roof. Support beams spaced evenly around the walls spanned from the floor to the peak of the dome. Billy Ray set down the crate in the middle of the floor, directly underneath the peak of the roof in the center of the room. Then he set down the light, which illuminated most of the room, but still left shadows along the walls. He took out a small compass and checked the position for North.

"I've heard that this dome," Kenny said, "was supposed to have some kind of electrical device inside to zap people with energy from the earth to recharge their natural batteries in their bodies, making them live longer and healing them of any diseases or illnesses. Unfortunately, the guy building it died before the whole thing could be finished, and the electronics mysteriously disappeared after his death. Conspiracy theorists say he was killed so the Integratron could never be used for its true purpose to benefit mankind."

"You're all about to find out what this dome can really do," Billy Ray said. "Lita, you've been spouting off all day about a change coming. You were right. I've got a device here that, when used inside this dome, is going to change everything for us, the world, and everyone."

"What the hell are you talking about Billy Ray?" Joey said.

"Yeah," Lita said. "What is this all about, man?"

"What are we doing here Billy Ray?" Kenny added.

"Tell us what's up, man," Pete said.

"Look, I don't know how much of this you guys will understand," Billy Ray said. "Lita studies a lot of metaphysical shit, so maybe she can wrap her head around this better than the rest of you."

"Just tell us, Billy Ray," Joey said. "We're not idiots, you know. Shoot, man."

Billy Ray looked at each of them in turn with a cold, hard, stare.

"Every ten-thousand years, during the Summer solstice," Billy Ray said, "an event called The Sha'Daa occurs, where doors to other dimensions open here on earth. The creatures from these dimensions inhabit the earth, change everything about our world, and a new age will be born. Tonight is the night of the Sha'Daa."

"You're full of shit man," Joey said.

"You're freaking me out Billy Ray," Kenny said, waving a hand.

"Christ on a crutch," Pete said. "You're crazy."

"No, it's not crazy," Lita said. "Mystics from all ages have talked about other dimensions, places in another space or time from our own. I believe what you're saying Billy Ray, but what does all this have to do with us, man?"

"There's more," Billy Ray said. "I've made a deal with some powerful entities from this dimension. The doors to their realm can't open unless someone on this side creates a portal. It will take all five of us to complete the ritual. In exchange for opening the gate, we all become rich and famous rock 'n' roll musicians in the new age of mankind."

"What the fuck?" Joey said, as he stared in disbelief at Billy Ray. "Are you serious?"

"That's some insane shit, Billy Ray," Pete said.

"Hold on a minute," Kenny said. "We help you open this gateway to another dimension, and in return, we all get fortune and fame. What's the catch?"

"No catch," Billy Ray said. "That's the deal."

"No, no, no," Kenny said, "there's always a catch. What kind of new age are we talking about here? A peaceful one, or are these beings coming here to enslave the human race? I want to know."

"It's nothing like that," Billy Ray said. "You're just paranoid, Kenny, you and your conspiracy theories."

"This change I've been feeling lately," Lita said," it hasn't felt like a negative thing. Maybe this is supposed to happen, and mankind will move into a new and wonderful era where there is no poverty, hunger, or disease."

"I hope you're right, Lita," Kenny said. "It all sounds pretty fishy to me, though."

"This must be what that salesman guy was talking about in the restaurant," Lita said. "This is what I'm supposed to do, not just for us, but for all mankind."

"I don't know about any mystical shit like Lita," Joey said, "but I for one could go for a change of pace in this shitty world. I'm tired of struggling to make ends meet, putting up with all the bullshit, just to make our music. I'm ready for the money to flow right about now. I'll try just about anything."

"Yeah, I agree with Joey," Pete said. "I'm ready for some change. I don't know if I buy into this whole 'beings from another dimension' bullshit, but hey let's see what happens. If Billy Ray is right, it can't be a worse world than we've got right now."

"All right," Kenny said, with a heavy sigh. "If you guys are in, then I'm in, too. Why the hell not?"

"Good, I'm glad that's settled," Billy Ray said. "You guys all get along the walls. Each of you are supposed to be at a different compass direction. Lita, stand in the South, Joey in the North, Kenny to the East and Pete to the West."

He pointed them each to the four positions of the compass. Lita strummed her twelve string guitar gently, the soft tones of the music amplified inside the dome.

"Wow, it sounds awesome in here," Lita said.

"Hey, I can hear you playing like you're right next to me," Joey said.

"That's one of the effects the dome has on sounds," Kenny said. "It amplifies from the positions directly opposite from each other. Pretty cool huh?"

"Yeah," Pete said, "I can hear you talking like you're here in front of me, Kenny."

"Knock off that playing, Lita, and you guys be quiet," Billy Ray said. "I want you all to hear what this thing can do. It's called a multi-wave oscillator. This device creates vibrations and sound that resonate at a certain frequency, which causes the portal to open. This dome was built on an energy vortex which amplifies the power, like a guitar amp, to help open the gate and keep it open long enough for the entities to pass through."

Billy Ray opened the wooden case up and took out a strange device that looked like a coil antenna attached to a large square battery. The antenna, similar in configuration to the old Celtic maze designs, was made of heavy gauge gold wire. He flipped a switch, and it began to vibrate with a low hum. Billy Ray turned a knob and the sound became louder, the vibrations stronger. He could feel it resonating throughout the domed chamber.

"Whoa! That feels freaky. My whole body is tingling," Kenny said.

"Yeah, weird wild stuff, man," Lita added, no longer playing her guitar.

"The hairs are standing up on my arms," Pete said.

"Wow, that is intense," Joey said.

The hum and vibrations continued to build, and they noticed an eerie green light coalescing around the antenna. The air inside the dome seemed to get thicker and swirl in a circular motion. A greenish-black blob seemed to form, rotating in the air between the antenna and the peak of the dome. The green light emanating from the antenna grew brighter and the shadowy blob began to take the form of a green-tinted black hole as it spun in the air.

"Whoa, that looks wild." Lita whispered.

"Yeah, crazy looking." Pete said.

The air in the dome spun around with hurricane force and was howling and whistling around them. The wind began to take on a more sinister sound, like the growling of some great beast, which seemed to come from the ever-expanding sphere in the middle of the dome. Kenny, Joey, Pete, and Lita were staring wide-eyed at the inky-green black hole. A trickle of blood flowed from their noses.

Kenny held his fingers under his nose where the blood flowed even more now. He held it up in front of his face in horror. "What the hell is happening?"

"I'm not feeling so good right now guys," Pete said, as he staggered against the wall, blood from his nose dripping onto his shirt.

"Is it supposed to be like this?" Joey asked.

"Something's wrong guys, I don't like this." Lita said. "What is that thing doing to us Billy Ray?"

It's working. Billy Ray thought. Soon they will be dead – sacrificed in the ritual of the portal. The gate is opening, and the Sha'Daa is going to happen right here, right now. The ancient and powerful ones are coming to lay claim to the Earth after their ten-thousand-year exile in the abyss. Nothing can stop it now! And I as the harbinger of its glorious coming will sit at the right side of The Great Lord of the Abyss and we shall crush mankind to death and enslave their souls!

Billy Ray's appearance seemed to shimmer in the green glow, and he began to melt into an amorphous blob-like shape as tentacles sprouted from all over his body. Glowing red eyes popped all over what had been his head. The roar of the vortex of the extra-dimensional gate was deafening, drowning out the screams around the room.

Strange shapes had started to emerge from the gate, their tentacles reached forth out of the greenish-black darkness. Their howling was heard over the deafening wind.

"Oh my god," yelled Kenny. "What happened to Billy Ray? What are those things coming out of the hole?"

Pete's eyes had rolled into the back of his head, and he gibbered incoherently. Drool dripped from his gaping mouth and mixed with the blood that poured from his nose and eyes.

"No, no, no, no, this isn't happening," Joey screamed, and blood flew from his lips.

Then, a sound floated above the tumultuous noise of wind and howling and screams. It sounded like the clear ringing notes of a guitar. It built in volume until the vibrations of the twelve strings seemed to resonate and fill the dome. Lita struggled to maintain consciousness and play the chords of the song. Her fingers trembled on the fret board, as she tried to keep the notes clear and loud. Blood dripped from her nose and eyes onto the body of the guitar, and onto the floor. Still she played on, her brow furrowed and her face set in a grim mask of concentration. The acoustics of the dome amplified the volume of the instrument, intensifying it. The sound wrapped around Billy Ray and penetrated his body, and every particle of his being. The antenna of the multi-wave oscillator vibrated erratically. The swirling dimensional portal wavered, and the wind in the dome died down.

Across the dome, he could hear the notes of the guitar as Lita strummed the strings in a progression of chords for the chorus of a song that Billy Ray recognized. Lita played more confidently, as she felt the magic of the music fight back against the power of the portal.

"Forget about fortune and fame," Lita said. "All we really need is love, and music."

What the hell is happening, thought Billy Ray. That damned guitar is stopping the Sha'Daa. He fixed his multiple eyes on Lita across the room, and lunged toward her, tentacles outstretched to grab the guitar and smash it to bits against her head. Just then the antenna on the multi-wave oscillator shattered into a thousand pieces. The inky greenish-black sphere of the portal collapsed in on itself with a rushing vacuum of air that sucked Billy Ray, and all the denizens of the abyss trying to escape, along with the multi-wave oscillator, into the diminishing hole and winked out of existence with a loud 'pop!'

Joey, Pete, Kenny, and Lita, stunned expressions on their faces, looked at each other from across the domed room. The blood that had flowed from their noses and eyes stopped pouring forth, and they all stood there exhausted and bewildered.

Lita finally broke the silence. She strummed a few notes on her lucky guitar and said, "Damn, looks like we need a new lead singer."

* * *

INTERLUDE SIXTEEN

The demonic horde poured onto the pawnshop like an army of ants. For every attacking creature that was brought down on the store's periphery, five more would take its place. In minutes every doorway and window was on the verge of being overrun.

Inside, the main floor became a dueling ground for hand-to-hand combat.

"Ashley, look out," a tiny voice yelled from below.

Leaping in front of the pawnshop's proprietor, the small figure intersected the Venusian dart's path, and was instantly thrust sideways and impaled upon the wall.

Spitting blue blood, Brian Finn coughed out his final epitaph, "Sure and begorrah, lass, when it comes to luck, I've always been fucked." The leprechaun's lifeless head slumped forward onto his chest.

Ashley had no time to mourn. Spinning around she blocked the overhand strike of a Martian axe, and riposted with her spear, piercing the red throat of the four-armed giant, dropping him like a felled tree.

Next came a duo of green battle-elves sporting long, sapphire blades that they flourished like living flames. In a mad flurry of staff work, Ashley and her spear bore their attack for a full minute before cracking the skull of one and disemboweling the other.

Gronk and Turbo, standing back to back in the side room, swung through a series of circular arcs, mowing down dozens of hell-spawn, zombies, and indentured human cultists with the orc's twin scimitars and the goth's twin Uzi's.

Dozens of demon-spawn were now pouring in through the pawnshop's doorways and windows every few seconds.

"Ashley," Barrax yelled from the other side of the main floor that was now a crowded battlefield, "we're getting over-run."

"Everybody to the basement," Ashley yelled, "now!"

Gronk, Turbo, Barrax, Frank, and Ashley, the last survivors, were within twenty feet of the massive steel door to the basement when the full flood of demon-spawn poured into the shop. All five stood their ground, lest they be overrun, and the basement's open doorway breached.

Now, Ashley, Astraea spoke in her mind.

Ashley reached into her shirt and brought out the Agimat talisman.

"Looks like the shit's about to hit the fan," Johnny said.

Ashley, startled, smiled at Johnny who had popped into existence next to her. She frowned for a split second at his untoward appearance. The Salesman's clothes were dusty and rent in several places, his fedora partially crumpled. In all the centuries she'd known him, Ashley had never seen the Salesman display any outward manifestation of weakness or vulnerability.

"Ashley," Barrax yelled, "into the basement, we've got to close the door."

Ashley and her five cohorts backed toward the basement stairwell, killing dozens of attackers for every foot given.

Though making no offensive moves, Johnny, smiling like a madman, stood his ground and absorbed the attack of multiple bullets, darts, arrows, grenade fragments, and phase-plasma rifles. Soon, he looked like a human pin cushion and dozens of bloody wounds appeared on his body. The Salesman was acting as a shield to Ashley's left flank.

"You don't have to do this," she yelled over the deafening roar of battle.

"Do what?" Johnny asked, his otherworldly voice cutting through the din like a knife through water. "Can't an old friend drop in for the occasional visit?"

The damage being done to Johnny's body was horrible to behold. He was beginning to look like a medical cadaver after a full autopsy.

"A good thing you're not human," Ashley spit out.

"On the contrary my dear," Johnny groaned, "for all my powers, my form is all too mortal, and yes, I feel every molestation and abuse given."

"Go," Ashley yelled to the others, "and close the door behind me."

"But," Barrax stuttered.

"I'll be fine," Ashley screamed, "Do it now."

I am ready, Astraea said.

Barrax, Frank, Gronk, and Turbo turned and ran. The vault-like door slowly slammed shut. Ashley and Johnny pressed back against it.

The crowded shop floor surged against them.

"I'm glad you came back, Johnny," Ashley said. "I… I've always had a thing for you."

Johnny grabbed her free hand, "in another time… in another world, my dear…."

Astraea, the incorporeal Libyan avatar of justice, flowed into the ancient amulet that hung upon Ashley's breast. It immediately began to glow with a blinding light.

"Aduro," Ashley screamed.

The heart of a sun was born.

*   *   *

CHAPTER SEVENTEEN: CROUCHING SEAL, SLEEPING DRAGON

by Jason Cordova

No battle plan survives contact with the enemy
                                    – Helmuth von Moltke the Elder

A pinprick isn't enough to harm someone of my stature, but it certainly can be annoying.

I yawned and shifted my body, shaking away the tiny pain which had jabbed me in my long, serpentine tail. I was vaguely aware of my surroundings and knew I was somewhere in the middle of a vast, frozen sea. I could feel ocean currents move around me, the steady ebb and flow massaging my ancient scales comfortingly. The water around me was frigid and icy, almost as cold as where I had been spawned millions of years before. It was a wonderful feeling, the cold. It made me sleepy and I started to drift off once more, content in my underwater realm and the retirement I had chosen.

"Wake up, Kasyarna," something small and pathetic called out from a short distance away, jarring me to wakefulness. I grumbled and told it to go away. "I will not go away until you open your eyes," it continued. "I'm late already as it is."

Stupid messenger imps and their work schedules. Still, they were effective at their jobs for that very reason, though this one being late was news to me. I had no idea what it was late for. I was retired. I lifted one eyelid and looked at the tiny face hovering before me. I curled my upper lip and revealed my sharp fangs to it, a not-too-subtle reminder to the imp that I could eat him and it wouldn't even be considered a snack. I flicked my tongue out and slapped the imp away. It did not go far, unfortunately. I finally asked it what it wanted.

"The Sha'Daa has begun. You are late to the battle, Great One!" it squealed. I heaved a mighty sigh and lifted my chin, stirring up the vast ocean floor and causing more than one school of fish to flee. Nearby, a larger predator instinctively darted after the fish before turning and swimming as fast as it could upon realizing that I was not a part of the ocean floor. I felt the thin veneer of mollusks and coral which had grown upon my face and down my neck fall off as I moved for the first time in an age. The last vestiges of sleep disappeared from me as I stared at the messenger imp.

"And?" I growled. *Damn it,* I didn't say. I was enjoying my rest and retirement. I had earned my retirement, unlike most of my brethren. I had won my fight in my Sha'Daa. So what did this little thing want with me now?

"You have been called forth once more by the Forces of Evil, O Mighty Kasyarna!" the creature screeched. I was beginning to wonder if the little bastard had a setting other than "excited". "General Fashad is counting upon you to defend this territory. Even now the Forces of Light gather their finest warriors to do battle against you. To kill you, O Undefeatable One."

I scoffed and rolled my eyes. The last time the Forces of Light had come for me, they wore tiny whale-skin boats, carried sticks that had chipped rocks tied to them, along with a shaman with an orca's tooth around his neck. I was a four-hundred-foot long sea dragon with impenetrable skin, fangs the size of a shark and claws that were bigger. I had almost felt guilty about eating their little shaman, though that momentary lapse into pity was gone long before I had fallen back asleep. I had assumed that my work was done, the Forces of Evil would rule the earth and I would be left alone for the rest of time. I really didn't want to participate in another Sha'Daa. Plus, the shaman had given me horrible indigestion, and I was almost certain that it had been one of his arms that was still lodged in my back row of teeth.

I reminded the imp of the previous times that an enemy had come up to my frozen wastes to do battle and how well they had performed. I went into gory details: death, dismemberment, using severed skulls to annoy the dolphins, which was always a great way to pass the time. None of the humans had left a mark upon my memory. Except for the shaman, who had sworn at me even as I was devouring him. That had impressed me.

"They have something called a 'Seal' now, great dragon," the messenger warned me.

I blinked, surprised. Those stupid little things that swim around me, chasing fish and playing in the waves above?

The imp must have seen my confusion, for he explained. "They carry weapons that are vastly more powerful than pointy sticks and magic spells. They have weapons which can harm you from a great distance, O Mighty One. They have magic sticks which fire death rocks at you."

I'd had enough of the imp's disorienting prattle. I reached down into my being and Concentrated, pulling out the imp's memories. He screamed in anguish and pain as I ripped his psyche apart in my search for more information, my own mind crushing his as I scoured everywhere for more details. He struggled in vain to prevent me from reaching the innermost depths of his mind, but I was too strong, too agile in my mental assault. His defenses were no match for me. I riffled through his mind until I found what I was looking for.

Rifles. Bullets. Missiles. Steel ships. Navy SEALs.

Man had come a long way since the last Sha'Daa, I recognized, as I started to work the kinks out of my long, sinuous neck. These humans and their new weaponry just might be able to hurt me – warriors, true warriors with the ability to cause much destruction in their wake. A challenge. I released my hold over the imp, which slumped to the ocean floor and groveled, mewling pitifully, the damage done. I reached up and scratched a stray barnacle off my pointed chin.

"Return to your masters, demon," I grumbled as I pulled my massive body off the sea bed. I winced as one of my hind legs cramped up, the muscle weak and constricted from too many years without moving. Damn, that's going to hurt later, I thought. "I will do as I feel is necessary."

"You cannot tell me… I cannot…," it whined, every last shred of dignity stripped away from the mental flailing I had given it. I slapped the imp away with a claw and told it to go. It fled into the icy darkness, leaving me alone once more. I looked around at my undersea dwelling, contemplating the risk of losing it all in the name of the Sha'Daa.

Yes, I am of this world, born unto a dying race that had once ruled the world while man was still flinging poo at his cousins. My kind was now considered evil, I suppose, though really

I've never gone out of my way to find a fight. More than a few have found me, but again, I've acted purely out of self-defense. I'm certain a lot of the others of my kind had considered me lazy, but they usually ended up as adornments and decorations on the walls of ancient hunters while I enjoyed my long naps and, even better, my longer life.

I closed my eyes and Concentrated once more. Somewhere out there the Forces of Light were fast approaching; it would be prudent for me to be ready.

I watched the inflated rubber boats approach. The warriors in the boats – the SEAL team – were very disciplined. No war cries, no chants, no shouts about how powerful they were and were coming to collect my skin. They were contemplative, their minds like iron, their wills unbreakable. They had worked together for a long time, while their skills were forged in trials which would have made my brothers blush in shame and envy. I felt something in my belly and was surprised. I felt… fear. I shook it off as fast as I could. I didn't have time to be afraid of a bunch of hairless apes with guns.

They abandoned their boats on an icy shelf near my hiding place, weapons drawn and ready. Silently they disembarked, their footsteps making hardly a sound as they walked across the thick ice shelf. Their weapons slowly tracked across the open space of the surrounding ice, searching for any sign of me. I chuckled despite my earlier fear. They were looking in the wrong place for a sea dragon. We prefer wetter surroundings, and the barren ice surface is the last place a giant dragon my size would hide.

I propelled myself upward through the ice shelf, erupting from it with a massive spray of salt water and ice shards in the midst of their scattered group. Momentarily blinded, I let loose a furious roar to provide some cover as I regained my bearings. I had hoped that my roar and surprise would disorient them enough for me to cleave through them in no time. I could hear them yelling and cursing in fear and terror as I crashed down onto the ice, my body already moving the instant my hind legs touched the ice. I snapped my head to the right and latched onto the lower torso of the nearest human, his face frozen in shock as my jaws clamped home. He screamed in pain and pulled the trigger to his machine gun as my sharp teeth ripped him apart.

Oh, damn that hurts! I thought, as the first few rounds from the gun shattered scales near my front leg upon impact. I winced and tossed him aside as more gunfire tore into my rear. I snarled and slid across the ground, leaving the wounded human to die as I tried to get away from the weapon. The bullets had easily penetrated my scales and I could feel the lead in my sides, the biting sensation creating a pain I was not familiar with.

"Grenade! Grenade!" a voice cried out frantically behind me. I stopped and looked back toward the wounded man, who shouldn't have been in any position to speak at all. I had nearly bit him in half and yet, he was yelling. What the Sha'Daa was a grenade?

Something small bounced towards my long tail. I watched as it rolled closer, random bullets glancing off of my thickest plates protecting my spine. This, I thought, this is a grenade? I should have scoured that imp's mind more thoroughly. What in the world does a grenade –

Pain ripped through my entire body as the small thing exploded, showering my hindquarters with fragments hotter than the sun. I howled in fury and anguish as I felt the blast tear at my tail, ripping through the sinew and bone which held it to my body. My ears, delicate and designed to help me hunt fish in the black depths of the ocean, were deafened by the concussive wave the grenade created. The flash from the explosion was bright, temporarily preventing me from seeing anything around me.

I blindly slashed my claws at where I thought the nearest cluster of the enemy stood, catching two of the SEALs across their bodies and flinging them aside. I stomped after them and kicked them both a few times for good measure. More gunfire erupted and I was faintly aware of some kind of projectile which screamed past my head. I blinked and swore loudly as it exploded, destroying one of the boats the SEALs had arrived in. The soldier swore as well, which would have been humorous had we not been in a fight to the death. The wash from the propellant of the missile forced my head backward, which probably saved my life, as another grenade detonated nearby. This will not do, I thought as another grenade bounced toward me. I flicked it back to where it came from and the human shouted out in alarm as it rolled to a stop at his feet. It exploded and the man's legs were cut out from beneath him, effectively taking him out of the fight.

I spotted three of the cursed humans setting up a larger gun and froze, unsure of just what it was. It looked like one of the guns they had been using, about as much as I resembled a sea snake. I figured that the new gun was far more dangerous than the guns they carried which had already torn me up, so I pushed back through the ice, sliding back into the frigid water as the massive new gun opened fire.

I watched from below the surface as the bullets of the new gun chewed up the ice, and praised myself for my intuition. You get to be my age, you know when to trust your gut. And my gut, at the moment, was screaming for me to destroy that gun and kill the men firing it. I looked back toward the second hole I had just created and watched as large bundles were unceremoniously tossed into the water. I smirked and swam closer, curious to see if the humans were retreating and offering me a sacrifice instead. As I approached the packages, however, I noticed something was odd. I Concentrated and felt the dangerous feelings of a man who was certain that he was about to kill me. I glanced back at the packages and realized that they were just as dangerous – if not more so – than the grenades. Though it didn't sound especially dangerous to me, the word "satchel charge" sent a decided chill down my spine. I turned tail and swam away as fast as I could.

The packages exploded. The tremendous noise and pressure were murder on my poor, sensitive ears. The concussive waves rocked me and threw my body against the under layer of the ice, cracking my back and loosening up some of the barnacles that had become encrusted on my spine over the millennia. I pivoted and swam back to the surface, breaking through a thin spot in the ice and watched as another SEAL tried to dive out of the way as I descended from above.

His reflexes weren't nearly as good as he should have hoped for. On the plus side, he did break my fall.

The SEALs manning the big gun desperately tried to turn and fire at me, but I was ready for them. I sucked in as much air as my belly could hold and threw up ten thousand years worth of fish and fish guts on them. The smell made me gag, but the corrosive material that splashed against them dropped them like stones. I grinned and spat as the nasty taste of fish made my stomach roil. Even if they had survived, they would not be fighting any time soon.

Then there was one. I charged forward and he dodged, tossing more grenades toward me. I avoided most of them, flicking a few of the closer ones away to explode harmlessly to the side. He fired his weapon at me, a few of the bullets smacking me square in the chest. I grimaced and stayed on target. He was the last, and after him I could get some blasted rest.

I was moving faster now, my attention entirely focused on the burly black warrior in front of me. He was nimble and dodged a few of my swipes as he fired at me with his gun. I roared in rage as another cluster of bullets penetrated my chest and the base of my neck, where my armor is weakest. I used that rage to propel me forward and I finally managed a glancing blow to the warrior's head.

He slid aside as I staggered, blood pouring from my many wounds. He bounded to his feet and shot me two more times before a surprisingly loud click! emanated from the gun. The SEAL swore loudly and barely managed to dodge my claws, rolling to the side as I chased after him, the two of us racing across the ice. For a human his size, he was quick.

He fired his weapon over his shoulder and I yowled as one of the cursed bullets cracked a tooth, sending the shard flying into the back of my throat. I gagged and coughed violently, tripping over my own two front legs as I struggled to dislodge the tooth. I hit the ice with a solid crack! and I think I broke something in my chest plate. I swore at multiple gods and goddesses for my misfortune and the human's luck as I crawled forward a few meters. I picked myself up and swallowed the blasted tooth. I knew it was going to hurt later, whenever it decided to pass.

Assuming I lived long enough for that to happen.

I scooped up a large chunk of ice and pressed it into a compact ball roughly the size of my prey. I twisted my body and hurled the ball of ice toward the warrior. He looked back and I could almost see the surprise in his eye as the giant ice ball came sailing towards him. Once again, the human managed to escape my attack as he threw himself onto his face, the snowball narrowly missing him. I cursed louder and slithered over the ice toward him, abandoning my legs so I could move faster in a straight line. We sea dragons are adaptable like that. There really is no other good way to swim through the ocean, and on ice the technique really isn't that much different. We just lose maneuverability.

I closed on the fallen warrior quickly. I had to act now, before he managed to get that damned rifle turned around and pointed at me again. I snaked my tongue out and managed to snag his ankle, wrapping around it and jerking the human. He yelped and slammed the end of his gun into my prehensile tongue. A salty tear trickled from my eye but I grimly held on, determined to end the fight once and for all. The human continued to pound on my tongue, drawing a short vicious knife. That was too much. I whined and finally released him. He rolled away from me, then ripped a short tube off the body of one of his men. It clicked open to double his size. He glared at me over it, gasping and wounded. I was no better, done, spent. All I wanted to do was to get out of there before he killed me. We stared at each other. I knew I could reach him but that tube promised more explosive death.

The fight had not lasted long, but it seemed like it had taken forever. I do know that it was the bloodiest one I had ever been in. I had to put a stop to this fight with the human before something serious happened to me.

I examined the young warrior before me. As a specimen of his species, he was marvelous. Strange markings on his arm aside, his body was near-perfect, almost as muscular as his distant ancestors whom I devoured so many centuries ago. His hair was nonexistent on his head, something I had never before seen willingly done on a human. His mind was strong and nearly impenetrable, his soul secure in the side of light. There would be no swaying of this man. He was a natural hero who would always stand defiantly against a villain. Unfortunately, that meant standing against me. I knew how this game played out and I honestly wanted no part in it. Gurak piss on the Sha'Daa. I just wanted to rest, recover. I just wanted to be left to my retirement.

"Truce, man-ape," I hissed to him, my wounded belly pressed down into the icy cold shelf, my damaged tail hanging on by a slender piece of bone and flesh. I was hurt, hurt far beyond anything I had ever experienced in my long life. I was immensely weakened. He was strong, his weapons powerful and his will unbreakable despite his numerous injuries and dead companions. The wounds didn't seem to bother the man before me, while mine gnawed away at my concentration.

Is this to be my grave? I gingerly ran my tongue across my injured paw, letting the saliva sooth the burning wounds as I kept a careful eye on him. My cracked tooth scratched the inside of my mouth, but it was merely annoying compared to what the gunfire had done to me. The bullets hurt more than something that small should, and their impact had cracked many of my scales while penetrating into my vulnerable muscles. I was almost afraid to look at my injured hind leg, aware that his fragmentation grenades had probably left me partially lame – assuming I survived. I needed to get back to the water, to sleep and to heal, but the man was blocking my path. I did not want to die. There had to be another way.

"What are you?" he asked, looking me over with a careful eye. I could hear the weariness in his voice, as well as the cold, hard determination. He would die before he failed in his mission, something that I had not expected in a man who was the last of his small group. He was alone against me, a creature more ancient than recorded history, and yet he was unafraid.

"You know what I am," I growled. I was mildly surprised I could even hear him after the explosion and damage to my ear. He asked me where I had come from. I waved towards the waves beyond with my injured left claw and he nodded. A short, awkward silence later I told him that I did not wish for my death just yet.

"Yeah, I don't really have a burnin' desire to die either," the man admitted after a moment. He looked back at the strewn bodies of his comrades and his features grew haggard. I pushed through my pain and Concentrated. I could feel the iron form in his soul, giving him inner strength to finish his mission. I also sensed, somewhere on his being, the taint of the cursed Salesman.

I knew how The Salesman worked: he'd offer some unwitting mortal human an object or item that seemed to be worthless, but could change the entire course of the Sha'Daa for the person holding the item. He was supposed to be neutral, but a few of the others I had spoken to long before believed that he served the hidden agenda within the Sha'Daa. One of my brothers, now dead, had even suggested that he was the very embodiment of the Sha'Daa. I just considered him a meddler at best. Give a worthless being too much credit and they become far more valuable than they really are.

So what had he traded with this man before me? I felt a sudden, burning urge to know.

"What did you receive from The Salesman?" I asked.

"That crazy guy?" the human questioned, keeping his weapon on me. Seeing my nod, he shrugged and looked away. "Information. He gave us information, told us that you wouldn't be prepared for the Sha'Daa, whatever the hell that is. Said that you'd be asleep and we would win our fight by default."

"Nothing in his world is free," I said, recalling how the messenger imp had claimed he was late and running behind. "What did he want in return?"

"My Satchel Paige rookie card," he replied. "It's my lucky baseball card. My mom gave it to me when I joined the Navy. Carried it for twelve years and never lost… never lost a man. Until today – the day it wasn't in my pocket."

It suddenly dawned on me that the warrior would not forgive me for causing the death of his men. His bond to them was far stronger than anything I felt. I had to do something, fast, before he killed us both. I had to try something, perhaps use the same technique that the thrice-damned Salesman used.

"I can raise them," I offered quickly, using his unspoken desires to placate him. He looked at me, his eyes thin slits on his black face. I explained, my words coming out in a rush. "I can raise them. If you will leave, and they leave with you after I raise them. A trade…" I let my voice trail off.

He accused me of lying but I shook my great head, aware of another wound near the soft plates at the base of my throat. I could lie, but there would be no point. We were at a stalemate, two pawns in a rigged game of chess. I would call a draw and we would both retreat, to live out our meager lives as best as we could.

"What's your name?" he asked me, his voice cracking. Surprised, I told him. He grunted and told me his. He looked back at his men and, for the briefest of moments, I could see his indecision. What was there to be uncertain about? I wondered.

He stared at me and spoke. "Well then, Kasyarna. Would they be fixed? Their wounds?"

"Their wounds would remain, but lessened," I said. "They will follow you, loyal soldiers of your clan. You will find great power leading them."

"Wait," he stopped me with a raised hand. "What do you mean, follow me? Will they be alive?"

"They will be raised," I said.

"No," he shook his head. "Will their souls be put back into their bodies?"

I suddenly realized what he was asking and I shivered. He was asking me to break the rules, to go against the ancient decrees lain down by the oldest of my kind. I was hesitant to break those rules, for they were what held our magics together and protected us from both the good and evil in the world. They were what allowed us to tap into the very fabric of time and life, to retain our immortality. I stopped and thought about that for a moment. Our immortality granted us much, but what was life without living? I had slept for so long, missed so much that I had been at a loss when the ship carrying the SEAL team arrived in my domain. What else had I missed? Why had the demons not awakened my brethren, the others like me scattered across the world? Deep down, I had my suspicions. I came to a decision far sooner than I expected.

"I will do as you ask, Master Chief Tyrone" I said. "I have a request of my own, however."

"Just Tyrone. What's that?" Tyrone asked me. I told him and he recoiled, visibly shaken. I tried to soothe his fears as I began to reason with him. He pursed his lips thoughtfully as I explained and, by the time I was finished, he was nodding. "Okay, yeah, they might go for that."

"As a token of my goodwill," I said as I carefully slid toward the fallen humans, "I will raise them and breathe life back into them, as you requested. Then you may decide whether to honor our agreement."

I leaned forward to the first of the fallen and breathed, letting the fabric between the dimensions slip as I flitted the soul back into his body. For once, the Sha'Daa wasn't using me but I it. The man on the ground gasped as life filled him once more. He clutched at his belly where I had disemboweled him but he no longer found a wound. He looked at his hands then back into my face and shouted in surprise, scooting back away from me, his hands fumbling for the weapon at his side.

"Stand down, PO!" Tyrone yelled. The confused man looked at him but, thankfully for me, followed orders. I moved to the next fallen warrior, and the next. Each time I reached down and breathed on the dead, breaking rules that were almost as old as the earth, I brought them back to life and ensured that they retained their souls. Each time I was, as I had learned from one of the sailors aboard the SEAL team's mighty ship, giving the Forces of Evil the proverbial middle finger. The gesture was intoxicating.

"There, Tyrone," I said, after I finished bringing back his last fallen soldier. I moved carefully away from the group and looked at the master chief. "My end of the agreement is fulfilled." Tyrone nodded and turned on his radio. After a moment of silence he looked at it, surprised, before laughing and pulling a small block out. He reached into his front pocket and pulled out a similar device, which I surmised to be a 'battery.' He put in the new battery and chuckled some more. I was momentarily afraid he had finally lost his mind. He then spoke into his radio, voice shockingly calm for someone who had just witnessed his men being torn apart and then brought back to life right before his eyes. I watched, silent, as he began to argue with someone else in his device. Partly out of respect – though mostly because I was just too tired – I didn't Concentrate on his conversation and instead, focused on examining myself. I winced. I was a wreck.

My tail had fallen off fully sometime when I had been bringing the fallen soldiers back to life. I stared in shock at the appendage which lay in the nearby snow, the tip twitching. It had been half of my body length and my rudder when I swam beneath the waves. I was no longer a four-hundred-foot sea dragon, merely a two-hundred-foot one. I continued my self-examination and felt that my hind leg still wasn't working properly, though I could feel the magic working through the flesh. My wounded claw would eventually heal, but I knew that a lot of the cuts across my armored foreleg would scar. I looked as though I had fought with an elder dragon and not nine puny man-apes. My respect for Tyrone and his men grew.

Tyrone interrupted my inspection. "We're good to go."

I grinned toothily as the SEALs all looked around at one another, happy to be going home and away from this Arctic hell. I was thrilled that I would finally see this new world that had been created while I had been slumbering away, blissfully unaware. I looked toward the small cove of ice, where the rubber boats had broken loose during the massive fight and were drifting out into the frozen sea. I realized that my new allies didn't have a way back to their ship. That could have presented a minor problem, except…

"You SEALs need a ride?"

I curled my nose near the damaged stump where my tail had once been and began to lick it, hoping that my saliva would eventually help it grow back. The captain of the large vessel had flooded what he called a "well-deck" and lowered a massive metal wall, the stern gate. It had allowed me to swim inside and deposit the SEALs safely in the protective innards of the ship amidst the tremendous shock of many of the common sailors aboard.

I looked over at Tyrone, who was leaning back on a large, green bag while listening to what he called music. I could hear the deep thumping from his machine and recognized, faintly, the ancient tribal beats of his people from long ago. It was familiar and comforting to my ears, though they were still slightly deafened from the multiple explosions the SEALs had caused when they tossed their grenades and charges at me. I settled down as the ship, nicknamed "The Proud Lion" by her crew, chugged slowly out of the Arctic Sea and toward my new home. It would be different from my frozen sea bed, but it would be welcome after so many years of solitude. I was amongst warriors of light now, and the Forces of Evil could find some other dragon to do their bidding the next time they came calling.

The land of Florida would be my new home. I was retired, after all.

*   *   *

INTERLUDE SEVENTEEN

Ashley felt her entire being fill with all-consuming fire, but she did not burn. The surrounding horde of attackers, and her shop, instantly converted to white ash that slowly, strangely dissipated, leaving her floating in a bright white void.

She looked down and saw that her own body had become a golden transparency. Amber energy sparkled and outlined her skeletal system and all her internal organs. Her clothes seemed to have evaporated, and a duller flame, in the shape of the amulet, flickered between her breasts. Looking back up she took note of Johnny, still holding her left hand, and she gasped.

The change to The Salesman's form was even more dramatic. For he now appeared as a sparkling, blue, incandescent nude demi-god, with an even brighter halo of blinding light about his head. He topped nearly ten feet.

Johnny bowed his head slightly, and a small drop of effervescent energy fell from his eyes and struck Ashley's hand. And then he was gone.

* * *

CHAPTER EIGHTEEN: NORTHLIGHT

by Deborah Koren

They move in tandem through the forest, light-footed and shifting shape with the shadows. Moriel mimics the sturdy form of a pine, watching Kasar – always the show-off – bound away in the shape of a deer. Of course, the humans spot him. Kasar wants them to. This is a game to him. A deadly game, perhaps, but a game nonetheless.

Moriel schools himself in patience and lets the humans pass by. They point after Kasar's form, and he hears their words:

"A deer –"

"Did you see?"

And the woman, the only one he fears, says, "Something was wrong with it. It didn't move right."

There are five of them: three men, one woman, and a girl child. The human males carry their supplies without grace, complaining and resting frequently, bodies soft and paunchy. Moriel equates them with the registrar caste back home in Tatis: running things from desks, fond of paper and files and passing judgments. Not doing things.

The woman is different. – physically small and compact, but agile and strong. She wears her backpack as if it is part of her, adjusting her stride to accommodate the weight without compromising her body's natural stance. She's the one who leads this group through the backcountry of the Sierra Mountains. She sets the pace, and the rest follow.

Moriel has not expected to find such a semblance of home caste structure here on earth. The priestesses have taught that the human women are docile, that it is the men who are the leaders and who pose a threat to the Sha'Daa. If they are wrong about this, what else might they have concluded incorrectly? Doubt is an unfamiliar emotion, and finding reason to question the priestesses' knowledge bothers him. His entire life's purpose from birth through death has been determined by them. They cannot be wrong.

His gaze draws back to the girl child again. Dark-haired like her mother, with blue eyes and a narrow face, twig arms and legs, and yet she carries her own little pack as easily as her mother. She walks behind the woman, sometimes trying to match strides, sometimes straying off the path to balance on logs or dart around nearby pines. The woman allows her to roam and play without a glance, and Moriel's gut tightens. He would not be so careless of his offspring had he been allowed…

But the priestesses have denied his petition to join the fatherhood. One does not question the rulings of the priestesses, and yet he has not forgiven them for taking away the only thing he has ever wanted.

You should not dwell on the past. Kasar comes up beside him, in his natural demon shape now. He does not strut – Kasar moves too fluidly for that – but the arrogance lurks in his casual stance and wide-set amber eyes.

Moriel shifts from tree camouflage form to his own body. He stands taller than Kasar, more powerful, his four arms conditioned and well-muscled.

It is not bad to have regrets, he says, mildly.

It is when you doubt. There can be no doubt today. The Sha'Daa is already upon us. Can't you feel it?

Moriel can, the vaguest rumble in the ground below his feet.

The priestesses amass their power. It falls to us to make sure no humans remain here to prevent the portal from opening.

The glory of Lasinir be upon us. Moriel means the ritual words sarcastically, but Kasar glows with pride. Typical. The reason the priestesses selected the unfledged stripling as his partner on a mission this important still evades him. If he had not seen Kasar's fighting prowess displayed at the skill trials himself, he might have risked their wrath and made comment.

Ten thousand years is a long time to wait, the stripling says.

Moriel hesitates, weighing thoughts he should not be having, then orders: We do not harm the child.

Kasar laughs. You are dwelling again. You must think practically, not through the veils of your past. We must destroy her caretakers. You cannot replace them. You are not a father at home, and you know even less of the caring for a human child. When the portal opens and we remake this world into an image of Tatis, she cannot survive. She will die anyway, but if you delay, her death will be cruel. It is not like you to be cruel.

Nevertheless.

Our orders are to eliminate all possible opposition.

Moriel scoffs. A girl child is opposition?

No, merely a casualty of war. She is in the wrong place at the wrong time.

Then I will kill her myself.

Kasar's laughter mocks him. You cannot do it! You, who have slain thousands to achieve this honor of safe-guarding the opening of the portal for our armies – you are undone by a child.

Continue your patrol, Moriel orders coldly. He lopes away quickly, knowing his lack of response only proves Kasar right. But he will find a way to keep her. To have his own daughter. If they succeed this Sha'Daa, then the priestesses will offer any prize. Kasar can have all the wealth and lands and prestige he wants. Moriel wants only the child.

The humans have moved fast while he and Kasar exchanged thoughts. He catches up to them in a shady meadow, where they pull food from their packs for the middle day repast.

Just watching the girl makes his heart ache to hold her and stroke her hair, to sing to her the tales of Lasinir and Meare, the true gods, and their children, the points of the compass. He has learned the human language for those: North, South, East, West. Caline – North – is his patron god, and the sons of Caline are traditionally granted a father's role. To be denied…

He changes shape to appear human, studies his two arms and finely jointed fingers. It isn't a true shape-shifting, merely a mimicry of shape, an approximation of the external appearance of something else to camouflage his true nature. Inside – he cannot change his internal organs into that which he cannot see. It is why the humans were suspicious of Kasar's deer shape. He did not actually become the creature he imitated.

An unfamiliar voice speaks, not one of the five humans. Moriel shifts again to hide in the tree shadows for a better look.

A stranger rests among the hikers. A fellow foot traveler, like them, tall, with night-black hair, in stained, cropped clothing that exposes suntanned arms and legs. When he smiles, sunlight highlights a gold tooth. He holds something in his hand, offering it to the woman. Some kind of knife.

The stranger smells different. Not human. Not demon either. Something different, and a smell Moriel has been taught to beware.

They call him Asil. Humans call him the Salesman.

Moriel looks for Kasar, but his partner is doing as ordered and patrols the perimeter. He wonders if Kasar would try to kill the Salesman. What a score that would be, to take out the biggest opponent to the Sha'Daa. Moriel knows better. The priestesses have cautioned that the Salesman cannot be trapped so easily. He is canny and with powers far greater than a mere demon's. Besides, Asil cannot truly interfere in the Sha'Daa. Moriel has been taught that too.

The woman nods and accepts whatever trade the Salesman has proffered. Metal glints when she unsheathes the knife.

Even so armed, Moriel cannot judge her a threat. The woman is strong, yes, but he has watched her hunt the silvery water prey with a slender pole and wire – and she has failed. No creature that could not catch such small things could defend against his skill, or Kasar's. He has tried his own skill against the fish she sought to catch and succeeded on his first try. It is not so different from diving for jaunas back home. One, two, or ten blades in her hand will make no difference. Humans simply cannot move fast enough to challenge him. A projectile weapon – now that might have given her an edge, but the Salesman has not brought her one of those.

Moriel shakes his head, baffled. What possible help has the Salesman really provided the human?

He blinks and realizes the Salesman has somehow left the clearing. It is a good thing Asil cannot fight them directly. A creature that moves like that would give them trouble, although Kasar would grin with feral delight and relish the test to his skills. And being cocky, young, and overconfident, he might full well lose that test.

The little girl grasps for the knife in the woman's hand, and Moriel flinches, wanting to snatch her back himself. The woman rebukes her softly and resheathes the blade. "It is not a toy," she murmurs.

"Moriel, son of Caline, I would trade with you."

Moriel does not jump at the soft voice, or the unexpected proximity. He pivots to see the Salesman standing nearby. Asil has retained his human guise, but he seems taller, less the traveler, more… leader. Moriel wonders if the Salesman could appear as a fellow demon, and silently he thanks Asil for not insulting them by assuming their shape.

The Salesman inclines his head in acknowledgement, and Moriel understands that the stranger can hear his thoughts.

I thought your trades were only with the humans, to defend against those such as I? Moriel sends.

"Normally. This is something extra. Something you want, not need."

There is nothing I want, except to complete my mission and see that the portal opens. You know that.

Asil holds up something small and blue, and curiosity compels Moriel to take a closer look, despite himself. The Salesman shrugs, almost embarrassed. "Bubbles."

What?

"Bubbles. Soap bubbles. It's a child's game."

That gives Moriel pause, and now he is wary again. The creature knows things he should not.

"Love is not so easy a thing to hide," the Salesman says, gently, "and your species is an emotional one."

Moriel keeps silent.

"I know you are here to make sure these people do not stop the portal from opening. Yes, I hope they do stop you, but the Sha'Daa is full of unpredictability, and you may succeed. If you do, and if you can protect the girl, then you might need these." He holds out the bottle of bubbles again. "To break the ice, to give her something, to distract her from what has happened around her."

Still, Moriel says nothing, but his hand twitches. It is a present the girl child would understand.

"Look," Asil says. "This isn't a trick. Children are innocent. You and I know that. Your partner does not, which is why I came to you. You care. You'll try to save her. And so… this might help you help her, that's all."

You do not give, you trade. What do you want from me?

The Salesman gestures. "How about your rank bracelet?"

Moriel closes his fingers over it protectively.

"It designates you a hunter, an assassin: a killer," Asil says. "That's not what you want it to say."

Nevertheless, it is what I am.

"You don't have to be."

Giving you the bracelet does not change who I am.

"No, only you can change who you are."

There is a trick, a catch, something in the trade that he knows he should distrust. Asil is his enemy, the enemy of the Sha'Daa. And yet… Moriel does want the bubbles, the child's toy. A token to give her.

He licks his lips and scans the surroundings for Kasar. This breach of security would allow his younger partner to take over the mission, and rightly so. Moriel has no business even talking with this figure.

And yet, Asil offers him something harmless, to help ease the child. And he wants that for her.

He tears the braided wire bracelet from his wrist and thrusts it at the Salesman, receives the blue bottle in return. Pictures of colored circles decorate the outside of the container. The white lid is sealed tight, and Moriel shakes it slightly to feel the liquid slosh inside.

"Thank you," Asil says. "Protect the child."

He vanishes as abruptly as he had appeared.

Moriel glances around again for Kasar, but the Salesman's presence appears to have passed unnoticed. Moriel contemplates the bottle of bubbles. He is not quite sure what it is or why this bottle will appeal to the child, but he wants to believe in the harmlessness of this trade so he can gift the girl child this small token. And Asil is right about one thing – the rank bracelet is a constant reminder of a destiny he was not allowed to follow.

It cannot be. The bottle is a trick, something to trap him or destroy him. Maybe the contents are poisonous to his species. On the verge of throwing the item away, he hesitates again. The Salesman has asked him to protect the child, and Moriel has detected no guile in the tone. But, doing as Asil wants, as his own heart wants, that is another thing entirely.

The humans finish their rest break and move on again. He smells the air, judging their distance. It is always the same; they move slowly, steadily. No threat at all.

You linger, Kasar says. Are you tired, old man?

Moriel does not need to see him to detect the sneer. He decides it is the last insubordination he will tolerate. Kasar thinks of anyone older than himself as aged, but Moriel is not old. These are his prime years, and Kasar needs a reminder that the mature are stronger, quicker, more powerful. He seizes Kasar by the throat, sweeps his legs out from under him, and has him pinned and choking on the ground before the stripling even knows what has happened. His under arms strike at Moriel, but Moriel shifts his form to pin the appendages. Moriel draws his knife, slices two parallel cuts across Kasar's left cheek, deep and designed to scar. It is the traditional mark that a stripling has crossed an elder and failed.

He releases Kasar, who does not even dare glare now. His eyes stay downcast, submissive, as it should be. Do not forget your place, Moriel murmurs.

I serve, Kasar says.

Moriel smells the fear, the humiliation, and the obedience. Tradition demands he allow Kasar to restore his honor now, and, here in this foreign dimension, only one way exists to do that. He can think of no way to delay any further. Then serve. Kill the four humans – not the child. He stresses the last. Neatly, swiftly.

The child will be spared.

Spare her the killings. Moriel's tone is still harsh.

You doom her.

The knife still rests in his hand, and he wields it again, striking a third gash below the other two on Kasar's face. Now, the stripling gasps, his stoicism lost, and puts a hand to his face. Serve, Moriel admonishes.

Kasar skulks away without another word.

They are committed now, but Moriel feels no regret. Asil would not have traded with the woman if she was not part of the Sha'Daa. Sparing the humans is a pacifist fantasy unworthy of someone of his experience.

The tremor of increasing power vibrates the earth more strongly now. Almost, the sound of the priestesses' chant resonates through the air. It intoxicates, that thrum of vitality, singing to him of home. The Sha'Daa is well underway. It won't be long before the priestesses build up the quantity of psychic power necessary to burst the interdimensional portal between

Tatis and earth. And once open, no mere human woman with a knife can stop them.

He tastes Kasar's first kill in his mind, as the stripling succeeds at his first true hunt. No more training, no more beasts. Now, it is for real. The ecstasy of the clean death feels like rain, washing their faces. Moriel relishes it as much as he knows Kasar does. A tremor rocks the earth beneath his feet – not the gateway opening, not yet, but the exultation of the priestesses. The walls between the dimensions are so thin now that they can share in Kasar's kill, and the assurance that no humans will stand to prevent them.

Another human is downed, and, this time, Moriel can smell the tang of blood in the air. It is a heady aroma, full of promise, full of power. Now, Moriel moves. He shifts into his shadow shape, seeking speed and stealth. Blood lust is something he understands, and, despite orders, Kasar may not stop at the adults.

He doesn't have to feel Kasar's thoughts to know that the stripling will kill the human woman last. It's his slight way of rebelling to the end. Moriel locates the woman easily enough by finding the girl. The child's scent is fixed in his mind now; it's like the sound of morning bells – crisp, beautiful, new. He could track her anywhere. Her mother smells of sweat and fear, but he does not detect the same foul scents on the girl child. She is not alarmed, and he grins in pride.

Their packs have been discarded. The woman clutches the girl's hand and runs through the forest. She sticks to the trail for better speed, Moriel guesses. Or because the shadowed woods around them now tremble with unknown danger. There is nothing humans fear more than the unknown.

He has promised the kills to Kasar, but, as he pursues, he knows now he must kill the mother himself. He can do it in a way the girl will not see. Kasar's discretion is not to be trusted, not where Moriel's unusual wishes are concerned.

The other two males are killed; one screams briefly. Kasar is either too excited and making mistakes, or the human put up more of a struggle than the stripling anticipated.

The woman does not turn, but Moriel sees her grip the girl more tightly. He keeps pace, loping through the forest to the side of them. Her fastest run seems almost slow motion to him. It is an unfair hunt. He stays in shadow form and streaks toward them. The knife the Salesman gave her swings in her hand, at the ready, but she does not know how to use it. But determination, fear, and self-preservation – more for the child than herself – fuel her. It is appropriate, and Moriel respects her for those true father-feelings. One must protect the young. Even Asil has said so…

He crosses the trail behind her and blurs in, one hand closing over her knife hand, twisting hard enough that the metal blade drops to the dust. Another hand wraps around her waist, the third around her mouth to prevent a scream, and the fourth hand separates her grip from the child's tiny hand. He bears her into the woods so fast the girl child spins and falls to the dirt and sees nothing.

He breaks the mother's neck, eschewing the traditional bloodletting of which Kasar is so fond. It is cleaner, quicker, and his respect for her position as the girl's first caretaker demands he show her some honor. Kasar has shed enough blood to satisfy the priestesses.

The woman's body seems small, limp, broken. He leaves her beneath a tree by the side of a tiny meadow where the golden bees flit from white flower to white flower. He shifts shape into human form. Male, older, the image of a human father he saw in a study deck once. The bottle of bubbles is in his hand, but he keeps it hidden, biding time. He wants to see how the girl child will react first.

She crouches, studying her mother's fallen knife where it lays in the dirt. Her head turns toward him as he steps out of the woods. He cannot speak the human language. He understands it – it was part of centuries of training – but his shape-shifting abilities do not include the working knowledge of how to form a human larynx, throat, tongue… Only his outside image appears accurate. But where the adult might fear telepathic communication, he does not think the young will mind. They are still open, still ready to learn and accept.

It is all right, he says, in the human language, in her mind, using all the soothing tones, colors, and feelings he can conjure.

Who are you? she asks in return, standing, and he smiles. He still smells no fear on her.

My name is Moriel. He wants to tell her that he is now her father, but prudence wins out. The thrum of energy beneath them rises. The last human threat to the portal has been extinguished. Now, it is merely a matter of letting the priestesses' power grow sufficiently to reduce the wall between their worlds to a tissue-thin film. Then the soldiers will pour through. It is dangerous to stay here, he tells the girl. Will you come with me to safety?

"Where is my mother?"

It may be an expected question, but that does not make it easier to hear, or answer. She has departed with honor, he says. She is too young to understand, but he owes her the truth.

She surprises him. "You mean she's dead," she says. "Like father."

He hadn't known. He had assumed one of the three males was her father. Soothingly, he murmurs, but you are not alone. I will care for you. I promise it.

It aches to say those words, in a good way. Years of daydreaming and wishful thinking put into words, real words. It does not require a rank bracelet and a priestess's blessing to be a father. To care for the young, one must simply do it.

"You promise?"

Yes, but you must come with me now, he says. It isn't safe here.

"Why?"

The question exasperates him. It is not the place of the young to question their elders. The human child is as stubborn as Kasar.

Because, he casts about for an answer that would make sense to her. Do you know what a volcano is?

She nods.

One is beneath us now.

She stoops suddenly and puts her palm against the earth. "Is that why the ground shakes?"

He stares at her, fascinated. You can feel it?

"Of course!" She almost rolls her eyes at him.

He has been taught that most humans are not well-endowed, psychically. Yet this mere child can feel the power of the two dimensions colliding, fluctuating, ripping. The priestesses have much to account for, he thinks.

"Mommy thought it was an earthquake, but earthquakes stop and this doesn't stop unless I make it."

Unless you…? Moriel stills himself, focuses on the girl. He must have misinterpreted the human words.

Abruptly, the thrum of power cuts off, and he floats, bereft, in a soundless, emotionless void. He gasps like a spiked jauna and fights the instinctive urge to return to his natural body shape.

"Like that," the girl says, innocently, blithely.

How did you–?

She says, "I think it."

You must not, he says, sternly. Let the earthquake go.

"Why?"

Because… you cannot stop an earthquake. It will damage you to try.

"It doesn't hurt."

He closes his eyes. Could your mother stop it?

"No."

Maybe her ability is localized, he thinks. She might be creating a ring of peace around herself, while the priestesses continue their work unknowing. Or maybe she really could close the door.

You've signed your death warrant, child, he thinks. If Kasar feels the damping force, he will be coming, and orders from a superior or not, he will be expected to destroy her. It's why they are here. Moriel knows he should kill her himself. Innocent yet, but somehow possessing the strength to block the priestesses. But he cannot. He would lose her forever. There is still time. He just has to get her to stop, or get her away from this area.

He remembers the bubbles then. He pulls the bottle out and kneels beside her. Her eyes light up.

Do you know what this is? he asks.

"Bubbles. Daddy used to play bubbles with me."

Show me, he says, and hands her the bottle.

Tentatively, she takes it. Then she grins and unscrews the cap, sets it down carefully face up on a rock nearby. She fishes in the bottle with a finger and pulls out a circle, no, a stick with a ring at each end, of different sizes. It drips with a vaguely oily substance. She raises the wand and blows at one of the rings. Whorls of iridescent colors shift and glitter in the sunlight as a string of bubbles, like beads spilled from a broken necklace, float sideways on the light breeze. She laughs and repeats the process.

A hole still remains where he should feel the strength of the priestesses, but it is lessened now. Distract her enough and the gate will continue. That's all he needs to do, distract her for long enough and it won't matter how powerful she is or what she can do. She'll just be a girl child, needing care, and he will be the one able to provide it.

Blow more, he encourages her.

She does, and he watches the bubbles drifting – until they pop mid-air, as if they have struck an invisible wall. The soapy bubble material leaves a residue in the air.

Panic and adrenaline grip Moriel as the realization strikes – he has not smelled Kasar coming, and that is not possible unless the girl is blocking more than the priestesses' power.

Run! he orders, and throws himself in front of the girl as Kasar materializes in his natural form. The stripling's four arms clench around Moriel's throat and chest, and Moriel knows he has to shift shape immediately or give the advantage of the fight to Kasar. But he hesitates, not wanting to reveal his true demon form to the girl. Not wanting to destroy the illusion they've created. In all his life, he has never hesitated in a fight before, but this time, he knows his wavering thoughts have killed him. Kasar breaks one of his legs with a stomp, snaps his human-shaped forearm.

Pain is like acid, striking through him, so vivid he is blinded by everything but the agony of it.

Kasar drops him to the earth and sneers. Sentiment and tears are for old men. This is the Sha'Daa! Only pain has a place here, and yours will be the first of our own lives sacrificed on our path to conquering this world.

Moriel screams aloud as Kasar breaks his other leg, and two fists thump into his chest, snapping ribs. His head falls back against the earth, and he looks at the girl who still stands nearby. She has not run as he commanded. Her eyes are wide, her mouth agape – not in horror, but something else. Shock? Anger? He cannot read human expressions well enough to tell. All he knows is the despair of failing her. It is not sufficient simply to want to be a father.

At her feet, a glint… the knife the Salesman had traded her mother, dropped in the dust when Moriel had borne her away.

Now, he does not falter or stop to think about the pain. He seizes the knife in his good hand, shifting his body longer, snakier, whip-fast. He twists upward. Kasar is quick. He seems to sense the incoming motion and swats with one of his hands at the blade. But Moriel smells the confidence on the stripling, and knows that Kasar assumes his weight and speed will be enough defense against an injured opponent. If he is smart, Kasar would shift, switching to a shorter body shape, or a taller one, anything but remain as he is. But it is always so with striplings. They assume they are superior and discard the cautionary measures they have been taught. Moriel evades the block and impales Kasar in the throat.

The stripling's death throes are graceless, all bulging eyes and four hands clawing for the blade embedded in him. Like a panicked child. Moriel sinks back to the ground and lets Kasar slump to his knees. The stripling tears the knife free and turns it back toward Moriel, but without it, his life's blood gushes more freely, and, knife still in hand, he pitches forward, dead.

Moriel knows he should shift now to his real body. His wounds will kill him, and the teachings claim it is dishonorable to die in another shape. The priestesses avow that no soul can be released under those circumstances, but Moriel laughs at that. A silly superstition. Regardless of the outer appearance, the matter is all his, from the shattered bones to the wet eyes he turns toward the girl child. Seeing one monster is bad enough. He will die for her in as close an approximation to human as possible.

Why didn't you run? he asks.

The girl child crouches, knees gripped with her thin arms, and ignores his question. "You can't keep your promise now, can you?"

No, he says. I could keep you safe only for a very short time, a heartbeat, from this one danger. He gestures to Kasar's body.

"I remember how to get back," she says. "I can follow the trail to the parking lot. There are people there. Don't worry."

It's what fathers do, he says. Even temporary ones. He pauses, then asks, Is it difficult?

"What?"

Stopping the earthquake?

She shakes her head.

Then stop it. Quench the trembling in the earth. Hold it still. Can you do that?

Her head bobs.

Can you do it alone?

She nods again, but fearfully this time.

It's important, he stresses. If you lapse… he searches for smaller words. If you let it go, you will die too. It will be hard to keep up, and you will be scared, but you must stay here until tomorrow, and hold true.

"I don't want to be alone." She reaches out and grips his fingers in hers. "I don't want to be alone," she repeats aloud.

No one does, but, sometimes, it must still be so. I will tell you a story, for as long as I am able. The story of Lansinir and Meare. Now… stop the earthquake.

The reverberations beneath him cut off again as she re-exerts her force. It's like a physical blow, that absence she creates, severing him from his world, his past, his existence.

No, only everything the priestesses had designated. He raises his wrist, looks at the non-existent rank bracelet.

And smiles.

* * *

EPILOGUE

Ashley, back in human form and fully dressed in torn, bloody clothing, suddenly found herself standing within the remains of her shop, watching the last dregs of smoke rise from the large circular pit of ashes she inhabited. The fire had been all consuming, the only treasure saved from its appetite, herself, at its tiny epicenter.

It took about twenty minutes for the surviving defenders and the three hundred refugees to climb out the well-disguised street-level exit from the nuclear bunker that was Ashley's sub-basement.

"Now that's what I call a deus ex magica, baby," Turbo said.

"Kid," Gronk said, "you're all right." The giant creature patted the goth's soot-covered shoulder with a huge hand, staggering the lad, and raising a small cloud of black ash that set several surrounding folks coughing.

A handful of hours yet remained in The Sha'Daa, but Ashley no longer felt its regard in this corner of Ireland.

Eire itself has survived, Astraea said in her mind. I cannot speak for the rest of the world.

"Do you think Johnny is alive," Ashley whispered, "that he will return?"

The stars themselves show only a dark path when it comes to that being, Astraea said. His fate – or its – is beyond even my comprehension. Considering the array of challenges that still lay upon his shoulders, I would judge his survival to be… unlikely.

Ashley rubbed the back of her left hand, which displayed a strange blue scar where Johnny's astral tear had fallen. She bowed her head. The faerie, Llewellyn, hovered beside the shop owner and kissed her brow.

Ashley smiled sadly, and gazed back at her fellow survivors, all three hundred of them, who were now gathering around her in the street, looking to her for leadership and purpose.

I must go silent now, Astraea said, *perhaps for years. This exertion has cost me much. I will sleep and one day return… Now, do what you must…*

Ashley stood tall.

"Oscar Wilde told us that ordinary riches can be stolen," Ashley said, raising her hands to get everyone's attention, "real riches cannot. In your souls are infinitely precious things that cannot be, and have not been, taken from you."

The surrounding buzz of multiple conversations ceased, and all looked up to the imperious figure who stood upon an upturned car. Ashley surveyed her surrounding crowd one more time and voiced a yell of pride and triumph that set everyone's heart surging.

"Erin Go Bragh!"

The reply was a deafening roar of approval that was heard as far away as Dublin.

AFTERWORD

by Michael H. Hanson

"I had been the author of unalterable evils;
and I live in daily fear,
lest the monster whom I had created
should perpetuate some new wickedness."
> – Victor Frankenstein, MD

That's right, we've put out a third Sha'Daa anthology! I'm beginning to believe this vision of mine wasn't a bad idea after all. Over a year has passed since the successful publication of the series' second book, "Sha'Daa: Last Call." Ed and I managed to catch our breaths before diving into the recruitment of new writers needed to make "Sha'Daa: Pawns" a reality.

Yes, this is the third book about that inevitable conflagration that is just around planet Earth's temporal corner. The Sha'Daa, that once every ten thousand years free-for-all brawl between humankind and everything evil in the multiverse is back! And humanity has a mere forty-eight hours to get its act together, and save itself.

The Sha'Daa has found a new home at Perseid Press, and I can now promise you that there will be many new anthologies in this series published in the years to come

Are you ready for The Sha'Daa? – Michael

AUTHORS

Prologue, Interludes, Epilogue by Michael H. Hanson

The son of a U.S. Army Sergeant and a Nurse, Michael H. Hanson is the fourth of five kids. Michael attended the Newhouse School of Public Communications, where, alongside his filmmaking activities, he found a few spare moments to study creative writing and poetry. He graduated in 1989. A transplanted New Yorker, he edits engineering society journals for a living, and occasionally dabbles in genealogy research and collects impressionist oil paintings. He spends his free time spinning both tales of the fantastic, and introspective poetry, in his small but cozy garden apartment. "Sha'Daa: Pawns" is the third published book set within Michael's Sha'Daa Universe.

http://www.shadaa.com/

Forces of Evil by Edward McKeown

Edward McKeown: I've loved science fiction since I found a copy of Andre Norton's Stargate (no relation to the TV series) on a lonely afternoon in the old Victorian building that was Alexandria Bay's little library when my Dad was assigned to Camp Drum. Norton led to Clark, Heinlein, Asimov, Resnick, Cherryh and a host of others Eventually I started writing on my own, taking the movies that played in my head in daydreams and fleshing them out into a host of short stories, and three series of books. In Robert Fenaday's Trilogy, I followed a fairly ordinary man's descent into violence and obsession as he traveled the stars looking for his lost wife, a naval intelligence operative. Then Shasti Rainhell, a genetically engineered woman-warrior inherited Robert Fenaday's ship and set off on her own adventures. Decades later but in the same Confederate universe, a disgraced pilot, Wrik Trigardt, chances across an ancient combat android named Maauro, and the two strike up an unlikely alliance to survive in a universe hostile to them both.

When not writing, I practice martial arts in various forms of Kung Fu and Tai Chi. Lately I've been dancing ballroom with my artist wife, Schelly Keefer. I do better with the Kung Fu but anything worth doing is worth doing badly.

http://www.sfwa.org/members/mckeown/ &

http://www.sfreader.com/authors/edward-mcKeown

Ed is a man of many talents. Not only did he write chapters for all three of the Sha'Daa books to date, but he volunteered to become a proofreader, a position which eventually morphed into Ed becoming the official "Editor" of both "Sha'daa: Tales Of The Apocalypse" and

"Sha'daa: Last Call" and now, "Sha'daa: Pawns." Ed also brought me into Janet Morris' recently revived 'Heroes In Hell' series where we met our current publisher, Perseid Publishing. Call it serendipity, luck, or simply fate, I can never be grateful enough that I met the talented, hard driving, force of nature that is Edward McKeown. Thank you, Ed. For everything. – Mike's note

Thanks, Mike. We have been a good team for The Sha'Daa, kind of the Yin and Yang of the work. Without Mike and his creative drive and guiding vision, we would never have begun this journey, without my "ant and the rubber tree plant" doggedness, perhaps we wouldn't have finished.

When Mike and I finished "Sha'Daa – Tales Of The Apocalypse," we plunged into "Sha'Daa – Last Call" with barely a pause. There had not been room in the first book for all the fine work we'd gathered. In editing "Tales" I got in as many different stories as I could, forcing me to push the longer stories or the second submissions from some of our fine authors into "Last Call."

"Sha'Daa Pawns" followed on the heels of the two earlier Sha'daa volumes, as we realized that there was more to say about this apocalyptic event, after we heard from the foot-soldiers of evil. The big joy of this volume was working again with many fine authors and helping them find their voices, then meeting the new voices that would add fresh spice to the Sha'Daa experience.

Whither from here? Who can say?

– Edward McKeown

Asylum by John Manning

A Halloween baby, John Manning considers his love of horror, dark fantasy, and generally scary tales his birthright. Although he has written a number of non-fiction articles for various magazines (and one tiny short story), it is only within the last couple of years that he has come into his own with the release of his first novel, Black Stump Ridge, a tale of supernatural horror set in the Smoky Mountains of East Tennessee, along with *Disclaimer*, a short story in "Lawyers in Hell" and *Brimstone Arsenal* which appears in "Rogues in Hell" (both volumes part of the shared universe series "Heroes in Hell," created by Janet Morris in the 1980s and edited by Chris and Janet Morris). Now he is testing the waters of the apocalyptic world of Sha'Daa with his story, Asylum, and another entitled Mr. Bassman in the upcoming "Sha'Daa IV – Catechism" that will follow this book. As if writing is not work enough, he is also editing his own horror collection called "What Scares the Boogeyman?" to be published by Perseid Publishing and scheduled for release Autumn 2012. Originally from Detroit, he now resides in Houston, Texas.

*

LibertyCon 24, Chattanooga, Tennessee. It was early Sunday evening. The dinner with the pros was finished and I was seated at a large round table savoring the memories of my first convention as a pro guest. Ostensibly, I was there to help promote the release of Lawyers in Hell earlier that month, and I did my part on panels and readings and autograph signings. I also did a little promotion for my first novel,

Black Stump Ridge, which had come out the previous January. After years of struggling to break into the fiction market, I was basking in the warmth of having two professional successes in the same year.

I suddenly realized that I was no longer alone with my reverie. Michael Hanson had taken a seat next to me. We talked – inconsequential small talk at first – and then he began to tell me about an anthology that he was writing. The more he talked, the more excited he became. I wasn't sure at the time where this was headed, so I listened patiently as he explained Sha'Daa and its ramifications for humanity. He told me about a canon character called Johnny the Salesman and the role he played in thwarting the ten thousand year cycle.

As Michael waxed on and on, Rich Groller, a long-time friend, took a seat across from me. He began explaining how he felt I should consider writing for Michael's series and that he felt I was a perfect fit to write this kind of apocalyptic tale. I started to talk about deadlines I was facing and projects I had pending when I suddenly realized I was being double-teamed. After a bit more discussion, I agreed to do a story for "Sha'Daa IV – Catechism". We all agreed that the deadline for this book, "Sha'Daa III – Pawns," was too short and I would never make it.

I came back to Texas, and, per instructions, downloaded what I needed to do my story. I finished it, submitted it, and was told it was accepted. I signed the contract and thought that was the end of my involvement in The Sha'Daa – at least until number five was ready for submissions.

Nope.

A couple of weeks later, I – and a couple of other writers, such as Larry Atchely, Jr. – got an email from Michael saying that they needed more stories for "Sha'Daa III – Pawns" and if they extended the deadline would I please send in another story? And, that is how I came to have a story in this book. Asylum. And, looking back over it all, I'd do it again. Thanks, Michael and Rich, for double-teaming me. -- John Manning

Hunter's Run by Art Sanchez

As a transplanted New Yorker living in sunny Florida, Arthur Sanchez believes he may be familiar with the sensation of stepping out of one reality and into another. In his story, *Hunter's Run,* he embraced the challenge of writing the story from the demon's perspective and hopes he was able to get the reader to root (just a little) for the bad guy.

Arthur has published over 100 short stories as well as two short story collections. He's presently working on an unsold novel and is guest-editing for Whortleberry Press on a new anthology due out in the summer of 2012 entitled: "Strange Mysteries: A Day At The Beach." For more information on Arthur's work, links to free stories available on the web, or to purchase a copy of one of his paperbacks, please visit:

www.arthursanchez.com

Or visit his Facebook page at:

https://www.facebook.com/ArthurSanchez1610

Keepsake by Mallory Makepeace

Mallory Makepeace was born on April Fools Day in 1980. Barely graduating from Mertier High School in Northern New York State, he was later kicked out of the U.S. Air Force after one year in service for frequent misconduct of a discreditable nature. He was next fired from his Resident Advisor position at Syracuse University after a mere month on the job.

After eight years of drowning his sorrows in beer, depression, and womanizing, he managed to acquire a Bachelors degree before running away to New Jersey. Divorced with no kids, Mallory continues his lifetime campaign to fail his way to the top.

"I am the genius that is me, and punks like Harlan Ellison, Isaac Asimov, and Steve King can kiss my flat, pale butt. You got it, baby, I'm back! Read my story first…. It's the best one." – Mallory

Fall from Grace by Jeff Barnes

As an Air Force brat, Jeff grew up in such exotic locales as Japan, Alaska, Texas, and Tennessee. After a botched attempt at college (sadly, they do not award degrees for partying and lack of work ethic), he ended up being hired by the FAA to be an air traffic controller. Jeff spent eight years in Anchorage and Dillingham, Alaska before moving to Paducah, Kentucky, then Nashville, Tennessee. From there he left active air traffic control to work in FAA headquarters in Washington, DC, where he has worked ever since. Aside from controlling, Jeff's 28 years of federal service have been spent in electronic warfare, system development, strategic planning, and computer security. Currently he is the lead safety engineer for the Aeronautical Information Management Directorate, as well as telecommunications infrastructure manager for the NAIMES 2 program. Jeff's masochism extends to working online to complete the degree he was too unmotivated to get when he was young. He is on track to complete his degree in Professional Aeronautics from Embry-Riddle Aeronautical University in 6 months. Since all that wasn't enough of a challenge (only taking up about 23 hours of each day), when his friend Rich Groller described "Sha'Daa," Jeff had an immediate story idea for the fourth book in the series. Rich was kind enough to introduce him to the writing group, and Jeff's idea was accepted. Then he found out there was still time to get his foot in the door with "Pawns," so he pitched an idea for that volume, too. The pitch was accepted and the rest was… well, you get the idea. Although he has been writing on and off for many years, this is his first published story.

Dust by Sarah Wagner

Sarah Wagner lives in West Virginia with her husband and two sons. Most of her work tends toward science fiction and fantasy but she won't thumb her nose at any good story that comes to her mind. Her stories have appeared in numerous magazines, ezines, anthologies, and her own collection of science fiction, "Hardwired Humanity." When she's not writing, she's either playing with her kids, watching so-bad-they're-good sci-fi B movies, or attempting to win her battle with laundry. You can find her on facebook, livejournal, and at her website: www.sarahwagner.domynoes.net.

Door 790 by Diane Arrelle

Writing under the name Diane Arrelle, I have had around 200 short stories published and I have two 2 published books, "Just A Drop In The Cup", a collection of short-short stories and"Elements Of The Short Story, How to Write a Selling Story". I live on the edge of the Pine Barrens (home of the Jersey Devil) in Southern New Jersey with my husband, currently one of two sons and my cat. I am proud to be one of the founding members, as well as the second president of, the Garden State Horror Writers, and I am also the past president of the Philadelphia Writers' Conference.

I began writing stories in college while taking the four-hour once-a-week class, The Geography Of South East Asia, which I needed for my teaching certification in social studies. It was really a long class, and begged to let my imagination roam. Growing up extremely rural and listening nightly to the ghastly ghostly tales that my older siblings forced upon me, I naturally turned to horror, since I am basically afraid of everything.

To support my writing habit for the last couple of decades, I have held a wide variety of jobs including Teacher, School Bus Driver, Waitress, Sales Clerk, Mystery Shopper, Newspaper Correspondent, Tutor, Freelance Writer, Senior Citizen Center Director, and I was also that person who stood around in a department store burning vanilla tinged milk and cooking tasteless crêpes to sell nonstick pots and pans.

My story in this anthology was inspired by a delightfully creepy resort my sister and I stayed at recently, and to my utter joy, it was my turn to tell her some ghastly ghostly stories to keep her up half the night.

You can visit my two websites at:
Writingtheshortstory.com and dinaleacock.com and I am on facebook and twitter.

Bloodstone by Gustavo Bondoni

Gustavo Bondoni is an Argentine writer with over eighty stories published in ten countries. His first two books were published in 2010: a collection of Gustavo's previously published stories, "Tenth Orbit and Other Faraway Places" was released in October, and his short novel "The Curse of El Bastardo" in November. His third book, "Virtuoso and Other Stories" was published in 2011. He can be found on his website at www.gustavobondoni.com.ar, and his blog, located at http://bondo-ba.livejournal.com/

Silver and Iron by Leona Wisoker

Leona Wisoker's work is fueled equally by coffee and conviction; her debut series, "Children of the Desert", is set in a world which is still struggling through a number of basic moral and developmental issues. The final result leaves room not only for serious questions but moments of laughter, and inevitably involves coffee.

Her short stories have appeared in Andromeda Spaceways Inflight Magazine, Futures: Fire to Fly Magazine, Alienskin.com, and Anotherealm.com. She is a reviewer for Green Man Review and the Sleeping Hedgehog; an editor for Damnation Books; and regularly blogs about writing and creativity.

Double Cross by Paul Barrett

Paul Barrett has lived a varied life full of excitement and adventure. Not really, but it sounds good as an opening line.

Paul's multiple careers have included: rock and roll roadie, children's theater stage manager, television camera operator, mortgage banker, and support specialist for Microsoft Excel.

This eclectic mix has allowed him to go into his true love: motion picture production. He has produced two motion pictures: "Night Feeders" and "Cold Storage." "Night Feeders" was released on DVD in 2007. "Cold Storage" won the Audience Favorite Award at the 2009 Dead By Dawn Film Festival in Edinburgh, Scotland, and has been picked up for DVD release by Lionsgate.

Amidst all this, Paul has worked on his writing, starting with his first short story, about Ziggy Stardust and the Spiders from Mars, at age 8. Paul has written numerous commercials and industrial video scripts in his tenure with his creative agency, Indievision. His script for "The Ozone Zone" won both a Telly and Communicator Award. He has three novels currently making the rounds to agents. Paul lives in Charlotte, NC with his partner, filmmaker Tony Elwood, and their two cats, Skittles and Ashe.

Tendrils of Gloom by Michael Griffiths

Michael D. Griffiths is a man who likes to keep busy. He has worked with the magazine Abandoned Towers since its inception, moving from Slush Reader to Marketing Manager.

In the past, his writing has been published in numerous periodicals and anthologies. He was awarded first place in Withersin's 666 contest as well as Golden Vision's Online Fiction Contest. He is on the staff of The Daily Discord, Cyberwizard Productions, SFReader, and writes book reviews for Innsmouth Free Press. His series "The Chronicles of Jack Primus" is available through Living Dead Press. Lately his attentions have turned toward the walking dead and, besides the various anthologies focusing on the subject his work had appeared in, he has begun a new Zombie Apocalypse series called the "Eternal Aftermath."

http://www.amazon.com/Eternal-Aftermath-Zombie-Michael-Griffiths/dp/1611990238/ref=sr_1_1?ie=UTF8&qid=1323985774&sr=8-1

The Bokor by Richard Groller

Richard Groller is co-author of "The Warrior's Edge" (with Janet Morris and Col. John Alexander), and a contributing author to "The American Warrior" (Janet and Chris Morris, Eds.), and to the "Heroes of Hell" shared universe series since it began in the 1980s. Nominated for "Military Intelligence" Professional

Writer of the Year in 1986, he has published numerous historical and technical articles in such venues as "Military Intelligence," "The Field Artillery Journal," "Guns and Ammo," and "The Journal of Electronic Defense." As a contributing writer to the "Heroes of Hell" series, he has been published in "Prophets in Hell," "Lawyers in Hell," and "Rogues in Hell" and has another story accepted for the next volume in the series. He is Editor of a volume of dark poetry called "The Book of Night" that will be published by Perseid Publishing in 2012. His short story L'uomo Nero will be published in 2012 in the upcoming horror anthology "What Scares the Boogeyman." When not writing, Rich is Director of Business Development for Dilijent Solutions, LLC, a Northern Virginia-based defense contractor involved with software- and engineering-related technical and managerial support for the Department of Defense and Intelligence Community.

The Saglek Incident by Bruce Durham

Bruce Durham lives in Mississauga, Ontario. He has appeared in Paradox, Lovecraft eZine, "Flashing Swords," "Return of the Sword," "Rage of the Behemoth," "Lawyers in Hell" and "Rogues in Hell," among others. In 2009 his short story The Marsh God was adapted into a graphic novel. The Marsh God and Homecoming won Preditors & Editors Readers polls for Best SF&F in 2005 and 2006, while Yaggoth-Voor from "Rage of the Behemoth" placed 2nd in 2009 and received 'Harper's Pen' and 'Prix Aurora' nominations. Currently he writes for Janet Morris and her Hugo Award-Winning "Heroes in Hell" series. You can visit his website at www.brucedurham.ca

Time for a Change by Larry Atchley Jr.

Larry Atchley, Jr grew up in Grapevine, Texas, and has been writing since he was a teenager, mostly poetry, fantasy, science fiction, and horror stories. He published two poems in a high school senior class anthology, and mailed poems out to several small press magazines in the early nineties, but without success. Frustrated with the process, he wouldn't try to have anything published until almost twenty years later. He became serious again about publishing his fiction writing after attending a writers' workshop presented by authors Sarah A. Hoyt and Amanda S. Green in 2010, which taught him a lot, and boosted his confidence in his writing. His first big break as a writer came later that year, in October, when Janet Morris and Chris Morris invited him to join a group of writers working on their shared-world series "Heroes in Hell," which they were rebooting with "Lawyers in Hell," and to submit a short story for the book. They accepted his story, Remember, Remember, Hell in November and it was published in the book in June 2011. Working closely with many of the other writers in the "Lawyers in Hell Writing Group" project led to him being invited to submit writing to other anthologies that some of the members were working on. In July, 2011, Larry had a poem accepted for a collection called "The Book of Night," edited by Richard Groller, to be published in 2012, which he read aloud in an author panel at the literary convention, LibertyCon. While at the convention, Michael H. Hanson, whom he collaborated with on their stories for the "Lawyers in Hell" anthology, invited him to submit a story for his shared-world anthology series, "Sha'Daa."

"It was a lot of fun researching and writing for "Sha'Daa." I love the series concepts of an apocalyptic event taking place on the Summer Solstice every 10,000 years and the character, Johnny the Salesman. When I first learned about the Integratron building from a travel show, I knew this was where my story, Time for a Change would take place."

Larry is currently writing stories for submission to several fiction anthologies, and is busy working on a fantasy novel. He is also writing non-fiction articles on a variety of topics that he hopes to have published in 2012. You can read his blog at www.larryatchleyjr.wordpress.com. Some of his other interests include photography, Qi-Gong, Kung Fu, martial arts, traditional archery, fencing, philosophy, mythology (especially Norse), paranormal studies and investigation, survivalist studies, bicycling, hiking, reading, collecting rare books, and spending time with his family. His wife, Sussie Atchley, is a professional freelance photographer, and his daughter Alina Atchley is an artist and jewelry maker. They live with their two terriers, Frodo and Rosie, and two cats, Samwise and Prue in the suburbs of the Dallas/Fort Worth Metroplex, in Texas.

Crouching Seal, Sleeping Dragon by Jason Cordova

Jason Cordova did not want to be a writer. He wanted to be many other things, first and foremost a professional baseball player. After that, a teacher, then a professional videogame player. However, with the deck stacked against him (as well as too many injuries to his shoulder, which killed the aspirations of videogaming and baseball), in 2007 he finally accepted the writing gig and sold his first book three months later. Since then he has had multiple short stories published and more novels in the pipeline.

He currently lives in Kentucky, very near the heart of thoroughbred country.

"I have to admit, when I was invited to do a story for "Pawns," I wasn't sure what sort of story to write. I knew it had to be from the villain's point of view but other than that, I had nothing. I was worried that maybe Michael had asked the wrong guy to play in his sandbox. Then subject came up of perhaps using a Navy SEAL team to fight in the "Sha'Daa" and realized that the story was right there. All I had to do was to break things and everything would be in order. Kasyarna came to life with the story (curmudgeonly was the best way I could describe him…) and the rest is, well, "Sha'Daa.""

Northlight by Deborah Koren

Deborah Koren writes fiction from California's Sierra Nevada mountains. When she's not writing or reading (or working at her pesky day job), she is out hiking, playing with her dogs and cats, fencing, watching "Combat!" reruns, shoveling snow, and frequenting the local library. Her fiction has appeared in several ezines, including: Anotherealm, AlienSkin, RaggedEdge Publishing, Gateway, and Kenoma, several of which have won awards. Several anthologies, such as Best of AstoundingTales.com, Ghelenden Revisited, and Cybertales: Live Wire, have included her stories. She has also had two stories published in the first two volumes of the "Heroes in Hell" series after it was resuscitated by its creator, Janet Morris.

"Anything having to do with apocalypses is appealing to me on general principles. Being asked to participate in an anthology with a unique vision of the potential end of the world and a great group of writers is even better. Don't call me Ishmael, call me Captain Nemo."
http://www.cimharas.com